HUDSON'S KILL

ALSO BY PADDY HIRSCH

The Devil's Half Mile

HUDSON'S KILL

Paddy Hirsch

A Tom Doherty Associates Book
NEW YORK

HUDSON'S KILL

Copyright © 2019 by Patrick Hirsch

A Forge Book
Published by Tom Doherty Associates
120 Broadway
New York, NY 10271

www.tor-forge.com

Forge® is a registered trademark of Macmillan Publishing Group, LLC.

The Library of Congress Cataloging-in-Publication Data
is available upon request.

ISBN 978-0-7653-9916-8 (hardcover)
ISBN 978-0-7653-9918-2 (ebook)

Our books may be purchased in bulk for promotional, educational, or business use. Please contact your local bookseller or the Macmillan Corporate and Premium Sales Department at 1-800-221-7945, extension 5442, or by email at MacmillanSpecialMarkets@macmillan.com.

First Edition: September 2019

Printed in Canada

0 9 8 7 6 5 4 3 2 1

To cousin Michael.
For your faith, your strength, and your inspiration.

HUDSON'S KILL

NEW YORK
September 1803

ONE

Saturday

Kerry O'Toole pushed the big iron key into the brass lock of the African Free School, and jiggled it back and forth. The lock was new and poorly set, and the key needed finessing before it turned properly. John Teasman, the headmaster, had ordered the lock fitted a week earlier, after a lumberyard owned by a black man named Bonsel was burned to the ground. Fires were not uncommon in New York in 1803—the city was still made mostly of wood, and accidents happened—but everyone was saying that the fire that put Bonsel out of business was different. The Irish, black, and American nativist gangs were all struggling for control of what they considered to be their quarters of the city. And they were becoming more brazen and violent by the day. The African Free School was on Cliff Street, in the old Dutch district, and while it was endowed by some of the wealthiest and most powerful families in New York, it was still a Negro business in a neighborhood claimed by the nativists. Teasman wasn't taking any chances.

Kerry twisted the key, and the tongue of the lock slid home.

The sound of a bell made its way up the street. She turned to the little girl in the long brown dress standing beside her. "How many chimes was that, Rosie?"

Two big, hazel eyes looked back. Rosie Tully's fine, dark hair was tied back in two pigtails. She held up five fingers on one hand and one on the other.

"Six bells. Very good. Now, shall we see if we can find a cab?"

Rosie's pigtails bounced.

Cliff Street was empty, but the sound of laughing and singing filtered up from the waterfront, just three blocks away. Kerry took a last look at the façade of the school, to be sure all the windows were closed. She slipped the heavy iron key into the pocket of her dress and touched the hilt of the long-bladed boning knife she kept there. She took the child by the hand.

Rosie was the youngest daughter of Tamsin and Seamus Tully, who owned Hughson's Tavern on the North River waterfront. They often asked Kerry to mind their youngest on busy days. And Saturdays were always busy. Kerry would go to the tavern for a late luncheon, then take Rosie to the African Free School. Rosie would look at the pictures in the books and pamphlets while Kerry prepared her lessons for the following week. They would read together for a while, and then go home to Kerry's house.

The little girl skipped ahead, tugging Kerry's hand, and Kerry felt her throat close up.

Rosie slowed, and looked up at her with solemn eyes. Kerry smiled and squeezed her hand. She shifted her thoughts. How many women in this city had lost an infant child, to disease, fever, or cold? She was more fortunate than most. She had lost, but she had gained, too. When her own child had died, three years before, her future had looked empty. It was bad enough that she was the daughter of an Irish gangster and a runaway slave. Times were changing, but mixed-race children were generally assumed to be the offspring of black prostitutes and their white clients. They had few prospects for marriage or choice of career. Servant. Thief. Whore. Kerry had made her way as a pickpocket for a while when she was younger, so, when Daniel died, she was on the point of throwing herself back into the cesspools of the city. But Justy Flanagan had pulled her back. He had helped her to read and write and try another path. And everything had changed.

———•———

There were no cabs, and when they reached Beekman Street every hansom that passed was occupied. So they kept walking, up the shallow hill to Chatham Row and around the Park. They crossed the Broad Way, traversing the spine of Manhattan Island, and walked down into the New Town. The heels of Kerry's boots clicked on the uneven cobbles, and she had to tread carefully to avoid turning an ankle. Landowners were throwing up townhouses and tenements as immigrants flooded into the city and demand soared. But the buildings here were thin-walled and rickety, the streets poorly paved. Most of the street lanterns in the area had been stolen, and those that remained were rarely lit.

The evening light threw long shadows in the lanes, and Kerry could feel the eyes on her, watching from dark windows and doors. This part of the city was still neutral territory, too far uptown for the nativists, and too new for the blacks or the Irish. Families were still moving in. But it wouldn't be long before the population settled. And then the gangs would stake their claims and the fighting would start.

Even then, she would still be safe enough. Her father was O'Toole, the bloody right hand of the Bull, who controlled the East River waterfront and the Irish gangs. And her cousin was Lew Owens, whose heavy-handed enforcers took a piece of every business run by someone with colored skin, from brothels to bakeries. Everyone who lived in this part of New York knew who Kerry O'Toole was, and if they did not, if they had just recently arrived in the city and mistook her for a soft mark, the long, thin blade in her pocket would set them straight.

They walked on, towards the north end of the town. Kerry lived with her cousin, in a tiny, two-room cottage in the rear of an enormous compound, bigger than any house in the old Dutch quarter on the tip of Manhattan. It was nearly impossible for a black man to buy property in the city, but Lew Owens had persuaded a lawyer to do the conveyancing for him, and he was now one of the few Negro landowners in New York. The compound was well-sited, at the cusp of the new developments and the ramshackle shanties of Canvas Town, where most of the city's free Negroes lived, and Owens' gang held sway.

A light onshore breeze blew up the hill. It carried the stench of woodsmoke, roasting meat, and open latrines. Chapel Street narrowed further, hemmed in by a high brick wall and a row of rickety wooden tenements, divided by deep, narrow alleyways. The street had not yet been paved, and Kerry could feel the dampness of the ground through the leather soles of her shoes.

There was a mewing sound. Rosie stopped and looked up at Kerry, huge hazel eyes, her fingers in her mouth.

Kerry smiled. "Was that a kitty-cat?"

The soft whimper came again, floating out of one of the alleys. Kerry peered into the darkness. She felt the hair rising on the nape of her neck.

Rosie's eyes were like saucers. Kerry bent to pick her up. "Don't be scared."

Her heart thumped. She took the knife out of her pocket. She balanced Rosie on her left hip and shuffled down the alley, the blade held out in front of her.

Nothing moved in the gloom. She stopped halfway down the narrow passageway, feeling the pulse in her temples, waiting for her eyes to adjust. Slowly, she began to make out a shape, crumpled on the ground, wedged into a niche in the wall. She edged closer, and saw it was a girl, wrapped in a kind of thin shroud, lying on her side. One of her shoes had come off, and the sole of her foot was pale in the dim light.

Kerry went down on one knee. She slipped the knife back into her pocket, and eased Rosie gently off her hip. Her heart was pounding. She tried to keep her voice steady.

"Look away, now." She turned Rosie to face the mouth of the alley. And then she turned back.

The girl on the ground was shivering, her eyes closed, her face wet with sweat. She whimpered again, the voice catching with pain, like rust on a blade. Kerry touched the girl's face. She was pale and freezing cold, and Kerry knew instantly that she had been cut somewhere, and that all the blood had poured out of her. She pulled the shroud back to see.

"Oh, Jesus."

The girl had been cut from her breastbone to her pubis, a long, smooth gash that had opened her up and let her entrails spill out onto the ground. Her arms were dark with blood, crossed over her abdomen, loosely cradling what was left of her belly. Her guts glistened, white against her dark skin. Kerry rocked back on her heels, bile burning the back of her throat. "Jesus. Sweet Jesus Christ."

The girl's eyes flickered open. They seem to look right through her. She muttered something, and tensed, as though she was hugging herself tighter. Kerry dropped to her knees in the mud and wrapped her arm around the girl's shoulders. She pulled her close, but there was only a halting sound, as though the girl was trying to catch her breath. And then, nothing.

Kerry grabbed Rosie up and hurried back to the street. She ran back along the puddled lane and up to the Broad Way. Two watchmen were ambling up the shallow hill, talking quietly to each other, swinging their long clubs. Kerry ran to them, Rosie clutched tight to her chest.

"Whoa there, missy!" The bigger of the two watchmen held out a hand.

"There's a girl, in an alley off Chapel Street . . ." Kerry stopped to catch her breath.

"There usually is, lass." The big watchman grinned, showing a badly chipped tooth.

"She's dead."

He frowned. "Are you sure?"

"Yes, I'm sure. I watched her give her last breath. I need you to get down to the Hall and tell Marshal Flanagan."

"Oh, Marshal Flanagan, is it?"

Kerry checked herself. "Yes. Tell him Kerry O'Toole told you."

The tiniest hesitation. "O'Toole?"

"Are you going to stand there and repeat everything I say, or are you going to fetch the Marshal?"

The man's face darkened. "I don't fetch. I'm not a goddamned dog."

"Right, then, leave her there," Kerry snapped. "And when some stall owner finds her tomorrow with a hole in her belly and her guts half-eaten by rats, remember that you were told she was murdered and you did nothing. I wonder what the Marshal will have to say about that, when I tell him."

She stood trembling, holding tight to Rosie.

"It's all right, miss," the second watchman said. He was wiry and narrow-shouldered, with long gray hair swept back from his face. He was staring at her hands. She looked down and saw her fingers were dark with blood, which had smeared on Rosie's dress. "We'll get word to the Marshal." The man's voice was soothing. He had a faint Cockney accent. "Whereabouts on Chapel Street?"

"By the Armstrong tenements. Third alley down on the left."

He nodded and smiled. He had strange eyes, with large, dark pupils and enormous irises. Like one of the husky dogs she had seen on the waterfront, years ago. She felt nervous and reassured at the same time.

"Thank you for telling us," he said. "Now are you all right to go on home with the child there? Do you need us to come with you?"

"No. I'm fine."

"Right you are, then. Good night."

The watchman with the broken tooth was staring at her, an odd look on his face.

"What?" she snapped.

"If it is a murder, like you say, the Marshal will want to talk to you."

Kerry held Rosie tight. "He knows where to find me."

TWO

Justy Flanagan knelt beside the body. "Hold the lamp higher, please, Sergeant."

It was a trick of the light, caused by the flickering candle, but Justy could have sworn the girl gave a slight smile. It could not be, though, because she was long dead, her limbs stiffening and her skin waxy and ashen.

She lay on her right shoulder, one arm draped so that her right hand was cupped loosely over her lower belly. The wound in her torso was a long, dark slash. Her entrails were a pale tumble of old ropes.

Sergeant Vanderool leaned close. "He must have been one unsatisfied customer." He bumped against Justy's shoulder. He smelled of grease and damp wool and whiskey.

Justy was a tall, narrow-faced man, with high cheekbones and long fair hair that flopped over a pair of blue-gray eyes. He was one of five Mayor's Marshals, but he wore no uniform. Instead, he was dressed casually, in a dark green coat and cream-colored whipcord breeches that were now soaked through the knees with God knew what. His boots were not doing much better. They were made of butter-soft brown leather, but they were getting old. He had taken them from the body of an English cavalry officer that he had killed in a skirmish during the Rebellion in Ireland, five years before. He had worn them almost every day since. They had been repaired over and over, but now that he could feel water seeping through the soles and stitching, he wondered if it was time for them to retire.

"That's a lot of assumptions you're making, Sergeant."

"That so?" Vanderool hawked, and spat against the wall. "What other kind of woman's going to be down this way but a *stephoer*? And only a man's going to do damage like that."

Justy looked around the dank, narrow alley. It was well past dusk, and the light from the lantern cast long shadows against the mottled walls and made the churned, muddy ground into a battlefield. Vanderool had a point. "Has anyone touched her?"

"No."

"Are you sure?"

The sergeant rolled his eyes. He was a slope-shouldered, pot-bellied man of about fifty years, with thin hair and a receding chin covered in stubble. "Mister Playfair," he called out. "Anyone been down here since you found her?"

"No, Sergeant," a voice came back down the alley. "No one but you and the Marshal."

"Satisfied?" Vanderool's voice was sharp.

Justy ignored him. He touched the girl's neck. She was as cold as the water soaking his trousers. He shifted position, took a breath, and slipped his fingers into the long wound that split her torso. The skin was as stiff as salt-soaked canvas; her intestines were slick and cold against the palm of his hand. He had to swallow hard to keep down the bile that seared the back of his throat. He closed his eyes and slid his hand into the body cavity, past the knuckles. It was freezing in the alley, but he could feel a trace of warmth under his fingertips.

"What in God's name are you doing?" Vanderool was aghast.

"Something I learned in France." Justy had spent time with the Paris police as a student, and had gone back the summer before to learn about the techniques their criminal detectives were developing. He sat back on his haunches, tugged a handkerchief from his cuff and used it to wipe his hands. "See how her legs are stiffening, slightly?"

"Rigor mortis. We all know about that."

"Yes, but it hasn't set in yet. It usually takes four hours or so, depending on the cold. And the core of her body is still warm to the touch. So we know a few things."

"Such as?"

"Such as she wasn't long dead when Mister Playfair found her."

Vanderool sniffed and shuffled his feet. "Come on, then. We need to get her out of here. There's a crowd gathering. We don't want to set them off."

Justy nodded. Vanderool might be an Irish-hating, nativist bully, but he was no fool. He knew the city well, and he knew that the alley they were standing in was only a stone's throw from the Canvas Town slums. Which meant the crowd outside was almost certainly made up of poor black men, most of whom would resent the presence of white faces on their turf.

He stood up, wincing as a sharp pebble poked through the sole of his right boot. Another reminder to have the damn things mended.

"Very well, Sergeant," he said. "Let's get her up to the morgue."

Vanderool barked an order, and Justy walked back to the street, stepping out of the way of two lads carrying a stretcher and a blanket. Perhaps a dozen men stood a few yards away, watching. They were all a little drunk and a little curious, speculating about what was down there in the dark.

There was no tension in the air, but the two watchmen were taking no chances. They stood in the center of the street, facing the crowd of black men, their clubs on their shoulders. Playfair was the bigger of the pair, an inch over six feet, and broad as a heifer. Justy had seen him in action before, and knew he was the kind who relished a fight and never held back. Tasty, in the vernacular. He caught Justy looking at him and grinned, showing a broken tooth.

Gorton was slighter and shorter, although not by much. His eyes flicked back and forth, scanning the faces in the crowd. He looked older than Playfair, with long, steel-gray hair and a face like a hatchet. Justy didn't know him well. He was a Londoner, a former soldier who had come to New York less than a year ago. A quiet, thoughtful man.

The stretcher bearers emerged from the alleyway. The blanket bulged obscenely. The men had tucked it in under the dead girl's body, to keep her entrails from spilling out.

A growling sound came from the crowd. Justy felt his skin prickle. Suddenly, men were shouting, loud and angry.

"What have you done?"

"They've killed him!"

"Damn them!"

Playfair and Gorton swung the clubs off their shoulders and planted their feet wide. Justy motioned at the stretcher bearers to stop. He stepped forward between the watchmen. "Gentlemen, please disperse and leave us to do our work."

"Looks like you've done your work already, you cossack bastard!" The voice was heavy and slurred with drink.

Justy held up a hand. "Someone called us here. A person has been killed. We are taking the body to the morgue. Please let us pass."

"Murderers!" The man was fast. He lunged out of the crowd, straight for

Justy, the dull gleam of a blade in his hand. Playfair swung hard, a killer blow, but the man slid in the mud, and the club slashed through the air above his head. The man recovered and sprang forward, his knife aimed at Justy's belly.

But Justy was no longer there. He had taken a long step forward with this right foot, so that he was side-on to the man. His left forearm kept the knife hand clear, and his right hand shoved the man in the back, driving him forward under his own momentum until he tripped over Justy's outstretched foot. He sprawled on the ground, his face in the mud.

Playfair stepped up and kicked the knife away. He raised the club.

"Let him go," Justy ordered.

Playfair lowered his weapon, a sour look on his face. The man scrambled to his feet. He went to pick up his knife, but Playfair lunged at him. "Go on, ya madge. I won't miss twice."

The man slunk away. There was a smatter of applause from the crowd. "Nice moves, Marshal," someone shouted.

"Frisk's over, gents. Time to go back to your cribs," Gorton said. He was still facing them, standing easy, his club on his shoulder as though he was out for a stroll. "Unless you want me to set the Marshal here on you, o' course."

There was a ripple of laughter. The workers began to drift away.

Justy looked for Vanderool, but the sergeant had disappeared. Scuttled back to his warm bed, no doubt, Justy thought, then chastised himself for the thought. The man had come immediately when he was called, after all.

Justy motioned to the stretcher bearers. They picked up the girl and walked slowly away from the alley. One of the men slipped on the mud, falling to one knee, and the stretcher lurched sideways, the body shifting so that the blanket slipped back, revealing the girl's face. Her eyes were still open, staring emptily up at the sky, her skin slack, her lips parted slightly.

Gorton pulled the stretcher bearer upright. He stood over the body for a moment, then smoothed his palm over the girl's face, closing her eyes. He pulled the blanket up. The stretcher bearers carried her away.

Gorton and Playfair were Watch wardens. The Watch was mostly made up of volunteers who worked during the day and stood in sentry boxes around the city during the dark hours, keeping an eye out for fires. But there were six professionals, full-time employees of Federal Hall, whose job was to patrol the city during the night. These wardens went in pairs from box to box, ensuring the volunteers were awake, and acting as runners in the event of a fire.

"Which one of you men found the body?" Justy asked them.

"Me," Playfair answered. "We was passing this way and I thought I heard a sound. Come down to see what was what, and there she was."

"Did you touch her?"

"Just to see if she was quick or dead."

"And?"

Playfair shrugged. "She was still warm."

"And then you came straight down to the Hall?"

"Mister Gorton came down. I stayed on stag."

Justy nodded. Playfair was the senior man, in terms of time served. "Is this your usual route?"

"We vary the routes. Captain's orders." Playfair looked smug.

"I see." Justy looked him in the eye. "Why didn't you raise the alarm when you found her? She wasn't long dead, so her killer might still have been in the vicinity. If you'd blown your whistle and raised the Watch, we might have had a chance at catching him."

Playfair scowled.

"The doer was long gone, Marshal," Gorton said. His eyes were fixed on a point over Justy's left shoulder.

"How would you know that?"

"Stomach wound like that, it takes a long time to die. No major vessels cut. No damage to the heart or lungs. Just a long, slow bleed."

"You sound as though you've some experience."

"I seen a lot of men die with their guts opened up. In Guadeloupe."

Justy nodded. He remembered reading Gorton's file. The man had been a corporal of the King's Marines. He had fought in the vanguard of the British force that had taken the Caribbean island of Guadeloupe from the French in a savage, almost suicidal action. The newspapers had been full of the story at the time. The assaulting forces had run out of ammunition early, and a resupply had been intercepted. But the British had attacked regardless, and taken the outpost using nothing but raw bravery and the bayonet.

Justy suppressed a shiver. He knew what it was like to face a wall of English bayonets.

He looked around at the muddy street and the ramshackle warehouses. Several were tanneries. There was a strong smell of fermented urine. It was a bad place to die.

"I'll assign one of your watchmen to stand guard here until the morning.

Instruct him that no one is to go down this alley until I return. Then go to the Almshouse. I need you there, in case anyone comes to claim the body. If they do, one of you stay with them, while the other comes to fetch me. Is that clear?"

"Aye, Marshal," they said in unison.

Justy followed the stretcher bearers along Chapel Street. The mud clung to the heels of his boots, and he could feel water sloshing around his sodden right foot. He had a sudden memory of Ireland, cool mud between his toes, and then of the ensign of cavalry who had owned the boots before him, sitting atop his horse, his pistol leveled at Justy's head. Justy had stood in the marshy water and waited, staring at the small, black hole of the pistol's muzzle. But the ensign had failed to cock his pistol properly. He had squeezed the trigger but the hammer had not snapped forward as he expected, and when he realized his mistake, his eyes had opened impossibly wide. Sky blue, the same color as the facings on his jacket. Justy had hurled himself out of the marsh, dragged the ensign off his horse, and stabbed him in the throat. The man hadn't needed his boots after that.

He heard footsteps behind him. Playfair was hurrying along the street, his feet squelching in the muck. The big watchman stopped and kept his eyes on the ground. "One thing I left out in my report, sir, before."

"Yes?"

"When I said it was me what found her, sir, well, that wasn't quite right."

"What do you mean? You didn't find her?"

"Not exactly, sir."

Justy sighed. "Be direct, Mister Playfair, please. I have an appointment."

Playfair had a sour look on his face. "Very well, sir. What I meant to say is, I did find the girl, but I was tipped off."

"By whom?"

"By a young woman, sir. She said she knows you. Asked for you by name."

"And did she give her name in return?"

"Kerry O'Toole."

Justy was glad it was dark and there were no streetlights in this quarter of the town. "Miss O'Toole found the body?"

"Yes, sir. She said she heard the girl breathe her last, and that we should fetch you."

"I see." In the dim light, far behind Playfair, the bend in Chapel Street looked like the entrance to a dark, narrow cave. Justy wondered why Kerry had come this way. "I commend you for coming to tell me the truth, Playfair. What was it that prompted you to do so?"

The sour look returned to the watchman's face. "I couldn't rightly say, sir."

Justy hid his smile. "Well, whatever it was, you would do well to cultivate it."

THREE

Justy leaned on the wall of a warehouse opposite the Owens compound and tried to ignore the stench from the Collect Pond that seeped over the Broad Way. It was a potent mixture of rotten fish, decaying meat, burned hops, and urine, made all the more pungent by a blanket of thick clouds that covered the city. He wondered how the people crammed into the new tenements on Elm Street could stand it. But stand it they did. They even used the pond as a source for drinking water.

There was a light burning in the window of Kerry's cottage. Justy knew she would be sitting in the armchair beside the window, reading by the light of a three-stick candelabra. Something by Swift or Richardson, he supposed. He felt a spark of envy. Most of the books on his night table these days related to the law.

He tugged his watch free of the fob on his waistcoat and squinted at the face. It was too dim to read, but he had heard St. Peter's bell strike nine, so he knew he was now catastrophically late for dinner.

Eliza would understand. She was twenty-two years old, a doctor's daughter with sparkling blue eyes and a mouth that rose on one side and fell on the other when she was trying not to laugh, which seemed to be all the time. They had only met twice, the first time in Philadelphia a month ago. He was giving evidence in court; she was handing out books to veterans at the City Hall. When they had met again, two weeks later, at the Governor's Ball, he was surprised to learn she lived in New York. He was even more surprised when she had taken his arm for a stroll by the Battery, and bombarded him with questions: about him, about books, and about how best to help the immigrants that were flooding the city, usually without prospects of any kind. He wasn't used to women talking about anything other than themselves or what they were wearing. It was a pleasant feeling.

He took a deep breath, walked across the street, and knocked. When Kerry opened the door, her face was shadowed by the candlelight behind her.

"You must be chilled to the timbers, standing out there all this time," she said.

"You saw me?"

"Like a spare peg at a wedding. I don't know how you managed to creep up on all them English during the Rebellion. They must have all been drunk or half asleep."

He shrugged. "Most of them likely were."

She looked down her nose at him, a half smile on her face. She wore a long dress and a heavy woolen shawl. Her hair fell in a dark wave over her right shoulder. He thought about the habit she had, of curling it around her right hand, over and over, as she read. He swallowed the vague sense of panic that rose in him. "May I come in?"

She stood aside. "There's no fire."

The room was small and plain, with a table and two upright chairs at one end, and a swept fireplace flanked by two armchairs at the other. There was a door opposite that led to her bedroom. It was ajar, and as Justy walked in, he heard a sound come from it. He looked at Kerry.

She smirked. "Jealous?"

He felt the heat in his face and she laughed. "Don't worry, ye drumbelo. It's just wee Rosie Tully. She's only five, but she snores like an old man."

"Seamus and Tamsin's girl?"

"They had their hands full tonight."

They each took an armchair. Justy nodded towards the bedroom. "Was Rosie with you when you found the girl?"

Kerry's face seemed to close up. "I couldn't leave her in the street."

"Of course not."

"I told her to look away. It was dark. I don't think she saw anything."

Justy nodded. "There's nothing else you could have done."

Kerry swallowed. "It was like the girl was holding on for someone to come. So someone would be there when she died."

The words hung for a moment in the chilly air of the plain room. There was a book on the small table between the armchairs. Wax from the candelabra had dripped onto its cover. *The Coquette, or, The History of Eliza Wharton.*

"Is it any good?" he asked.

"I'm not sure many men would say so."

"I heard it was written by a woman."

"Too lowbrow for you, then?"

Justy drummed his fingers on the arm of his chair. "Tell me about the girl."

"She was lying on her side." Kerry's voice was tight. "She had a kind of thin robe wrapped around her. One of her shoes was off. She was crying. I tried to turn her, and then . . ."

Justy waited.

"She'd been cut open. She had her arms wrapped around her." Kerry swallowed. "But the innards were spilled out of her. She was half-frozen."

She bent her head and her hair fell across her face.

"Did she say anything?"

"No."

"Did you see anyone?"

"No."

"Did you take anything from the alley?"

She looked up. She shook her head.

"Just one more thing, then. Why were you down there in the first place?"

"What? Are you worried about me now?" Her voice was clotted.

"As a matter of fact, yes. That's a dangerous area, Kerry."

"Why? Because of all the darkies? Did you forget I'm half darky myself?"

"That has nothing to do with it. That girl you found had darker skin than you, and that didn't save her. Now why were you there? It's hardly the most direct way to here."

Kerry took a deep breath. The light caught her face for a moment, showing the strain around her eyes. "The direct way is along Elm Street."

Justy nodded. The week before he had stood in the center of a line of watchmen at the corner of Elm and Barley Streets, holding back a crowd of angry black men who were intent on tearing the heads off a crew of construction workers. At first he had thought it was an ordinary labor dispute between blacks and whites, but then he saw that the builders had begun to dig up the old Negro burial ground.

The cemetery had been closed nearly a decade ago, in 1794, but the city appeared to have gone back on its promise to leave the ground untouched. The workers didn't know who had employed them, and there were no records at Federal Hall of anyone applying for permission to start work on the site. After Justy had stopped the dig, the workers had not returned, but the long, dark scar of open ground in the corner of the old burial ground remained. Justy was not superstitious, but even he had to ask how the spirits of the thousands of men, women, and children buried over the years might take exception to being disturbed so callously in the name of progress. And how they might react.

"You might do better to stay on the Broad Way in future." He pulled out his watch.

"Nice tatler," she said.

He nodded. It was not a particularly thin piece, and it was made of silver, not gold, but it was precious to him. Jacob Hays, the High Constable, had presented him with it on his first anniversary as Marshal, two years before.

"No dummy?" Kerry smirked. It had become the fashion for men to carry two watches on their person, one of which was a fake, a disk of cheap metal painted gold tucked into the opposite fob pocket from the real watch. The idea was to confuse thieves, who would not know which of a man's twin watch chains was attached to the genuine article. But Kerry had been one of the best pickpockets in the city, and she knew all it took was a little patient surveillance. Wait until the swell draws his thimble from its pit, and then have at it.

Twenty-five minutes past nine. He tucked the watch away. "I'll leave you be, Kerry. Thank you for telling the watchmen to send for me."

He was halfway to the door before she spoke. "How's the doctor's daughter, by the way?"

He stopped and turned slowly.

"It's a small town, Justy. You can't walk a girl along the water for more than an hour in this town without some cove noticing."

"Is that so?"

Kerry's mouth twisted. "I didn't know you liked the fair ones. Or maybe it's not her looks that draws you. Her father's a wealthy man, I'm told, for a nimgimmer. A big house here, and a spread across the river, too. She's quite the catch."

His face burned, and she laughed. "Boys a dear, you always were easy to rake." Her voice was bitter. "But don't worry. I know you're not the kind to whore yourself. Not like me."

"Kerry . . ."

"I'll see you, Justy."

It was like having a door slammed in his face. He took one last look at her, sitting in the shadows, staring into the empty grate, then he turned and walked out into the night.

FOUR

A tall black man dressed in a long, old-fashioned coat opened the door to Dr. Reginald Cruikshank's townhouse. His lined face and patient eyes made him look like a statue of a saint carved in mahogany, with a halo of graying hair.

Justy stepped up under the porch, out of the rain. He pulled the dripping hat from his head. "Justice Flanagan. I'm very late, I'm afraid."

"All the other guests are in attendance, sir." The footman took the hat, and stood aside to let him into the hallway. A hum of noise came from deep in the house. There was a strong smell of candle wax, cigar smoke, and brandy. Justy struggled out of his wet coat. The ornate clock on the sideboard told him he was nearly two hours adrift.

"Sir?" The footman took the coat with one hand, and held up a mirror with the other. Justy used his fingers to fumble his hair into place. He looked the man in the eye. "What's your name?"

"Nicholas, sir."

"Well, thank you, Nicholas."

The slightest bow. "You are most welcome, sir."

A door behind him swung open, and the sound of a small crowd filled the hallway.

"Oh, Justice, at last!"

Eliza Cruikshank seemed to float down the hallway. A shiver ran through him, hot and cold at the same time, as though all the blood had been sucked out of his head and into his belly. The first time he had met Eliza, she had worn a long-sleeved, high-necked dress; the next time she had worn a ball gown.

Now she was wearing a strapless sheath of translucent white silk that barely covered her breasts.

He closed his mouth. She smiled and touched his cheek. "You're so late, you bad boy!"

It was the fashion to have tousled hair, but Eliza's was in more than the usual disarray, and there was a smear of lipstick at the corner of her mouth. Justy smelled the musty scent of brandy and champagne on her breath. The tingle in his groin evaporated.

"I'm very sorry, Eliza. There was an emergency. A young woman . . ."

"Oh, another woman?" She pouted. "Was she as exquisitely dressed as I?"

She twirled. The sheath of silk clung tight to her belly and thighs. Justy thought of the girl, lying in the mud, the gaping wound in her abdomen.

Eliza smirked. "You're just like Daddy. He thinks it's scandalous. But it's the latest thing. And I like it. Nathaniel likes it too, don't you, Nathaniel?"

"Yes, Miss Elizabeth," the footman said.

"Good." Eliza linked her arm through Justy's, and pulled him down the hall.

"His name is Nicholas," Justy whispered.

"Who?"

"Your footman."

She tossed her head. "Oh, Nathaniel, Nicholas, it doesn't matter. They're all Ns."

"What do you mean?"

"Daddy's slaves. They're all named N. The male ones, anyway. After Narcissus. He was the Emperor Caligula's secretary or something."

Justy felt cold. "Claudius."

"What?"

"Claudius. Narcissus was Claudius' secretary." He stopped. "Eliza, I didn't know your father had slaves."

"Well, of course he does, silly. He does have a thousand acres to farm."

"But he's a member of the Manumission Society, isn't he?"

"Oh, darling. Half the members still have slaves. You can't free them all at once, you know. Daddy says it would ruin the economy." She patted his arm. "Now come on and have a drink."

————•————

The Cruikshanks' withdrawing room was high-ceilinged, fifty feet square, carpeted by a thick rug of a gold and red design, and lit by a single enormous chandelier. The ladies were gathered around the fireplace, perched on arm-chairs and chaises, cooing over a baby in a bassinet. The gentlemen stood in a half circle beside the window, glasses in hand, arguing about whether the plans for the development of New York should be published or drawn up in secret. The third group, and the loudest, was a mix of men and women, all of whom were in various states of drunkenness. Two men were singing as a tall woman with a long nose danced in a circle, her arms in the air. Another man was asleep on a chaise longue, a half-full wineglass balanced precariously on his chest. The others were either watching or playing a rowdy game of cards on a small table piled with banknotes.

Justy stopped in the doorway. "Eliza, I thought it was just dinner."

"Oh, it was, darling, but then Piers and Sophie and the others popped in and now we're playing cards." She pulled him towards the group of young people. "You know everyone, don't you?"

Her entourage. She had introduced them to Justy at the City Ball, when they were in somewhat better repair. The dancing girl was Sally Olivetti. The singers were Jean Moulin and Michael Hogg. Constance Burr, Trudi Wolff, Piers Riker, and Chase Beaulieu were playing cards. The man asleep on the chaise was Peter Romanoff. They were the idle offspring of the richest families in New York.

Chase Beaulieu was a fair, stocky man of about twenty. He had the bleary look of a hardened rake coming to the end of a three-day drunk. He made a disgusted sound and threw down his cards. "The Devil has stolen my luck. Again."

The singing stopped and the ladies squealed as Piers Riker leaned forward to gather up his winnings. He was in his midtwenties, with long, dark hair pulled back from his head to show a high forehead with a sharp widow's peak. His face was narrow and his features were severe: a long nose and pointed chin, with a tiny rosebud of a mouth in between.

Justy watched him rake in the notes and coins. His father was Tobias Riker, a Wall Street merchant of Dutch origin who owned the Millennium Bank and sat on the boards of the most powerful institutions in New York. That included the Tontine Coffee House on Wall Street and the Common Council, which controlled so many aspects of life in the city, including policing.

Piers Riker did not work. He was content to ride his father's coattails, drinking, whoring, and gambling the money his father made. He finished scraping his winnings into an untidy pile and smiled at Beaulieu. "Perhaps you should have a leprechaun sit beside you, Chase, to bring you better fortune." He looked up at Justy. His eyes were small and quick, like a bird's.

Eliza's hand tightened on Justy's arm. "A glass of wine, darling?"

"Come now, Eliza." Riker's eyes were bright. "We mustn't force our pretentious tastes on Mister Flanagan. Surely you have a good common ale to offer him? A bumper of Switchback, or Pharaoh, perhaps?"

"A flicker of diddle!" Beaulieu laughed, his face flushed. "That's what a doxy had me buy her at the Shipmates last week. It's gin, I believe. Or geneva." He frowned. "Not sure, actually."

"Nobody cares what you ordered, or for whom you ordered it, Chase." Eliza's voice was cold.

"Sorry, Eliza." Beaulieu's eyes were glassy.

The baby began to wail. A nurse in a long white apron started across the room, but a tall, bony woman waved her back. She had lank blonde hair and skin that looked as pale as vellum against the purple silk of her dress. She looked into the bassinet, an uncertain look on her face, and the child's wail turned into a full-throated shriek.

Eliza whispered in Justy's ear, "Mindy Shotwell. Do you know her?"

Justy shook his head.

"From Albany. Her husband is Charles Shotwell, the one by the window in the awful yellow coat. He's a banker of some kind. English. No money of his own, which is why he married her. She came with a considerable dowry, which she needed because she was over thirty when they wed. And that was a few years ago. It's a miracle she was able to have a child. Here, I'll introduce you."

She pulled him by the arm. The infant was squalling now. Mindy Shotwell lifted it out and rested it gingerly on her shoulder. It had a shock of red hair that made it look as though its head had caught fire. It wriggled and fussed for a moment, and then let out a long, wet fart.

The room fell silent.

"Good God, Charles," one of the men by the window said. "What on earth have you spawned?"

The men brayed. The ladies tittered and waved their handkerchiefs. Mindy Shotwell's face was crimson. The nurse took the child and hurried away, its head like a rust stain on her crisp, white apron.

Eliza plastered a smile on her face, and led Justy to the group of men by the window.

"Gentlemen, may I present Marshal Justice Flanagan."

The men nodded and hummed and hah-ed, giving polite grins as Eliza introduced them by turn. Charles Shotwell was the last. He appeared unaffected by his son's outburst, or the ridicule it had inspired. He was a balding, pug-faced man of about forty, whose belly was barely confined by a yellow-and-black-striped waistcoat. He wore a single watch chain, stretched so tight it looked as though the timepiece attached to it might pop out at any moment. He was a little drunk, and sweating, so the hair around his balding crown looked like a slick of black paint. He hooked a thumb into his empty fob pocket and beamed a smile at Justy. "Never met a policeman before," he said.

"It that because you've done nothing wrong, or because there's not enough of us to go around?"

Shotwell honked. "The latter, more than likely."

Justy found himself grinning back. "I suppose I'll have to keep an eye on you."

"Let me make it easy and have you to lunch sometime."

"I'd like that."

"Hark at you, Charles," one of the other men said. "Always trying to sell someone something."

They all laughed, Shotwell loudest of all. His face flushed, revealing a long, straight cut on his left cheek, from his ear to the corner of his mouth.

"That's a nasty slice you've got there," Justy said.

Shotwell flashed his grin and touched the wound. "Here's a tip for you. Never shave yourself. Especially in the aftermath of a brisk evening. If your valet happens to be out of commission with the colic, go to a barber. Or wear stubble for a day."

His fellows chortled at the idea of going to work unshaven. Somewhere in the house, the baby was shrieking. Shotwell's wife was seated on a divan, looking stricken. Shotwell pulled the watch out of his pocket, looked at it blankly, and tucked it away again.

"What time is it, old man?" he asked one of his fellows.

The man's watch chains looked like they'd been detached from a ship's anchor and gilded. He hauled on one of them and produced something the size of a small apple. "A quarter of eleven, Charles. Past your boy's bedtime, I'd say."

"Past my bloody bedtime, too," Shotwell said. He tossed back his glass, turned to Justy, and stuck out his hand. "Damned good to meet you, sir."

"And you, Mister Shotwell. Good night."

Eliza led Justy back to the card table. Chase Beaulieu and Piers Riker were still playing. Chase Beaulieu let out a large belch.

Eliza grimaced. "Oh God, Chase."

"I'm merely communing with the infant," he slurred.

"You're disgusting."

"Yes. Awfully sorry."

Riker played a card, and Beaulieu groaned. He threw his cards down. "That's it. You've cleaned me out. Again."

Riker glanced at Justy. The tip of his tongue appeared, like a worm wriggling between two stones. "Join us, Flanagan, do. We're playing primero."

"No, thank you."

"Really? You might win some money. Something to supplement your policeman's salary. Not that we should be paying you anything at all, of course. Father says the very notion of a standing army in the city is an abomination."

"Father might change his mind if he was robbed at knifepoint or had his house burgled."

Riker smirked. "One has people to protect oneself from that sort of thing."

"And if one isn't wealthy enough to have people?"

"Well then, it's every man for himself. The very principles this fine republic was built on. We certainly don't need to pay vast sums of money to a bunch of . . . what's the phrase the guttersnipes use? Cossacks. Or is it crushers? I suppose you'd know better than I, given your provenance."

Justy smiled. "Both terms would do very well. All the time and money you've been spending in Dover Street brothels appears to have paid off."

Chase Beaulieu scoffed. "Oh, not Dover Street, old man. Piers has gone to the dark side." He held his hands up in the air, like a half-bit magician, and declaimed in a loud voice, "To Canvas Town!"

Everyone laughed, except Riker, whose face had turned as white as card.

Beaulieu appeared not to notice. "We went up there earlier. I'm damned glad I wasn't on my own. The place is all dark alleys and crooked lanes. Like a damned labyrinth. And I forgot to bring my ball of string!" He hiccupped and slapped the arm of the divan. "Ball of string!"

"Shut up, Chase!" Riker's voice was a lash.

There was silence in the room.

"Sorry," Beaulieu mumbled. He pushed himself to his feet. "Excuse me."

He took three careful steps away from the card table. He stumbled against Justy. He sniggered. "Sorry, old fellow. Would you mind helping me to the door?"

Justy had the impression of a man who had once been strong as an ox, but had let himself turn to fat. He steered Beaulieu away from the table.

Beaulieu muttered something.

"What was that?"

Beaulieu's head twitched, like a dog threatened by a stick. "I must speak to you," he whispered. "But not here."

Justy could feel eyes on his back. Riker and the others, watching him from the card table. He glanced at Beaulieu, saw the sweaty skin, the clear, darting eyes. Beaulieu was not drunk. He was scared.

"Hughson's?" Justy murmured.

"No. Piers' father goes there sometimes."

"The Merchant's, then. Tomorrow?"

"No. Monday. At six o'clock. And mind you are not followed."

They had reached the door. Beaulieu made a show of fumbling with the handle. "Thanks awfully, old fellow." His voice was a loud slur. He pushed out into the darkness of the corridor.

Justy walked slowly back towards the card table. Riker watched him.

Justy met his gaze. "So much for Princeton men being able to hold their liquor."

Riker smiled slightly. "Chase went to Columbia, with all the other shopkeepers' sons. Speaking of which, I saw your High Constable today, at the Tontine. Stuck out a mile, of course, in that awful red coat of his. Very gauche."

"I wonder if you'd have the courage to tell him so to his face."

"I don't see why not. The way he was groveling to my father, I shouldn't think he'd be much trouble at all in a contest between gentlemen. Perhaps you'd like to place a wager on that."

"You against Jake Hays? It sounds like quite an entertainment, but I'd rather not see the Bowling Green sullied by what little you have in the way of brains." He turned to Eliza. "I think I should go."

"Coward."

Justy stopped, his skin bumping all the way up his spine to the nape of his neck.

Riker's voice: "I'm calling you a coward, Flanagan. Didn't you hear?"

"Oh, I heard."

Riker lolled back in his chair. "Then you are not a gentleman. A gentleman would not allow himself to be so insulted. A gentleman would call me out."

Justy was aware that the entire room had gone quiet. "I would call you out, Riker, but in case you hadn't noticed, it's raining outside." He turned to look the foppish young man in the eye. "And if you had any experience of firearms, you'd know that pistols don't work particularly well in wet weather."

One of the men beside the window barked out a laugh. "Well said, sir!"

The laughter rippled outward, and soon everyone was roaring.

Riker's face was tight. "Filthy bog-lander. A waste of rations, like the rest of them. Lazier than Negroes and more expensive. We should burn the scum in the ships they arrive in."

Justy felt ice cold. Eliza pulled at his arm. He patted her hand. "Is that champagne and brandy you're drinking, Eliza? I'll have one of those, if you don't mind."

Riker was shuffling the cards, his tiny mouth twisted in a smile. Justy pulled out a chair. "What did you say you were playing?"

"Primero."

"Never heard of it."

Riker's eyes glittered. "I'll teach you."

———◆———

Justy was lying. Primero was just one of the many card games he had learned to play, at university in Ireland, and on his travels throughout Europe. He was not a particularly skilled gambler, but he could read men well, and he had a strong stomach for risk. It had been years since he had played that particular game, but he found it was like slipping on an old leather glove, and once he had flexed his fingers, won a little and lost a little, he began to take his revenge. He had to start small, as he had very little money to play with, but soon the pile of notes on his side of the table grew fat. Riker drank heavily, which made it easier, and within an hour, Justy had cleaned him out.

He stood up. He knew he had gone too far. He should have allowed Riker to escape with some money, and a little face, but the cold rage inside him had made it impossible to stop.

"One more hand," Riker slurred.

"You're drunk, Riker. Let it end here."

"One more hand. Give me the chance to win it back, for God's sake."

"You have nothing to wager."

"My carriage. It's worth a thousand pounds at least."

"No carriage is worth that."

"You haven't seen it. Or the horses."

Justy didn't need a carriage. He didn't need a horse, let alone two. He had no room to keep them, and he was well aware of the cost of maintenance and stabling. But the vengeful part of him wanted to crush Riker.

He looked around. Eliza's guests had left their places and were standing around them, watching. It was late, and the room was heavy with the smell of candle wax. The rain drummed on the windows. Eliza was perched on a chaise on his left, her back straight as a ramrod, her hands clenched in her lap. She shook her head slowly, her eyes bright.

He sat down.

FIVE

Sunday

New York was a big city, more than sixty thousand people, spread over two square miles. The number of people living in the spider's web of streets at the tip of Manhattan Island grew every day, but the town itself was growing a good deal more slowly. A special survey commission was working on a plan to develop the land north of the city, but surveying took time, and no one wanted to start moving earth until the commission released its recommendations of how the city should be built and where the main roads should go. Which meant that newcomers were resigned for the time being to cramming themselves into the slums and shantytowns of the Hudson and East River waterfronts.

The crush of people made New York a dangerous place to live, and the more people that arrived in the city, the more that died there. Some died in work accidents, buried in landslides or crushed under cart wheels; others died drunk, falling into the rivers or freezing to death; many, like Justy's mother, died in the bouts of yellow fever that tore through the city every few years.

A very few met their end at another man's hand, but that number was growing as the torrent of newcomers turned the poorer parts of the city into a pressure cooker. The black, Irish, and nativist gangs that competed for control of New York's underworld preferred to maim rather than kill, as murders attracted unwanted attention. When things went too far, the gangsters either disposed of the body or made it look like an accident. An obvious murder was a rare thing.

And the murder of a young woman rarer still. Justy could count on one hand the number of violent female deaths he had encountered in his four years as a Marshal. He rested a candelabra carefully on the corner of the smooth granite slab, close to the girl's head. She was young, pretty, and dark-skinned, with a long nose, a narrow face, and a high forehead. In the soft light, her skin looked as smooth as a piece of silk. The nails on her fingers and toes were trimmed and filed. Her hands and feet had neither calluses nor bruising, none of the usual signs of hard work. She was well cared for, well nourished. The robe she had been wearing was made of fine wool, and embroidered at the edges in blue and gold thread. Even with the appalling gash in her torso, she looked like someone's precious daughter. And yet no one had come.

His eyes were gritty. He had gone back to his lodgings after Eliza's party, and tried to sleep. But he had snapped awake just a few hours later, bathed in sweat, unable to recall whatever it was that had disturbed his dreams. He had dressed, intending to go to the Federal Hall, but his feet had carried him up-hill instead of down, through the still-sleeping city to the mean alley where the girl had died. He had looked over the scene in the thin, early morning light, then walked to the Almshouse, where bodies were kept in an old wine cellar until they were claimed by relatives or friends.

He felt a tickle in his nose. The air was heavy with the smell of lavender. The nuns who ran the Almshouse had stuffed bunches of the herb into sconces around the cellar to mask the smell of death. Justy had argued for the establishment of a proper morgue, with proper ventilation and some windows to see by, but his superior, the High Constable Jacob Hays, made the undeniable point that a corpse was rarely left unclaimed for more than a night, so the cellar was really all the city needed.

"What do you make of it, Mister Gorton?" Justy asked.

Gorton stepped out of the shadows. He slipped something into his mouth and leaned forward over the body. There was a crunching sound, and Justy smelled coffee.

"Professional job, I'd say," Gorton said.

The cut was a livid purple gash that ran from the girl's sternum down the length of her torso. The nuns had washed the corpse, and removed the girl's entrails. Someone had bound the body cavity closed with a bandage, but the cut still flared at both ends, like a split sack of cotton.

Gorton ran his tobacco-stained forefinger down the length of the gash. "This cut's precise. No hesitation. A clean line. Means the doer had a sharp knife and he knew how to use it. But this . . ." He pointed at the end of the cut.

Justy picked up the candelabra. The long, vertical gash ended two inches below the belly button, but Gorton was pointing lower down, at a thin, horizontal cut, less than a half-inch wide, just below the upper line of the puff of hair above the girl's pubis.

"I missed that." Justy leaned in, and felt the skin bump, all the way up his spine. "A filleting knife, you think?"

"Could be. It was something narrow, anyway."

Justy placed the candelabra carefully on the corner of the slab. It was a moment before he could speak. "So he stabbed her to death, and then cut her open? Why? What kind of monster does something like this?"

"One who knows how to cut up bodies well enough, I'd say. A huntsman perhaps." Gorton's voice was grim. "Or a butcher."

The faint chimes of a church bell floated down to them. Justy looked towards the sound, hoping to see someone at the top of the long flight of cellar steps. "Eight o'clock. Half the city's either at work or at mass by now. The other half's at breakfast. And no one has come to claim her. Do you think that's strange?"

"Depends on the girl. I grew up in Whitechapel. Kinchin would go missing all the time from round there, and no one ever gave a dry bob for 'em. Begging your pardon."

"This isn't London. And that girl doesn't look like the kind that's disposable. She looks like the kind whose parents will have been going mad with worry all night."

"That's if they even knew she was out of her bed. Eight's still early for some. Mayhap the parents haven't even seen she's gone yet."

Justy nodded. Gorton was making all the right points. But something inside him knew that the watchman was wrong, and that there would be no anxious parents hammering at the doors of the Almshouse or Federal Hall on the girl's account.

"I don't think anyone's coming for her, Mister Gorton. Which means we'll need to find out who she is ourselves."

"We?"

Justy gave him a long look. The candle flames lengthened in the still air. "Haven't you asked yourself why I dismissed Playfair, but asked you to stay with me?"

Gorton gave the universal soldier's shrug, the one that said officers frequently did things that made no sense at all.

"What made you tell Mister Playfair to correct himself last night?" Justy asked.

"Don't know what you mean, Marshal." Gorton's tone was wooden.

"I don't know you, Gorton, but I know Playfair well enough. He's not the kind of man to go back on a story once he's told it. Not without some convincing."

Gorton's stare was impassive. It was a moment before he spoke. "It was the young woman. Miss O'Toole. I reckoned if she really knew you, she'd pay you a visit, and then you'd find out what happened from her. It seemed like too great a risk."

"So you don't like to take risks?"

"Only when it's worth it. There was no profit in having you believe that we was first to find the girl, far as I could tell."

"If there had been, would you have stuck to your story?"

Gorton was silent. The candlelight accentuated the lines in his face and the gray in his hair. They made him look like an old man. But he still looked fit, rangy and muscled, with the sharp face and quick eyes of a hunting dog.

"You were a marksman in the King's Marines, weren't you?" Justy asked.

"And a scout." Gorton's eyes slid over Justy's, making the briefest contact. "Like yourself."

Justy had a sudden memory of sliding on his belly through a patch of wet grass, his face blackened with burned cork, his knife slippery in his hand, his eyes fixed on the red coat between the trees, his stomach liquid with fear. He shook the thought away. How did Gorton know? He had not made a habit of blabbing about his part in the Irish Rebellion, but he supposed it was inevitable that people would find out. "I hope you won't hold it against me."

Gorton smiled slightly. "We're all friends now, Marshal. They never sent Marines to Ireland, so you won't have milled any of my mates."

The whites of his eyes looked yellow. His irises were almost black. Less like a hunting dog. More like a wolf.

"You've kept your skills up, too, Marshal," Gorton said. "Judging by the way you dealt with that cove last night. Nice moves, like the man said."

"It gets more difficult every year. Owney Clearey does his best, but I'm a poor student."

"Clearey the pugilist?"

"I train at his gymnasium. Or I did, at least. I haven't been in a while." The last time, more than a month ago, Clearey had given him a tiresome lecture on using ordinary household objects in a fight. The edge of a dish could crush a man's windpipe. A rolled-up sheaf of papers could gouge out an eye. Anything could be a weapon, properly aimed, properly applied, with maximum force and maximum speed and maximum aggression. And so on and so forth. Justy had lost interest and not gone back since. As such, he had felt slow the previous night, and ill-prepared for a tussle. But the man had been drunk and clumsy. Which made both of them lucky.

He looked down at the girl. The soft light of the candles made deep hollows of her eye sockets, and turned the gash in her abdomen into a dark pit.

"Someone might come, I suppose." His own voice surprised him, a murmur that seemed to float up between them to the vaulted ceiling.

"But you doubt it."

"I do." Justy nodded. "What's your first name?"

Gorton looked surprised. "Jeremiah."

"Well, Jeremiah, you likely know this already, but Marshals work alone. I couldn't get a constable or a watchman to help me on an investigation, even if I wanted to. But that doesn't mean I can't hire on help on my own account."

"You're offering to hire me?"

"I am. These injuries might tell us something about the doer, but until we establish her identity, it'll be very difficult to catch him. I'm not going to be able to do any of it on my own."

"You'll pay?"

"Two dollars fifty a day. The same rate you get from the city."

Gorton looked as though he was tasting the idea, rolling it around on his tongue like a chunk of rock sugar. "I can't give you that much time, Marshal. I'll still have to do my warden's work. If I call in sick, they won't pay me. They might even fire me."

"So you work a double shift: with the Watch at night and with me during the day."

"When would I sleep?"

"You catch an hour's kip here or there. It's just two days. Three at the most. Nothing for a corporal of Marines. You must have spent whole weeks awake on your feet in Guadeloupe."

"I was a younger man then."

"Three days. It's all I need."

Gorton pursed his lips. "Why me?"

"What do you think?"

A shrug. "Because I'm an incomer. Because I'm not long in town. So I'm not in anyone's pocket yet."

Damn, but the man was sharp. "That's part of it, right enough. But you have the air of a man who might like this kind of work." He looked into Gorton's eyes. "Most of all, though, it's because you care."

"Do I?"

"I saw you earlier, Jeremiah. You closed the girl's eyes. And you covered her face."

"So?" Gorton's strange eyes were unreadable.

Justy felt the heat leap into his face. "Look. You can walk out of here now and leave this to me. The chances are I'll make a little headway, but I won't get the whole story. Come Sunday, we'll put the tib in her eternity box and forget about her." He leaned forward. "Or you can stand with me, find out who this girl was, and help me get the beast who cut her open like an animal. And we can make the bastard swing." The pulse was hard and fast in his throat.

"So you are Irish after all, Marshal, I was beginning to wonder." Gorton smiled, for the first time. "Two fifty a day?"

"Double your money."

———•———

Sister Marie-Therese of the Incarnation, the senior vestal of the New York order of St. Ursula, was waiting for him at the top of the cellar stairs. She was a petite, thin woman, with small button-like eyes set deep in the sockets of her skull. She was at least a foot shorter than Justy, but somehow she still managed to look at him down her long, pale, blade-like nose.

"Have you completed your inspection, Marshal?" A trace of an Irish accent, so faint that Justy couldn't place the region.

"For now, yes. But I'll return later. This afternoon. Unless she is claimed, of course."

"You think she will not be?"

"I don't know. Would it be a problem if she were not?"

The nun gathered up the rosary that was tied around her waist. She began clicking through the beads. "She is not Catholic."

"So what? We've had all sorts in here in the past. People of all colors. Even Dutchmen."

He smiled, but the sister's mouth tightened into a thin, white line. "She is not a Christian."

"What difference does that make?"

"Regardless of what my predecessors might have permitted, Marshal, I remind you that this is a house of Christ. We do not welcome those who reject His word."

Justy felt his face flush. "And how, precisely, has the young woman lying dead on a slab down there done that?"

The beads clicked. "She was a Mohammedan. As such, she explicitly rejected Christ's teachings."

"How do you know she was a Mohammedan?"

"Sister Claire O'Connor pointed it out. She washed the body when it came in. She saw the girl's hands and forearms were painted with red dye recently. She lived for several years in Africa and knows their customs. She tells me young Moorish girls paint themselves this way."

"I didn't see any marks."

"They are very faint. And her skin is . . . quite dark." The sister sniffed.

"I must insist that you keep the body here until she is claimed or identified, Sister. Regardless of her religion. Or her color."

"You insist?"

"Request, then. On behalf of the City of New York."

"It is impossible. A heathen, in God's house? It is blasphemy."

Justy could feel the pulse in his temples. "This is my commandment, that ye love one another, even as I have loved you."

The clicking stopped. The nun's voice was cold. "I do not care to have a theological debate with you, Marshal. I have my sisters to think about."

"And what will they think if you toss a girl's body out, to be thrown into some waterfront drainage pit with the dead dogs and the slaughterhouse leavings? And on a Sunday, too."

Sister Marie-Therese's skin seemed to tighten across the bones of her skull. She and Justy stared at each other. She gave a sharp nod. "Burial day is Friday next, so you have until Thursday night. If she is not claimed by then, I shall arrange for her removal."

"One more thing. I would like to speak with Sister Claire."

"Certainly not."

Justy sighed. "Think of it this way, if this girl really is a Mohammedan, Sister Claire may be able to help me identify her. And the sooner I can do that, the sooner I'll have her out of your cellar."

She considered the point. "She is sleeping now. You'll have to come back later."

"I shall. Thank you. In the meantime, did she say anything else about the girl?"

The nun looked as though she had smelled something rotten. "Her clothing. Her nightshirt, or whatever it is you might call it, is of exceptionally high quality."

"Go on."

"Sister Claire tells me there is a Mohammedan family that lives north of the city that sells this kind of cloth. But it is very expensive, made of a fine wool. Very lightweight, with some exquisite embroidery on the hems. Remarkable workmanship, I must say." Her tone was grudging.

"I thought it was rather thin."

"Indeed it is. Very thin, yet extremely warm. Sister Claire says Mohammedan ladies usually wear such garments indoors. Or under an outer cloak of some kind."

"So it's not the kind of thing one would expect a young girl to be running about in, at night?"

"One would not *expect* a young girl of that age to be out of doors at night at all, Marshal. Mohammedan or otherwise." She folded her hands together over her belt. "Now, if you'll excuse me, I have my rounds to make."

SIX

Hughson's Tavern was a deceptively sturdy wooden structure, built at the end of Liberty Street, on the southwest corner of Courtland Market. Three stories high, with a steep roof, the tavern leaned precariously over the dank swirl of the Hudson River. It had an infamous history. Sixty years before, John and Sally Hughson had been convicted of acting as a go-between for criminals, fencing goods stolen by slaves from their masters and selling them on to free New Yorkers who liked a bargain. Today the tavern was just a tavern, run by Seamus Tully, a farm boy from County Tyrone.

The door was wide open. Kerry lowered Rosie to the ground, and the little girl ran inside. She squealed as her mother picked her up and swung her in the air, then settled her on her hip.

"I hope she wasn't too much trouble, Kerry girl." Tamsin Tully's voice was a combination of West African lilt and Irish brogue. She wore a long apron over her indigo skirt, and her shirtsleeves were rolled up to show a pair of strong forearms.

"Not at all," Kerry said. "She helped me at the school this morning, didn't you, Rosie?"

"We tidied the books," Rosie said.

Kerry winked at her. "I thought I'd better not bring her round too early, Tam. In case you had a late one last night."

"And so we did. I didn't get to my bed until three. But Seamus was square. I'm usually up at six to clean the place, but he let me rest on and did it all himself. I only just got up."

"That's why you look so dimber, girl."

"Ah, you're great." Tamsin lowered Rosie to the floor. "Will you come in for a damper?"

"I will. But only for a moment. I've to be back at the school this afternoon." She had to duck under the lintel. "Jesus! Why did the bloody Dutch build their doors so low to the ground?"

Tamsin laughed. "To keep the bloody Africans out, of course."

They hugged each other. They were both tall women, but the resemblance ended there. Kerry was slim and wiry, with long, straight hair and caramel-colored skin, while Tamsin was dark and voluptuous, with big almond-shaped eyes, and a broad halo of tight curls. She was seventeen when Seamus Tully had spied her at the Fly Market, shopping for pears for her mistress. He was smitten on sight, but she was a slave then, and forbidden from any kind of relationship that might result in a child. So he saved every penny he had for five years, and then he went to her mistress and persuaded her to sell Tamsin to him. He bought her, freed her, and married her, all on the same day.

Kerry held her friend by the shoulders and looked down. "I thought I felt something. How far along are you?"

Tamsin smiled. "Four months."

"I thought you were done with all of that."

"I thought I was too. I suppose God has other plans for me."

Kerry smiled back. "Congratulations, then."

"Thanks." Tamsin patted one of the stools at the counter. "Come on now. I'll get you a cup of coffee. There's bull-dogs in the basket there."

Kerry settled herself, and lifted one of the flour-dusted sweet rolls to her nose.

"I have to tell you something, Tam. We had a bit of a scare last night, Rosie and me."

The child was balanced on her mother's knee. She looked up, with big solemn eyes. Kerry smiled at her. "We took a roundabout way home, along Chapel Street. I didn't want to go up Elm Street. You know, past the old burial ground."

Tamsin nodded. "It's a desecration, what they're doing."

"Aye. Anyway, while we were there, I heard a sound come from one of the alleyways. There was a girl down there."

"She was crying, Mammy," Rosie said.

Kerry took a breath. "I couldn't leave Rosie on the street, Tam."

"She was on the ground," Rosie said. "She was hurt."

Kerry touched her hair. "Did you see anything else, Rosie?"

The little girl shook her head. "You said to look away."

Tamsin placed her gently on the ground. "Why don't you find your dolly, Rosie. Let Mammy and Auntie Kerry talk for a little."

The girl ran into a back room. Tamsin's face was tight. "We sent her to you to be safe."

"And she was safe, I promise. I went straight to call the Watch. And then straight home."

They sat for a moment, as the sound of the street filtered into the tavern. A man calling out the price of his apple pies. Two women fighting over something. Kerry looked at the basket of sweet rolls. She had lost her appetite.

"I'm sorry, Tam, I had to go down there. That sound the girl made, like an animal with its back broken. What kind of a person would I be if I'd have walked on?"

It was a moment before Tamsin nodded. "You're right, I suppose. I just don't like the thought of Rosie being there. Growing up in this city, she'll see such things soon enough."

Kerry reached forward and took her friend's hand. Tamsin squeezed. "So what of the girl? Raped, I suppose."

"I don't think so. She was cut, like you gut a rabbit. Here to here." She drew a line down her stomach.

Tamsin shuddered. "Dear Lord Jesus, this city. It gets worse every day. Did they get the doctor to her?"

Kerry shook her head. "She died."

"Oh, no." Tamsin closed her eyes for a moment. "Did you recognize her, at all?"

Kerry shook her head. "She was young. Thirteen or fourteen, maybe. She had some odd togs on, too. Nothing but a kemesa made of some soft cloth. A nightgown, maybe. She was abram underneath, like she'd just come from her bed."

"Did you see her hands?"

"Soft as gingerbread."

"So, not a worker. A curtezan, then?"

Kerry shrugged. "She didn't seem so well-used."

A floorboard creaked. A short, bearded man stood in the doorway that led to the upstairs rooms. He had wide shoulders and sharp green eyes, and Rosie was balanced on his hip, chewing the end of one of her pigtails.

"This one woke me up, asking for her dolly," the man said, and kissed Rosie's forehead.

"Sorry, Seamus," Tamsin said. "Let me take her."

"No, she's grand." Seamus Tully bounced his daughter a couple of times, and she giggled.

"How dost, Kerry?" he asked.

"Well enough, Seamus. What time did they go to last night?"

"Last night? This morning, you mean."

"Well, it's good business, if nothing else."

"That's true." He pulled the pigtail gently out of his daughter's mouth. "Justy Flanagan was by earlier."

Kerry shifted on her stool. Tully's eyes sparkled. "Nice to hear youse are back to talking."

"I wouldn't go so far." She winced at the sound of the bitterness in her own voice.

"Oho! So he's still hunting coney down in the First Ward, then?"

"Enough, Seamus!" Tamsin squeezed Kerry's hand. "He's a fool. They're both fools."

Tully was unfazed. "He told me about that girl you found last night."

"Did he?"

"He thinks she might be a Mohammedan. Something one of the nuns at the Almshouse told him about the duds she was wearing. A kemesa, he said, made of some kind of soft wool, with an embroidered edge. It made me think of that shawl I bought you for your birthday, Tam, remember? The red one."

His wife narrowed her eyes. "The one you used to mop up spilled brandy at Christmas, you mean?"

He grinned. "Aye, well, I bought it from one of the Mussulman families that lives up by Hudson's Kill. I was told it was the best cloth in the city."

"Good thing the bingo washed out, then," Tamsin said. "I'll fetch it."

"Thanks, *a chara*." He kissed her on the cheek as she squeezed past, taking Rosie from him and balancing the child on her right hip in one swift motion. He watched his wife as she swayed up the steps, and then winked at Kerry, who tried to smother her smile.

"Thanks for looking after Rosie for us, Kerry."

"No bother. She's like my own."

"I see that." He squeezed her hand. "I worry sometimes she makes you think of Daniel."

And there it was, the desperate ache in her throat. The sensation of standing on the edge of a chasm, the wind at her back. She had been just seventeen years old when she had given birth to the boy. They had just celebrated his second birthday when he fell ill with colic and was taken to the sanatorium at Turtle Bay. Away from the city, Daniel had escaped the yellow fever that ravaged New York that summer, but he could not escape the fire that tore through the hospital and burned it to the ground. Kerry had to content herself with burying a box of ash.

Tully walked to the counter, refilled her cup, and handed it to her. The hot coffee eased her throat and warmed her hands. She smiled at him. "She's a lovely wee girl, Seamus. I'm happy to have her, anytime."

"Well, we're grateful." Tully poured himself a cup. "So what about this girl, then? You think she might have been Mohammedan?"

Kerry shrugged. "She looked like a hundred others. Darker than me. Not as dark as Tam."

Tamsin returned, carrying a red shawl. "Is it the same cloth?"

Kerry weighed the material in her hands. "It's close." She examined the embroidery on its hem. "I'd say the girl's shirt was finer, but the edges are the same."

Tully put an arm around his wife. She rested her head on his shoulder and turned into him. Her hands crossed over her belly, cradling the slight bulge.

"Kerry?" Tully was staring, a worried look on his face. She could feel every hair on her body standing on end. An image flashed in her mind, the girl's hands dark and sticky with blood, crossed over her belly, holding herself. Her own stomach felt suddenly hollowed out.

"Tell me about these Mussulmen, Seamus."

He shook his head. "Not much to tell, for they keep to themselves. You know the kill?"

"Well, I've never been there, for I'm not mad. But I know where it is."

Hudson's Kill was a small tidal stream that decanted into the river of the same name. It was surrounded by marshes, which had an evil reputation amongst both the Negro and Irish populations. They said spirits lived up there, selkies and kelpies that drifted up from the sea to hunt for children in the night.

"They built a kind of compound up there, years ago," Seamus said.

"Compound? I thought you said it was a family."

"It was, ten years back. A dozen or fifteen of them settled on the meadowland south of the kill. Not anyplace I'd like to live. Swamp and mosquitos in summer and floods and ice in the winter. But they set about draining some of the land and building on it. A lot of buildings. Well made, too. Not your usual Canvas Town kips."

"So how many live up there now?"

"A lot more than a dozen. But there's no way to find out. The way they've built the place, there's only one way in and out, and there's always a couple of stout fellows standing about there to help with directions, if you take my meaning." He gave her a sharp look. "So whatever it is you're thinking of doing, don't."

Her temper flared. "You can read minds now, can you?"

"No need, when I can read your face. You look like you're measuring a man for his coffin." He tried a smile. "You'd be terrible at cards."

"Aye, well, I'm not thinking about playing games just now."

Seamus Tully nodded slowly. "I can see that."

SEVEN

Justy's office was a ten-foot cube with a bare wooden floor and a single window, too high in the wall to look into the street. It smelled musty, making him suspect it had been a storeroom, but he appreciated the spare austerity of the space. A table, a chair, a lockable drawer, and the armchair for visitors. Plenty of light and no distractions. Apart from the anti-Catholic tract that someone had placed carefully in the center of the desk for him to find that morning. "A Short and Sure Method for the Extirpation of Popery." Justy folded it in half and pushed it to the side.

Gorton sat stiffly in the battered leather armchair opposite him, clicking the nail of his right index finger with his teeth. He saw Justy watching him and put his hands in his lap. The skin around his cuticles was red and raw.

"That's a bad habit you have there," Justy said.

Gorton gave him a blank look with his wolf's eyes, and Justy felt himself redden. He felt for his purse in the inside pocket of his coat, pulled out five dollar coins and stacked them on the table. "Here. Two days. Payment in advance."

Gorton looked at the coins. His Adam's apple bobbed and his fingers fluttered in his lap, like a bird preening its feathers. Then he leaned forward, scooped up the money, and sat back in one smooth movement.

"So how do we start?" he asked.

"With the shoes."

Gorton's face was blank. Justy smiled. "You said earlier that you thought Miss O'Toole might come to see me. In fact, I went to see her. She told me that when she found the girl, she was missing a shoe. But I saw no shoes in the alley. It's possible Miss O'Toole was mistaken, of course. But I examined the dead girl's feet this morning, and saw no cuts or bruises. Which leads me to the conclusion that she was indeed wearing shoes, and to the inevitable question, where are those shoes now?" He gave Gorton a frank look. "Sister Marie-Therese says the girl's robe was expensive. It stands to reason, then, that her shoes would be, too. They, along with the robe, are the best clues we have as to who this girl was."

Gorton thought for a moment, then cleared his throat. "It was muddy down there, after the rain. A small pair of shoes could easily get squashed down the muck."

"Perhaps you're right, Mister Gorton. I should go back to take a second look."

Gorton stood up. "No need. I'll speak to Mister Playfair. Between the two of us, we'll find them. You can count on it." Gorton flashed a ragged row of sharp, tobacco-stained teeth, and then he was gone.

———————

"You could have got him for half the price, Justice."

Jacob Hays was standing in the doorway. He was a barrel-shaped man, a foot shorter than Justy's six feet, but broad in the shoulders and stout in the belly. His dark hair was swept back from a high forehead, and it curled over the collar of the long red overcoat that he always wore when he was on duty. He grinned at Justy, then walked across the room and peered down into the street below. "So, what do you make of him?"

"Gorton? I think he shows potential."

"He's a gambler. His commanding officer in Guadeloupe wrote and told me. Money fairly flows through the man's fingers, he said. That's why you could have got him cheap."

"I'd prefer to pay a man what he's worth."

"Very commendable." Hays picked up the tract on Justy's desk. "Another one?"

Justy shrugged. "My weekly love letter. I have a whole drawer full."

"You keep them?"

"I don't like to waste the paper."

Hays flopped into the armchair. "I've just come from the Tontine."

"On a Sunday?"

The Tontine Coffee House was a gathering place on Wall Street. Brokers and businessmen used its well-appointed rooms to trade anything from a shipload of tobacco to a portfolio of stocks and bonds. There were several such meeting houses, but the Tontine was the most exclusive. Its senior membership included the richest and most powerful businessmen in New York, if not the country, which made it a waypoint on the career path of any politician aiming for a place on the national stage.

Hays waved his hand. "You know my ambitions extend no further than my current office. I have no desire to be a damned alderman, or anything else. I was feeling them out."

"And?"

"And it turns out that I have considerable support. But there are complications."

Hays had fought for years to become both High Constable and Captain of the Watch. The twin appointments gave him oversight of the city during both night and day, but comparatively little power to stop the rising tide of crime in New York. He had lobbied for more constables, both to assist the Marshals in investigations and to break up the increasing number of riotous assemblies. He wanted to do as the French had done and the English were trying to do: create a permanent police force for the city. The previous Mayor, a Federalist, had supported the idea. But the new Mayor, Edward Livingstone, was a Democrat-Republican, a Jeffersonian, which made him a fervent opponent of anything that had the whiff of the English about it.

Which was why Hays had spent his Sunday morning drinking coffee. Livingstone was a politician, and the lifeblood of any politician was money. In New York City, money meant Wall Street. And, as Justy knew from his own experience, the biggest money dined and traded at the Tontine. Hays had been making the case that the best way for Wall Street to secure its money was with a police force.

"What complications?" Justy asked.

"This damned plan for the city's expansion, of course. It's become a bargaining chip. Every speculator in the city wants to know where the main roads will run, and where the most valuable plots of land will be. And because my constables guard the door when the Commission meets, they think I have some inside knowledge. They say they'll support me, if I can tip them. Me! The High Constable! Who the hell do they think I am?"

"I see the difficulty."

"Do you, indeed?" Hays snorted. "Well, talking of difficulty, what's this about you ordering a watchman away from his post last night? I've already had an inquiry from the Council about it."

"I needed a guard. A girl was killed, and—"

"I know all about that." Hays made a dismissive gesture. "Someone went too far with one of Lew Owens' stable, I presume."

"Why? Because the girl was black?"

"That, and the clothes she was wearing. Or not wearing. Some kind of exotic robe, wasn't it? Hardly the sort of thing a respectable young woman would wear."

"You've been talking to Sister Marie-Therese."

"Have I?"

"Did she mention the markings on the girl's hands? Moorish girls decorate themselves thus. And one of her nuns thinks the robe was of a Moorish design."

"Yes, she told me about the Mohammedan theory. But I find it hard to credit." Hays leaned back in his chair and examined the ceiling. "Do we even have any Moors in New York?"

"Not many. A small community of about a dozen settled just south of Hudson's Kill, ten years ago now. Runaway slaves, the story goes. Led by a fellow who calls himself Umar Salam. They escaped from the Carolinas in a boat and were lucky enough to be picked up by a Quaker schooner, which brought them here."

"And you know this . . . how?"

"I dropped in to Hughson's this morning. Seamus Tully told me what he knows. A few of their menfolk do some trading in the market. Fish from the river, eels from the marsh, and some fine cloth, imported from the East. The men keep to themselves, and the women are rarely seen, but Seamus says the community has grown over the years."

"Grown how?"

Justy shrugged. "Mohammedans newly arrived in the city, looking for those that share their beliefs. Other runaways, perhaps."

"Hmm." Hays thought for a moment. "The good sister implied she was reluctant to keep the body in the Almshouse. You appear to have convinced her otherwise."

"Mohammedan or not, she was a girl, Jake. Barely thirteen, I'd say. The bastard that killed her stabbed her in the belly first, then split her like a goddamned sausage."

He let that sink in, but Hays said nothing.

Justy felt his face flush. "This is bold-faced murder, Jake. Not some waterfront frisk gone too far. A young girl, slaughtered and dumped. No one's come to claim her, and no one will. Which leaves us. We have to speak for her. We have to act for her. And that means finding her killer. To do that, I need to know who she is, and I can't find that out if she's been tossed in a nameless grave by some stiff-necked harridan in an overstarched wimple."

There was sweat on his upper lip.

Hays held up his hands in surrender. "Fair enough. How long did the sister give you?"

"Until Thursday evening."

"And you're using Gorton?"

"On his own time. Unless you can spare him from his rounds."

"Well, I can't. We're damned short-staffed at the moment, as you know."

"I do."

Hays grasped the lapels of his red coat, like a knight testing the fit of his armor. "Well, I'd ask you to luncheon, but I have a meeting with the Mayor."

"Is the police force on the agenda?"

Hays gave a thin smile. "It's my only agenda, Justice. As you know."

"Go gcuire Dia an t-ádh ort."

"I hope that's not some leprechaun's curse."

"It means may God place His luck upon you."

"May he, indeed." And Hays strode out of the room, the tails of his long coat unfurling behind him.

Justy watched him go. Jacob Hays had hired him and mentored him, and Justy had come to know the High Constable well in the last few years. He was a conscientious man, the kind who considered every possibility before making a decision. The kind who followed every lead of an investigation, wherever it led, and who kept meticulous files. Born in New York, Hays had watched the city grow as he had grown, and he knew every square inch of its streets. He knew about the Mohammedan community living on the edge of Canvas Town, Justy was sure. So why was he pretending he didn't?

EIGHT

Sister Claire looked as though she had been pulled off a potato field in County Kerry and stuffed into a nun's habit that very morning. Her forehead, cheeks, and nose were scarlet red and peeling, and her hands were as wrinkled and brown as a worn pair of shoes. She had the patient, ageless air of a woman who has spent her life helping others, without expecting anything in return.

She sat straight-backed in an upright wooden chair, feet crossed at the ankle, the toes of her heavy shoes suspended an inch from the stone floor. She raised her face to the afternoon sun that lit the small space, with its two chairs and long, wooden table.

The girl's body was laid out on the oak. It was covered from toes to neck by a white sheet, which made her skin look much darker. The removal of her organs and the cool air of the cellar had forestalled corruption of the body, but there was still a distinct smell in the small room. Justy found himself breathing though his mouth.

The sister seemed unaffected. "I thought it might be easier to see her here, rather than down in that terrible place." Her accent was soft and educated.

"I'm surprised Sister Marie-Therese allowed it."

"Sometimes it's better to beg forgiveness than ask permission."

"Speaking of which, I have a man coming later to sketch a picture of the girl. It may help us identify her. I haven't told the vestal."

"What she doesn't know won't hurt her." The nun's blue eyes were bright with mischief.

The girl's cheeks were gray and slack. They pulled the corners of her mouth so that the purple lips were dragged slightly open over her even teeth. Her eyes were half-open. The nun had tried to smooth them closed, but they seemed fixed in place, and the whites were like two empty slits in her dark skin.

"She has gone to God," Sister Claire said.

"That's not what Sister Marie-Therese thinks."

"Indeed." The nun smiled faintly.

"She told me you spent some time among Mohammedan people."

"Ten years in Araby and another seven along the Slave Coast. In that time I came to learn that we are all very much the same. We all share the same essential beliefs."

"So why the objection to having a Mohammedan in the Almshouse?"

Sister Claire shrugged. "Partly because of partisanship. If someone's on their side, it means they're not on ours. And partly because people only see the differences between peoples, not the similarities. Look at us and the Protestants. There is nothing to tell between us, and yet there's so much hatred."

Justy looked at the girl. "So what can you tell me about her? Is she Mohammedan?"

"Almost certainly." The sister hopped off the chair. She barely went as high as Justy's chest, but she was tall enough to reach over the body and take hold of the top of the sheet. She flicked it back, and Justy felt his stomach lurch. The edges of the cut sagged into the cavity of the girl's body, making it look as though someone had taken a spade to her torso and dug a long furrow there. The skin was gray, and mottled black and purple along the length of the gash.

The sister took one of the girl's hands and rotated the arm so that the sunlight fell across it. "Do you see these marks?"

An intricate wreath of markings spread across the back of the girl's hand. The tattoos were faint, like pencil marks on a gray wall, climbing like tendrils up each finger and past her wrist.

"She has more on her other hand, and her feet. They are not permanent, as you see. But they are not easily washed out. I would say they were done several weeks ago. A month, perhaps."

"What do they mean?"

"They can mean a number of things, depending on who wears them, and where. In some places women wear these designs all the time. In others, they only decorate themselves so on special occasions. Like a religious festival, or a coming of age. Or a wedding."

"She seems too young for either."

"She does. And yet . . ." Sister Claire leaned over the table, lifting the dead girl's elbow so that she could rest the girl's hand on her body, the limp fingers settling just below the cut, on a slight curve in her belly.

Justy felt sweat break out on the back of his neck. "She was pregnant?"

The sister nodded. "I would say three months gone. Perhaps more. Young girls can often hide the signs for longer."

"My God." Justy leaned on the table. There was a sharp taste in his mouth.

"You saw this?" The nun pointed at the girl's lower abdomen. She had pulled the sheet down to the girl's upper thighs, exposing her pubis. The small, diagonal cut was obvious now, an emphatic, dark gouge under the wisps of hair.

"Yes."

"I examined the wound. The knife, or whatever it was, was stabbed upwards, at an angle. Like this." She made a fist, and demonstrated. "The blade went directly into the womb. It would have caused a massive hemorrhage."

Justy's mouth was sticky. "So why cut her open?"

"To be sure she didn't run? The precision of the second cut suggests to me that this is a man familiar with a knife. The apparent lack of hesitation indicates he is accustomed to killing. If so, he would have known that the first wound would likely not have killed her immediately. She might have been able to get to the street first, perhaps to someone's house. But it's impossible to crawl too far with one's entrails exposed."

"It depends," Justy murmured. He had the sudden memory of a young English skirmisher, slashed open by a flail of canister fire, dragging himself back across the open ground towards his own gun line. The fight had stopped for a moment, an unaccountable lull, and every man on both sides had watched the trooper hauling himself across the churned grass, his guts draped like white ropes over one red-coated arm. Christ, how the man had screamed. Over and over, foot by foot, for nearly fifty yards, before an Irish marksman hushed him.

He sat back in his chair and rubbed his face. "How is it you are so calm, Sister?"

She smiled. "People think nuns do not live in the real world. That we shut ourselves off and stay remote from life. Many do, of course. But those of us who choose to step out of the cloisters see more of life than most. We live among the poor and the desperate. We are daily witnesses to the depravity of humankind, the way we treat each other, and ourselves."

"You're saying you've seen worse than this?"

"I'm saying I am no longer surprised by what human beings can do to each other. People commit far worse atrocities than this, every day. And for all sorts of reasons. For money, for country, for independence. For God."

"So how do you keep doing what you do?"

She smiled, and it was like watching a flower open. Her blue eyes shimmered. "Because just as we are capable of the most depraved acts, we are also capable of the most glorious. I seek to tilt the balance. That is all."

NINE

Gorton led him through a winding passageway crammed with people. The Sunday market was as busy as any other day. Hawkers shouted out the prices of their wares, and the air was thick with smoke from charcoal braziers and grilling meat. It was midafternoon, and the sun was still high in the sky. The shopkeepers had strung canopies made of sail canvas and colored silk over the passageways, so that the light was filtered into a patchwork of colors, and the market became a labyrinth. Justy's nostrils twitched at the scent of perfumes and spices; they flared at the sharp stink of new leather. He smelled dried fish, fresh flowers, raw spirit, and wools still damp with dye. His ear caught a half-dozen languages that he knew, and several he had never heard before. He kept his eyes on the back of Gorton's sunburned neck as the watchman led him through the press of people, wondering how a man so recently arrived in the city knew his way around Canvas Town so well.

Gorton stopped. He shrugged his knapsack off his shoulder. "This is the place."

The shop was little more than a large cupboard, the doors of which had been flung wide open to display hundreds of pairs of colored leather slippers. They were arranged in rows on the inside of the doors and the cupboard itself, making a kaleidoscope of color twelve feet high and ten feet wide. It was a moment before Justy noticed an old man squatting in the corner of the tiny shop. He wore a grubby white robe and a battered black hat that looked like an upside-down flowerpot perched on the back of his head. A stringy beard curled like a wisp from his chin. His gnarled brown fingers flicked at a string of beads, his watery eyes fixed on Justy's face.

"His name's Khaled," Gorton said. "I asked around earlier, and everyone says he's the only man in the city makes stamps like these." He rummaged in the knapsack and handed Justy a pair of small red shoes. They were well used and slightly damp, and the leather was thin on the ball and heel of the soles, but they were of high quality. The uppers were supple and the dye had not run, and the shoes were lined with soft calfskin. Justy pictured the girl's delicate feet, and her round, manicured toenails. "So you found them in the mud in the alley after all?"

"Got lucky."

"They seem very clean."

"Gave 'em a quick bougie. Reckoned Mister Khaled here might not recognize them, else."

Justy let it go. He knelt and held out the slippers to the old man. "Did you make these?"

The shopkeeper sniffed them, and ran his finger along the inseams of the heel and the sole. He twisted the top of the upper inside out and showed a blue smudge on the leather. Then he did the same with a shoe plucked from the display. It showed a small blue K. He nodded and grinned, stubs of stained teeth like a shipwreck.

Justy showed Gorton. "What do you think? Is it the same mark?"

Gorton peered at the smudge, then looked at the new shoe.

"I wouldn't stake my cockles on it, but the workmanship's comparable."

Justy turned back to the old man. "Who did you make these for?"

The shopkeeper shrugged. He made a wide gesture with his hand.

"Do you understand me?" Justy asked.

The shopkeeper shook his head. Gorton snorted. "He kens well enough, I think."

"Perhaps. Do you have the sketch with you?"

Gorton dug in his knapsack and took out a leather tube. He tapped out a sheet of vellum from it, unrolled it, and handed it to Justy.

It was no death mask. The artist had worked quickly and taken some license, shading the sketch here and there to give the impression of life and health. The girl's eyes were closed, but her lashes seemed to quiver on the page. Her cheeks were full, and her lips were slightly parted, as though she was sleeping, and had just taken a breath.

"Do you know her?" Justy showed the shopkeeper the picture. The change in him was slight, but Justy caught the hesitation, the way he shrank into himself, as though Justy had pulled a knife.

"You know who she is, don't you?" Justy said.

The old man shook his head. He began flicking through the string of beads.

"Stop that," Gorton barked. "The Marshal asked you a question."

"That's all right, Mister Gorton." Justy squatted. He held the sketch closer. "Can you tell me her name?"

The shopkeeper shook his head for a third time. He opened his mouth, showing them the wreckage of his teeth. It was a moment before Justy realized what the old man was telling him. He could not speak English. He could not speak at all. It had happened some time ago, judging by the appalling scarring, but someone had cut out his tongue.

———•———

"He is a Sufi. A mystic."

The man's voice had the bass rumble of a distant landslide. He was a black wedge in the slot of blue sky between the awnings. Justy squinted and saw a dark-skinned, dark-eyed man in homespun, mud-colored breeches and a cheap linen shirt, sleeves rolled up to reveal a scrawl of runic tattoos. His face was covered in a wild thicket of hair. Two other men stood behind him, tall, loose-limbed, and scrawny, with the still patience and blank eyes of former slaves. One's face was scarred with tribal tattoos. The other looked as though someone had torn at his mouth and his forehead with a fork. Their shirts were smeared with blood.

Justy stood up. "I thought mystics were supposed to dwell in caves and live on charity."

A wall of strong, white teeth appeared in the tangle of the man's beard. "Charity? In this town?" He laughed. His men stared.

The shopkeeper sat cross-legged on the floor of his tiny shop, wedged into the corner, his blank, rheumy eyes watching and not watching at the same time.

"How did he lose his tongue?" Justy asked.

"Who knows? Perhaps he cut it out himself." The man took a step forward. Justy forced himself to stay still.

"What do you want here, Marshal Flanagan?"

Justy felt as though he had been slapped. "You'll step back now, cully, if you don't want me to burn that goddamned muzzle of yours to the roots."

Silence. The street around them had emptied. There was only the big, bearded man and his sidekicks, and the old shopkeeper with his empty eyes.

The big man stepped back. He held his hands in the air. "Allah would not be pleased if I allowed my beard to be trimmed, whether by a knife or by fire."

Justy felt his stomach unwind. "And the Mayor would not be pleased if I started a blaze in the middle of Canvas Town."

"The Mayor?" The man snorted. "I think he'd be pleased to come up here and fire Canvas Town himself. I think he'd like to burn every free Negro in the city off the island of Manhattan."

Justy had to stop himself from nodding. Edward Livingstone was a strong supporter of immigration, but only on the condition that the immigrants were white. And Protestant.

"What's your name?" Justy asked.

"I am called Zaeim."

"You're a fishmonger?"

"I am."

"And how long have you been in New York?"

The man shrugged. "Years now. I have lost count."

Justy showed him the sketch. "Do you know her?"

The man cocked his head on one side. "Is she dead?"

"Why do you say that?"

"Her eyes are closed."

"Perhaps she's asleep."

The man's eyes flicked up. There was a flash of anger, and then they flattened again. "A lawman does not inquire about a sleeping girl."

"I'll ask you again. Do you know her?"

The man shook his head. "I do not."

Justy handed the sketch to Gorton. "Zaeim. That's an unusual name. Is it Moorish?"

"Why do you want to know?"

"The girl may have been Moorish. I want to speak to people in that community."

"Why?"

"That's my business. New York's business."

The man laughed. "New York's business. That's good, Irishman. Very well. I am Moorish, but this girl is not one of us. Now you can go back to your white hall and make your report."

It was Justy's turn to step forward. "Your people have lived here quietly for more than ten years, Mister Zaeim, but if I return to Federal Hall with nothing to say, that will end. Word will get out, as it always does, and the next time you come face-to-face with an Irishman, he will be at the head of a mob, howling for your blood and intent on burning your miserable tents to the ground. Now take me to someone who speaks for your people. Preferably someone who doesn't smell quite so strongly of fish."

The beard bristled, and the line of even, white teeth appeared again.

"Very well," the man said. "Follow me."

Justy prided himself on his sense of direction. As he had followed Gorton through the market, he had the general sense that he was heading slightly downhill, towards the Hudson River. But now, with Zaeim leading the way, he became almost instantly lost. The big, bearded man moved fast through the crowd, turning left and right until their way was barred by a row of canvas-draped shacks. They were unusually high, almost double the height of the other dwellings, but before Justy could look at them closely, Zaeim pushed through a doorway that was little more than a crude tear in a sheet of worn sailcloth.

One moment Justy was walking through a dark, narrow tunnel, with his head bent and the musty smell of damp burlap in his nose. The next he was blinking in the sunlight. The chaos of Canvas Town was gone. In its place was a quiet, open courtyard, bordered by low, smooth-walled buildings with tiled roofs, as sturdy and well built as anything in the First Ward.

Zaeim had disappeared. His men had not followed them. Justy and Gorton were alone.

There was an impression of space and light. Water tinkled and gurgled in a fountain in the center of the courtyard, which was shaded by the shivering, silvery leaves of a buttonwood tree.

For a moment, Justy relaxed. And then he saw Gorton looking up at the rooftops.

"We're like fish in a fucking barrel in here," he muttered, turning in a tight circle.

Something plucked at Justy's insides, and he started towards the entrance they had come through. The rough hessian curtain screening the doorway was twitched aside, and one of Zaeim's men appeared, a club in his hand. The sunlight glistened on the sweat that beaded on the ridges of the scars that ringed his mouth and made a rough curve across his forehead. Justy tried to think what might have caused that kind of scarring, and when the man scratched at his ragged beard, he remembered an illustrated pamphlet on agricultural labor that he had read in a coffee house. It had included a drawing of slaves working in a strawberry patch. To stop the slaves running away, they were chained. And to stop them eating the fruit, they were muzzled.

Justy was suddenly very aware of the folding knife that he kept tucked in the top of his right boot. He eased himself slowly back towards Gorton until they were standing shoulder to shoulder. The man in the doorway stood still, watching them.

"He will not let you pass. Not without my instruction."

They spun around. Zaeim was striding towards them from one of the buildings. He was no longer dressed in his workman's clothes, but in a long, white robe. Instead of boots, he had sandals on his feet, and while his beard still looked like a thorn bush, his hair was wet and slicked back neatly from his forehead, and a small, white cap was perched on the top of his head.

Gorton's hand was a blur. A long, curved blade flashed in the sunlight. He took a half step towards Zaeim. "You'd better get to instructing, then. Lest you want me to fill yon pretty fountain with your claret."

Zaeim stopped. "Soft, Mister Gorton. I am unarmed."

Gorton scowled. "How do you know my name?"

"I know everything about you, Jeremiah. Where you live, how long you have been here, what you do, and what you have done. Which is why I know that you know what this is." He held out a white rod, about two feet long, tipped with what looked like horsehair. "And what it means."

"What is it?" Justy asked.

Gorton kept his eyes on Zaeim. "It's a sign of office. It means he's the gaffer here."

"You are fortunate to have such a sharp and knowledgeable fellow by your side, Marshal." Zaeim's teeth gleamed. "I am indeed the gaffer, as he says."

"So you are Umar Salam?" Justy asked.

Zaeim bowed his head.

"And Zaeim?"

"Zaeim is my people's word for leader. That is what I am. But Umar is who I am."

"Why not say so before?"

"Because I do not wish to attract attention, either to myself or to my people. You are a Catholic, Marshal, so you have some sense of what it means to live and worship in a way that people of other religions find objectionable."

Justy thought about the folder full of anti-Catholic tracts in his desk. "Stow the chive, Jeremiah," he said.

Gorton hesitated.

"If he wanted us backed, it'd be done by now. Put it away."

Gorton slipped the blade into the long sheath on his belt.

"Thank you." Umar spread his arms wide. His teeth gleamed. "Welcome to Mimo."

"Mimo?"

"It has several meanings. Property. And sanctuary."

It took only a few minutes for him to show them around the compound, a collection of a dozen dun-colored buildings of various sizes, all surrounded by the high wall that separated the community from Canvas Town and the rest of the city. The place was spotless, and deserted. It was an island of quiet in the middle of the bustling riot of New York. The windows of the buildings were curtained, but he caught a glimpse inside one, and saw a small, neat room, with blankets and several low cots stacked neatly against one wall.

"Where is everyone?" Justy asked.

"Working. We are almost completely self-sufficient here. We fish the sea, we farm the meadow, we make clothes, and sell them in the markets."

"And who are your people?"

"People of the Faith. Anyone who believes or wishes to learn is welcome, wherever they have come from."

"I've heard you came up from the Carolinas."

Umar's beard bristled. "Do you intend to send us back?"

"I'm not a slave catcher."

Umar had stopped beside a pile of what looked like sections of reed fencing, stacked up against a half-built wall. He used his horsehair switch to point at a large, square hut with a steep roof. "This is our kitchen. We cook communal meals here. The refectory is on the other side."

A long, low, barrack-like building ran along what Justy reckoned was the north wall of the compound. It had just a single door. A figure in a light blue robe appeared in the doorway, and then was gone.

"What's in there?"

"That is where we make the garments we sell. The cloth comes from India. We buy it by the bale, and fashion it into clothes and shawls."

"May I see?"

"Of course."

Inside was a single room containing several long tables, with benches on either side. Bales of cloth were stacked up against one wall. Light streamed in through long, narrow windows close to the ceiling. A dozen women were sitting around the tables, working on pieces of cloth. They all wore robes of different colors, and when Justy and Umar entered the room, they pulled the edges of the cloth to cover their heads and faces.

"Why do they do that?"

"It is our religion. The Prophet, peace be upon him, said our women must cover themselves in the presence of men who are not of their family."

There was a small cart loaded with neat stacks of shawls beside the door. Justy smoothed his hand over the cloth. "The girl in the picture I showed you was wearing a robe like this."

Umar shrugged. "We sell a great many of such things."

"She had drawings on her hands. Tattoos."

"Like the ones on Mister Gorton's arms and chest?"

Gorton smirked.

"How do you know so much?" Justy demanded.

Umar flicked at a fly. "You have your spies around the city, Marshal. I have mine."

"To what end?"

Umar sighed. "Do I really need to explain this to you, an Irishman, whose people are fenced into the sinkholes of New York, to drown and freeze and sweat to death with yellow fever? Like you, we worship God in a way that these people believe is unnatural. They call you Catholics devil-worshipers, but they tolerate your presence because you are white. Imagine what they would think of us, Negroes who follow the Qu'ran, eat only with our left hands, and cover our women. They would think us Satan incarnate. And they would treat us accordingly."

"Not all the leaders of the city think that way. There are many who believe in the principles that this country was founded on. They will defend your right to worship as you please."

"Will they?" Umar leaned on the doorframe. "They may believe we have those rights, despite the color of our skin, but will they fight for us? I doubt it. So I have to protect my people in a different way. I send my people into the city, to learn things about those who would threaten us, and I use that information when I need to."

"There are that many of you?"

"We are not so many. But we have been here a long time now, living in the shadows. And our number is growing. Our dark skins allow us to move about the city unseen, to mix with the servants and slaves who make this city work, and who know everything that goes on. No one notices another Negro, so long as he stays in his place. And everyone talks. We simply listen."

The women had stopped working and were watching them, twelve pairs of eyes, swathed in colored wool.

"Why did you even let us in here?" Justy asked.

"Because I have heard about you, Marshal. You are a tenacious man. When I heard you had shown an interest in our community, I knew you would not stop until you had gained entry to this place. As you said yourself, better that you come invited than in the van of a mob."

"And so you can show me what you want me to see."

"I have nothing to hide, I assure you."

"So what's in there?" Justy pointed to a door on the other side of the room.

"Just storage." Umar pulled the door open. There was a tiny room, piled high with bales of cloth. A cloying smell of incense was in the air. "We received a shipment, two days ago." He closed the door. "Is there anything else I can show you?"

The man with the muzzle scars led them back through the market to a small clearing flanked by a number of tiny stalls selling food and drink. And then he disappeared into the crowd.

Gorton held up two fingers to the owner of a coffee stall and sat down, chewing a nail.

"So, what did you make of that?" Justy asked.

"Big place."

"Right enough. You could fit a hundred folk in there. I'd like to know how the hell he managed to build it without anyone knowing."

"He's probably been at it for years, slow and sure."

"Aye, but a place that size? How do you keep something like that quiet?"

Gorton shrugged. "Like he said. No one pays much heed to what goes on in Canvas Town. Least of all to a bunch of blacks."

The shopkeeper arrived with the coffee. He poured it into tiny cups from a long-spouted pot, and placed a plate of sweetmeats dusted with powdered sugar on the table. The coffee smelled strong, and was musty with dark spice. It was surprisingly sweet.

Gorton smiled at the expression on Justy's face. "It's Arabic. They like it so your teeth ache."

"Your file said you spent some time in North Africa."

"I saw plenty like your man Umar there. Petty chiefs of small tribes. Two camels and a dozen followers, most of 'em."

"This one seems a little more than that."

Gorton nodded, thoughtfully. "He do, don't he?" He bit into one of the pastries.

"You were in Gibraltar, too, I saw. What was it like there?"

Gorton grinned. "It was rum. Good food. Good weather. Good people, too. You get all sorts in Gib. Gyppos, Frogs, Spaniards, darkies, the lot. I liked it."

"So why did you leave?"

The watchman considered Justy for a moment before answering. "I was drummed out."

"Your file says you have an honorable discharge."

"I do, on paper. But I was drummed out, just the same."

"You'll have to explain."

Gorton popped another sweetmeat into his mouth and chewed, his sharp chin moving in a small, tight circle. "I had a fight with my sergeant major in Gib. Battered him with a pick helve after I caught him flogging rifles to a gyppo trader. My lieutenant took my part in the inquiry, but I found out later that the captain was in on the scheme. The lieutenant got a promotion, a commission on a ship of the line. I got the shaft. The captain gave me a choice: transport back to Blighty for a five-year stretch in Pompey nick for assault, or a clean ticket out of the Corps. I didn't reckon I'd even make it back to the barracks, knowing what I did about what they were up to, so I took the discharge and marched straight down to the port. Took a billet on the first ship out. Happens it was sailing to Savannah and then up to here."

He sipped his coffee.

"Why are you telling me this?" Justy asked.

"You asked." He shrugged. "Truth is, I mean to make a place for myself here, and like that cove Umar says, you're not the type of man leaves stones unturned. I reckon if you checked on me proper, you'd find out eventually. Maybe not the whole story, but enough to know something was off. I'd prefer you got the whole bever from me."

His eyes were steady. Justy felt suddenly uneasy. He drained his cup. "How is it you know Canvas Town so well?"

Gorton nibbled at the edge of another sweetmeat. "I like it. Reminds me of Gib. Besides, every city I've been to there's a quarter like this. The food's always good and cheap, and it's the best place to go to understand the way a place is headed."

It was late in the afternoon, but the square was still full of people jostling, squabbling, and bargaining. The sun strobed through the awnings in shards of light, picking out pieces of the crowd: a blue tunic, a silver brooch, a plum-colored shawl, an emerald-green hat.

Justy sat up.

Gorton caught the movement and snapped forward. "Ware hawk?" His sharp face made him look like a hunting dog sniffing its quarry.

"No. It's nothing." Justy stared into the crowd. "I just thought I saw someone I knew."

"A young fellow? Tall and spooney, with a green hat?"

"You've a good eye."

The watchman pushed a hank of gray hair back from his pale eyes. "I told you I was a marksman in the Corps. They used to put me in the rigging, with orders to aim at the officers."

"Remind me to stay on your good side."

Gorton grinned. "So who was that in the hat? Want me to go after him?"

"No. I'm not even sure it was who I thought it was." Justy drained his coffee, and dug in his pocket for a coin. "We should go. We've a great deal more to do, and not much time to do it."

TEN

Kerry saw Justy too late. She knew instantly that he had caught a glimpse of the big green caubeen that topped her disguise. She backed quickly into the shadows of a spice stall and looked across the square. Justy was scanning the crowd. She smiled. His right boot had a hole in the sole. And his coat looked loose. He needed someone to look after him. She scowled at the thought of Eliza Cruikshank. The tossy-locked florence.

She felt someone's eyes on her. She recognized the watchman from the night before. His long, narrow face. And his sharp eyes. He was staring right at her, but it was impossible for him to see her, she was sure. She eased herself back further into the darkness, but the man didn't look away. She held her breath.

Justy said something, and he and the watchman stood up and walked into the crowd. Kerry exhaled slowly. Perhaps he hadn't recognized her after all. The woman minding the stall was looking at her, eyes like two pips in an old brown apple. Kerry blew her a kiss and she chuckled.

Kerry was dressed as an apprentice boy, in black coat and breeches, brown woolen hose, and cheap black clogs. Her long, dark hair was curled tight and pinned under the big green hat. It was a good disguise, one she had worn almost every day when she was a teenager, when she had trawled the Broad Way and the markets, cutting open men's pockets with a quick, thin blade, and walking away with their wallets. She had been an excellent tooler, quick and careful, and not too greedy, until a pistol ball in her shoulder had made the point that if she continued with a life of crime, it was liable to be a short one.

So she had given up life on the cross. But she had kept up her skills, by practicing here and there. And she had held on to the disguise.

She had gone from Hughson's Tavern to her home, to dress in the clothes and the shoes and the old green country hat that she kept locked away in a small chest on top of her closet. It had been nearly a year since she had last put on the disguise, but she remembered all of it: how to stand like a man, and how to walk like one, uncaring, with a slight slouch, her hands in her pockets, and her head forward. And, best of all, how to slip into character, how to adopt the attitude of ownership and privilege that came with being male.

She had walked down into Canvas Town, thrilling with the feeling of sudden freedom. No one condescended to her; no one fell silent when they registered her presence; no one eyed her in the way so many men felt free to eye a woman, regardless of her class. She had become just another apprentice, invisible, and able to go, almost unchallenged, wherever she wanted.

She had known Canvas Town well when she was younger. It was her cousin Lew's home ground, and most of the city's black population had spent at least some time in its encampments. But it had changed as the men who owned the land had begun building on its southern and eastern bounds, hemming the shanties into an increasingly narrow strip of land along the shore of the Hudson River and forcing them upland, across the steep ground of the old forts on the Star and Foundry Redoubts, and down to the edge of the marshland around Hudson's Kill.

Kerry had never been this far north before. The squatters had stripped the old forts bare, and used the wood from their palisades to make walls and pathways between the shacks. There was a low hum of sound and the smell of sewage and cooking food, and when she glanced through the open doors of the shanties and tents, she saw people of all colors huddled around low tables, eating and talking.

She kept moving, threading her way through the crowd, along a narrow lane that dropped steeply out of the old Star Redoubt and seemed to lead roughly north.

The wall surprised her.

It was about eight feet high, covered in a rough stucco of mud and straw. The shacks and lean-tos were built right against it, so it was impossible to follow it around. She backtracked and came up another lane, and then another, each time meeting the same rough, windowless wall.

It was nearly an hour before she found the entrance. There was a clearing at the end of an alleyway, an open space around a gap in the buildings that was just wide enough to allow a carriage. A big, sunburned man with a black wedge of a beard leaned carelessly on the wall, taking bites from a strip of dried fish. He kept his eyes on Kerry as she approached.

She rolled her shoulders. "How dost do, my buff?"

The man's eyes were dark and bloodshot, like squashed flies on a handkerchief. He tore another piece of fish off with his teeth, leaving a thread of saliva on his beard.

Kerry ignored the worm in her guts and tried again. "I'm told as how you can buy good cloth hereabouts. Like silk, they say."

"Who's they?" The man's voice was rough.

"People about the place. A friend of mine bought a shawl for his blowen a year or so back. I thought I'd see about doing the same."

The man sniffed, hawked, spat. He half-turned to look into the entrance.

"Faisal," he called. "Customer."

A small round man in a long brown tunic and baggy white trousers appeared. His beard was cropped close to his dark skin, and his head was shaved. His nose was small and hooked, like an owl's beak. "Yes?"

Kerry dug her hands in her pockets. "I came about buying a shawl. For my tib. It's her birthday next week."

"Who told you to come here?"

"A friend of mine. He did for his wife last year and she was right pleased."

"I'm sure she was. Our cloth is of excellent quality." His small, dark eyes skipped up and down. "But expensive."

There was a handful of coins in Kerry's pocket. She jiggled them in her hand. "I ain't as well breeched as some, it's true. But I'm warm enough."

The man looked thoughtful. "We close at dusk. But I can make an exception, I suppose. Wait here."

He disappeared through the entrance, turning sharply left to avoid a blank wall that prevented Kerry from seeing inside. A moment later, there was a squeaking sound, and the man reappeared, pushing a handcart laden with bolts of colored cloth.

"How about this one?" The man pulled an orange shawl from the top of the pile. It was slightly coarse, and Kerry guessed it was made of old wool.

The man smiled. "Yes, you are right. Not for a true lady." He flipped through the bolts, and pulled out a pale blue length of cloth. "Try this. Lambswool."

The cloth was luxurious, as soft as fresh cotton, but with the texture of a light blanket.

"It's rum. But the shawl my friend bought is finer than this, I'd say."

"Indeed? His wife is a lucky lady, then. Such garments are very expensive."

"I told you. I have coin."

The man held up his hands. "Of course. Forgive me." He fumbled at the bottom of a stack of bolts of cloth and eased out a single rose-colored shawl.

"Here." He held out the scarf. "This may be what your friend bought for his wife."

Kerry's fingers tingled as she ran her hand over the material. It was like stroking a kitten.

The man chuckled. "Beautiful, is it not? Let me show you." He shook the shawl open, so that it floated in the air for a moment, like a pink cloud.

Kerry glanced down at the cart. The edge of a square of pale yellow cloth had pulled loose from the bottom of the pile. It looked like silk, edged with gold embroidery.

"What's that?"

"Ah." The man cocked his head to the side. "That is not for sale."

"It's on your cart."

"A mistake, I assure you."

"It's dimber."

The man nodded. "It is very rare. Made from the hair of a goat that lives high in the mountains of a place called Kasheer, very far from here."

"May I touch it? Just to see?"

The man's head bobbled side to side. Neither a yes or a no. Kerry reached out her fingers. The cloth was as fine as silk, but softer. She knew instantly that it was the same cloth that the girl's robe was made of.

"How much is a shawl made of this?"

"It is not for sale."

"Everything's for sale."

"It is too much."

"What did I say before?" Kerry snapped.

The man gave her a long look. He quoted a number.

Kerry laughed. "You're cracked."

The man shrugged "I told you. It is very rare."

"Rare as rocking horse shit."

The man sighed. He held up the shawl that he had unwrapped. "Did you like this one?"

"I did. Until I saw that other. Now I think I might have to save up a bit longer."

"I see." The man began to fold up the shawl again. "Perhaps you will think about it and come and see me again."

"Perhaps."

The man gave a thin smile. "But before dusk the next time, please."

ELEVEN

The salesman pushed his cart back into the compound, turning left at the wall. There was no way of seeing inside, Kerry decided. She felt the sunburned guard watching her. He popped the last scrap of dried fish into his mouth and wiped his fingers on his beard. She nodded casually, thrust her hands deeper into her pockets, and sauntered back down the alleyway.

There was a bend in the path, and as she made the turn, she heard someone step close behind her. She picked up her pace, widening her stride, her heart thundering as she fumbled for the knife that she had hidden inside the band of her breeches.

A huge hand clamped over her fingers. An arm wrapped around her neck, pulling her backwards, off her feet. She arched her back and kicked hard, and was rewarded with a grunt. But it was a lost cause. The man who held her was bigger and stronger. He spun her to the side and dragged her through a doorway. And then, as quickly as he had grabbed her, he released her, and sent her staggering forward.

She spun around, hauling at the knife, the breath like fire in her throat. But there was no one there, just a length of loose hessian that served as a door.

"Sit down, girl. And put the chive away."

She turned back. She was standing in the middle of a small, mean room, walled in by loose planks of wood. The roof was a poorly stitched patchwork of rough sacking and tattered sailcloth. A dim light filtered in through its holes and seams, and a single stub of candle guttered in a sconce nailed carelessly to one wall. The place smelled of dried mud and stale sweat.

A man with a shaven head and skin like polished mahogany sat on a low bench on one side of the space. Lew Owens wore his usual clothes, a pair of cream riding breeches, black leather boots, and a white shirt that emphasized the breadth of his shoulders and the darkness of his skin. He was leaning back on the wall, his long legs thrown out in front of him, crossed at the ankles.

She scowled. "I should have known it was you."

His laugh boomed in the tiny space. "*Noswaith dda*, cousin."

Her face was still hot. "Try your Taffy patter on someone who gives a damn."

"It means good evening."

"I don't give a strap. What do you mean, having your dogs grab me off the street?"

"Would you have come if they'd asked nicely?"

She said nothing.

"I didn't think so." Owens patted the space on the bench next to him. "Don't be hot with me, now. Come on and rest your cooler and I'll put you flash to what's what."

She sat down. There was no point in doing otherwise. The man who had ambushed her would be waiting outside, she was sure, and there would be more of her cousin's men scattered about the area, as he never traveled without a half-dozen trusties with him.

Lew Owens grinned at her. He was only thirty-three years old, but in just ten years he had clubbed and stabbed his way to the top of the filthy, vice-ridden heap that was Canvas Town, and then extended his reach far beyond. He owned a stake in almost every gambling house, oyster bar, brothel, and dance hall in the Fourth and Sixth Wards, and collected a protection fee from many more. He was tall, handsome, and as black as the coal he had been forced to mine in Cape Breton, before he escaped.

He was just ten years old when he arrived in New York. His aunt took him in. She too was a runaway slave, who had fallen in love with an Irish gangster named O'Toole. Three years later, she died giving birth to her daughter, Kerry.

Kerry hated her cousin and loved him in equal amounts. She hated him because he was a violent, merciless criminal; she hated him because he was a parasite, feeding off the lives of the poor, the desperate, and the addicted; she hated him because he reminded her of what she was: high yellow, mulatto, half-breed, and unwelcome in either community.

But she loved him, too. He had put a roof over her head, food in her belly, and clothes on her back, and never asked anything of her. His protection gave her a measure of freedom, and made her feel safe in a city that was dangerous for a woman with her skin color, not to mention her ambitions. He was family.

"It's a shame I have to come all the way down here to get a glimpse of you," he said. "What's it been, two months since we broke bread? Three?"

"You only have to walk around the back of your house and knock on the door, Lew."

"No. I respect your privacy. But perhaps we should arrange something more regular."

"As you like."

A low murmur of voices came through the thin wall behind them, followed by a rhythmic grunting. The candle guttered and dripped wax onto the bench between them.

Kerry screwed up her face. "Christ, Lew. This isn't one of your vaulting-schools, is it?"

"Not mine. Longhair Torrance. You know him?"

"No."

"Course you don't. Well, don't worry, he knows how to keep snug."

"It's not that I was worried about."

"Well, you should be." Owens narrowed his eyes. "What were you doing up by Jericho?"

"Why do you call it that?"

"On account it's got a wagging great wall built around it, and no one knows what's inside. Now what were you doing there?"

She shrugged. "I wanted to buy a shawl."

"You didn't get dressed up in that rig to buy a blasted scarf, Kerry. Tell me."

She leaned back to look at him. "You look a bit worried, Lew."

"I wouldn't say worried. But that big bastard Absalom is giving me enough of a headache without you twisting the puzzle."

"Absalom?"

"Umar Salam's what he calls himself now, but he was named Absalom when he washed up here with nothing but the rags on his back. More than a dozen years ago now."

The grunting intensified. The wall behind them began to shake. Kerry leaned forward. "And he's the topping man in Jericho?"

"He is. Styles himself a high priest of some kind. Goes about harping on the word of the Prophet or some fudge."

"And that bothers you?"

"It does when it cuts into my business. Telling folk that borrowing money is an offense against God? I've had twenty-three coves pay me back in full in the last half year."

"I'd have thought you'd be pleased."

"Don't be daft, Kerry. If some clunch pays me back, it means I can't squeeze him for chink. True, I only got a trickle out of most of them, but those twenty-three trickles made for a healthy little stream that's not flowing into my purse no more. And that's not all. The bastard's been after my best doxies, too. Preaching at them about turning away from sin and making a paradise on earth. Ten of them, he's turned. And no cherry-colored cats, neither. White girls, every one. I've had to put lads on the door of every one of my houses, but his word gets in, somehow, and they get out. Never to be seen again."

"What are you saying? He kills them?"

"I don't know. That's another reason I want to get in there. To find out."

The noises from the room behind them stopped. Owens rolled his eyes. "I thought he'd never finish. Now I've pattered enough. Time for you to tell me what you were up to."

It was dark in the small room. A cart clattered past on the narrow street, and, somewhere, a woman laughed. Kerry thought about the horror she had seen the night before.

"Did you hear about the girl who was milled?"

Owens shrugged. "She wasn't one of mine, if you're asking."

"I'm not. She looked more like a princess than a curtezan. But no one's claimed her."

"And you think she came from Jericho?"

"Maybe. It was the kemesa she was wearing that twigged me. Made of a fine nab that the Mohammedans sell. I wanted to look for myself."

"And?"

"Some cove name of Faisal showed me a clutch of shawls, all made of good cloth, but nothing like what that girl had on. But I saw he had another piece, hidden away on this cart. I asked about it but he got all scaly and said it wasn't for sale. It was the same nab the girl was wearing, though, I'm sure of it. He said the wool came from a long way from here."

"So it came in on a ship." Owens scowled. "Umar must be going snacks with that fat madge Flanagan."

"How do you figure?"

"The Bull runs the waterfront, don't he? How else is Umar going to get his goods off the hard? But it's not a dockside deal I'm worried about."

"What? You think they're planning a move against you?"

"Maybe. Flanagan has his eye on my turf. And old Absalom's for sure gathering a crew. You don't do that for no reason. I don't know how many he's got behind those walls of his now, but it's a sight more than the dozen he brought with him from the Carolinas. That Faisal cove you met hails from Araby. That hackum guarding the gate is New York born. So there's all sorts in there, including plenty of runaway slaves. The kind that don't shirk in a tilt, if you catch me."

A shout came from close by in the lane outside. Several voices joined in, and a woman screamed. There was the sound of something heavy collapsing.

The sack curtain in the doorway twitched. The man who stepped inside seemed to fill the space. He was built like Owens, with the same shaved head and broad shoulders, but he was half as big again, in every direction.

"What plays, Jonty?" Owens asked.

"Bit of a ruck going on, Chief." The man's voice was a deep Barbados drawl. "Some simkin went and pulled down the front of Tanny's libben. Looks like a nob. Says she buzzed something precious out of his pit. The boys have him outside."

"Something precious, eh? Let's have a gun." Owens sprang up, and the big man named Jonty backed up out of the doorway.

A blanket of cloud had rolled in across the city with the dusk, and the night was pitch dark. There was no street lighting in Canvas Town, and no torches for fear of fire, but two of Owens' men carried lanterns, attached to long poles. Two more had a tight grip on a tall, thin man with a shock of white hair. His narrow face was bruised on the right cheek and bleeding above the left eye. He wore a crushed-velvet coat and whipcord breeches, white hose, and a pair of dainty shoes with large silver buckles.

Owens stepped close. "Slumming it, are we?" His voice was silky, the Welsh accent strong.

"There's been a mistake." The man's voice wavered. His accent was English, cultured.

"I'll say there has, *bach*." Owens looked over the man's shoulder. A small crowd had gathered, dark faces lit up by the flickering lanterns. "You think you can come down here and do what you like, do you? Accuse folk of theft? Tear down their homes?"

The trickle of blood on the man's temple showed black against his bone-white skin. "That . . . that woman stole from me, while I was . . ."

"While you were what?"

"While I was . . . inconvenienced."

"While you were up to your nuts in guts you mean." Owens bared his teeth, triggering a rumble of laughter from the crowd.

The man tried to turn around to see who was laughing, but the two men held him steady.

"Look at me." Owens voice was a lash. "Do you know who I am?"

The man nodded. "You are Lew Owens. Mayor of Canvas Town."

Owens laughed. "Mayor? Yes, that'll fadge. I'm the Mayor, which means I make the laws, and I make sure people stick to them." He looked around. "And there's a law against tearing down peoples' kips, ain't there?"

The crowd murmured its approval.

"Now where's Tanny?"

A petite woman pushed through the crowd, past the Englishman and his captors. She wore a long-tailed red tunic over a grubby petticoat that looked as though it might have been pink. She was about twenty years old, light-skinned and dark-eyed, with long, black hair piled in untidy hanks on the top of her head.

Owens smiled. "Evening, Antoinette."

"Lew," the girl simpered, and made a parody of a curtsey.

"What's this about you buzzing this cove, then?" Owens' tone was friendly.

The precarious pile of hair shook. "Not me, Lew. You know I don't play them kinds of games with my gentlemen. I know the rules."

"He says different."

The girl pouted. "Well, he's a liar then, ain't he?"

Owens turned to the Englishman. "We may not have any grand cribs or flash halls like you have on Wall Street, mister, but that don't mean we don't take pride in where we live. It don't mean we allow any flash cove to come down here and do as he pleases."

The man nodded. "I understand. I didn't mean to damage the lady's . . . house. I'll pay."

"Yes you will. But not 'til you've learned a lesson." Owens nodded at his men. "Let him go."

For a moment, it looked as though the Englishman might collapse. His knees shook, and his face grew even paler. But then he recovered, smoothing his coat, and tugging at his long cuffs.

"Right, lads." Owens' voice was sharp. "Get down to Tanny's kip and take it apart. Every scrap. Anything worth a rag, bring it here. And burn the rest."

"No!" the girl shrieked.

Owens held up his hand to stop the men. He loomed over Tanny. "What's wrong, *geneth*? Worried about what they'll find?"

"There's nothing in there, I swear it, Lew, I swear!"

"In that case, the next step's to search you. And I mean everywhere. Maybe I'll have Jonty do it. He's a clumsy bastard, mind. Big fingers, too. Like bloody bananas."

Jonty folded his massive arms across his chest. The girl's eyes were wide. She lifted her skirt and fumbled inside her drawers.

"Here." She held out a silver medallion on a thin necklace.

"I told you," the man said.

"I don't give a nun's grot." Owens examined the medallion. "Plate. The chain's worth more than the coin."

"It has sentimental value."

"Oh, it does?" Owens grinned. "How much value? Shall we say an eagle?"

The man gave him a sour look. He dug into the pocket of his breeches for a coin.

Owens tossed him the medallion. "Right then. And remember this: there's only one man can go about tearing down another's libben, and that's me." He stared at Tanny. "Carry on, lads."

"No!" Tanny clutched at the men, but they shoved her aside.

Owens' grin was a wolf's snarl. "The only reason I'm not going to break all your fingers and pull out your front teeth, girl, is because you've still got some miles left in you." He stared at the crowd. "The next cove or cooler I catch thieving won't be so blessed with good fortune."

"What about the nob?" someone shouted from the back of the crowd.

"Oh yes, the nob."

Owens took a step forward and drove his fist into the Englishman's stomach. The man's hair flapped limply as he doubled over. Owens stepped behind him, put his boot on the man's backside, and shoved. Kerry jumped back as the man went sprawling through the doorway into the shack. Owens nodded at his bodyguard.

"Teach him a lesson, Jonty. But hold off killing him. I don't want anyone asking questions."

The big man had to bend low to get through the doorway. The sack curtain fell into place behind him.

"No!" the Englishman's voice was muffled, and then there was only a series of hard thumps, like a cleaver chopping meat.

The lantern light gleamed on Owens' skull as he walked towards the crowd. "Anyone got anything to say? No? Be about your business, then."

He watched as they shuffled away into the darkness. There was a low rumbling sound in the distance. Owens squinted at the dark sky. "We're in for a right old soak, unless I'm much mistaken. Good thing too. Fill up those rain barrels. Save us dipping into the Collect and risking an early death."

The two men sent to pull down Tanny's shack returned. One carried a small sack. Owens looked inside. His lip curled. He pulled out a small wooden doll and waved it in front of Tanny. "What do you think I'll get for this, Antoinette?"

"Burn it, if you must." Her face was hard.

Owens laughed. "You're a stiff one, ain't you, *geneth*?" He dropped the doll back into the sack and threw it to her. "Let this be a warning to you. From now you do business up in the fort. See Miss Violet. She'll give you a room. Fifty percent to me, twenty to her. And no trying to put a hole in the bucket. Fair enough?"

Tanny nodded.

"Here." Owens flipped the man's coin in the air. Tanny's hand was like a snake striking. She grinned a row of surprisingly even teeth, then snatched the sack to her breast and hurried away.

The sky rumbled again, louder this time. Owens held out his hand. A fat drop of rain splashed on his palm.

He laughed. "Perfect weather for peeping." He turned to Kerry. "Let's walk."

TWELVE

Kerry and Owens stood in the darkness, under the awning of a shuttered shop, watching the entrance to Jericho. The rain made a roaring sound, hammering on the wooden awning, churning the fifty yards of open space between them and the opening in Jericho's walls into a sticky sea of mud. The big, bearded sentry that Kerry had seen earlier was still in his place by the entrance, huddled under a small lean-to, wrapped in a heavy cloak.

Kerry shivered and shifted her feet on a plank that was just wide and thick enough to keep their feet out of the muck. "What are we doing here?"

Owens was wearing a long coat that he had taken from one of his men. It was buttoned to the neck, to cover his white shirt. He had his hands shoved deep in his pockets, and he ignored the rainwater that leaked through the awning and ran in a thin stream off his head. "You said you wanted a look at Jericho. Here we are."

"I've already seen this much."

"And what did you see?"

Kerry shrugged. "Some cove selling shawls. Another standing guard. A single entrance in a high wall, and no way of seeing inside."

"So what does that tell you?"

"I don't know. That your man knows how to build walls? What does it tell you?"

"It tells me old Absalom has something to hide." He nodded at the sodden sentry on the entryway. "And the fact yon hackum is still sat there in the rain tells me he either pays his crew well, or he's put the fear of God in 'em."

The deluge seemed to slacken for a moment, but then the sky made a sound like a heavy cart being dragged along a cobbled street, and the rain redoubled in strength. It pounded the soaked ground, bouncing up and soaking Kerry's hose to the knee. The sodden wool began to sag down her calves, and she bent to pull them up. "Blast your top lights, Lew. I know there's a real reason we've been standing here for the last hour in this grubshite. Why don't you spill it?"

Owens grinned. "Aren't you wondering where I sent the lads?"

"Not really."

"We've been trying to find what other ways he has to get in and out of the place, but no luck. So this weather's perfect for having a proper snitch about. Hugger-mugger-like. Even if old Absalom's got men on his ramparts, they won't be even half as sharp as normal. And they won't see anything through this bloody rain."

"Are you sure? I can't see that new gorilla of yours moving about unnoticed, even if it was pitch black outside."

"Who, Jonty?" Owens tutted. "That's not very nice of you, Kerry. Jonts is a good lad. He's had a rough time of it. He was a slave on an apple farm outside of Roxbury, until he got freed a few months back. His owner had a horse that dropped dead of overwork, but rather than buy a new one, the bastard put Jonty in the harness instead. Treated him just like he did the nag. Flogged him. Kept him in a stable. Even put a nosebag on him."

Kerry imagined Jonty curled up on a pile of muddy straw, shivering in the cold.

"Anyway, you're right about him being useless for night work," Owens went on. "He's got his hands full with young Mister Lispenard, who you met earlier."

"The gent with the floppy hair? You know him?"

"I wouldn't say I know him. But I know who he is. We're standing on his land."

Kerry blinked. "I thought he was English."

"Aye, well, he was born here, but he lives in London now."

"He doesn't seem too bothered about people squatting on his land."

Owens chuckled. "Oh, he cares. He's spent all the inheritance his father left him, and he needs to sell up, if he's to keep living in style. He wants to give our people the hoof just like all the other landowners."

"What's he doing down here, then? Spying?"

"Not at all, *geneth*. He just likes a bit of dark meat every now and then. Can't help himself."

Kerry wriggled her toes in her wet shoes. "How do you know all this?"

"He keeps some rooms down on Liberty Street. Only comes over once a year, but keeps them staffed with a brace of mop squeezers. One of whom does a little work for me on the side."

"I wondered why you pulled your punch on him earlier."

Owens' grin flashed. "I had to put on a bit of a show."

"Jonty too?"

"He knows how to make some convincing enough sounds, make the crowd think he gave the dirty mutton-monger a pasting. He'll have had Mister Lispenard back to Liberty Street by now."

"So much for laying down the law."

"You don't kill the goose what lays the golden eggs, *geneth*."

There was a tearing sound above them, and water gushed over Owens' head.

"Dumb glutton!" He stepped sharply to the side, and his heel slipped off the narrow plank. He lost his balance and fell back against the doorway of the shop, soaking his breeches.

Kerry giggled. "So much for hugger-mugger."

"Your brown arse." Owens struggled to his feet. A sheepish grin made him look suddenly like the lanky, scrawny teenager that Kerry had played with when she was a child.

"Come on." She pulled him onto the plank and shuffled sideways so that he could fit under the shelter beside her. She put her arm around his waist and pulled him close. He wrapped his arm around her shoulder. She smelled the coconut oil that he used as an emollient on his scalp.

They stood for a moment, watching the entrance to Jericho, listening to the rain.

"What's got you so charged here, *geneth*?" Owens' words thrummed against her arm.

Her chest tightened. She saw the girl on her side, the gray ropes of her entrails. "I saw the lass die, Lew."

"That's not it. Folk die all the time in this city. Black folk more than most. That's not enough to get you dressed up in those duds, trigging it from school, and standing about in this weather. You should have been off to your libben and a nice warm fire long ago. So what is it?"

His arm was a warm, heavy blanket on her shoulders, his hand on her upper arm.

"I think she was with child." Her voice was small against the dull roar of the rain.

"What makes you say so?"

"Just something about the way she held herself."

"You think him that killed her knew?"

"I don't know. Could be. But either way, it was two lives taken that night, not one."

The rain was a wall of sound around them, hissing on the rooftops and gouging trenches in the muddy street.

"I miss him too." Owens' voice was a low rumble.

She had to hold herself, her nose tingling, the breath high in her throat, her body like a string wound tight. She thought about her son, her darling Daniel, his high forehead and his tiny feet, and the smell of him, warm milk and crushed cookies. His skin like silk against her lips.

Owens' arm tightened, hugging her against him, and she let the tears slide down her face, fat and silent in the dark.

"So what will you do?" Owens asked.

She waited for the cramp in her throat to ease. "I don't know. What can I do?"

He nodded across the lake of mud at the sentry shivering in the rain. "Like you say, you could get in there. Find out for sure who the girl was, and why she was hushed."

"How? You've said yourself you can't find a way in."

"Not me. But I reckon you could walk right through that gate, if you had the right story. If you happened by one of Absalom's sermons and pretended you're a curtezan looking to escape your splitter, he'd welcome you, like as not."

"You said he only wanted white girls."

"You could say you're Spanish, or Italian. That's white enough, wouldn't you say? I could get you set up. You already talk flash, and you've plenty of experience putting yourself out of twig. Shouldn't take much for you to learn how to act the mab."

She twisted out of his embrace and stared at him.

He shrugged. "Just a thought."

THIRTEEN

Monday

The weather had cleared in the night and a stiff onshore breeze drove the woodsmoke that belched from the city's chimneys up Manhattan Island, revealing a flawless cobalt sky. The rain had scrubbed the cobbles of the streets in the night, pushing heaps of mud and straw and ordure to the curbs, where it stood, steaming in the morning sun. Down in the estuary, the tide was turning, and the air was full of the roar of water as the Hudson and East Rivers churned.

Justy was grateful for the cool air. He had slept badly, something dark tormenting him in the night. He could not remember the dream, but the feeling of unease stayed with him, like mist covering the ground on a winter morning.

He walked down the Broad Way, stepping into the street here and there to avoid the men employed by householders to sweep up the muck in front of their residences. Some of the men were servants or slaves, dressed in smart livery. Others were freelance street sweepers, young, ragged boys who hooted and called to each other as they swung their shovels.

It was still too early for the wealthier of New York's denizens to be about, and there were few carriages on the Broad Way, but the wind carried a hum of noise up the streets from the East River waterfront. The markets on Catherine Street and Maiden Lane opened before dawn, and Justy could hear the stall holders calling out, and the carts rumbling on the cobbles of the Bowery, bringing meat and produce from the farms north of the city.

He recognized the tall, lean figure of Gorton approaching him from a hundred yards away. The watchman's eyes were pink and bloodshot, and garnished with two dark half circles. He was munching on a chonkey, and as he got closer, he wrapped the uneaten half of the pastry in a handkerchief and tucked it into his coat pocket. "Good morning, Marshal. I thought I might catch you coming this way."

Justy stopped. "Good morning, Jeremiah. A fine day. Although you look as though you're ready for your bed."

"I am that. It feels like days since I last saw the straw. But I wanted to catch you before I got my head down. I'll walk with you and peach you the whole scrap."

"Go on then." They began walking.

"When you went to speak to Sister Claire, I went back to my libben to couch a hogshead. But before I got my head down, I asked the mollisher what rents me my room about our Mister Umar. Turns out he's a bit of a cushion thumper."

"Is that so? Where does he preach?"

"Up by the creek. Most evenings, she thinks. Not that she's been to one herself."

"Perhaps we should go tonight, then."

They had arrived at Federal Hall. Two carriages had pulled up at the bottom of the steps. The first was familiar, a red-painted covered cabriolet, pulled by a white mare. Behind it was a dark blue four-seater, drawn by two chestnut horses.

Justy stopped. "Thank you, Jeremiah. You should get some rest. What time do these assemblies take place?"

"Six of an evening. Just after it gets dark."

"Be back here at three, then. We'll have a bite and then go and hark at this fellow's patter."

He watched Gorton's rangy frame lope back up the hill to the Broad Way. Then he turned and knocked on the door of the little red carriage. "Eliza?"

"Don't come in." Eliza's voice was only slightly muffled by the canvas cover.

"Why? What is it? And what are you doing here at this hour?"

He glanced up at the rear of the cab, where the driver sat. The man looked away quickly, but not until Justy had caught the faint smile on his face.

"I have been up all night, composing a letter." Eliza's voice was softer now, and Justy had to press his ear against the canvas to hear. "In the end, however, I have not been able to convey my feelings adequately on paper. Father will be quite distressed when he sees how much of his vellum I have expended in the effort."

"I'm not sure I understand, Eliza, I—"

"Please do not speak, Justice. It is hard enough for me to say what I have to say, without hearing your voice." There was a long pause. "I have come to tell you that I do not wish you to call upon me any longer."

"Eliza, if this is about Riker, I apologize. I allowed myself to be drawn out."

"Please, Justice. Piers is a cad. Everyone knows it. But I expected more from you."

"I'm sorry, Eliza."

There was another long pause. "I am sorry, too. This is the last time we shall see each other. I have brought your . . . winnings with me."

Justy glanced behind him at the blue carriage. A jarvie was perched on the high driver's seat. He was dressed entirely in white: breeches, hose, waistcoat, jacket, shirt, and necktie, in stark contrast with his dark skin. His hair was shaved tight around the back and sides of his head, which was crowned with a high hat made of white silk.

"I am leaving for Greenwich this morning." Eliza's faint voice recaptured his attention. "I shall be away for quite some time. I don't know how long." She took a breath. "Please spare us both, Mister Flanagan, by not calling upon me again."

She knocked twice on the roof of the carriage. Justy had to jump back onto the sidewalk to avoid his feet being crushed by the wheels of the cab as it rolled away. He could feel the eyes of a handful of onlookers, early birds who had stopped to watch the show. His face burned.

He watched the little red carriage plunge down the hill towards Water Street. And as the heat of his embarrassment faded from his face, he felt something else. A sneaking sense of relief.

He turned to look at his prize. It was a kind of phaeton carriage, a four-seater sprung drag of an unusual design. Most drags were open to the elements, but this one had a low-slung cab painted a glossy midnight blue. Its door handles, railings, wheel hubs, and coach lights were all made of brass, polished to a high shine. The two chestnut horses, a gelding and a mare, stood quietly in the braces between the shafts, their coats as glossy and groomed as the carriage itself.

The white-uniformed driver straightened up on his seat. "Mister Marshal Flanagan?"

"Yes."

"Your carriage, sir. With Mister Riker's compliments."

The rig rocked and creaked as the jarvie descended from his perch. He went to the horses and began talking softly to them, stroking their noses and feeding them something that he took from the pocket of his white coat. They nuzzled him, fat tongues licking his face.

Justy walked slowly along the sidewalk, unable to take his eyes off the vehicle. The paintwork was so thick and smooth that it looked like lacquer. Two red pennants stirred in the breeze from a pair of six-foot whips angled from the back of the cab. The jarvie gave the horses one last pet, then hurried to open the nearside door.

It was hot inside the cab, but there was none of the customary stink of mold or damp, just the rich scent of warm leather and wood polish. Justy sat on the upholstered bench and ran his hands over the furnishings. The seats were stuffed thick with horsehair, and upholstered in leather. The floor was covered by a scarlet rug. The walls of the cab were padded in royal blue silk. The windows were curtained by lengths of sumptuous blue velvet. It was so quiet in the cab, he could hear his heart beating.

"Is everything all right, sir?" The coachman had put his hat on. His white clothing reflected the sunlight. The effect was blinding.

"Yes. Quite all right. Thank you."

"Where to, sir?"

Of course. He couldn't leave the damned thing here outside the hall. He ran his hands over the soft, tufted leather of the seat beside him. By God, it was a beautiful vehicle. And it was his! He leaned back in the seat and chuckled to himself.

The coachman stood patiently, waiting, his eyes on the ground. Watching him and not watching him, at the same time.

Justy gathered his thoughts. Where to? A good question. Where did one keep a carriage and two horses? Was there a stable near his lodging? He had a vague memory of one somewhere on Church Street. But how much would it cost? And what about a driver? It looked as though the white-clad jarvie was willing to help him get the rig to a stable, but what then?

He felt his mood sour. There was no way he could keep the damn thing. It was too expensive, and he didn't need a carriage, anyway. He would have to sell it.

Damn it.

He sighed. "Do you know Hughson's Tavern?"

FOURTEEN

Seamus Tully placed a mug on the bar. He hefted a large copper kettle with a thin spout, and poured coffee in a long, steaming stream.

Justy sniffed the brew, then sipped. He looked up at Tully. "So. How much for a week?"

"Six bucks."

Justy grunted. He knew the price was fair. Possibly even cheap. The carriage itself took up a lot of room. And horses ate like, well, horses. And six dollars wouldn't kill him. He could afford that for a few weeks. He didn't want to rush the sale, after all.

"She's a beauty," Tully remarked. "How'd you come by her?"

"Game of chance."

"Ah." Tully wiped an invisible spot of dust from the gleaming varnish on his counter. "Well, I don't know about the rattler, but I do have the name of a cove who'd have those prancers."

"I'm sure you do. How much, do you reckon?"

"Seventy-five each, maybe."

Justy sipped his drink. He knew the horses were worth double that amount, but if he needed to sell them quickly . . . "I'll think about it."

Tully inclined his head. "Ho! An angel among us!"

The jarvie stood at the door, uncertain in his white suit of clothes.

Tully beckoned. "Come on in, big fella. All are welcome at Hughson's."

The jarvie approached the bar. He kept his eyes on the ground.

"Thanks for help with the coach." Justy jerked his head towards the bar. "Can I buy you a glass of ale?"

The man stood mute, twisting his silk hat in his hands.

"Come on, now. One drink for your trouble."

Justy nodded to Tully, who filled a tall glass and placed it on the bar. The coachman considered it for a moment, glanced first at Justy, then at Tully, and then lifted the glass and drank off half the contents in a single swallow. He put the glass back and exhaled in a long sigh.

Tully chuckled. "You look like a man who hasn't seen a beer in half a lifetime."

"Nor have I, sir," the jarvie said. His voice was deep, with a lilt of the islands about it. He picked up the glass and sniffed it, then took a second, much smaller swallow.

"What's your name?" Justy asked.

"Hardluck, sir."

Justy coughed on his coffee. "Hard luck, you say?"

"That's right, sir. My mother called me that, on account I was born on the ship on the way from Africay."

"She should have called you Goodluck, then, for it's a miracle you survived."

"So everyone says. She figured the slavers might throw me overboard, rather than have another mouth to feed. So she named me Hardluck, hoping they'd think that bad fortune would come to them if they took me. And the name stuck."

Tully refilled the man's glass. "That story deserves one on the house."

The driver looked at Justy. Then he looked at the ground.

"Come on now, Hardluck," Justy said. "Have a seat. You'll not dirty your clobber, if that's what you're fretting about."

Hardluck hesitated for a moment, then slipped onto the stool. He sipped the froth off his beer. "I broke down the rig and cleaned the wheels, sir. I stabled the horses, too. Mister Tully keeps a good clean post." He nodded solemnly to Tully, who raised a glass in acknowledgment.

"Well, I'm most grateful to you," Justy said.

The jarvie stared at him for a moment, surprise in his face. And then he looked down. "I didn't feed them, for they had hay first thing this morning."

"Don't worry about it."

They fell silent. Justy looked at the sediment in the bottom of the mug. There were women he had met in Ireland who claimed to be able to read tea leaves left in the bottom of a cup. Could they do the same with coffee? he wondered. And what would they say? What was in his future? Would he find out who killed the girl in the alley? Would he ever find a woman he liked? Would he find someone to give him a half-decent price for the carriage and pair that was currently draining his purse?

He thought about the short trip that he had taken in the cab. The vehicle was so well sprung, it felt as though he was riding a cloud. The leather on the seats was like butter, and the windows and doors so well fashioned that he could hardly hear anything as they drove along.

He glanced at Tully. "It's a pity to sell it."

"Aye. She's a beauty, right enough." Tully began polishing a pewter mug.

Hardluck swiveled on his seat. His eyes bulged. "Sell it, sir? The carriage?"

"I'm afraid so. I mean, it's a beauty, and the horses too, and I'd love to keep it, but I've no use for a carriage of my own. And then there's the cost."

Tully put down the mug. "You could afford it, Justy. If you really wanted. Fence the horses and get yourself a couple of cheaper nags. Maybe even get permission to use the city stables."

Justy considered the point. "I suppose it's possible. But even if I did choose to keep it, who'd drive the blinding thing? I can barely handle a cart. I'd throw a wheel or have it turned over in a ditch in half a day."

Hardluck was suddenly on his feet. "Driving's my job, sir. Mine!" He looked like a man who had just been robbed.

"I'm sorry, friend." Justy kept his voice soft. "I can tell you love those beasts, and you've put your whole self into looking after that rig. Anyone can see that. But that part of your life's over now."

Hardluck stared at him, sweat breaking out in large beads on his face. "Don't sell me, sir."

Justy frowned. "Sell you?"

"I'm a good worker, sir. And I can find a way to keep your costs down. I'll buy feed direct from the farms. And I won't eat much, I promise."

"Hardluck, what the devil are you talking about? You are Mister Riker's man, and much as I hate to say this, you must go back to him."

The jarvie gripped the counter with one large hand. His entire body was quivering. "No, sir. I am your man now."

"What?"

"Mister Piers said so. Carriage, horses, and driver. All yours. That's what he said."

Justy stared. The tavern seemed to shrink around him. "There must be some mistake."

"No mistake, sir." Hardluck fumbled with the buttons of his coat, then pulled a long, cream-colored fold of paper from his inside pocket. "He told me to give you this."

Justy looked at the paper. The florid script. His pulse thumped in the roof of his mouth.

Tully leaned across the counter. "Read it, then."

Justy's mouth was dry. "I, Piers Andrew Riker of the town of Trenton, New Jersey, do give and grant to Justice Flanagan, Mayor's Marshal of the City of New York, a certain Negro male, named Hardluck, about thirty-three years of age. I now quit my right, title, claim, and interest in said Negro male to said person, and bind myself to warrant and defend against all others et cetera et cetera Piers Andrew Riker."

"Is that legal?"

"He's got two witnesses. And his father's an assistant justice of the peace. I'm quite sure that'll settle the matter."

They both turned to look at Hardluck, standing beside the bar in his white suit of clothes, his eyes on the ground. He had twisted his absurd white hat entirely out of shape.

"Tamsin's not going to like this too much," Tully muttered.

Justy laughed.

"You think this is funny?"

"You have to admire Riker, Seamus. He is a creative bastard. What better revenge for his humiliation than to humiliate me even more in return? By turning me into a goddamned slaver!"

"So what are you going to do?"

Justy stared at the sheet of vellum, at the names of the two witnesses. The first signature he knew well: Eliza signed her name with a distinctive flourish, and she had printed her name clearly beneath. The second was a mere scrawl, and the writing under it looked like the hand of a palsied man. It was a moment before Justy was able to decipher Chase Beaulieu's name.

He thought about the anger in Piers Riker's face when Beaulieu had told the room about their jaunt to Canvas Town the evening before. About Beaulieu stumbling to the door, whispering that he wanted to meet. The fear in his voice.

He looked up at the jarvie. "Tell me, Hardluck. Do you know a Mister Chase Beaulieu?"

"Of course, sir. He and Mister Piers are quite close."

"Have you seen him recently?"

"Why, yes, sir. I drove them both on Saturday afternoon."

"Whereabouts, exactly?"

Hardluck looked awkward. "To Barclay Street, sir. St. Paul's."

"The Holy Ground?"

"Yes, sir. For lunch, Mister Piers said. They came back just after the Trinity bell struck three."

"And what kind of state were they in?"

"Pretty fair. Although Mister Chase was complaining that Mister Piers had spilled garlic broth over him."

Which meant they had been in one of the few oyster cellars that served shellfish stewed in the French style, with white wine and garlic. "And then?"

"Then Mister Piers told me to drive up Church Street, sir."

Justy felt excitement clutch at him. Church Street ran parallel to Chapel Street. "How far?"

"I drew up just past the Quaker house."

Only a few hundred yards away from where the girl had died.

"Which way did they go?"

The driver hesitated. His fingers twitched, as though he was pulling on the carriage reins.

"Which way, Hardluck?" Justy kept his voice soft.

"Left, sir. Down the hill."

"Into Canvas Town?"

The driver nodded.

"And what time did they return?"

"Near six, sir." The driver's voice was a murmur. He avoided Justy's eyes.

"Tell me."

"They were hurrying. Mister Chase was very drunk. He cast up on the sidewalk before he got into the cab. It was dark, but I could see Mister Piers' coat was wet. I thought perhaps Mister Chase had taken his revenge and spilled drink on him."

"But?"

"But later, when I was cleaning the carriage, there was blood on the seat."

"Human blood?"

Hardluck shrugged. "Just blood."

Justy sat up. His fingers tingled and his head felt light. Piers Riker. Was it possible? He was a notorious rake, and Beaulieu had intimated that he had been spending more time in Canvas Town than usual. Perhaps the girl had been a prostitute after all.

"Tell me, Hardluck. Does Mister Piers like to hunt?"

"Oh yes, sir." The driver seemed relieved to change the subject. "He is a very good shot."

"And does he dress his kill himself, in the field?"

"I believe so. Mister Riker's huntsman has often commented on his skill with a knife." He caught himself, and frowned.

Justy patted him on the shoulder. "That's all right. Thank you for being candid with me. Now finish up. We have a great deal to do today, and not much time to do it."

FIFTEEN

Kerry paid a street sweeper a penny to take a note to the African Free School. In the note was a lie. It told John Teasman she was taken ill, and needed a day or two to recover.

It was less than a mile in a straight line from her home to the heart of Canvas Town, but there was no direct route, only a slow zig-zag through the crush of narrow lanes, and it took most of a half hour for Kerry to reach the fort. It was an old watchtower, built by the British after they took New York from the Continental Army in 1776. They had heaped earth on the already high ground a few hundred yards back from the shoreline, then built a palisade, first of wood, and later of quarried stone. Most of the stone was now gone, but the foundations remained, and when Canvas Town moved north and encompassed the old lookout point, an enterprising madam had commandeered the fort, built some rudimentary dwellings inside it, and turned it into a brothel.

There was only one point of entry, from the south, up a shallow earthen ramp that was paved with wooden planks. They squelched under Kerry's feet as she walked up the slope, her skirts hitched up to keep them from dragging on the damp wood. The ramp was hemmed in by flimsy shacks made of whatever materials their builders had scavenged: worn sailcloth, scorched barrel staves, ripped bedsheets, burned window frames, discarded roof tiles, and waterlogged pallets. Women stood in the makeshift entrances, many with their breasts uncovered. Some were obese, others were emaciated, some were very young, and some looked very old, although Kerry knew they could not be. They all had the feverish look of the poorly nourished, and many bore the scars and pockmarks of disease. Some gave her blank looks as she passed. Others

scowled. Either she was a busybody, come to lecture them on the evils of their
way of life, or she was competition. Either way, she wasn't welcome.

She reached the top of the ramp and found her way blocked by a large, pale
woman dressed in a sleeveless purple ballgown. The woman had powdered
her breasts liberally and forced them into a corset, making them look like two
snow-covered drumlins. She had piled her graying hair high on her head in
the old style, and she had two large, black beauty spots, one on the right side
of her chin, the other under her left eye. Her lips were smeared with red wax;
her eyelashes with lamp black, so that they looked like spider's webs.

The effect was clownish, until Kerry looked into the woman's eyes. They
were iron gray, and as empty as a freshly dug grave.

"You're Lew's cousin." The woman had a strong, Northern English accent.

"And you must be Miss Violet."

"Aye." The madam's gaze was steady and unblinking. "Tanny's in't Rose
Room. But she's busy now, so you'll have to wait."

"Very well."

Miss Violet turned on her heel and walked away across a small, roughly
circular courtyard that was covered with sand. The space was ringed with a
number of small huts. Opposite the entrance to the courtyard was a bigger
building, made of brick, with a black door. Miss Violet disappeared through it,
leaving Kerry alone.

Kerry counted eight individual huts. They looked old and weathered, but
they were sturdily built, with proper roofs and doorways, each of which was
painted a different color. The paint looked fresh, and expensive. Beside each
of the huts there was a low bench and a covered wooden pail. Kerry went to
the bench beside the pink door and sat down.

In the lanes and alleys around the fort, business in Canvas Town was in
full swing. The cries of food sellers and stall holders mingled with the hum
and buzz of people hurrying back and forth, buying and selling and passing
the time of day. And business within the fort was in full swing, too, despite the
early hour. It sounded as though every one of the huts was occupied, and the
courtyard was full of the barely muffled sound of grunts and sighs and giggles
and squeals.

A shuffling sound came from behind the pink door, then a click, and it
swung open. A man strode into the courtyard, moving quickly, his shoes scuff-
ing in the sand, his head down.

Tanny leaned in the doorway. She looked older in the daylight, her white dress a little grayer, her skin showing the faint marks of childhood smallpox. She gave Kerry a sour look. "You're Lew's cousin, then, are you? Come to learn the trade?"

"Something like that."

Tanny folded her arms. "Lew said you'd pay me for the time."

"Did he? And how much would that be?"

"Five bob."

"Not bad for a day's work." Most working men made between six and fifteen dollars a week. Kerry made four.

Tanny snorted. "A day? That's five for the hour."

Kerry laughed. "This ain't Cherry Street, hen, and just because I'm togged in buntings and a snicket don't mean you can treat me like some judy hick." She stood up to leave.

"Talk flash, then, do you?" Tanny's grin made her look ten years younger.

"Have done since I was a titter. Which is how I know you're looking to kimbaw me."

Tanny shrugged. "I'm just trying to make a rag. If I spend the day nattering with you, I'll have no chink to show for it, and Miss Violet'll make me wear the bands."

Kerry smiled. "Nice try, Antoinette. Lew told me he's already agreed to pay you and Miss Violet, so you won't have to worry about not getting your rations. In fact, do me right and I'll take you to luncheon, too."

A door banged open across the courtyard, and a man half-fell out of the sky-blue hut, clutching his breeches closed with one hand. With the other, he blew an extravagant kiss. And then he stopped dead in the center of the space. He looked around, as though he was lost, and then bent double and vomited into the sand.

Tanny watched, dead-eyed, as the man limped away. "Aye, well," she said. "I could use a little time off anyway."

———•———

She led the way to a small coffee house, ordered eggs and a soft loaf, and gave Kerry a refresher on the hierarchy of the New York demimonde. There were a handful of prostitutes in New York who could charge five dollars for an hour of their time. But none were dark-skinned, and none did business in Canvas Town. There was a strict hierarchy, and everyone in it knew their place. At the bottom of the heap were the bunters, desperate women who lived in the alleyways and middens of the growing city, begging or prostituting themselves and spending most or all of the proceeds on drink. Next came the buricks, also called cracks or drabs. These made enough to afford to put a roof over their heads, but were either too old or tired or diseased to do much more than subsist otherwise. They plied their trade where they could afford their lodgings: in the fetid, poorly constructed sinkholes of New George and Charlotte Streets, along Laycock Lane, just east of the Common, or in Canvas Town, like the women Kerry had encountered on her way into the fort.

Tanny was a member of the next, broadest band of prostitute, called a curtezan. These were women and men in their prime, and depending on their looks or skills or business savvy, either did business as an independent operator, or as a case-vrow, attached to a particular brothel or bawdy house. There were benefits to both arrangements, but downsides, too. Tanny told Kerry she had started as a case-vrow in the fort, and enjoyed protection, room, and board. But she was young and pretty and in demand, and she soon came to resent surrendering most of what she made to the house. She had left the fort the previous year and set up as a squirrel, as New Yorkers put it, in her own nest. She had to pay some money to one of Lew Owens' pimps and maintain her own premises, which could be expensive. But she kept everything else that she made, and she kept her own hours. She was able to operate where she pleased, in her own place, or in certain taverns, or with the John Street vestals, women who did most of their business in the theater district. She was disappointed that Owens had ordered her back to the fort, but she accepted that her world was governed by rules, and that she had been caught breaking them. She was confident that within a year or so, she would be able to go back to operating independently.

She was equally sure that she would never ascend to the highest level of the prostitute's universe, that of the gentry-mort. These men and women catered exclusively to New York's upper classes. A handful even came from that class themselves, but had fallen on hard times and were forced to sell themselves from time to time, to maintain their lifestyles. These part-timers were called high-fliers or lady-birds. Most professional gentry-morts operated independently, with a handful of clients, but some preferred to work as case-vrows, in the most exclusive, highly discreet establishments on Cherry Street, or in the Holy Ground, the notorious district behind St. Paul's chapel that was owned by the Episcopal Church, but was nonetheless home to several well-appointed mansions of ill repute.

Tanny had never worked Cherry Street or the Holy Ground herself, but she knew many of the gentry-morts who did. She mixed with them in the infamous third tiers of the Park Street and John Street theaters, or at a balum rancum, the lewd parties thrown by wealthy and dissolute New Yorkers, where prostitutes were hired to dance and mingle naked with the invitees. But while associating with them was one thing, joining their ranks was quite another. Not that Tanny wasn't pretty, or popular or skilled enough, she assured Kerry. Just that she was too dark and too petite and a little too rough around the edges.

"Not like you," she said. They were back in the Rose Room, which was a tiny space, with a wooden floor, lit by a single window. There was a wide bed with a thick mattress, a tired-looking armchair, and a small table. But it was clean and tidy and free of dust. The walls had been whitewashed, the floor scrubbed, and the window rinsed, so that the sunlight sparkled on it.

Tanny made Kerry turn in a circle. "You ain't got much of a breech on you. And you don't sport much of a dairy, neither. But that don't mean much. Some of these gentry-morts are so spider-shanked and hatchet-faced you'd think they were coves. But some like it that way, I suppose."

"What about my color? Could I pass for white?"

"You ain't turnip-pated like the English or the Cloggies. But you might pass for Spanish. Them coolers got that dark hair and olive skin, and there's plenty of coves like that well enough. Plus you simper nice, and you got a good set of grinders, and that helps. Lift up your skirt."

Kerry did as she was told, bunching the folds of material at her waist.

Tanny raised an approving eyebrow. "That's a rum set of games there. You want to show 'em off as much as you can. You got any buntings with a long slit in them? Or any other rig what'll show some skin?"

"I'm a teacher, Tanny. I don't have any togs like that."

Tanny's white, even teeth were like a light in the dim little room. "Just as I hoped. Time for us to do a bit of shopping."

SIXTEEN

Justy settled on the luxurious cushions of his new carriage and closed his eyes. It was not yet noon, and yet he was exhausted. It was all the administration. When he had arrived at his desk, he had found it piled with papers. Writs of protests from attorneys; the schedule for the security detail guarding the secret Planning Commission; summonses from the court; and the inevitable tract about the horrors of popery, complete with a picture of Satan dressed as a nun. The only document he was really interested in was the duty constable's report from the night before.

It had been an unusually slow night, for a Sunday. There were only two reported incidents. A group of women who had drunk too much at a birthday celebration had decided to relieve themselves in the middle of John Street, just as the Mayor's wife was leaving the theater. And someone had alerted a watchman to a large gathering of men on some waste ground behind George Street. The watchman had gone to investigate, but the crowd of men had disappeared.

The carriage lurched over a bump in the road and Justy sat up, rubbing his face. He could not shake the thought of the dead girl, lying in the muck of the alley. It made him feel uneasy, almost panicked. It was not what he usually felt. He did not think of himself as a hard-hearted man, but he had seen enough death and investigated enough murders to know he had to keep himself at arm's length from the victims. But this was different. Perhaps because the girl was so young.

He thought about his dream. He still could not recall it. But he remembered the feelings. The same panic he was feeling now. The same unease. The same anger. He thought of Piers Riker and felt the anger flare. He wanted to drive down to Beaver Street and push himself into the man's smug, sallow face and demand to know his whereabouts on Saturday night. But he had to investigate the watchman's report first. Hays would never forgive him if he did not. Large gatherings of men usually meant trouble, especially in that quarter of the city. And the wrong kind of trouble might mean fire. And because New York City's buildings, old and new, were still made mostly of wood, fire was Jake Hays' principal concern.

George Street wasn't far, and Justy could have walked. But he took the carriage. And why not? It was convenient, it was luxurious. It was his. He ran his hands over the buttery leather of the seat for what seemed like the hundredth time, wondering at how soft it was, as the cab rocked gently along the street. And then he heard the muffled sound of the driver, clucking his tongue at the horses, and he felt a chill in his guts. Hardluck was his, too. His slave.

Damn Piers Riker.

Well, it would not be so for long. He would have freed the jarvie on the spot, except that giving a man his freedom was not as simple a matter as opening the door and letting him walk away. It was a legal process that required paperwork and signatures and witnesses and official stamps. And not merely to satisfy the law. Hardluck would need written proof of his status that he could carry with him, if he was not to be grabbed up by runaway slave catchers. And those papers took time to arrange. Time that Justy did not have enough of, not if he was to investigate mysterious gatherings of men, and not if he was to find the killer of a girl whose only misstep was to have become pregnant. He hated himself for it, but Hardluck would have to wait.

The carriage pulled smoothly to a halt, and Justy looked out of the carriage window onto a strip of taverns, brothels, flop houses, and oyster cellars that tipped downhill for a ragged quarter mile. George Street, or Laycock Lane, as most New Yorkers called it. The lane was just one of several quarters of the city that laborers, longshoremen, soldiers, and sailors went to spend what little money they made on cheap drink, food, and sex, but it was by far the most lively.

The Bull owned every building on the street. He owned the grand four-story brownstones and the old wooden steep-roofed Dutch barns; he owned the cottage-style taverns and the shaky brick tenements with their rickety balconies. He owned the stables and the pigsties and the outhouses. He owned the strips of wasteland that the street bunters did their business on, and the square yards of payment where the penny-rum sellers flogged their rot-gut liquor. They all paid the Bull. The hundreds of men and women who lived on Laycock Lane paid rent, and the hundreds of streetwalkers and stallholders who set up shop there each evening paid a tax. In return, they could do whatever they wished, free from the interference of Federal Hall and the prying eyes and preaching mouths of the upright men and women who considered themselves the moral heart of the city.

Tickler's Alley was the entry point to a quarter acre of wasteland tucked behind a stable. It was the former site of a pie shop, owned by one Maurice Tickler, that had burned down a few years before. The old painted sign TICKLER'S PIES still adorned the wall of the alley and gave it its name. The land was deserted, which was unusual, as it was popular with bunters, who did business on the stony, patchy grass and slept there afterwards. It was also the best staging point for twenty armed men intent on wreaking havoc on Laycock Lane.

The sound of boots crunching on loose stone made him turn. A heavyset man stood in the entrance to the alleyway, dressed in a rough linen coat and a farmer cap. Prelim "Cooper" Corrigan, one of the Bull's trusties, nicknamed so because he liked to nail his victims into barrels half-full of spoiled ale before rolling them down hills until they learned their lessons or died. Not that he had ever been caught.

Corrigan nodded. Justy ignored him.

Corrigan stood aside to let another man pass. Ignatius Flanagan was a half-foot bigger and wider than his bodyguard. He seemed to fill the alleyway up.

"Uncle," Justy said.

The Bull nodded. "Well met, Justice. How did you know I'd be here?"

"I didn't."

"You mean you didn't happen by for a visit?" He feigned disappointment. He was immaculately dressed, as always, in an indigo coat over a black waistcoat and matching breeches that strained to encompass his swollen belly and barrel chest. The Bull didn't drink, but he liked to eat, sweets in particular, and Justy saw a light dusting of powdered sugar on the lapel of his coat that spoke of a mid-morning doughnut or pastry. Or two. He had become as big as a prime bullock in recent years, but he was still fast and strong, and word had it he would occasionally make an example of someone, to prove he was every bit as brutal now as he was aged twenty.

"I heard there was a bit of a rumpus last night," Justy said.

"Not much to tell. A gang of hackums crewed up here, then stepped into the lane. They were all set to get cracking when some upstanding citizen stopped them."

"You saw this?"

The Bull shook his head. "I was tucked up in my scratcher. Prelim Corrigan was the duty man, and Lizzie Toms told him."

"Lizzie Toms the madam?"

"You're familiar with the Buttered Bun, then, Nephew?"

Justy said nothing. The Bull's mouth twitched into what passed for a smile. "Well, Lizzie telt Prelim some matelot glimmed what was afoot, and stepped out to stop it. She said he dropped the front man and the rest piked on the bene."

"They just ran off? How many were there?"

"Twenty or so, she reckoned. All strapped with torches and toasting forks."

"And the sailor?"

The Bull shrugged. "You'd have to ask Lizzie."

"Lizzie Toms won't talk to a Marshal."

"She will if I make the introduction." The Bull smirked, a mean, yellow slit in the gray slab of his face. "I can tell her to sort you out, too, if you fancy. It's quite a covey of gigglers she's grown in there."

"I'd rather you didn't."

"You sure? Only I heard you might be looking for some comfort."

"You are misinformed, Uncle." Justy felt his face burn.

The Bull laughed, a hard bark. "Come on, then."

They made their way down the alley to the street. The Buttered Bun was an old wooden house, three stories high, built in the Dutch style with a steep-pitched roof. It was flanked by two poorly built warehouses made of crumbling red brick. With its brown shingles and fresh white paint, it looked like a little old lady sandwiched between a pair of drunken soldiers.

Justy had never met Lizzie Toms, but he had heard plenty. The streetwalkers brought in by the Watch had a hundred names for her: ape leader, fustiluggs, Munster heifer, meer fussocks, pocky trot, platter-faced jade. All of which made him expect a large, middle-aged, overweight woman, with heavy legs, and a wide, round face marked with smallpox scars. So he was surprised by the petite, slim, blonde-haired madam who emerged from the back of the small, neat reception area in the front of the brothel. Lizzie Toms looked as though she was barely out of her teens. She was dressed modestly, in a high-necked blouse and a long, dark blue skirt. Her hair was styled simply, pulled back from her face and secured with a bow of black silk, like a man's. Her skin was pale, and as clear as a glass of river water. She dipped a small curtsey when she saw the Bull. "How now, Mister Flanagan?"

The Bull made an awkward little bow. "Good day to you, Lizzie. And how many times must I tell you to call me Ignatius? How goes the day?"

"Tol-lol, I suppose." Her eyelids fluttered. "Ignatius."

The Bull seemed to swell up a little. Justy was shocked to see a smile twist his lips, and wrinkles appear around his eyes. He slapped Justy on the shoulder. "This here's my nephew. Justice Flanagan. You've not met him, I take it."

The eyelashes fluttered again. "No. But I've heard of the Marshal, of course." Her voice was soft, almost meek. Could this be the same woman that the streetwalkers despised as a brutal, vindictive madam who whipped her girls for the slightest infraction?

"Are you Lizzie Toms?" Justy asked.

"I am, sir."

"And this is your establishment?"

"It is. Thanks to your uncle, who has been so kind to me." She gave a shy smile that somehow included them both. "You're most welcome here."

Justy imagined he could hear the grin splitting the Bull's face. "My uncle tells me you witnessed the fracas last night."

"That's right, sir." She went to a counter in the corner of the small foyer, and perched on a tall stool, her hands posed daintily in her lap. "A group of men, perhaps twenty or twenty-five, coming out of the alley opposite. Some were carrying torches, others had swords and staves."

"What did they do?"

"Nothing at first. They lined up across the street, blocking it off at the top end, all shouting and waving their weapons. They looked to be readying themselves for a fight."

Justy nodded. "What then?"

"A man stepped out in front of them. He was a big Negro, with a long beard. He made some speech about putting the torch to the sinners. The usual tilly-tally that one hears from the reformists. It sent his men into a frenzy. Which is when the sailor came out."

"From here?"

The madam nodded. "He was sitting just where I am now, drinking stout and port wine."

"How do you know he was a sailor?"

"He came with his shipmates. They were telling sea stories. You know the way they do."

Justy nodded. "So what did he do?"

"Well, he was as cool as you like. As soon as he heard the big Negro shout, he got up and strolled past me, into the street. The man had his back to him, of course, and the sailor walked right up to him and said something. I couldn't hear, but the Negro stopped sudden and whirled around, a blade in his hand."

"You saw the knife?"

"Oh yes. A long one. A carving knife, perhaps. It flashed in the torchlight, clear as the day. The man was fast, but the sailor twisted away. He caught the man by the wrist, then hit him, very hard. And down he went." She slapped her hand hard on the counter.

"And then?"

"Then he stepped over the man. 'Who's next?' he asked, and they all just looked at each other and started backing up the street."

"They left their man behind?"

"I thought they might, but the sailor called out to them, 'Hey! Take your litter with you!' and waited until four men hurried back to pick the man up and carry him away."

"And that was that?"

"That was that."

Justy thought. "You said the lead man was black. What about the rest of them?"

She shrugged. "It was hard to see. Some of them, sure."

He looked around the small space. The counter was a good vantage point to watch the door of the brothel and the street beyond.

"You said the sailor was here with some shipmates."

"That's right. They were eight men altogether. But he was the only one left down here. The rest were upstairs."

"And he stayed down here the whole time?"

The madam's blonde ponytail bobbed. "The whole time."

A careful man, then. Keeping watch for his mates. Drinking some, but not too much, and not allowing himself to be tempted by Lizzie Toms' girls. A wise precaution on Laycock Lane, where there were as many thieves working the crowds as there were cobbles on the street.

"Do you know anything about these sailors? What ship they were from?"

"No. But it can't be a galleon, because they said they didn't have a doctor on board, and those big ships always do."

"Why did they need a doctor?"

"Why, for their man. The blood was running out of him like a river."

"So the knife did catch him?"

"Just here." Lizzie touched her side, under her left arm. "Opened him right up. One of his men pulled his shirt open and I saw the whites of his ribs. But he stayed on his feet."

"A hard man," the Bull said.

"And big with it. He had to duck his head to get out of the door there."

Which meant he was several inches taller than Justy. "Where did they take him?"

The madam shrugged. "I've no idea. The Almshouse, perhaps. It's closer than the hospital. But wherever he is, he won't be hard to find. A man as big as that, with his hair that red, and a beard like a bonfire? There can't be two of the like of him in this city."

———⬥———

Lars Hokkanssen lay, eyes closed, on a straw-stuffed mattress on a raised pallet in the corner of a long, pale room. He was naked, the lower part of his body covered by a threadbare sheet of coarse linen, and his torso wrapped in a thick cotton bandage. Blood had leaked through the cotton in a long, fat curve from his sternum to the pit of his left arm. His skin matched the whitewashed walls. His red hair and beard looked like red paint, spilled on the pillow.

A nun stood over him and pointed. "The blade ran over his ribs here, but it slid through here, under his arm."

"Deep?" the Bull asked.

"Two fingers, at least."

The Bull grunted. Justy felt the ground soft under his feet. He felt his uncle's eyes on him. He held up a hand. "I'm fine."

"He walked away, Nephew." The Bull's voice was soft. "That says something."

"I don't know. He's a stubborn bastard. You'd have to chop the legs off him to get him off his feet."

"I knew there was a reason I liked him." The Bull's hand was heavy on Justy's shoulder. "Men like that are hard to kill."

Justy nodded. He knew exactly how hard it was to kill Lars Hokkanssen. For six months they had fought together in Ireland's Rebellion of 1798, hunting English soldiers, fighting them face-to-face, and then, when the Rebellion was crushed, running from them like rats. Lars had been beaten and shot and slashed and blown up and burned, and he had always walked away. Except once, when Justy had carried him through the Kildare marshes with a lead ball deep in his right thigh. Seven long days and nights. Lars said he owed Justy for that one, but Justy knew it was the other way around, that from the first moment they had met, Lars had watched over him and protected him, every step of the way.

"The last time I saw him looking like this, we were up to our bellies in a Kildare swamp. I thought he was done for."

"He told me once that you carried him out," the Bull said.

"Did he?" Justy shook his head and looked down at his friend. "I don't know. The place was crawling with soldiers. I was ready to give up, but he wouldn't let me. He was the one with the bullet in him, but he never flagged. I'd say he carried me as much as I carried him."

Lars' lips twitched and his eyelids fluttered, and Justy felt relief envelop him like a warm blanket. He winked at the Bull. "He was a heavy bastard, mind. It was like carrying a slaughtered pig."

His uncle smiled. "I've always thought of him as a big, strong fellow. But he looks weak, lying here. And a lot smaller than you'd think. Scrawny, almost."

"A blessing for the sisters, I suppose. Less of him to wash."

"Aye. A dirty business it is, swabbing down a sailor. Not that they'd have to worry about the old rantallions."

"Why's that?"

"Ah, you know what they say about the bloodnuts." The Bull wiggled his little finger. "The bigger the fire up top, the less that burns below." He winked at the nun, who looked as though she had sucked a lemon.

"That's a boggin' lie!" Lars' voice was a hoarse scratch, like a rake on a gravel path. He tried to prop himself up on his elbows, but fell back, groaning.

"Settle down, ye big cods-head." Justy laughed, blinking back the tears that had suddenly blurred his vision. "What the hell were you thinking, charging into a tilt on your own like that?"

"Someone had to." Lars' voice dropped to a whisper. He gave a slight smile. "I didn't see any coppers about to keep the peace."

The Bull smirked. "Well said, jack."

"Is that so? And where were all of your lads, then?" Justy snapped.

Lars chuckled, quietly. "Now, now, gents. No fighting in church." He closed his eyes and breathed out, a long wheeze.

Justy squatted beside the bed. "Can you move, big fella? We need to get you to a doctor."

Lars said nothing. His face was as pale as the sheet he lay on. The nun put her fingers to his neck. "His blood is slowing. If you move him now, you could open his wounds, and if you do that, you'll kill him."

"Can we bring the doctor here, at least?"

She shook her head. "There's nothing a doctor can do for him now. He's been well stitched, and we can keep him as comfortable here as he would be anywhere. You need to let sleep do its work, now. Sleep and prayer."

Justy closed his eyes and rested his head on the edge of the bed. He heard Lars breathing, hoarse and shallow, and he felt the pressure build inside him, a potent mix of fear and rage, making his heart pound so hard he could feel it in the roof of his mouth.

The Bull's massive hand was warm on his shoulder. "We'll get the man that did this, Nephew. Don't you fear. That black bastard Owens has had it coming for a while now. It's time to balance the scale."

Justy rubbed his face. He stood up. "How can you be so sure it was Owens?"

"Who else? That crew last night was a bunch of blackfellas, wasn't it? Owens' lads, for sure. The madge has been chipping away at my holdings for years. Cloying my best doxies and sending his lads to tilt outside my boozing kens. And now this? He's asking for a scrap."

"And you'd be happy to give it to him, I suppose."

"If that's what's needed." The Bull's eyes were hard.

Justy looked down at his friend. His red hair. His paper-white skin. He felt drained. "Can you not settle this some other way? Why not meet the man and talk?"

"Talk?" The Bull laughed. "Why don't I take a bow and sell tickets for a voyage up my windward passage while I'm at it? The time for talk is over, boy. Now it's time for us to fight."

"Your fight, not mine." Justy's voice sounded hollow in his own ears.

"Is that so? With your friend lying there with a gash like the East River in his guts?"

"I won't help you set the city alight just because a friend got hurt."

The Bull's lip curled. "Well, that's your business. But don't expect me to take this lightly. I've been too soft for too long on your account. Times gone, I would have burned Owens out the moment he made his first move, then drowned every one of his rats in the Collect. But you asked me to hold back. And so I have. But no more. The madge wouldn't have tried something this bold unless he thought I was weak. So I have to show him he's mistaken."

SEVENTEEN

Once again, Gorton led him through the crush of Canvas Town, to a rough clearing, where a small crowd had gathered. Men and women, of every shade of black, white, and brown, stood under the awnings of the buildings and in the mouths of the alleys, or sat on cloaks and makeshift cushions. They all had the washed-out look of the poor. There were lanterns strung along the sides of the square. As Justy watched the people settle, he heard a church bell on the faint northerly breeze.

A man appeared, dressed in a baggy shirt and loose trousers. He carried a large wicker tray, heaped with chonkeys. He weaved through the crowd, allowing each person to take a pastry from the pile. Umar was already there, standing on a low platform, watching his man work. He wore his long, white-sleeved robe and his small white cap. His black beard looked enormous against the white tunic, and his dark skin gleamed like oiled teakwood. His men stood behind him in the shadows, scarred faces and gleaming eyes.

"Listen to the words of the Prophet, peace be upon him," Umar began. "The Devil has given up trying to lead you astray in big things, so beware of following him in small things. Life and property are sacred. If anyone has lent you something, return it to him. Hurt no one, lest they hurt you in return. Lend money if you wish, but God forbids the charging of interest. Your capital is yours to keep. That is the word of God."

It was a good opener. There was a low buzz of chatter. A man sitting on the ground in front of Justy snorted. "No interest? Keep all your money? No taxes? Some chance. The bloody church'd go broke and fall to pieces."

There was a ripple of laughter, and then the crowd fell silent as Umar began to speak again, taking pauses between each sentence, so that his speech acquired a rhythmic, hypnotic cadence. "No white man has superiority over a black man. Just as no black man has superiority over a white, except by piety and good action. We are all brothers and sisters, and nothing we own is ours, unless it was given freely and willingly." Umar's delivery was smooth, and even. His voice was deep and resounding, and it carried right across the silent plaza. The effect was lulling, and Justy leaned against the wall of the building beside him and let the voice wash over him.

The shack was made of pieces of driftwood, parts of a ship or its cargo that had washed up on the river shores. The builder had not used new nails, but had hammered bits of scrap iron into the wood, or reused the rusted nails that were there before. Many of these had not gone deep into the wood and bent or sheared off, and as Justy leaned on the wall, the ball of his shoulder rolled onto one of these shards of metal.

He stood straight, rubbing his arm. He felt as though he had just woken up. Umar was still speaking, his voice low and deep. The crowd was bewitched. They watched him, slack-faced and glassy-eyed. Even Gorton was staring, following every word, nodding slightly as Umar's words swirled around them, like fragrant smoke. "Those who are merciful will be shown mercy by the merciful. Be merciful to those on the earth, and the One above in the heavens will have mercy upon you. God does not look at your appearance or your possessions; but he looks at your heart and your deeds. It does not matter what you are, who you are, or what you have done to survive. You might walk the streets and sell yourself, you might commit the most depraved acts, in order to live. God sees all that we do, but he is merciful. He forgives. Those who repent, believe, and do good deeds: God will change the evil deeds of such people into good ones. This goes for all, brother and sister, no matter what deeds they have done in the past, or been forced to do."

He stopped. The crowd seemed to lean forward. He stretched out his hands, and for a moment, he looked like a man feeding lumps of sugar to a herd of ragged horses. "These are the words of the Prophet. The world's comforts are not for me, he said. I am like a traveler, who takes his rest under a tree in the shade, and then goes on his way. Allah be praised."

He stepped back off the platform, and the crowd sighed.

"Quite a speech," Justy said.

Gorton looked startled, as though he had been caught at something. There were two spots of color, high on his pale cheeks.

"Everything all right, Jeremiah?"

Gorton blinked. His eyes cleared. "Aye, Chief. Quite a speech, as you say."

A small crowd had gathered around the dais, mostly women, most of whom had the worn, gaudy look of street prostitutes. One of them looked a grade more exclusive, a tall, lithe woman in a pale blue dress and brown linen shawl. She looked like she might be Spanish or Greek, with olive skin and long, dark hair that she had piled up on her head so that its tresses fell and framed her face. Her cheeks were rouged, her eyes heavy with dark makeup, and her lips were a deep, liquid red. Umar was listening to her, his head cocked slightly on one side, a slight smile on his lips. Then he laughed, and she laughed, too, swaying back and twirling a lock of her hair, and Justy realized to his horror that he knew that gesture, and that the woman was not some street bunter.

It was Kerry O'Toole.

EIGHTEEN

Kerry had spent the afternoon with Tanny in the cast-off stalls on Greenwich Street. There was a line of them, heaped with gowns, petticoats, and corsets, all salvaged from the grand houses around Cherry Street, William Street, and Wall Street. Most of the clothes came from housemaids, who either stole them or received them as gifts from their mistresses, and most were long out of style. Ladies these days dressed in the European fashion, in loose, gauzy slips that showed off the figure and often revealed almost as much of the wearer as they covered. These modish gowns occasionally found their way to Greenwich Street, but they rarely spent long on the stalls. If they weren't reserved for special clients, they sold quickly, and for a far heftier price tag than a Canvas Town working girl could afford.

The result was that most of the area's prostitutes dressed in the older styles, so they looked more like their clients' mothers and grandmothers than their wives or paramours. Which, Tanny pointed out to Kerry, often worked in the working girls' favor. "You'd never twig by looking at 'em how many of these coves just want a cuddle from their mammies. Oh, they do want to tumble, in the end. But most of 'em want to be babbied a bit first." Tanny shook out a heavily embroidered petticoat, held it up against Kerry, and then tossed it back on the pile. She raised an eyebrow. "Some of 'em even like a bit of a spanking."

Kerry snorted. "I think you're having a laugh at me."

"I am not, girl. I put 'em over my knee, pull down their britches, and wallop 'em, just like they're little boys." She slapped her palm down on the pile of clothes, sending up a cloud of dust. Her eyes twinkled. "I can see you thinking what your man might say if you did similar."

"I haven't got a man, Tanny."

"Aye, but you know some, don't you?" She smiled. "Well, don't try it, anyway. It's not the kind of thing most men like their sweethearts doing. It's their little secret, ken?"

"I can see why it might be."

———•———

Tanny had found the blue dress at the bottom of a huge pile of dowdy frocks that reeked of stale sweat. It was a long-sleeved formal gown, with a high, stiff bodice and an extravagant train. She had torn off the arms below the shoulder, then deconstructed the bodice, so that it wrapped snugly around Kerry's chest. "We'll wedge something under there to push your heavers up a bit," she said.

While Kerry had cut off the train of the dress and hemmed it, Tanny had worked on a petticoat, removing most of the lace at the front, and adding some at the back. "To make it look like you've crackers worth talking about."

She had oohed and aahed over Kerry's long, dark hair as she brushed it straight, oiled it into tresses, and piled it up untidily in the fashion. "Make it look like you just got out of bed after a tumble. Even if no lass ever looked like that after a half hour on her back."

Lastly, she had painted Kerry's face with rouge and lipstick, the tip of her tongue showing, pink as a rose, between her teeth. Kerry found herself thinking about Justy. Would he run away to a bawdy house once a week for a spanking? He hadn't known his mother much longer than she had known her own, and her mother had died giving birth. No, Justy would not like a spanking, she decided.

Tanny chuckled. "Something's put color in your cheeks, girl, and it ain't this powder. Who is he, then?"

"Just someone I know."

"Interested, is he?"

"No."

"Well, he must be made of stone, because you're a dimber lass. A bit lacking in curves, maybe, but your hair's so fine, and your skin's like silk. You've got a smile like sunshine, too. When you let it show, that is."

Her fingers were soft on Kerry's cheek. "And why don't you ever smile, girl?"

The question took Kerry by surprise, and it had surged inside her, the darkness and the pain, like something alive, trying to scrabble its way out of her. Her throat tightened, and her skin bumped. There was a sudden wetness in her eyes, but Tanny had not pulled away. Instead she had kissed Kerry lightly on the forehead, and whispered to her, "Don't cry now, girl. Don't ever cry. Don't ever let them see what they do."

———•———

Tanny had worked a miracle. "We'll call you Rosa." Daughter of a Spanish sailor. Shipwreck turned streetwalker. Dark eyes, red lips. Two pads of linen hidden in the bodice of her dress thrust her breasts upwards, and the extra material in the back folds of her petticoat pushed up the back of the gown, making it uncomfortably tight.

Tanny had patted her belly. "You've got to suffer for beauty, girl."

The blue dress bought her a different kind of freedom. On the way to see Tanny, she had attracted all kinds of looks: curious glances from some men, suspicious stares from others. Some women had looked angry, or resentful; others had shouted abuse at her, or asked for help. She was an outsider. Now, strutting beside Tanny, hips swinging, she was part of the landscape. Few people gave her a second glance, and those that did so, did so differently. One man whistled at her, another leered, and a third followed behind her for a few paces, whispering propositions, asking how much for this or that, until Tanny spun around, lifted her skirts and kicked at him. The women ignored her, except for a trio who leaned out of a window and spat in unison into the street. They were thin, sallow-skinned, and black-haired, dressed in colorful silks. Tanny spat back and cursed them. "Don't mind them. Bloody ladyboys. Jealous 'cause they've even fewer curves than you."

As they walked, Kerry asked what Tanny had heard about Umar. She was aware he existed, and had heard about his gatherings, but said she knew nothing about him poaching white girls from brothels owned by Owens and the Bull. There were plenty of all-white houses in the city, but none in or around Canvas Town, or not that Tanny had heard about. And, she insisted, she would know.

They arrived at the gathering. There was a small crowd sitting in the small open space, munching on their free pastries. Kerry had stood at the side as Umar spoke, amazed at the way he was able to control the crowd with his voice. He was better than any priest that she had ever heard, not that she went to church.

And suddenly, the address was over. The space was filled with a low chatter, as people discussed what Umar had said. Kerry watched the faces, some still slack and bewitched, others twisted in skepticism and scorn. And a few were wide and open, radiant and transported.

Tanny grabbed her arm. "Did you hear him?"

"I did."

"That part about God not looking at appearances. About him not minding if you sell yourself. Do you think that's true?"

"I don't know. They say Jesus let Mary Magdalene wash his feet, and she was a curtezan."

"She was. And she was blessed." A deep voice, behind her. Kerry spun around, and found herself face-to-face with Umar. His robe was made of a rough linen, but it was as white as sea spray. She could smell the cedar oil in his hair and beard.

"And what is your name?" he asked.

"That's none of your bloody business." Tanny pushed past. The wide-eyed look was gone. Her face was pinched with suspicion, and she drew herself up as tall and straight as she could. "You may be sharp with your tongue, Mister, but you'll have to put your hand in your pocket if you want anything from us."

Umar's teeth flashed in his black beard. "You are Antoinette. I have heard about you."

Tanny scowled. "Who's been spinning dits about me? I'll strip the skin off 'em."

"I believe you would, Antoinette. Which is why I will not name names. Only to say that those of your sisters who spoke of you mentioned only your virtues."

Tanny snorted. "What sisters I have are dead, Mister. One of the pox, and the other of being born. I ain't got no sisters no more."

Umar made a slight gesture towards a trio of women standing in the shadows of a stall at the back of the clearing, watching them. They were dressed in plain gray shifts and scarves covered their heads. "What of these? They are your sisters, are they not?"

Tanny hesitated. She squinted at the women.

"Who are they, Tanny?" Kerry asked.

"I only ken two of 'em. Josie Box and Cass Wade. I know 'em from the theater. But I ain't seen them in half a year. I thought they was either dead or gone up to Boston."

"They are with me now," Umar said. "Doing God's work."

"God likes it the French way, then, does he? Because that's what Cass specializes in."

Umar burst out laughing. "A sharp tongue, but an even sharper mind. I see I was not lied to."

"Oh yes? And what else did they say?"

"That you have a hard shell, but one that shields a kind heart."

"Someone kens how to patter and flatter, it seems." The words were hard, but Tanny's tone had softened.

Umar turned to Kerry. "And you? What is your name?"

"Rosa." The name felt unfamiliar on her tongue. Kerry realized she should have spent as much time practicing her lines as she had rehearsing her walk.

"You are from New York, Rosa?"

"As much as anyone else, in this city." Her stomach felt like a flock of birds taking off.

He nodded. "And what brings you here today?"

"I was told I might hear something of interest."

"You did not come for the food?"

"I can feed myself well enough."

"I imagine so." It was like being eyed by a snake. "And was it of interest? What you heard?"

"I have never heard a churchman say that what we do might be smiled upon by God."

"And why not? Women are bought and sold all the time, and the transactions are blessed by God as marriages. Why should God not bless a transaction when a women sells herself on her own terms?"

"It would be a better world if women did not have to sell themselves at all."

Umar inclined his head. "Perhaps. But that is not the world we live in."

Kerry felt her cheeks burn. "Aye. In this world, men make the blessings, and men make the deals. And they take a cut of the proceeds, whether it's marriage or whoring."

The cold eyes flickered. "And where is your man this evening?"

It was a moment before Kerry realized what Umar was talking about. She tried to think what Tanny might say about Lew. "Sat in his libben, sipping Bristol milk, I expect. Getting fat off the sweat off our backs."

"I didn't take Mister Owens for a sherry man."

"I don't know what the bastard drinks. Nor do I care to." She was surprised by the force in her own voice.

Umar's teeth showed in the black of his beard. "I would like to continue our talk, Rosa."

"Oh, you would?"

Umar's grin widened. "No, I don't mean that. I thought you might join us for dinner."

"Us?"

"These ladies." He gestured towards the group of women behind him. "And some others. Birds of a feather, if you will."

"What about Tanny? I'm not going without her."

Umar's dark eyes flicked up and down, taking in Kerry's blue dress, the brown shawl, and the red, red makeup. "In that case, she is welcome."

———————

Kerry had expected to be led through the lanes to the front of the compound, but Umar took them the opposite way, into the thick of Canvas Town. Tanny walked beside her, clutching her arm tight, whispering away. How handsome Umar was. How mysterious. And what was a rancid old doxy like Josie Box doing with him? She was thirty, if she was a day. Cass she could understand, she being so pretty and all. And why were they dressed like that? Almost like nuns. And Josie and Cass were no nuns, that was for sure.

A sharp right turn, and they were all suddenly crowded together in a large, low-roofed room. Kerry turned around to see one of Umar's bodyguards pulling a wide door closed behind them. His cheeks and forehead were adorned with the symmetrical welts that African tribes used as tattoos. He had a broad, sword-like blade shoved into his belt.

The room had packed earth for a floor, but the unmistakable dung-and-straw smell of a stable still hung in the air. Light came from a lantern on a large, low table, and several others set in sconces along the wooden walls of the room. Heaps of cushions formed impromptu chairs.

There were three other women already there, sitting on the cushions. They were all white and dressed in the gaudy mismatch of clothes that suggested they were in the same profession as Tanny, although they gave no sign of recognizing her. They were all very young. Umar settled himself cross-legged beside them.

"Rosa, Antoinette, allow me to introduce Abby, Gladys, and Prim," he said, and the women nodded cautiously at each other.

Umar clapped his hands, and a door at the other side of the low room swung open. The trio of women in gray shifts entered, and placed jugs and cups and plates loaded with food on the low table. There was a whole leg of lamb, sliced thinly and dressed with a thyme and mint sauce. A jointed chicken, stewed with dates and apricots. A dish of spiced carrots, another of herbed potatoes and a pile of flatbreads. Kerry found her mouth falling open slightly.

Umar spread his arms. "Please, help yourselves."

The women fell on the food, loading the flatbreads with meat, and stuffing their mouths. Tanny plucked a leg of chicken from the bowl, and tore off a piece with her teeth. She squinted at Umar. "Any ale?"

"No ale, Antoinette. My religion forbids it. I hope good water will suffice."

Tanny shrugged. She took a cup from the table and swigged. "Nice and fresh, at least."

After a few moments, Umar nodded to the women in gray. They stood up as one, took their plates from the table, and left the room without a word.

Umar looked at Kerry's empty plate. "You are not hungry, Rosa?"

"Not really." It was a lie. Her stomach was beseeching her to tuck in to the food, but a small voice at the back of her head told her that the display of generosity was dressed-up trickery, and she would do well to be on her guard.

"You think I might be trying to poison you?" He laughed, and took a slice of lamb, rolled it up in a flatbread, and took a large bite. He chewed, watching her. "How long have you been with Lew Owens?"

Kerry swallowed down the tight feeling in her chest. "Since I arrived in the city. A few months ago now."

"And where did you come from?"

"My past is my business."

Umar's teeth flashed. "Of course. Forgive me."

One of the women was staring at Kerry. She wore an off-white sleeved gown that was yellowed around the neckline and under the arms. Her blonde hair was teased into an unruly heap on top of her head, and lipstick was smeared slightly at the corner of her mouth. She looked grotesque, a child in her early teens, dressed like a parody of a lady.

"What house you in?" She had the hard voice of a woman twice her age.

"The Hayloft," Kerry said.

Owens owned six bawdy houses in and around Canvas Town, but there were at least a dozen brothel owners who kicked up a monthly tax to him. Tanny had advised her to tell people she worked directly for Lew, in his oldest house, the Hayloft. It was located in the Holy Ground, outside Canvas Town, and therefore likely to be the least well known.

The blonde woman picked up a chicken wing and twisted the bones out of it, then popped the meat into her mouth. She sucked each of her fingers, one by one, her eyes still locked on Kerry. "I heard the Angel keeps the Loft tied down tight. Likes to use a cat on runaways, they say. Whips 'em herself, and takes pleasure in it, the dirty cow."

Kerry felt Tanny stiffen beside her. She smiled. "I heard the same. But the Angel doesn't run the Hayloft. Slack Annie's our abbess, as I'm sure you know."

The blonde woman grunted and looked away. Umar seemed amused. "You are all with Lew Owens, are you not?"

The three women nodded in unison. The youngest had thin ginger hair and a spray of freckles. She looked about fourteen. "Lew looks after us. He's nice." She had a thin, high voice.

"Is he? He takes half of everything you make, does he not? And then you have to pay for lodging, in a house that he owns, guarded by his men, who will not let you go about of your own accord. How did you slip away tonight?"

She snickered. "Tam Corley was on the door. He fancies one of the girls. We paid her to take care of him for a bit. He won't dare blab to Lew."

"Very swift of you, Abby." Umar's eyes twinkled.

Kerry had a sour taste in her mouth. But the girl was charmed, simpering under Umar's gaze.

"I meant what I said earlier, about God not judging women in your profession, Abby," he went on. "I think it reprehensible that Mister Owens takes advantage of you so." He showed his teeth. "I would like to offer you an alternative arrangement."

The girl gasped, recoiling as though she had been slapped. "Don't talk so! He'd kill us!"

Sharp lass, Kerry thought. Abby and her friends were risking a severe beating just for sneaking out of their house. If her cousin Lew found out they were discussing leaving him for another pimp, he would disfigure them. Or worse.

Umar patted the girl's hand. "Don't worry, Abby. No one will hear anything of this conversation, I promise you."

Abby tittered, tossing her ginger curls, and putting her hand over her mouth. She glanced across the table and Kerry froze. The girl's eyes were like marbles, hard and cynical in the child's face, and Kerry saw she was playing a part. These women weren't here by accident, she realized. They must have known that Umar was recruiting from her cousin's brothels. No doubt one of the "sisters" had gotten word to them that Umar could make them a better offer. This was all part of the negotiation.

Umar looked around the room. "Here is what I propose. If you leave Owens and come with me, I will allow you to keep three-quarters of what you earn. You will have fewer assignations, but they will be more lucrative . . ."

"What's that mean?" the blonde woman broke in. Even in the poor light, Kerry could see there was something moving in the heap of hair piled on her head.

"Fewer men to service, but more money each time, Gladys," Umar explained.

"All the gelt in the welt won't do us no good if we're dead." Gladys scratched at her scalp. "Which we'd be as good as, if we skipped. If we did this, and I'm not saying we would, how would you keep that black bastard clear of us?"

"You would live under my protection. Behind my walls."

"In Jericho?" Kerry asked.

Umar slid his gaze over to her. "In Jericho. Yes."

"Would we have to dress like them sisters of yours?" the third woman asked. She was the oldest of the three. She looked feverish, sweating through her threadbare red dress, her forehead marred by spots that she had tried to cover with a gloss of pork fat and a dusting of powder.

"Not if you don't wish to, Prim," Umar said. "The sisters wear what they wish. Life is simple behind my walls, so they dress simply."

"Like sacks of potatoes," the woman named Prim muttered. She crammed a slice of lamb into her mouth, wiping the juice off her chin.

For a moment, the only sound was a loud chewing noise.

"What if we didn't like it?" Kerry asked. "What if we wanted to leave?"

"You would not be the first. Several have done so. They took the money they made and left with my blessing."

"I've never heard of any such," Tanny said.

"Of course not. They did not stay in the city. Not with the likes of Owens seeking them."

"What if we say no tonight?" Gladys asked.

Umar shrugged. "Then you say no. Smuggle yourselves back into Owens' house. Think on my proposal. No one will know you were here. No one will know what we spoke of."

"These judys know." She tilted her chin.

Umar's eyes flicked to Tanny. "No one would dare tell Mister Owens of this meeting. Would they, Antoinette?"

Tanny scowled. "Not if they wanted to keep their face arranged just so."

"You see, Gladys? Anyone who tells Owens anything will have to admit they were here too. And by their own volition. Owens won't let that stand." He paused to look at each of them in turn, hard eyes in a blank face. "And neither will I."

It was so quiet, Kerry could hear the two guards breathing behind her.

Abby spoke first. "I'll do it."

"Abby!" Gladys snapped.

"More chink for less prink, Glad."

"And Owens after you for the rest of your days."

"Cass Wade don't seem that bothered. Besides, I don't aim to stay in this city for much longer. I want to save some plate and get out. I can't see that happening with Lew Owens running me."

Prim sneered. "Gunna move to Ohio, are you, Abby? Raise goats and chickens?"

"And why not?" Abby sounded defensive.

"Get raped by a horde of bloody savages, more like. Giving it away for free when you could be making good money back here? You're baked."

"Fuck off, Primrose, you shabby madge." But there was no heat in Abby's words, and Kerry had the sense that these three women squabbled like this all the time.

"What about you, Gladys?" Umar asked.

The blonde woman scratched at her scalp again. "More gelt sounds good, I won't deny. But I'm afeared of Lew. And that big bastard, the new one, whats-hisname."

"Jonty," Prim said, picking her teeth with a wishbone.

Gladys shuddered. "Brute."

"You would go back to that?" Umar's voice was smooth. "To being man-handled and misused by Owens' trusties? I promise you there will be none of that with me."

Gladys glanced at Prim. "Cass said as much."

"She's a lying slag," Prim said. "You can't trust her. She's probably taking a cut of whatever we make."

Umar raised his hands. "I won't deny it. She will receive a bonus for every one of you that joins me. As you will, if you persuade any of your sisters likewise."

"How much?" Prim's voice was like a trap, snapping shut.

"Ten dollars."

The three women exchanged looks. Kerry could see them calculating how many others they could convince to join them.

"I don't know," Prim said, finally.

Gladys reached for her hand. "You can't go back on your tod, Prim. He knows we're thick. He'll squeeze you."

Prim's face was pinched. There was fear in her eyes. "Right, then."

"Good." Umar's head swiveled. His eyes glittered, like quartz in a chunk of stone.

Kerry looked at Tanny, the question in her eyes. Tanny gave a single nod.

"Aye," Kerry said. "Count us in."

NINETEEN

Tuesday

It was hard for her to open her eyes. The lids felt as though they had been weighted down. The insides of her mouth tasted like raw cotton soaked in musk. She was lying on her back, on a low bed with a thick mattress. It was warm in the room, and dim. There was a candle in a sconce on the wall. The light around it was soft and hazy, as though she was looking at it through a sheet of gauze. Below it was a bucket with a lid, shoved into the corner of the room. The door opposite her bed was only a few feet away. There was a small stool in the corner on the other side of the door.

A cube. A box. A cell.

Kerry tried to sit up. Her limbs felt both loose and heavy, like links on an iron chain.

The door opened, and the gauzy veil wafted. Umar stood in the doorway. His white robe looked urine-yellow through the veil of smoke. He was carrying something that looked like a large pair of coal tongs. He placed the instrument beside the bed and leered at her.

"Welcome to Jericho, Kerry O'Toole."

———————————————

After they had finished eating the sumptuous meal, Umar had led them back through the winding, undulating lanes. Or perhaps it was a different direction altogether. Kerry couldn't tell. She didn't know the quarter, and with no points of reference, she had no idea which way they were going. She didn't even know where the river was, she realized. The other women were quiet, their heads down as they walked. Even Tanny was silent.

Kerry hadn't eaten. Her senses were sharp, her body vibrating with tension.

as she watched over the heads of the other women as Umar led them down the dark, muddy alleys. She was acutely aware of the man following her, the tattoos on his face, the blade in his belt. She had the feeling that if any of them decided to change their mind and break away, this man would cut them to pieces. So there was no way back. The only way out was ahead.

They came to a wall covered in a sheet of rough cloth. Umar pulled it aside, and led them through a tunnel into an open space. The ground underfoot was smooth, level, and dry. There was a faint smell of herbs. Kerry saw the stars, and felt her spirits lift.

Umar led them across the open, airy courtyard into a low building. They walked along a dark passageway into a large room, furnished with soft chairs. There were hangings on the walls, and several carpets scattered over a wooden floor. A polished dining table was set with an ornate candelabra and a large cutlery box made of pewter. There was a sweet scent in the air.

Umar pointed them towards the chairs. One of the women in gray shifts appeared with a tall, silver pot, and a collection of small glasses.

"Mint tea," Umar said, as the woman poured. Kerry's mouth was almost painfully dry. She waited until Umar had drained his own glass before she sipped the drink. It was strong and sweet, but refreshing.

Umar smiled at her. "You call this place Jericho. I call it Mimo. In my language, it means sanctuary. A safe place. You will be safe here."

His voice was smooth and soft in her ears. Her tongue felt warm and thick in her mouth. There was a light pressure inside her skull, and she giggled at the thought of her brain growing, like a balloon expanding inside her head. Umar was talking, his voice low and easy, like a caress. She lay back in her chair and looked around. The other girls were lying back, too. Tanny was already asleep, her mouth slightly open. She was snoring. Kerry giggled again. And that was all.

She stared at Umar, crouched on the stool beside her bed. Her brain had divided into two. Half of it, or perhaps most of it, was stupefied. But a small part of her was still razor sharp. It told her the incense she had breathed the night before was some kind of drug, and the mint tea was likely doped as well. Umar had drunk the same tea and breathed the same air, so it was clear that he had developed some kind of tolerance, but to the women, who were only used to strong drink, and perhaps not even that, the drug was highly effective.

The clear, insistent voice in her head spoke on. It told her that Umar knew who she was, and had known from the outset, and that she should have realized it the moment he included Tanny in his invitation to supper the night before. Lew had told her that Umar appeared only interested in white women. Which meant that Tanny could be in trouble.

Umar went to the sconce opposite Kerry. It held a candle and a kind of wire box, designed so that a small dish could be set above the candle flame. Umar used a cloth to remove the dish, and tipped its smoldering contents on the floor. He stamped them out, then did the same with the other sconce. He left the door ajar and sat down on the stool.

"Where is Tanny?" She could barely whisper.

Umar grinned. "How wonderfully selfless of you. To think of your partner in subterfuge before yourself. Don't worry. I am taking care of her. She is not what I typically look for when I seek out additions to my stable, but I have learned recently that one or two of my clients like an occasional dip in the dark pool. So she might be of use. Not least as a reminder to you."

She said nothing.

Umar watched her. "I meant what I said last night. Do you remember? I said you are safe here. And you are. Even though you are a spy. Nothing will happen to you. But you must listen carefully to what I tell you now, and you must promise to do what I say. Do you?"

Kerry felt a huge weight on her chest, as though something was pressing her into the thin mattress.

"Your cousin's men have surrounded the place," Umar said. "No doubt they are waiting for some kind of a message or signal from you. No such signal will come, of course, and after a day, he will assume that you are a hostage, which is precisely what I want."

"He won't care."

"You're wrong. His pimp's heart may be mostly turned to stone, but my spies tell me there is one spot, as soft as a silken cushion, that he retains for you. So you can imagine how pleased I was to see you at the gathering last night, dressed in your ridiculous disguise. You make a poor whore, Kerry. You should stick to dressing as a man."

Her eyes were heavy. He grasped the door to the cell and swung it quickly back and forth several times, dragging what smoke there still was in the room into the black corridor outside.

He sat back again. "You are my insurance, Kerry. Owens and Flanagan are preparing to attack me, but you will keep them off balance." He held up a finger. "Now I know that devious mind of yours is already scheming ways to escape or get word to your cousin, but I must warn you, if you make any such attempt, you will suffer for it."

He bent and picked up the instrument that he had placed on the floor. She had thought they were tongs for putting coals on the fire, but up close she saw they were pincers, a huge V of black iron, with two brutal points like the fangs of a snake at each end.

"Do you know what this is?" His tone was light, conversational.

She shook her head.

"It's an ancient tool, used for punishing adulterous women. It looks crude, but it is carefully designed." He reversed the pincers, and pushed the fangs against his chest, above his heart. "These points are placed thus, above and below the offending woman's breast. And then the pincer is closed."

The iron made a scraping sound as the fangs slid together. "The points are not particularly sharp, as you see, but when enough pressure is applied, they penetrate the skin, and cut into the flesh around and behind the breast. Once the pincer is fully closed, the breast can be torn quite easily from the woman's body."

He turned the instrument in the air, as though inspecting it for the first time. "The breast-ripper causes a great deal of pain, of course. That is its purpose. But I have not determined whether women with heavier breasts find its application more painful than those that are less well-endowed."

She said nothing. Her throat seemed to have closed tight.

His eyes glittered. "I can see the rage in your eyes, Kerry."

She was boiling with it. Her mind felt as though it was on fire, screaming at her to hurl herself at him and tear his eyes out. But her body was slack and useless, still sodden with the drug. And then he spoke again, and the fire inside her turned into ice.

"I would not use this on you, of course. You are too valuable to me. But young Antoinette? Now, she has a fine set of heavers, has she not? I imagine she would suffer considerably if I punished her."

He snapped the pincers together, *clack, clack, clack.*

"And I shall punish her, if you do not do exactly as you are told. Do you understand?"

Kerry nodded. She understood perfectly. Umar was evil, a man who trapped women and sold them, and who would not hesitate to tear their flesh from them, to further his ends and gratify himself. She believed every word he said. He was the Devil.

TWENTY

Justy sat shoulder to shoulder with Hardluck on the narrow driver's seat of the carriage. He had surprised the driver by climbing on top of the cab, insisting he needed the air. He had lain awake until long past midnight, worrying. He had gone from the gathering to The Merchant's to meet Chase Beaulieu, but Beaulieu had not come, and Justy had sat in the noisy coffee shop, wondering why Kerry had been talking to Umar, all dressed up like a doxy. His fears had pursued him all the way to his lodgings, like a bad smell, and kept him up until the small hours. Sleep had come, eventually, but the same unremembered dream had come with it, and he had woken with his sense of panic redoubled from the previous day.

Hardluck was still dressed in his white coat and breeches.

"Do you not have any other duds?" Justy asked.

"No, sir. This is all I ever wear. I've no need for other clothes."

"What about when you clean the carriage, or muck out?"

Hardluck frowned. "I generally do so in my drawers, sir."

Justy felt the anger lift in him, like hot water in a pot. "Well, you'll be a free man by the end of the week. And then you'll never have to wear a ridiculous rig like this again."

The driver said nothing.

"You don't seem very enthused by the prospect of freedom, if I may say."

"I'm sorry, sir."

Justy laughed. "I have to say, I fancied I'd get a rather different response."

Hardluck pulled gently on the reins to steer the horses out of the way of a cart that two men were pulling up the street. He was hunched forward now, his back no longer straight, and his face had sagged. His cheeks were wet.

"Hardluck?"

The driver wiped his face with his sleeve. "Forgive me, sir. I don't mean to seem ungrateful. I feared this might happen. I just hoped you might change your mind."

"Change my mind? I would have thought you'd want to be set free."

"To do what, sir?" His eyes were brimming again. "This is my life. It's all I know, this carriage, these animals. Without them, I'm nothing."

"That's nonsense, man! You're a human being, and freed of your chains you can be anything you want to be. You can live where you please; you can work as you please."

"As I please?" The driver's voice wobbled. "I've no skills beyond those of a carriage man, and I doubt Mister Riker will pay me for work that another of his slaves will do for nothing. Especially with things on his estate the way they are."

"Riker? You'd really go back to that family?"

"Where else? I can't stay here. I don't know this city, and I'm not a young man. I don't know how to make a start in a place like this."

They had reached Trinity Church. The traffic was heavier now, with carts coming up from the docks, and carriages carrying people up from the big houses down by the Battery.

"Is Mister Riker's estate having problems, then?" Justy asked.

"Sir?"

"Just now you said he'd be unlikely to employ you, things being what they are."

The muscles in the driver's arm tensed as he tugged on the reins to pull the horses around. "I mean the estate is suffering, sir. Mister Riker concentrated the land on sweet corn five years back, but we've had dry summers and hard winters the last three seasons, and a plague of ear worms that ate any corn that survived."

"What did he used to grow?"

"All sorts. We had big orchards. Apples and peaches, but he cut the trees down. They took too many men to keep up, he said, and corn makes more money. If there is any corn to pick."

"He still seems to live pretty well."

"He sold off some of the land last year. And some of his people, too. There used to be forty of us, altogether. Now there's only ten left."

And Riker had other businesses. His bank, which no doubt would keep him afloat until his fortunes turned around.

They pulled up at the steps of the Hall. Gorton stood there, a strained look on his face.

Justy jumped down. "Everything all right?"

"Riverman reported a body in the water. Up by Rhinelander's Quay."

"Where's Sergeant Vanderool?"

"Already down there. The riverman said he looked like one of the quality, so Old Hays told me to get you over there."

"Get in."

Gorton's face was gray and sagging, and his eyes were sunk deep in dark hollows. He clung tight to a strap as Hardluck turned the carriage around.

"Long night?" Justy asked.

"Long enough, sir," Gorton said.

"What did you learn about our friend Umar?"

"Precious little, sir. I spoke to a few of the folk at the gathering, but there's not much to tell. They go every night to listen to him, and he says much the same thing, but that's all.

"Does he ever ask for money?"

"No, sir."

"Try to convert them?"

"No, sir. All he does is make his speeches, then he talks for a while, and then he disappears."

"Did you follow him?"

"I tried." Gorton looked down. "He slipped away. I tried to tail him, but he was too quick, and I don't know that quarter too well. Sorry."

Justy's thoughts returned to Kerry. She must have taken it upon herself to find out who the girl was. He felt vaguely sick at the thought of her, with her reddened lips and tousled hair. He pushed the feeling away. Perhaps she had done better than Gorton, dressed in her disguise.

"Anything else?" he asked.

"No, sir."

"Well, I don't know how else we can find out who that girl was unless someone inside that compound tells us. And I'm damned if I know how to get inside."

Gorton smiled slightly. "I've been thinking about that. I was thinking I could join his crew."

"You don't think he'll twig what you're up to?"

"Perhaps. But I've been thinking on something he said when we were inside there, the other day. That you were lucky to have me with you."

"So I am. But that doesn't change the fact that you're white and Christian, and a member of the New York City Watch."

"Well, he's not likely to get one of his own kind into the Hall, is he? He might jump at the chance of having a man inside."

"But what would be your incentive?"

Gorton bit his nails and examined them. "I don't suppose it's a secret I like a flutter, sir. No doubt it's in my file."

"That's true. It is."

"Well then. I could tell him I was strapped and needed the chink."

Justy shook his head. "I don't like it. It's dangerous."

"Not so dangerous as some situations I've been in, sir."

Justy looked at Gorton's haggard face, and the dark circles under his eyes. He looked as though he had aged ten years. "I promised you I would only prevail upon you for two or three days. And by the look of you, I've worn you thin enough already."

The carriage pulled to a halt, and Gorton sat upright. "Don't worry, sir. I know I look fagged, but a couple of hours' couch and I'll be right again. I can go up and have a poke around this afternoon. See what I can see. I'll report back tomorrow morning, sir. If that's rum with you."

"Very well. But if you even get a sniff of anything tricky, get yourself out of there."

"Will do, sir."

They both got out, and Justy watched as Gorton walked away from the wharf. Something nagged at him, like a pill on a cotton sheet. The watchman seemed different. Not just tired, but unusually deferent. Gorton had called him "sir," over and over, even though he was one of those old salts who, once out of the service, refused to bow to officers. Justy couldn't remember him calling him "sir" before today. Marshal, occasionally. Or Chief. But not sir. Not once.

"Over here, Marshal."

Sergeant Vanderool was standing on the end of a wooden pier, a gaff in his hand. The wind gusted and blew his thick hair up like a brush. Justy's eyes streamed in the cold air. It was so clear he could pick out people on the New Jersey shore of the river. He imagined he could smell the farmsteads on the hook, the fermenting apples and the cow shit. He thought about Riker's fields, the blighted corn chewed to a black mush by the pests.

"What do we have, Sergeant?"

"Nothing so far. I have a man looking under here." Vanderool hammered the end of his gaff into the boards of the pier.

Justy nodded. The tide would have pulled the corpse into the dense thicket of pilings under the network of wooden boardwalks and piers that made up the North River waterfront. Finding a body down there was a difficult, dirty job. It was almost pitch dark under the piers, and the water was thick with sewage, fish guts, rubbish, and the dead and decomposing bodies of rats, cats, and dogs. The sighting of a human corpse was not unusual. Accidents often happened on the waterfront and drunkards frequently fell in and drowned. And, inevitably, the river was used as a dump by gangsters, on the rare occasion they went too far and killed someone.

"Got him!" a voice floated up through the gaps in the planks, directly beneath him. There was a splashing sound, and then a curse. "There's no room down here, Sergeant. If we try to get him on board, he'll tip us over. We'll put a spike in him and tow him out."

"Go on, then."

Another splash, and then the dory's bright green bow nosed out from under the pier into the river. There were two men aboard. One pushed at the pilings with an oar; the other held tight to a pike pole that was shoved into the water. The boat rocked in the wind.

"Get out of the chop," Vanderool ordered, and the oarsman pulled the boat around the end of the pier. Justy followed along above them as they slid down towards the shallow water of the slipway. How anyone had thought the body was clad in a gentleman's clothes was beyond Justy. It looked like a wet sack, submerged by the pikeman, who was leaning on his pole, making sure the body was securely hooked and would not float away.

Vanderool climbed down into the boat as the pikeman pulled the body close and unhooked it. The corpse floated face down, and Justy saw a band of white collar between a dark coat and a head of wet hair. Perhaps the observer had not been mistaken after all.

"Turn him over," Vanderool ordered, and the pikeman bent over the stern of the dory, bracing his knees on the gunwale as he reached into the water and grasped the corpse by the shoulders. He grunted, flexed his knees, and twisted the body hard, so that one of its arms flew up and slapped on the water as it rolled onto its back. The body was on the wrong side of the boat for Justy to see, but Vanderool lurched back, as though he had been struck. His face was white.

"What is it, Sergeant?" Justy said.

Vanderool clutched at the gunwale of the rowboat and sat down with a bump. "I saw him at the Planning Commission. Only yesterday."

"Who is it?"

The boat turned slowly in the eddy. The dead man was missing a shoe. His breeches could have been dark blue or green or brown, but soaked in seawater, they appeared black. His waistcoat was pink, embroidered and obviously expensive. His hair was long, and it looked lighter now, in the sunlight, plastered across his pale forehead. His eyes were half-open, so that the whites showed. Water seeped out of blue nostrils and purple lips.

The man in the water was Chase Beaulieu.

TWENTY-ONE

The Beaulieu mansion was an ornate pile, faced in white stone, that took up a generous length of Mill Street. Old Morgan Beaulieu, a pirate, smuggler, and fervent anti-monarchist, had built it with the money he made sailing molasses up from the French West Indies, in small, fast ships that could outrun the Royal Navy. The land on Mill Street was sunken and swampy, and had never been particularly sought after, but it plunged in value after New York's Jewish community built their first synagogue there in 1730. Morgan Beaulieu watched the newcomers drain the land and fill it properly, and he knew a bargain when he saw it. He made sure that he built his mansion big enough to look down on his neighbors.

The old pirate's only son, Franklin, was famous on Wall Street for selling every security he owned just before the market collapsed in the Panic of 1792, and buying them all back after. It was good timing, for old man Morgan had squandered most of his wealth before he died, and Franklin had to work hard and ruthlessly to turn what was left into a meaningful investment. The windfall had refurbished the mansion, restocked Mrs. Beaulieu's wardrobe, and sent their only son, Chase, to college.

The mansion was built right up to the pavement in the European style, with no fence or railings to keep away the passers-by. The door was lacquered continental blue and had a large knocker at chest height. Justy took a deep breath and lifted the big brass ring, but just as he was about to let it fall, the door swung open.

He found himself looking down a long corridor that appeared to go all the way through the house. There was bright light at the far end of the passage, and an impression of green, as though a door to the garden had been left open.

Deep in the house, a woman was crying, the chest-racking sobs of the recently bereaved.

He had done his best to examine Chase Beaulieu's sodden corpse on the dockside, but word had traveled fast. A constable had come hurrying down to the water, carrying an order from Jacob Hays. The body was to be delivered immediately to the Beaulieu residence. The Beaulieus were not to be disturbed.

Justy had released the corpse and gone to the Federal Hall. But Hays was nowhere to be found. So Justy had come here. He knew he was disobeying a direct order, but Beaulieu was a close friend of Piers Riker, so, in Justy's eyes, it was unacceptable to leave this stone unturned. He had found no injuries to Chase Beaulieu's head in his cursory examination on the dockside, and there seemed to be no blood on his clothes. The amount of water that poured out of his mouth when Justy pressed on his chest suggested Beaulieu had drowned. But had he fallen in, drunk? Had he been pushed? Or had someone drowned him? Justy had to know. And to know, he had to ask questions of the Beaulieus, and examine their son's body.

"Hullo?" His voice echoed in the hallway, but there was no response. "Mister Beaulieu?"

Silence. The faint sound of crying had stopped.

The hallway led through the house to a small, high-walled garden. It looked a little like a piazza in a small Italian town, with large, dark gray flagstones underfoot and roses climbing the walls. A man sat alone by a fountain in the center of the garden, at a small table set with a jug and a flask of what looked like brandy. He was slumped in his chair, staring into the middle distance, a half-full glass held loose in his hands. He didn't seem to notice Justy.

"Mister Beaulieu."

Franklin Beaulieu was built like his son: stocky and broad in the shoulders. He had the same round face, topped with a sweep of hair, except that the older Beaulieu was now thinning and the blond had turned to steel gray. His plump cheeks and smooth complexion might have made him appear youthful, except that his skin was now pale, and his blue eyes seemed to sag in his face.

Justy felt a stab of guilt. "I'm sorry, sir. I did knock. The door was open."

Beaulieu lifted his hand slightly in acknowledgment. "Caraway must still be upstairs with Clara. Seeing to things, I don't doubt." His voice was faint. He looked into his glass. "So many things to see to."

A bird flew into the garden, twittering loudly. It circled the table twice, and then landed on the rim of the jug. It had a rust-colored breast and bright blue feathers. It looked around, taking in first Justy and then Beaulieu, and then it took off again.

Beaulieu watched it, damp eyes, a faint smile on his face. "*Siala sialis*. Strange to see it on its own. It's ordinarily a very social animal." He sounded dreamy. "Like my boy Chase."

Justy's guts twisted with the full insult of his intrusion. He made a small bow. "I'm truly sorry for your loss, sir. My deepest condolences."

"What's your name?"

"Justice Flanagan."

The name seemed to mean nothing. "Have we met?"

"No."

Beaulieu tossed back his drink. His watery blue eyes took in Justy's clothes, the weathered topcoat, the tailored but worn breeches, the old, comfortable boots. "You're one of the surveying chaps he was working with, I suppose."

"No. We had a friend in common. Elizabeth Cruikshank. I . . ."

"Would you mind . . . ?" Beaulieu interrupted, waving his empty glass in the air.

Justy walked to the table. He could see now that Beaulieu was quite drunk.

"Thank you." Beaulieu watched with fierce concentration as Justy filled his glass. "I shall have Caraway bring you a cup."

"Not for me, thank you."

Beaulieu grunted. "Unusual for one of Chase's friends to refuse a drink."

"As I say. We didn't know each other very well."

The financier squinted blearily. "So what do you surveyors do? Just walk about, measuring things, I suppose."

Justy wasn't sure whether it was the brandy erasing Beaulieu's memory, or simply that he wasn't listening. He wanted to move on quickly, to get down to the nasty business of asking a man if he could examine the body of his son for foul play, but his instinct told him to wait.

"Chase never talked about it," Beaulieu went on. "Said he was sworn not to, or some nonsense. I don't think he enjoyed it, not one bit. Started drinking again. Staying out late. We didn't talk, of course, but a father knows when something's ailing his son. Can't think why Tobias thought he'd be interested in that kind of work."

Justy's pulse jumped. "Tobias Riker?"

"Yes. You know him?"

"I know his son."

"Ah, yes. Piers. A good friend to Chase. Told his father Chase needed a job, and Tobias got him a position. Very generous. But surveying? Requires a knowledge of mathematics, I'd have thought. Not Chase's strong suit, by any means." He peered into his glass.

"Sir?"

A large man in a long frock coat stood in the doorway, a frown on his face.

"Ah, Caraway." Beaulieu waved his glass in the air. "This is Mister . . . um . . ."

The man's frown deepened. "I know who he is, sir. Flanagan."

"You know each other?" Beaulieu's tone suggested that he was shocked that his butler knew anyone outside of his household.

"He's a Marshal, sir." Justy caught the slight burr of a Donegal accent in the butler's voice.

"A Marshal? I thought you said you were a surveyor."

"No, Mister Beaulieu. I'm a friend of Eliza Cruikshank."

The financier looked confused. "Then why are you standing here, prattling on about surveying?"

"And how did you get in?" Caraway approached slowly. He had the lumpy features and scarring around his eyes that spoke of bare-knuckle fights, either for fun or for money.

"You left the door open."

"And you just walked in like you'd been given an invitation?"

"I called out. No one responded."

"Well, we've been busy. As you might imagine." He looked older in the sunlight. Still strong enough to carry a grown man up several flights of stairs, and doubtless still fast enough to take care of himself in a clutch.

Justy turned to face Beaulieu, keeping one eye on the butler, just in case. "I meant no disrespect, Mister Beaulieu. I came to offer my condolences. I should not have come unannounced. I apologize."

Beaulieu sighed. "Did you have questions?"

"Do you know what your son was doing last night?"

"I knew very little about his comings and goings, Marshal. We did not speak, as I have said."

Justy braced himself. "Could your son swim?"

Beaulieu stared. And then he folded forward in his chair, his head lolling.

His glass shattered. The butler bent over his master, and Beaulieu reared back, moaning, his eyes half-shut, like a man overcome with drink. But then his hands went to his face, and his shoulders shook.

Justy turned away. He was already way out of bounds just being here. Push the man too far, and he would complain to Federal Hall, and that would be the end of it. Hays would put him into the street without a word. He would have to find another way. He walked towards the door.

"Wait." Caraway loped towards him. "You're the Bull's lad."

"His nephew. But that's the extent of our relationship."

Caraway nodded. "I heard you were at odds."

"I wouldn't say we cared enough about each other to be so."

The big butler was silent for a moment. Then he seemed to come to a decision. "Mister Chase was out with Mister Piers yesterday."

Justy's scalp prickled. "Do you know where they went?"

"He didn't say. Just told me he was waiting on Mister Piers. When the carriage pulled up, he went straight out." The big man frowned. "That was the last time I saw him. Alive."

Justy gave him a moment. "Is there anything else you can tell me, Mister Caraway?"

The butler blinked. "You asked about Mister Chase being a swimmer . . ."

"Yes?"

"Well, he could swim just fine. His mother's from Nantucket, so he was half brought up on boats. And I've seen him in the water myself, a brace of times. Like a fish, he is. Or was."

TWENTY-TWO

"No!" Hays meant to whisper, but his voice carried clear across the lobby of the Tontine Coffee House. Trading had concluded at five, and apart from a few clusters of gentlemen tying up business or debating where to have supper, the place was almost empty.

"You will not speak to anyone in the Riker family. Absolutely not." He smoothed the lapels of his long red coat.

"Piers Riker was there, Jacob, and at the right time." Justy matched his tone. "He was with Beaulieu, and now Beaulieu is dead. And Beaulieu was the only man who could have told me how Riker got blood on him."

"Who said anything about blood?"

"His driver."

Hays was pale. "You spoke to his driver? One of his slaves? Without his permission?"

Justy looked down at the intricate parquet flooring of the lobby. "Not quite. He's not Riker's driver anymore. He's mine."

"Yours? What the devil are you talking about? Make sense, man!"

Justy sighed. "I played cards with Riker, a few nights ago. He ran out of ready cash and bet his carriage. He lost. It wasn't until the next day I realized the jarvie was part of the package."

Hays was still for a moment. And then a smile spread slowly across his face. "You're a dark horse, aren't you, Flanagan?"

"It was just a few hands of primero."

Hays chortled. "Well, you may have won the trick, but young Riker seems to be ahead of you in the game, wouldn't you say? Turning you into a slaver, by God! A very pretty jig." He glanced across the lobby towards the Club

Room. "Perhaps I misunderstood the boy. He sounds as though he could be every bit as sharp as his papa, if he put his mind to it."

"Except that he may have handed me a witness to a murder that he committed."

"For God's sake, Justice!" Hays seized Justy's arm and pulled him into a corner of the lobby. "Keep your damned voice down. And do not use that word in connection with Piers Riker in this place. Or anywhere else, for that matter."

"You don't think I need to see how Riker responds to Hardluck's statement?"

"Hardluck?"

"The driver."

"Hardluck? What kind of a name is that?" Hays held up his hands. "Never mind. I don't want to know. But the fact is the man is a slave. Is he not?"

"For now."

"And you would challenge Piers Riker, the son of one of the most powerful men in New York, with the word of one of his former bondsmen?"

Justy felt himself flush. "Why not? The man's a human being, with eyes and a brain, like anyone else."

Hays sighed. "Of course, of course. But the fact remains—"

"What are you so afraid of, Jake?"

There were low, padded benches arranged around the outside of the lobby, and Hays sank onto one of these and slumped back against the wall. "What do you think I'm afraid of?"

"Tobias Riker?"

"He's a powerful man, Justice. He leads the committee that controls the purse strings that pay for the Watch and the Constabulary and the Marshals. If he decides to choke us, he can. And then what is there to keep the city from sliding into mayhem?"

"You really think he would do that?"

"If it meant saving his son."

"So you do think Riker might have killed the girl."

Hays snorted. "Of course I do not. I meant save the boy from scandal, not from the gallows. There is absolutely no evidence that Piers Riker killed that girl."

"He was in Canvas Town."

"He and a thousand others."

"What about the blood?"

"What about it? Perhaps he got into a fight. Perhaps he fell into a butcher's shop. Perhaps he had his fortune told by some witch, who cuts the heads off chickens and sprays the blood about. There are a dozen ways to get claret on your clothes in that quarter. And you know it."

Justy placed his hand on the wall and leaned over the High Constable.

"Chase Beaulieu was with him. At that same card game the other night, he made a point of telling a story about how he and Riker went to Canvas Town the previous evening. Then he came and whispered to me that he wanted to meet me. He was pretending to be drunk, but he was afraid. He didn't come to our rendezvous last night, and now he's dead. You don't find any of that a bit suspicious?"

Hays folded his arms. "Very well. How did he die?"

"I don't know. We hardly had him out of the water before you had the lads take him away."

"I had to move quickly, Justice. I couldn't dawdle while Franklin Beaulieu's boy was stretched out there for all to see. The newspapers—"

"Oh yes, the scandal."

Hays ignored the jibe. "I gave you plenty of time to examine him, didn't I?"

"Only for a cursory examination. I wasn't going to strip the corpse down right there on the timbers to get a proper look. Think what the newspapers would have done with that."

"I'd rather not."

Justy took a breath. "I went to the house just now to ask about a proper examination, but—"

"You went to the house?" Hays' face was crimson. "I gave specific orders!"

"I had a few questions. Questions that needed answers."

"Such as what?"

"Such as could Chase Beaulieu swim."

Hays scowled. "And could he?"

"Very well, as it happens."

"Even when he was drunk?"

"There's nothing to say he was drunk, Jake. There wasn't even a whiff of ale on him."

"Nor would there be after a few hours in that water."

"Perhaps, but even so, being soused so doesn't remove a man's ability to swim. What's more, even the briefest dip in the Hudson is enough to sober up the most top-heavy lush, and pretty sharp. So there are still plenty of questions. None of which I can hope to answer if I can't get a look at the body. I need to find who their doctor is. Ask him to let me see if there are any injuries. Or at the very least give me a report."

Hays grunted. "Good luck. You won't see that particular corpse again until it's being lowered into a hole in the ground. And you might not even see that."

"Why not?"

"Really, Justice? Why on earth would the Beaulieus let you within a soft mile of their son? He's a notorious drunkard. People will assume that he got soused in the most disreputable part of town, fell in the river, and drowned. That is scandal enough. And if he was murdered . . ." Hays checked himself.

"If there was evidence of murder, wouldn't they want to know who killed him?"

"Not necessarily. Imagine if they found out that his killer was someone influential. Perhaps even someone they knew personally. Or, even worse, someone they did business with. On whom their very fortunes depended. What then?"

The door to the Club Room swung open, and a short, narrow-shouldered man wearing the red sash of a military officer stepped into the lobby. His coat was dark green with black facings, and there was a single silver epaulette on his left shoulder. He was stooped and white-haired, and his left foot dragged slightly, scraping on the parquet floor as he walked. As he drew closer, Justy saw the officer suffered from terrible wounds. His coat and breeches had been magnificently tailored, but the left side of his body still looked somehow shrunken, and an old burn scar spread out of his collar and over the side of his face, past his left eye. Both of his hands were scarred in the same way, ridged and white where the skin had pinched and gathered, and red and shiny between the fingers and close to the wrists.

His eyes were startlingly blue against the scar tissue. They flicked over Justy briefly, before locking onto Hays. "Are you coming back, Jacob? Fair warning: I'll drink the rest of the bottle if you don't."

Hays stood up. "Forgive me, Cornelius. May I present Justice Flanagan. One of my Marshals. Justice, this is Cornelius Swift."

"Major Swift." Justy shook the man's hand, conscious of the unnatural smoothness of his burned skin. "I see you wear a cavalry coat, sir. Have you ridden here with your company?"

"My company?" The uninjured half of Swift's mouth lifted into a smile. "You've got a sharp one here, Jake. He knows his uniforms."

"Marshal Flanagan has a military background," Hays said.

"Irregular," Justy said.

The blue eyes appraised him. "Yes. You do have the look about you. But you didn't serve in our little tilt with the redcoats. You're too young for that. And you weren't a whiskey smuggler."

Justy smiled and shook his head.

"No. You don't seem the type, Irish or not." The Major leaned forward slightly. "Of course, that's it. Ireland. You got your scars back in the old country, didn't you? In that nasty little set-to with the English in ninety-eight."

"My scars?"

"On your soul, young fellow. Those of us that have them can see them, plain as day."

Justy felt hot. "You are correct, Major. Ireland it was."

"Well, I'm glad you made it out."

Justy nodded. He wondered where Swift had received such brutal scars himself.

"Fort Clinton," the Major said, reading his mind. "Made the mistake of standing with the guns, which attract rather a lot of attention, as you know, and these were surrounded by rather a lot of powder. I was an infantry officer, not an artilleryman, or I might have noticed. When the Hessian grenadiers came at us, the whole lot went up. It got rather hot, as you can see."

"And now you command a company of dragoons."

"I'm better on a horse these days." Swift gave him a lopsided smile and turned to Hays. "Well then, Jacob, what about it? We still have some business to discuss, do we not?"

Hays was about to reply when he was stopped by the sound of a bell tolling. It was far away, but ringing fast and urgent, and quite clear in the lobby of the Tontine. Not the Trinity bell, whose deep tones had struck five more than a half hour ago, but something smaller and lighter. Sounding the alarm.

Hays and Justy were already running for the door. There was no need for either of them to say the word.

Fire!

———◆———

Hardluck had heard the bells and was already pulling up beside the steps of the Tontine.

"Well, God bless your card-sharping skills," Hays said, settling himself on the soft leather of the cab. He fingered one of the velvet curtains and hummed. "Damned fine carriage, Justice. Damned sharp driver, too. Well done."

"He's a slave, Jake."

"Yes, yes. Unacceptable, of course." Hays yelped as they sped around a turn. He grinned. "Still, damned well played."

They made the turn onto the Broad Way, and Hardluck pushed the horses to a canter. It was early evening, and the working day was over for most, but traffic was mercifully light, and the carriage sped up the hill, passing crowds of onlookers who were pushing up the street to see why the alarm was sounding. They passed the first bell, on the watch post at Maiden Lane, and the next at Vesey Street. With the cab window down, Justy could hear the big bell tolling from the tower of the New Gaol. And then he saw it.

Not a fire. A riot. A crowd of men, crammed into the top of Laycock Lane, loud and incoherent with rage and bravado and drink. It looked like Owens' crew against the Bull's; black against white. Justy counted twenty or more farmers' caps, but he could not see his uncle.

"How many?" Hays' face was as red as his coat, and his eyes were wide with excitement.

"Sixty?"

"Stop the cab!" Hays hammered on the roof of the carriage.

Justy put a hand on Hay's chest. "Steady, Jake. Wait for the lads to come."

Hays grinned. "They're already here."

He pushed Justy aside and jumped out of the cab. Behind them, a city carriage had drawn up, and watchmen, in their long coats and leather hats, were jumping off and climbing out of its cab. Gorton and Playfair were there, ordering the men into two ranks. When Playfair saw Hays, a wide grin split his face.

"Look now, lads! Topper's here, so you'd best show your best side."

The men roared their approval, and one of them tossed a billy to Hays. He plucked it out of the air, and swung it. "Right, boys! Time to go a-hunting! Follow the red coat!"

The watchmen cheered and several made trumpeting sounds as Hays made for the crowd. Playfair ordered them into a rough arrowhead behind their

High Constable. "Shoulder to shoulder, lads! Room enough to swing, but not enough to let a man through. If he tries, lay him low, and we'll pick him up later!"

They let out a roar as Hays lifted his club and broke into a charge. Several of the rioters turned at the sound, and tried to fight, but Hays' club swept them aside. The phalanx of watchmen followed his lead, laying out left and right with short swings to shoulders and the sides of heads, accompanied by hard jabs to kidneys and the smalls of backs. The idea was not to bring a man down, but to break the crowd up; to shock the rioters, to stun them, and force them to move away. Once out of the melee, the theory went, the pull of the crowd waned, and most rioters give up the fight. Not all: a handful tried to push back into the fray and were hammered for it. And those who tried to attack the watchmen were put down hard.

Gorton and Playfair made a good team. Gorton took up the rear, walking backwards, using short swings and jabs of his club to keep anyone from attacking their flanks. Playfair moved in the center of the phalanx, directing his men and calling out targets. If a gap in the ranks appeared, he moved to fill it, hammering his club into the space. He was nimble and brutal, stepping right to drive his elbow into a man's sternum, then skipping left to rake his club down the side of another's head, almost tearing his ear off. The rioters peeled away, one by one, clutching bellies, noses, ears, and arms, as Hays led his men into the heart of the melee.

Justy watched for fire. The last time a gang of hackums had spoiled for a fight here, they had brought torches, and Justy knew that fire must have been part of the plan. But he could see no flames in the crowd now. It was all hand-to-hand fighting, which the Bull's men, younger, harder, and better armed, were certain to win.

And then he understood.

"Hardluck! With me!"

He jumped down from the cab and sprinted away from the melee, along the Row. Several lanes led south, parallel with George Street, but Justy ignored them, knowing they led only to the backs of the grand houses that faced the Park. The next street was Frankfort Street, and Justy made the turn and hurled himself down the hill. Behind him, the thin soles of Hardluck's fancy shoes skittered on the graveled surface of the sidewalk, but Justy didn't look back. He passed one alley, then another, and when he reckoned he was level with the back of the Buttered Bun, he stopped.

"It's a diversion," he said, as Hardluck skidded to a halt beside him. "They mean to set fire to the Lane."

"Yes. But not this end."

"Of course!" Justy set off again, cursing himself, and blessing Hardluck at the same time. Together, they hurtled down the shallow hill. People jumped off the sidewalk to get out of the way, and Justy had to leap into the air to avoid tripping on the arms of a cart that someone had left half in and half out of a doorway. They plunged across William Street and ran to Rose Street. A man stood at the corner, selling fruit from a tiny stall. Justy stopped in front of him, breathing hard. "Have you seen any gatherings of people?"

The man blinked. "Gatherings, sir?"

"Groups of men. More than two or three."

"There was a work gang came by a few moments ago. Looked like slaves. A bloody shame, that. I—"

"Which way did they go?"

The man jerked his head in the direction of George Street. Justy slapped him on the shoulder and ran on. Rose Street was little more than a narrow lane, flanked by old, steep-roofed Dutch houses that had somehow survived the Great Fire. They seemed to lean over the passageway, blocking the light, and as Justy passed one of the alleyways that led down the backs of the houses, he smelled the distinctive, oily smell of a whale torch.

"Fire!" he yelled. "Fire!"

The alley was a crooked passage that jinked left around the back of one house, then right around another, and then left again into a wide, sloping lane. It doubled as an open sewer for the businesses along Laycock Lane on one side, and the Frankfort Street houses on the other. Justy knew this because he had grown up with the Bull, and had visited the area many times. But the men he was chasing did not know.

There were six of them. The passageway's twists and turns had disoriented them, and they were unsure of exactly where they were. The alley looked like any other, and there were no signs to tell them what was a house and what was a tavern or a brothel or an oyster cellar. One of the gang, a tall, bearded man, had been carrying a sack loaded with torches, and he had put his burden down and begun to distribute the brands. But only two were lit, and as Justy charged towards them, the men froze.

Justy was screaming. Not words, for there were no words in his head. It was a wild, keening cry, the same that had come out of him what seemed like a hundred years ago, charging with two hundred others across a rutted field in County Kildare, straight at an unwavering line of silver and red. Scarlet coats and steel bayonets, glittering in a pale light. An Irish morning, damp and heavy with the smell of wet grass and cannon smoke from the last barrage. His breath like a ragged knife in his throat, his heart like a greyhound, alive inside him.

He had not thought of death or injury then, and he did not now, even though two of the men, big, muscled, dark-skinned lads, had blades in their hands. The bearded man with the torches was shouting, handing the burning brands to two of his men, and a part of Justy's brain told him he had seen the man before, but no sooner had the thought flashed through his mind than he was on them.

The first of the two knifemen grinned. He saw a tall, well-dressed white man sprinting at him, screaming like a moon-touched fool. Easy meat for his blade. It was a bone-handled carving knife, stolen from a magistrate's house in Albany a few weeks before. The man had sharpened it until it was like a razor, and he held it casually by his side in his left hand, ready to pull it across Justy's face and open his cheek to the bone.

He did not see Justy's own knife. It was a special blade, a rejected prototype of a folding bayonet made for the King's Army that Justy had found in a cutler's shop in the English town of Sheffield, more than five years before. It was special, not because of the carved walnut shaft, or the six-inch blade, but because of the spring in the mechanism, and the catch in the handle.

Justy had no memory of taking his knife out of his boot. Perhaps it was when he smelled the smoke, or perhaps when he first saw the men in the alley, but it was there in his fist, the wooden haft warm and familiar in the palm of his hand, the metal catch a cool nub under his thumb. He squeezed, and the vicious sliver of steel appeared like magic, and the knifeman took a sharp step back, his eyes wide, his own blade slicing upwards for the parry.

Too late. Justy flicked his blade downwards, and the knifeman yelped, dropping his weapon as Justy's edge cut deep into his wrist. Without breaking stride, Justy barged on, throwing an elbow up into the man's face, barely registering the soft crunch of his nose breaking like an eggshell under the blow. He glimpsed Hardluck on his right, taking on the bearded ringleader and the second knifeman, but he kept moving. Hardluck would have to handle them as best he could. It was the lit torches that Justy wanted.

He screamed again, and one of the torchmen dropped his brand and ran.

The bearded man was walking backwards, his eyes on Justy's blade, and when Justy lunged at him, the man threw the flaming torch up into the air and took off after his fellow.

Justy let him go. He stopped, and watched the torch curve upward in a wide, high arc, turning over and over, sparks flying, towards the building on Justy's left. For a moment it seemed the momentum of the throw had put out the flames. And then the stave landed on the roof.

The house had been built more than a hundred years ago, in the early English style. Its walls were thick slabs of straw and plaster, sandwiched between heavy wooden beams. Its roof was made of thatched, dried reeds. Justy watched the point where he thought the torch had landed. He held his breath. For a moment there was nothing but the blue sky above the pale thatch. And then, the faintest wisp of smoke.

"Fire!" He ran for the back door of the building, dipping his shoulder, ready to batter his way through. But instead of wood, his shoulder hit stone, and it was a split second before he realized that someone had tripped him. He rolled hard to his right, knowing that the next blow would be aimed at his head, and he felt a searing pain in his ear as a stave hammered into the muddy ground where his face had been. He glimpsed the bearded man above him, his eyes wild and bloodshot, his mouth like a red hole in his beard, and then he rolled over again, fast, into the gutter that ran down the center of the alley, and he scrambled to his feet.

There was mud in his mouth and his eyes. The left side of his body was soaked. He spat and wiped the filth off his face. The bearded man was growling like a wolf, winding up for another swing, his eyes on the knife in Justy's right hand. He did not see or hear Hardluck, who walked up quickly behind him and hammered his fist into the nape of the man's neck.

The man's eyes rolled. He dropped into the gutter like a felled steer. Hardluck flexed his fingers and grinned. Behind him, the two knifemen lay propped against the wall. The one Justy had hit had a bloody mask for a face. He had tried to stop the bleeding in his wrist with a strip of his shirt, but had lost consciousness. The other simply looked as though he had fallen asleep.

Justy nodded. His heart was pounding, and he felt a throbbing in the side of his head. He reached up gingerly, and felt skin where there should not have been any, and then the feeling of someone driving a nail into his ear.

Someone above them screamed, and without a word, Hardluck threw himself at the back door of the house. He crashed through the flimsy wood, and disappeared. Justy ran after him, folding his blade and shoving it into the top of his boot.

He found himself in a windowless hallway that was already thick with smoke. Hardluck was gone, and Justy dropped to his knees, grubbing along the packed earth floor until he came to a stairwell. He crept upwards, listening for shouts, but he heard nothing, and before he had reached the landing, he was turned back by the smoke.

Someone ran past him, down the stairs, and he turned back, his eyes streaming and his throat burning. He choked, then vomited, and let himself go, rolling down the stairs until he was sprawling on the floor of the hallway again. His head reeled. He had no idea which way he had come. The smoke was like a filthy blanket, warping itself around him, scorching its way down his throat. He fumbled in his sleeve for a handkerchief and stuffed it into his mouth. His eyes were streaming. He crawled along the floor, feeling his way. He saw a dim light ahead, and forced his way onwards, the wadded handkerchief in his mouth like a gag, his arms and legs like lead.

And then the light went out.

TWENTY-THREE

Someone had torn his chest open and thrown a shovelful of hot coals into the cavity. It was the only explanation. His throat was on fire. His mouth was full of ash. His tongue was a useless chunk of charred meat. He could not stop coughing, and every spasm felt as though it tore another strip of flesh out of his gullet, and made the coals in his chest burn brighter.

Justy tried to open his eyes, but they were stitched closed by a thousand burning needles. Something slapped him in the face, and he felt cold water soaking his hair and his clothes, and pouring down his cheeks. Like a blessing.

He swallowed his cough, tilted his head back, and let the water soak into his eye sockets. He rubbed them gently, and blinked his eyes open. Two faces looked down at him. One square and hard, the other round and soft. It was a moment before he recognized them. Ignatius Flanagan, the Bull. Jacob Hays, the High Constable.

"Justice prevails," Hays said. A faint smile twisted his lips. A bucket dangled from his hand.

"Hardluck?" Justy choked. It was like dragging a tangle of fishhooks out of his gullet.

The Bull jerked his head. "He dragged you out by the scruff. Lucky you were wearing that topcoat or you'd be bacon by now."

Justy propped himself up on his elbows. The jarvie was crouched on the pavement on the other side of the street. His tie was gone, and his suit was scorched and torn, turned mostly black with soot and smoke.

The Bull smirked. "I reckon you owe him a bonus, Nephew. And a new suit of clothes."

There was a tremendous crash as the front of a building collapsed into the street in a shower of sparks and smoke. And then a wild hissing as a line of men and women doused the debris, sending up clouds of dirty steam. They hurried back to the hand pump on the street corner to refill their buckets, and several of Hays' watchmen stepped quickly across to what was left of the house. They used long, hooked poles to hack and pull at the smoldering timbers and thatch. In the darkness, lit by torches and the light from the other taverns and oyster houses, the hole in the row of buildings looked like a missing tooth in a beggar's grin.

"If there's anyone owing, Mister Flanagan, I'd say it was you," Hays said. "Imagine if that place had gone up, as they planned it to. The whole street would be ablaze. Your street."

"My street, Marshal. But your city."

Hays acknowledged the point with a stiff nod. "I am already in your nephew's debt."

He held the bucket out to Justy. "Drink. But small sips only. You know the drill."

Justy sat up and scooped out the water with his hand. It was an effort not to gulp. A small crowd had gathered around them, to see how much damage had been done, but now that the fire was out, they began to drift away. A handful of the Bull's men stood in a loose clutch behind their leader, some with bloodied faces, all carrying staves, their eyes watching out for trouble.

"Did everyone get out?" Justy's throat closed around the words.

"I wish I could say so." The Bull's face was grim. "There were three girls in the top room. No one's seen them. If they didn't burn or choke, they're buried under that lot now."

Justy stared at the heap of wet, smoldering ash that spilled across the narrow street. He remembered the terror he had felt as the smoke burned its way into his mouth, his throat, his lungs. Better than burning? He couldn't say. He turned away.

"You saved many more, Justice," Hays said. "If you hadn't tackled those men, hundreds might have died."

"How did you know they'd be back there, anyhow?" his uncle asked.

Justy rubbed his throat. "I don't know. It just felt like a diversion. And given they kicked off in Tickler's Alley, I figured the fire would be set in the opposite place. Well, Hardluck figured."

"I should have seen it," Hays said. "My blood was up, I suppose."

"Aye, well. Mine too," the Bull said. He nodded to Hardluck, who was still standing a few feet away in his blackened clothes. "Good thing for all of us your man has his head screwed on."

Hays watched his men tear down the last of the burned building. One of them wrenched at a stubborn bundle of thatch, jerking it loose so that it flew across the road and landed at Hays' feet. He prodded it with his toe. "Old reeds. The thatch went up like a candle, did you see? Not many buildings like that on this street, which suggests this took some planning."

A man pushed through the crowd. Cooper Corrigan's wide face was pale, his Adam's apple jumping in his throat.

The Bull stepped in front of him, put a meaty hand on his chest and shoved him back. "What are you doing here? You're supposed to be minding Dover Street."

Corrigan pulled his hat off. His hair stood up, wet and slick. "I put Daisy in charge, gaffer."

"Look me in the eye, you bastard!" The Bull's voice was like a whip. "If I'd wanted that lump Daisy in charge, I'd have told him myself. It's your job to look after the libben when I'm not there. So why the dumb glutton are you here instead?"

The big Irishman gaped. "Liam . . ."

"Stop stammering like that's a pudding on your shoulders and not your head. Liam who?"

"My boy, gaffer. I gave him a punishment for stepping out without my say. I sent him here to clean the jakes."

He was still staring at the smoking ruin of the building. The Bull followed his gaze. "Well, you won't need to worry. The jakes is out the back. The fire didn't touch 'em."

Corrigan's face crumpled. "I told him he had to work in the house an' all. Empty the girls' slop buckets an' that."

The Bull swore.

"How old was the lad?" They turned at the sound of Hardluck's voice.

Corrigan turned on him. "Mind your own, snowball. If it hadn't been for one of your lot sniffing at him, I wouldn't have had to trounce him."

"I carried a lad out," Hardluck said. "A tall streak, all arms and legs. Thirteen or fourteen years, maybe. I laid him down by the pump there."

"Was he alive?" the Bull asked.

"He was senseless, but he was breathing. His legs and arms were burned, I think. I laid him down and washed his face off."

The frantic filling of buckets had stopped, but a watchman still stood by the pump. Hays walked over and spoke with him for a moment, and then returned. "The lad was taken up to the Almshouse with the rest of them. He was awake and breathing. Likely burned, but alive."

"Oh, thank Christ!" Corrigan's voice wobbled. He put his hands over his face.

The Bull cuffed them down. "It's not Christ you've to thank. It's that man there."

Corrigan scowled. He glanced at Hardluck. "Thankee for the life of my son," he said.

Hardluck said nothing.

"A pretty trick for a snowball, to walk into the fire and come out whole." The Bull chuckled. "Seeing as you left your post and this man saved your boy, Cooper, I think it should be you buys him a new set of clothes. I'll take it out of your next wage. Fair enough?"

Corrigan's face turned purple. He opened his mouth and snapped it shut. He nodded.

"It's about time you got a grip on your boy," the Bull said. "What was it this time?"

"I caught him carrying on with some guinea girl. Right where my missus keeps her stall, if you can believe it."

"Not one of Lew Owens' motts, I hope. I don't want that bastard getting any more custom."

Corrigan shook his head. "She didn't look like a doxy. I only got a glimpse before she ran off, but she was a wee slip of a thing, dressed fancy, with her hair tied up in ribbons and little red shoes on her feet."

TWENTY-FOUR

Wednesday

It was impossible to sleep. Every time Justy swallowed, he felt as though some-one was pouring boiling pitch down his gullet. Every time he closed his eyes, he saw the girl, her abdomen split open, the whites of her eyes. Eventually he gave up, dressed in his spare clothes, and walked through the dark streets to the Federal Hall.

He had plenty of paperwork to do after the events of the previous day. A report to file on Chase Beaulieu; a second on his interview of Beaulieu's father; a third on the riot and fire.

And a fourth on Liam Corrigan, who was barely alive, according to the nuns. Justy and Hays had rushed to the Almshouse the moment Cooper Cor-rigan mentioned the girl with the red shoes, but the duty sister had turned them away, and not even Hays' bluster could gain them entrance.

Gorton had processed all the men arrested in the riot, and written a de-tailed report. No one had been killed in the fighting, but nine men were sent to the Almshouse with serious injuries. Gorton had identified all the white men involved as members of the Bull's crew except one, a man named Shard who had received a blow to the head in the melee, and had complained loudly about his treatment before passing out in a faint. He was carried up to the Almshouse and left in the care of the sisters. "Well-drest. Well shod. Well school'd," Gorton had noted in his careful script. The Negroes, he reported, all said they had been plied with drink and handed weapons, but none could say for certain who had led them down to George Street and encouraged them to riot. Attached to the report was another note from Gorton, saying he needed to rest after the night's events, and would report to Justy in the evening, to see if he wanted to continue working on his investigation.

"A waste of five dollars," Justy muttered. As the Wall Street traffic built up below his window, he sat and thought about Jake Hays' refusal to let Justy interview Piers Riker. Why was he so opposed? Tobias Riker was an influential man, it was true, but Justy and Hays had investigated powerful men in the past. Riker was on the Common Council, but he did not have complete control of the purse strings governing Hays' budget. Nor did he have a casting vote in the decision to expand the Watch and create a police force for the city. Was there something else? He turned the thought over and over in his head, but it was like a puzzle box, and he had no idea how to open it up.

When the Trinity bell sounded seven, he walked down the hallway to Hays' office. The High Constable was already there.

"How's the hero of the day?"

"A little scorched." Justy placed his report on the desk.

Hays flicked through it. "Lew Owens up to his tricks, I presume."

"I don't think so. I think something else is going on. I think there's a connection to a man named Umar, who's been trying to stir things up between the gangs."

"Umar?"

"He's the top man in the Mohammedan community I told you about. That compound his people have built up by the meadows is quite a place. He calls it Mimo. The word means sanctuary, and the place is a damned fortress."

"You've been inside?"

"He invited me in. I was asking about the girl, to see if she was one of his people."

"And?"

"He said he didn't know the girl."

"And the compound?"

"Empty. Except for a few women working on the shawls they make."

Hays stood up suddenly, his chair grating on the floor. He walked to the window. "And you think this man Umar is trying to stir things up between Lew Owens and your uncle. Why would he do that?"

"I have no idea. That's what I want to find out. Which is why I want your permission to take a section of men up to the compound. Have a proper look around."

Hays turned to face him. "No."

"No?"

"No. You will not confront this Umar. You will not go near that compound."

Justy laughed. "Is he on the police council, too? I can understand you not wanting me to brace Riker, but this hackum? He nearly set the city ablaze last night. What's his hold on you?"

Hays' face was crimson. "His hold on me? How dare you!"

"How dare I? How dare you! I'm doing my best to solve a murder and rein in a man who's trying to breach the peace, and you won't even let me get started. Don't speak to Riker, don't speak to Umar. Who can I speak to? God? Neptune?" Justy leaned over Hays' desk, his fists pushing the papers aside. "There's been something rank about this from the start, Jake. From the moment that girl got killed. The line you fed me about not knowing anything about these Mussulmen? It's bawbels. You know this city better than any man, and I'm damn sure you know who Umar is. No doubt you know what he's up to, as well. And the way you're carrying on, I half-believe you're part of it."

Hays was very still. The color had drained from his cheeks. He stood with his hands clasped behind his back, his eyes blank, but unwavering.

Justy felt the heat come out of his own face. He pushed himself upright. "Did you really expect me to do nothing, Jake? You know I'm not the sort to shy away when some cove barks at me. When something doesn't smell right, I don't scowre off, I put my nose to the ground. That's what makes me good at what I do. That's why you've kept me here."

Hays said nothing.

"Well, Jake." Justy spread his arms. "Say the word. Tell me I'm finished, and I'll walk out of here. But I won't let this go. Warrant or no warrant, I'll go on poking at this rat's nest until something breaks. Go ahead."

They stared at each other, letting the silence fill in the space between them, until Justy nodded, turned on his heel, and walked out of the door.

TWENTY-FIVE

He walked up to the Almshouse. It was still early, but he hoped the nuns would have fed their charges by now, and that Liam Corrigan would have a full belly. It should make him more willing to talk.

He took the backstreets, staying off the main roads that were a crush of people, carts, and carriages hurrying to work at that time of day. It wasn't until he had turned into one of the wealthier residential streets that he registered the sound of hooves behind him. When he turned, he saw a carriage, driven by a slim black man with a wide hat and a narrow face. The carriage stopped and a giant climbed out of the cab. He was shaven-headed and dressed like a sailor, in a short coat and long trousers made of dark brown wool. The coat was buttoned to his neck, and because he was almost as dark-skinned as the color of the clothes he wore, he looked like a moving shadow, a man-shaped hole in the light of the day.

He held the door open and jerked his massive head.

Lew Owens sat inside. He wore black breeches and a black waistcoat, unbuttoned over a white shirt that was open at the neck and rolled to the elbows. He could have been a waiter taking his break, except that the waistcoat was made of velvet, the breeches of finest whipcord, and the shirt of pristine linen. His oiled, shaven head gleamed like a cannonball on a hot day.

He gestured to Justy. "Come on up, Marshal."

"And why would I do that?"

"Because I've got something that you need to hear."

"Spill it then, Owens. For I'm not getting in that cab."

Owens plucked at a speck of dust on his trousers. "It's about Kerry."

"What about her?"

He grimaced. "I fear I may have put her in bad loaf, Justy."

Justy felt panic squirm in him. And then his dream came to him. The girl on her side in the alley, her back to him. His hand on her shoulder, rolling her gently on to her back. Her face. Kerry's face.

"What did you do?"

"I sent her into Jericho."

"Jericho?"

"The Mohammedan place."

"What do you mean, you sent her in?"

Owens said nothing. Justy climbed inside. The carriage rocked as the big bodyguard climbed up beside the driver, and then they were moving.

Justy sat for a moment, fighting to get his feelings under control as his dream played, over and over: Kerry cold. Stabbed. Slashed. Dead.

"Tell me," he said.

Owens folded his arms. "I asked her to go inside. See what that bastard Absalom's up to."

"Absalom?"

"Umar Salam. Absalom's his slave name. Or it's the name he arrived here with. Anyway, he's up to something, and I want to know what." He looked at his hands. "So I set her up with one of my girls, to see if she could find out anything."

"So it was your idea to tog her up like a whore."

Owens winced. "She'd have climbed the walls on her own, if I hadn't had the idea. It was that girl she found. She was blazing about it. Not just that some-one had milled the lass, but that no one would claim her. She reckoned the titter had a bellyful, which made it worse."

Justy felt a cold, clear urge to stab Owens in the face, to tear him open. "When did you last see her?"

"Two days ago. At breakfast. I sent her up to the fort, to see a girl named Tanny."

"Short, light skin, red dress?"

Owens frowned. "You know her?"

"I saw the both of them, at a gathering on Monday night."

"Aye, well. No one's seen either of them since. Tanny's not been back to the fort, and Kerry's not been back to her libben. I figured she got inside, like we planned. But I've had neither word nor no sign from her."

"What sign?"

Owens made a face. "She was to signal she was safe by chalking the wheel of a cart or a carriage. I've got a crew up there, watching. But there's been rotans driving in and out all the time, and not a mark on any of them."

"That doesn't mean anything. She just might not have got close enough."

"Maybe. Maybe not."

Justy pressed himself back against the cushions of the cab. His nostrils were full of the cloying smell of coconut oil. He felt sick. His mind unspooled, like a reel of fishing line with a whale on the hook. Too fast to stop. Too fast to think.

"Why are you so concerned about Umar?"

"He's up to something. He's trying to set me and your uncle at odds. Poaching his doxies and passing word it's me that's been doing it. Sending blackfellas to start fights in his gin shops and bowsing kens. That tilt in Laycock Lane? That was his crew, not mine. But the Bull doesn't believe me."

"I believe you."

Surprise, for an instant. "You do?"

"I saw a man at the riot last night. He was with Umar on Monday, too. He looked like a ringleader. But why set you two against each other?"

Owens shrugged. "I don't know. Could be he wants us to kill each other, so he can step in and take over. Or maybe he just wants us weak, for when he's ready to fight and carve out a piece for himself. Either way, he's getting ready for something behind them walls of his."

"Jericho."

"Aye. But it'll take more than a few trumpets to get in there."

Justy nodded. He felt calm now. The dread was inside him, like a worm working its way into his guts. But he could ignore it while he decided what to do.

He said, "What do you have in mind?"

"I'll go to your uncle. If we band together, we can take the bastard. He won't expect that."

"What makes you think the Bull will help?"

"He's close to Kerry, isn't he?"

"Not really. And even if he was, why would he believe she's in danger? You don't know for sure yourself."

Owens shook his head. "You're a cold one."

"I'm calling it how he'll see it. Apart from anything else, the Bull won't believe you care enough about Kerry to get into a fight for her. Truth is, I can hardly believe it myself."

Owens' eyes were steady. "She's the only blood relative I have left."

"One you tried to put on the street when she was barely a titter."

"That was a long time ago. Before we got close. Before Daniel."

Daniel. Justy remembered the last time he had seen the boy, laughing in his mother's arms, the spring before the fever had struck, before they had hurried him out of the city. There had been no funeral service that he knew of, and he had no idea where the child was buried. Kerry had refused to talk to him about it. And then they had drifted apart.

"Again, I believe you. But the rest of New York thinks that Lew Owens doesn't give a dog's cock for anyone but himself. That's what the Bull thinks. It's what he knows. So he won't help you. He'll think you're trying to lure him into a scrap with Umar. To bleed him. Or worse."

"So what do we do?"

Justy looked into the street. People hurrying in the thin sunlight, to work or home or lunch or church. While Kerry was locked up, perhaps bloodied, or broken, or dead. He felt like ice.

"An eye for an eye, Owens."

"Meaning?"

"Meaning if you've killed her, then I'll kill you."

"She's not dead, boyo." Owens' voice was quiet. "If she was, I would know. I would feel it. And so would you."

Traffic was heavy and the carriage was moving slowly. They were in the new build, to the north of the city, and Justy stared out of the window at the half-made houses as they inched along. The view opened up at a junction in the road, and he was suddenly looking down a sweep of freshly laid cobbles that ended abruptly at the edge of the ramshackle chaos of Canvas Town. In the sunshine, the slum looked like a colorful regatta of small boats, jumbled up in a crook of the river. But then the wind gusted, carrying the stink of the cesspits and middens up the hill; the sun disappeared and Justy saw the place for what it was: a tip of broken masts, torn sails, ragged sheets and blankets, ingeniously piled up and stitched together, the most concentrated mass of people in New York, a rookery to rival London's Cheapside.

And to the north, close by the river, were the dun-colored walls of the Mohammedan village. There were people in the marshland around Hudson's

Kill, small figures stooped between the grasses. Justy marveled at how Umar had hidden his Jericho in plain sight. The compound was invisible to the casual observer, screened by rickety buildings and crooked scaffolding, so that it looked like an extension of the sprawl. But now, knowing what to look for, Justy saw the full spread of the place. He walked around the interior walls in his mind, trying to recall the tour that Umar had given him and Gorton. But it was hard to match what he had seen then with what he was looking at now. It was like trying to fit a jigsaw piece into the wrong space. Perhaps he simply couldn't remember which way they had gone in.

"He's a fly cove, isn't he?" Owens read his thoughts. "He's walled up tight in there, like a rat in its nest. But there's a way in, boy. There always is."

❖

The carriage lumbered around a turn and down the hill, rocking on its axles as they moved off the cobbled road of the New Town and on to the muddy lanes of the slum. They pulled to a halt by an alley, and Owens led him through the back door of a shack and into a small, dim coffee shop. Four men sat at a small table under a window, playing cards, but they all stood up when they saw Owens. He gestured, and all but one hustled away, through a curtain made of strings of beads, and into a back room.

The window looked out onto the front gate of the compound. A hugely fat black man stood there, dressed in a stained gray smock and a battered straw hat. He filled the entryway like a prize bull, chewing slowly and spitting an occasional stream of tobacco juice into a puddle.

Owens turned to the remaining card player. He was a gaunt-looking man, with knobby wrists and elbows that had been polished to a high shine, like bits of weathered walnut.

"Have you seen anything?" Owens asked.

The man jerked his chin at the gateway. "Just yon bacon-fed gundiguts stood there. He hasn't moved since long before noon. Not even to piss."

"No traffic?"

"A carriage went in a while back. Nothing since."

Justy looked at the sentry. He was like a wall, his jaw moving slowly, his eyes invisible under the wide brim of his hat. He was the only way in. There were other ways, of course, hidden in the chaos of shacks and lean-tos abutting the walls, but Justy had no idea of where they were, and no time to find them. He had to get past the guard.

His fingers twitched. There was an easy way. He could stroll up to the sentry, ask an innocent question, and then attack, hard and fast. He imagined the knife in his hand, the blade like a lash across the man's throat, the spray of blood. He would be covered in gore, but he would be inside in a second, and that was what mattered.

"Don't," Owens said.

"Don't what?"

"Don't stick a blade in some poor cove that's done nothing more than stand in a doorway minding his own. I believe they'd call that murder up by Federal Hall."

"Ware," the card player said.

The sentry stepped back against the wall beside the gate. A pair of chestnut horses appeared, and then a four-seater sprung drag, with a low-slung cab painted a glossy midnight blue.

Justy felt as though all the blood in his body had been sucked into his feet. "Hardluck!"

The jarvie ignored him. He sat slouched in his seat on the top of the cab, wrapped in a dark cloak, his face shadowed by a hood. He flicked his whip hard against the backs of the horses. They snorted and jolted into a canter, hauling the cab hard along the rutted street.

Justy stared at the carriage as it rattled past. The curtains on the windows were drawn tight. He watched the carriage turn, wanting to convince himself that his eyes had tricked him, but there was no mistaking the two red pennants streaming from the whips on the back of the rig.

He shook himself awake, leapt into the street and broke into a run. His boots skidded in the mud as he made the slight turn in the road, but he stayed on his feet, and saw the carriage ahead of him, the driver's whip rising and falling. He ran down the shallow hill, gaining on the cab as it slowed to make another turn. And there was a sudden tug at his foot as the sole of his boot came loose, and he tripped and went hurtling forwards, his shoulder slamming into the dirt.

There was a ripping sound as the seam of his coat split down the back, and then he was rolling, over and over, pain shooting up his right arm and down his right leg. He stopped on his back. His right shoulder was numb, and his hand was tingling. He lifted his arm, and saw a long tear in the sleeve of his coat, and blood on his fingers. There was a grating feeling in his knee. The sole of his right boot was hanging by a few threads.

"Come on, then." The card player loomed over him, a slight smile on his face. He held out a hand like a shovel. It was warm and dry and as hard as iron. He pulled Justy to his feet.

Justy wiggled the fingers of his right hand, and winced as pain rippled up his forearm. "Did you see which way it went?"

The man shrugged. "It turned left, so up to the Broad Way then down to the town, I shouldn't wonder."

"Where's Owens?"

The man shrugged again.

Justy felt the cold sweat of shame. He had been a damned fool. Piers Riker had wanted to find out what he knew, so he had set a trap. And Justy had blundered right into it. Riker had baited Justy into a card game, wagered his carriage, then lost it on purpose. But he never had any intention of giving up the vehicle, or its driver, Justy saw that now. Hardluck was his spy, reporting back to his master, who had now reclaimed his carriage. And what recourse did Justy have? Was he going to take Riker to court, to claim a carriage and a slave won in a card game?

Across the street, a small boy in an indigo shirt was watching from the doorway of his house. He was grinning, his hand over his mouth. Justy looked down at his feet, at the sole of his right boot flapping on the mud. The whole of his right side was covered in filth. His sock was sodden with what looked like horse piss. He sighed. He was a dupe. He was a fool. He had let everyone down. Especially himself.

TWENTY-SIX

Kerry lay on the floor, listening. She had no idea what time of day it was, or how long she had been in the cell. There were no windows, and no natural light came through the gaps in the door. There was no sound.

Before he left, Umar had replaced the small burning dishes above the candle sconces, and refilled them with several small blocks of brown resin. The cell instantly filled with smoke again, and Kerry fell into a deep, dreamless sleep. When she awoke, she found a bowl of food and a cup of water on the stool beside her. She was able to sit up and eat and drink and use the bucket, but the effort left her exhausted, and she fell back to sleep. The next time she woke, the bowl was gone and her latrine bucket had been emptied, and the room was once again heavy with smoke.

Her mind had screamed at her to get up.

She had forced herself to sit up, but as she tried to swing her legs off the bed, her arms folded under her, and she fell to the floor. She was too weak to move.

She drifted. The dirt floor was cool under her cheek. There was a faint breeze from under the door, not much, but enough to waft the smoke up and away from her mouth. She felt her head clear, slowly, as though she had opened her skull and was removing wadding from around her brain, piece by tiny piece. She felt her senses return, and when the pain in her elbow had sharpened to a point, she rolled over onto her back, flexing her arm, wiggling her toes, and feeling the almost unnatural sensation of the breath in her lungs and throat, and the blood pumping in her limbs. She looked around the room, took in the bed, the stool, the lidded bucket, and the sconces. She took a deep breath and pushed herself to her feet. She took the burning disks from the sconces and tipped the twists of resin, hissing, into the latrine bucket. Then she lay down on the floor again, and watched the thin cloud of smoke as it slowly dissipated.

She listened. Her ears sang with the silence. Her cell could not be the only one. No one ever built a single cell. She wondered who else had been locked away. She imagined herself in the middle of a row of small boxes, each with their mean cot and latrine bucket. She wondered if the others would be drugged. She wondered about Tanny, and she shivered at the thought of the brutal tool that Umar had shown her. The evil bastard.

She heard the faraway sound of a door opening, somewhere outside. She eased herself slowly up onto the bed, lay on her back, and closed her eyes.

She concentrated, listening to the sound of someone approaching. But not straightaway. More doors opened, one after the other, and she realized she was right, that she was in one of a row of rooms. A single person was making their way down the passage, entering each room in turn, doing something that didn't take long, and then moving on to the next room. Not delivering food, or attending to the latrines: the movements were too quick, and there was no noise other than the shuffling of feet on the bare ground.

She counted seven doors, and then it was her turn. She slowed her breathing. She felt the air on her face as the cell door swung open. The person stopped. She felt them watching her. And then the door closed and the footsteps continued down the passageway, shuffling along, opening doors, performing the small task and moving on. Twelve cells in all, she counted, and then the person opened another door and she was left with the silence.

Her mind raced. Whatever task the person had performed in all the other rooms had not been done in hers. Was it the drugs? Had the person realized there was no smoke in her room? Why stand and watch her, and then leave? She strained her ears, wondering what she should do next. There were no locks on any of the doors, as far as she could tell, presumably because all the occupants of the other cells were drugged, and could not leave. But even if she was able to get out of her cell, which way should she go?

First, a reconnaissance. She had heard enough of Justy and Lars' stories to know that a mission's success was usually dependent on the amount and quality of scouting done beforehand. She would just go into the passage and try the doors, to see whether they were even locked.

She was on the point of swinging her legs out of the low cot when she heard one of the passage doors open. Then the sound of footsteps on the packed floor outside, moving towards her. A man, judging by the rapid, heavy sound of the boot heels on the floor. She shut her eyes and lay flat on her back.

Her door opened. And closed again, and the man was on top of her, dragging the thin pillow from under her head and pressing it over her face.

"Quiet now, missy!" Half hiss, half whisper, his breath heavy with the smell of raw liquor. She struggled, but his body was heavy on her, crushing her. She could feel the hard boards of the bed under her shoulder blades through the straw. She screamed, but the pillow muffled her voice.

He thrust at her, and pressed his hand hard over her face. "No one can hear you!" he sang in a half whisper. "They're all sleeping."

She was finding it hard to breathe. Panic bubbled in her chest. She squirmed under him, but his thighs and chest trapped her. He grunted, and reached down, lifting his groin off hers, just enough so that he could get his hand down and loosen his breeches. She got an arm loose and punched him in the side of his head. He cursed, and pushed down hard on the pillow with one hand, lifting himself off her, then drove his fist into her solar plexus.

It was as though someone had reached into her chest and squeezed her lungs together. She felt like a fish, gulping for air. He hiccupped with laughter, and pulled himself out of his breeches, and she felt him, stiff against her thigh. She had the sensation of being transported to the corner of the ceiling, where she huddled in the shadows, watching as he dragged her skirts up and began to paw at her underdrawers, as her arms flailed weakly at his shoulders, dragging at the pillow, trying to pull it away from her face, desperate to breathe.

She was barely aware of the door to the cell slamming open, but she felt the man stop, and the pressure on the pillow over her face was lifted. She pushed it away from her mouth and sucked the air in.

"You heard Absalom." A hoarse, loud whisper, a woman's voice. "This one is not to be touched. Now get out, or I will cut off your pizzle, and feed it to the gulls."

The weight came off her, as the man climbed off the bed. A woman stood there, a long knife in her hand. She pushed Kerry back down as the man hurried out of the door, hunched over with his back to her, fumbling with the ties to his breeches.

The woman wore a long, saffron-colored robe. She leaned close, and Kerry smelled a dark scent, musky and floral at the same time. "Let him run," the woman whispered. "If he is drunk enough to come in here, he is drunk enough to kill you if you try to fight him, no matter what Absalom says."

Kerry felt the energy go out of her. She slumped back on the bed, blinking back the tears pricking at her eyes. The woman went to close the door. Her eyes were dark in the wan candlelight, and made darker still by rings of heavy makeup. Her lips were stained a shade darker than her skin. She tugged the skirts of Kerry's dress down, and sat on the edge of the bed.

"I saw you took the charas out of the burners."

"Charas?"

"It is a drug. He makes us put it in all the rooms."

So this woman was the person she had heard working her way down the line of cells earlier.

"Who else is here?"

"Women. Young women." The woman hesitated. "Girls."

"The woman who came with me? Where is she?"

"The dark one? Absalom has her in another place."

"Has he hurt her?"

The woman glanced at the door. "She is unharmed. But he will destroy her if you do not do as he tells you."

Kerry thought of the breast-ripper. She felt something nameless rise in her, roll on the surface, and submerge again.

The woman's fingers were warm on her cheek. "Such smooth skin. You remind me of my daughter. Have you seen her, I wonder?"

Kerry felt her chest tighten. "Your daughter?"

"Rumi. She ran away. Four days ago."

Kerry opened her mouth to speak, but closed it again at the sight of the fear in the woman's eyes. She knew that look. She had seen it in the looking glass enough times. The terror of the unknown, not for oneself, but for one's child.

"What do you know?" the woman whispered.

"What was she wearing, when she ran away?"

"Red shoes. Her favorites." She smiled, and then the smile disappeared. "A golden robe. He made her wear it."

She stared into Kerry's face, her eyes darkening slowly, like a dying fire. And then, "She is dead, isn't she? I can see it."

Kerry wanted the bed beneath her to give way, and the earth to swallow her up. The woman's face seemed to collapse, melting like the candles in the sconces on the wall, until she looked a decade older, her eyes sunk deep in their sockets. "How?" she whispered.

"A knife." Kerry's throat was tight. It was hard to speak. She touched her belly. "Here."

The woman closed her eyes. "She was with child."

Kerry said nothing.

A whisper. "Where? Where did she die?"

"On Chapel Street. In a lane by one of the warehouses."

The woman was still holding the knife. Her knuckles were white around the handle. She looked down at the blade, as though seeing it for the first time.

"I'm sorry," Kerry said.

And suddenly the tip of the knife was an inch from her right eye. She froze.

"My Rumi is dead, stabbed like a pig in an alley, and you are sorry?"

It was an effort to look past the knife, and into the woman's eyes. But it was like looking into two holes, dug deep into the earth.

"I couldn't save her."

The woman's eyes were wide. "She was alive?"

"Only for a moment. She had lost too much blood."

"Did she say anything?"

"No. I held her, and she died."

The woman dropped the knife, and put her face in her hands. She quivered, like a tree in a storm. Kerry sat up and put her arm around the woman's shoulders.

"We've been trying to find you. To tell you."

"Where is she?" The woman's voice was muffled.

"In the Almshouse. She's being cared for."

"I must have her. I must wash her, and say prayers, and bury her in the correct way."

"I can take you to her."

The woman shook her head. "We cannot leave. If he catches you, he will kill you. And if he does not catch you, he will kill your friend."

She sat up, and wiped the tears from her face with the edge of her robe. She smiled, weakly. "I am sorry about the knife."

"There's no need to apologize."

The dark eyes searched Kerry's face. "You know what it is to lose a child, I think."

Kerry nodded. "A long time ago."

"She must have been very young."

"He. His name was Daniel."

The woman took a deep breath, and when she exhaled, her eyes were full of tears again. "I am sorry for it."

Kerry nodded.

The woman took her hand and squeezed it between her palms. "My name is Sahar."

TWENTY-SEVEN

Justy's landlady was a petite Chinese woman who had once run a brothel for the Bull, so she was accustomed to seeing men in various states of disarray. She sized Justy up with a single glance, led him down the hall to the kitchen, sat him in a straight-backed chair, and poured him a large measure of foul-smelling liquor.

Only when Justy had handed back the glass did she speak. "Your friend is here."

"Friend?"

"The big sailor. Hockson, or whatever. I put him in the parlor and gave him some tea."

Lars was sitting in one of a pair of uncomfortable chairs in the formal front room, sipping from a blue-and-white cup that looked like a thimble in his fist. He had shaved his scalp and his chin, and his skin looked soft and vulnerable. He toasted Justy. "Lovely cup of chatter broth your Mrs. Chow makes. Very tasty. I might have to pop by more often."

"You'll do no such thing. She's my landlady, and that means she's off limits."

The big man simply smiled and took another sip.

"You look a sight," Justy said.

Lars looked gaunt and hollow-cheeked without his beard. There were dark circles under his eyes, and bluish patches on the bony parts of his face. He wore his captain's coat, but his right arm was supported by a sling and bound against his body to stop him from moving it and opening the wound in his side. But his eyes were as bright and quick as ever.

He smirked at Justy. "Maybe you should have a peep in a shiner at your-self."

Justy looked down at his filthy clothes. He had taken off his boots and hose at the door, to prevent him tracking mud into the house, but his feet were streaked with dirt. "Shouldn't you be in your scratcher, still?"

Lars sniffed. "Maybe so, but I heard a few things last night you might want to know about."

"You can tell me while I change."

In his room, Justy stripped and scrubbed the dirt from his hands and feet. The cut on his forearm was bloody and painful but once cleaned, he saw it was little more than a deep scratch. His knee looked more serious, swollen and bruised, but not broken, as far as he could tell.

"So what's the chat?" he asked, pulling on a clean pair of drawers.

Lars sat on the bed, nursing his arm. "I heard the Lane near went up in flames last night."

"Did you, indeed?"

"Surely. Your boy Liam was full of the tale."

"Liam Corrigan?" Justy frowned. "The nuns told me he was half-dead."

"Not at all. His hands got burned a bit, but he's fine otherwise. The nose gents only stopped you coming in to be sure he got some rest. You know what cluckety old hens they are. The way you looked didn't help, by the way, with your face black and your clothes still smoking. You looked like the Devil himself."

"You saw me?"

"No, no. I was in me scratcher. One of the novices told me. Jenny O'Neill. A sweet girl. You scared the life out of her, poor lass." Lars grinned. "I had to comfort her, of course."

"Of course." Justy jerked the drawstring of his drawers tight. "Is that it?"

"It is not. The boy's father was in to see him first thing this morning. There's a nasty piece of work, by the way. He was giving the lad a quare hard time, saying that's what happens to young men who go chasing African girls, they get burned alive. Then he told him not to say anything to the law, if they should come by. I put two and two together and figured it all had something to do with that wee girl they have down in the cellar."

"How did you do that, exactly?"

Lars smirked. "Well, it wasn't too hard, even for a dumb tar like myself. Young Jenny had told me about how a young black girl was brought in to the

morgue a few days ago, cut open something terrible, and that you were chasing the doer. Then there's you banging on the door, half-burnt to a cinder, de-
manding to question a young lad who's in trouble with his dad for chasing
after a Negro lass. Chance it's the same girl, I thought, and had a whid with
young Liam after his father had left. And the boy spilled the whole damned
thing."

Justy laughed. "I should put you on the payroll, Lars. What did he say?"

"Well, first I asked him if she was a Mohammedan. Jenny told me one of
the sisters reckoned she was, from the ink on her arms. The boy said she was
indeed, and some kind of princess, too. And all shut up in a castle! You'll have
to tell me what the hell he was blabbing on about."

"There's a compound up in the north end of Canvas Town. High walls. Like
a bloody fortress. Built by a cove name of Umar, an escaped slave from the
Carolinas. Seems like an intelligent man, although he built his fortress right
by a marsh, which doesn't seem so smart."

"Oh, I don't know. Sounds smart enough, if he's a rice man."

"How's that?"

"Well, if he's a Carolina fella, he likely piked off from one of the rice plantations on the coast down there. Men who've farmed rice know all about how
to flood and drain land."

Justy stared at Lars.

"What?"

"You're a bloody genius is what." Justy grinned. "Hand me those breeches."

It was slow work lacing the drawstring.

"So, did young Liam tell you any more about his princess?"

"Not his princess. A princess. She told him she was some kind of royalty."

"How does a butcher's boy meet a Mussulman princess?"

"She was a wild one, it seems. Liked to sneak out of the place and go
a-roving."

"Risky."

"Aye, well, that's the point, isn't it? Anyway, she came by his stall one day
about a half year ago. She caught his eye, and nature took its course."

Justy stopped fiddling with the laces. "You mean . . ."

Lars smirked. "He's a handsome lad, if a bit wan around the gills. You
should see the younger nuns buzzing about him."

"Good God. Where did they go?"

"Down the alley near his cart, he said. His mammy often shabs off for one reason or another and leaves him minding the stall, so it was as simple as that."

"Good God," Justy said again. He sat on the bed beside Lars. "And that was where they met every time afterwards, I suppose."

"So he said. But after the first time they only met in the evening. She said it was too risky going out in the day. So he'd find an excuse to go by the compound each morning. On the days she could get away, she'd leave a sign. At the end of the day, he'd take the cart home, then go back again to Chapel Street. She'd be there, waiting for him. They'd nug it up for an hour or so, and then she'd sneak home."

"How often did this happen?"

"Once or twice a month."

Justy finished lacing his breeches and examined the cut on his arm. It had stopped bleeding. He took out a clean shirt and eased it on. "Did he know she was pregnant?"

"Oh, I'd say so." Lars' face was serious. "Jenny had told me as much, so I asked the lad."

"And?"

"And he folded up like a reefed sail. Turned away and faced the wall. And not another word out of him."

Justy pulled on his coat. Mrs. Chow had sponged the soot off it, but it was still damp. It would have to do. "Did the lad say what kind of sign she left? Or where?"

"No."

"Never mind. I'll get it out of him."

Lars sat up, cradling his arm. "Go easy on the lad. He's had a bad shock."

"I'm sure he has, Lars." Justy pulled his good shoes from under the bed and eased them on. "But I need to know what he knows."

———•———

Liam Corrigan's thin face was topped with the same slick of black hair as his father's. His skin was so pale it looked almost blue against the stark white of the sheet that the nuns had tucked around him, up to his neck. The burns on his arms were painful, but not severe. They had sponged them carefully, spread them with salve, and wrapped him in bandages.

Justy sat on one side of the narrow cot. Lars the other. The boy's eyes snapped wide open, flicking left and right between them.

"It looks like you know who I am," Justy said.

Liam said nothing. He stared hate at Lars.

"Don't look at him," Justy snapped. "Tell me about the girl. What was her name?"

The boy said nothing.

Justy leaned close. "If you stay silent, son, if you don't talk to me, she'll never be claimed. Her mother will never see her again. She'll be thrown into a pit with the dead dogs and the rubbish." Justy paused for a beat. "She won't even have a name."

He let the sounds of the ward fill in between them, the shuffling of the nuns as they walked up and down between the beds, the soft words.

"What was her name, Liam?"

Liam Corrigan's eyes were as green as a sunlit meadow, but they darkened then, as though a storm cloud had suddenly built up and blocked out all the light in the sky. He closed his eyes, long lashes wet on his cheeks, and when he opened them again, they were filled with pain.

"Rumi."

"Rumi. And where did she come from?"

"Jericho."

"You said she was a princess. What did you mean?"

"It's what she said." The tears were running freely down his cheeks now. "It's how she was able to get out. Her father was a top man, so she had the run of the place."

"A top man, or the top man?"

Liam shrugged. "I can't remember."

"We'll come back to it. So Rumi slipped out to see you."

The boy nodded, the straw in his pillow crunching under his head. "Once every few weeks."

"And you met in the alley where your parents kept their stall?"

"Aye."

"How did you know when she wanted to meet?"

"She'd throw a red shawl over the wall near the candle-fencer's place."

Behind Justy a door banged hard.

"How dare you!" Sister Marie-Therese of the Incarnation's cloak streamed behind her as she bore down on the ward. Her white headdress made her look like a clipper under full sail. Patients began sitting up in their beds. "This is a house of God, not a jail. You have no jurisdiction here."

Justy let her come. He waited until she had stopped in front of him, every inch of her five feet quivering in righteous rage. And then he leaned over her and pushed his face close, so that his nose was almost touching hers. "I am a Marshal of this city, Sister," he said. "I have jurisdiction everywhere."

She hesitated. "This boy is a patient."

"This boy is a witness to a murder. And if you're unhappy with me questioning him here, I'm quite happy to have him taken next door."

The front door banged again. The sound of Cooper Corrigan's boot heels reverberated off the walls as he marched down the ward. His face was red, and one leg of his yellow breeches was damp. He looked as though he had been pulled out of a tavern.

"What the fuck is going on here?" Corrigan snarled. "What are you doing talking to my son without me?"

"Your son is a witness in a murder inquiry, Corrigan. I'll question him any time and any place I care to."

Corrigan's face turned from red to purple. "I'll burn you down, ya madge."

Justy folded his arms. "Oh, aye? Pop me in one of your barrels, will you?"

"You goddamned black-joke bastard!"

"It's all right, Da."

They turned to look at Liam. He was looking up at them, his eyes as dark green and wet as a winter sea. "It's all right." His voice cracked. "I have to confess."

"Confess? Confess what?" Corrigan's eyes looked as though they might pop out of their sockets. "Don't say a word, son."

"I have to, Da. I'm sorry. I'm sorry for all of it." He closed his eyes, and his body shook once, and when he opened them again, he looked straight at Justy.

"I killed her."

Corrigan made a sound like an animal in pain. Justy kept his eyes on the boy's. "Tell me."

Liam swallowed. "Two weeks ago, she left the sign like she always did, and we met on Chapel Street. She told me she was in pig. We got into a fight. I told her we had to get buckled, but she wouldn't have it. She slapped me, and ran off. That's when Da saw her."

He glanced at his father. "I checked the wall every day after, like always, and she left the marker last week. Thursday it was. Only she never came. I was worried, like, for she never missed a meeting. So I waited all night. The next day, the marker was still there, so I knew something was queer. I stopped at our place and stayed as long as I could. But she never came. And then on Saturday, I went up in the evening." He took a deep breath. "And she was there."

He closed his eyes again, the tears running down his face in a stream. Justy fought the urge to reach out and tell the boy that everything was going to be all right. He waited.

"She was lying in the dirt, holding her belly. There was blood. A lot of it. She said she'd been chived. I tried to put my hand on her, down there, to stop the bleeding, but she pushed me away. She said it was useless, that she was done for."

He stopped, and the nun eased herself slowly onto the bed. She patted the sheet over his chest. "It's all right, Liam. You don't have to say any more. You didn't hurt the girl. You found her. It wasn't your fault."

"Aye, son." Corrigan stepped closer, relief on his face. "You did nothing wrong. You tried to save her, right?"

"You don't understand." The boy's voice was almost a wail. "She told me I had to save the child."

Justy could feel a pulse in his mouth. "What do you mean, Liam?"

"She said the baby was alive in her. That she couldn't live, but the child had a chance. I told her I didn't know what to do, but she said she'd show me. She told me to take out my knife."

There was a sharp intake of breath. The nun's face had gone as pale as her wimple.

"Go on, Liam," Justy said.

"She opened her robe." Liam's voice was a whisper. "She showed me where to cut. She told me to make like I was working on the stall, opening a hog . . ." His voice broke. "I couldn't stand it. The blood. The sound of her crying. The smell of it." His eyes pleaded. "She told me to reach in and take out the child. I put my hand down, but her guts came tumbling out of her. I tried to hold them in, but I couldn't. And she was moaning something terrible. And then she went quiet." He closed his eyes. "And then I ran away."

He looked up at the four faces staring down at him. "I'm sorry," he said again. And then his eyes filled with tears and he began to cry, deep, long sobs that echoed in the long, silent candlelit room.

Sister Marie-Therese put her hand gently on his cheek. Her eyes lifted to meet Justy's. "Are you finished, Marshal?"

"Yes." It was an effort to speak. "I'm finished."

It was cool on the steps of the Almshouse. The wind was in the west, a gentle breeze carrying the sounds of Canvas Town up to the Broad Way. Justy sat on the top step with Lars, trying to make sense of what he had just heard, and trying to decide what he should do now.

The door creaked behind him. Corrigan and Sister Marie-Therese came down the steps to face him. Corrigan looked like a man with a weeklong hangover. His face was pale and sweaty, and his hair flopped wetly on his forehead.

"He didn't do it," Corrigan said.

"Do what, Cooper? Carve the titter open with one of your knives? Pretend like it's a hog, wasn't that what he said?"

"He didn't stab her, Marshal." The nun's voice was firm. "She had already been dealt a killing blow when he arrived. This . . . the rest was an error in judgment."

"Error in judgment? I'll say."

"He's fourteen years old, Marshal. A child. The girl too, by the look of her. They'd have no idea of how babies come into the world."

"Aye. We never taught him anything like that," Corrigan insisted.

Lars laughed. "He seems to have worked out how to make a bairn, though, doesn't he?"

Corrigan said nothing.

Sister Marie-Therese sighed. "What the boy did was horrifying, I agree. But he did it out of ignorance, not out of spite. You heard him."

"I heard a pretty tale, Sister," Justy said. "How about this one: Liam meets his titter in the alley, and she tells him she's pregnant. He loses his wits. Maybe because he doesn't want a bairn, or maybe because he does, but she tells him she's not going to have it with him. Either way, he stabs her. Then he cools off. He realizes that his old man's seen him with this lass, and maybe not just him. If he's not careful, he'll swing for this, so he comes up with a plan. He cuts her up, the way some ignorant drumbelo that's got no idea how a woman works might do. Then, if he does get lifted, he's got a tearful ditty of love and despair to spin, one that'll have us all crying in the aisles."

"My boy never . . ." Corrigan was red-faced, fighting for the right words. He fell silent.

"You give the lad too much credit, Marshal," the nun said. She glanced at Corrigan. "The truth is, Liam has neither the brains nor the knowledge to think up a plan like that. Even if he did, he hasn't the cool to carry it out. The boy's as soft as butter. Not the hard nut you imagine."

"Not a hard nut?" Lars' voice was tight. "He used a butcher's blade to split the lass open like a she was a fucking oyster!"

The nun snapped her fingers at Corrigan. "That knife at your belt. Is it the same as the one your son has?"

"Aye." Corrigan tugged the blade free. It was a standard butcher's knife. Fine at the tip, and brutal at the base: two inches wide, and heavy enough to split bone and cut sinew.

"There's your proof," she said to Justy.

"Proof of what?" he said.

"Sister Claire showed you the wound in the girl's abdomen. That knife could never have made a wound like that. Do you think it likely that the boy carried two blades? That he stabbed her with one and cut her open with the other?"

Justy said nothing. The vestal was right. The knife that had stabbed the girl had gone deep. But the cut was not even a half-inch wide, meaning the killer had used a long, thin blade, and not the brutal butcher's cleaver that Corrigan carried.

"The boy will still have to see a judge for what he did," he said.

Corrigan nodded, but the relief had flushed his face red.

"Don't get your hopes up too far, Cooper," Justy said. "There's nothing to say that it wasn't the wound that he inflicted that killed her. Sister Claire will have to give evidence."

"My boy's not a killer."

"That's for the beak to decide."

TWENTY-EIGHT

Sahar and Kerry sat in the quiet, the thin cloud of charas smoke hanging above them. They held hands, and Kerry talked about Daniel, how small he had been when he was born, and yet how loud. A scream that could crack a window. She told how the child had been taken from her, and given to a wet nurse, and how her own milk had dried up, so that when she got him back again, she could not feed him. She told how the boy had grown quickly, but got sick easily, and when the yellow fever had struck the city, she had taken him to a sanatorium near Turtle Bay for safety, but the building had burned to the ground. And she had never seen him again.

The two women cried and held each other, and used the edges of their dresses to dry their tears. And then they sat quietly, the silence singing in their ears.

"The man who took your child from you. Where is he now?" Sahar asked.

"He's dead." Kerry looked into her eyes. "I killed him."

It was a moment before Sahar spoke again. "I want to kill the man who took Rumi from me. But I do not know who he is."

"Umar knows."

"He will not tell me. He wants nothing but loyalty and obedience from me. From all of us. If I tried to find out who killed Rumi, he would kill me. And he would do it easily. He kills, and does not give it another thought."

"Who has he killed?"

She smiled sadly. "He killed the man who owned us, on the island. He killed a man when he stole the boat that brought us here."

"He was escaping. You all were. Sometimes you have to do what you have to, to survive."

"And the women? The girls? What about them?"

Something fluttered in Kerry's chest. "What girls?"

"The girls he brought here, the ones that fell ill, or were barren."

"What are you talking about?"

Sahar smoothed her hand over the blanket. "You think this is a house of prostitution."

"Isn't it?"

"Do brothel owners keep their women drugged and shut in dark rooms?"

Kerry shook her head. "I suppose not."

"No. They do not. But Absalom does, because these women are not here to provide pleasure to men. To some men, of course, but that is not the reason the women are here. They are here because they are white, and their children will be white also."

"I don't understand."

Sahar grasped her hand. "He is breeding them. Babies. Little white babies, like precious birds, or rare horses."

"For sale?"

Sahar nodded.

It was a moment before Kerry realized that she was holding her breath. She exhaled, a long sigh. It made sense now. Why Umar was stealing white girls, why Tanny and the other streetwalkers had heard nothing about a rival brothel. Because there was no brothel. Why Umar had called it a stable. Because it was full of brood mares. Which meant the stallions were white men.

"You said some girls fell ill, or were barren. What happened to them?"

Sahar nodded. "They disappeared. One day they were here, the next they were gone. We never heard anything about them."

"How many?"

Sahar shrugged. "Ten? A dozen? Perhaps more."

"What about the white women in gray robes? What do they do?"

"They are his recruiters. He calls them his angels, but they are whores, addicted to charas. They live here, in a room beside the refectory. He gives them charas, food, shelter, protection. In return, they bring him girls."

Kerry leaned back against the wall. Perhaps it was the drug, but she felt somehow insulated from the horror of what Sahar was telling her, as though it was too much for her mind to cope with. But she could see the scheme laid out in front of her, as plain as a map.

"We have to get out of here, Sahar."

"We cannot. He will hurt your friend. If he catches you, he will do it in front of you. If you get away, he will cut her to pieces and deliver her to you."

Kerry's stomach flipped at the thought of the breast-ripper. Acid on her tongue.

"We can't sit and do nothing." She walked to the door. And then she turned and faced Sahar.

"Do you really want to find the man who killed Rumi?"

Sahar's eyes were as dark as a thundercloud. "I do."

Kerry nodded. "Then I have an idea."

TWENTY-NINE

Justy and Lars sat at a table in Hughson's Tavern, staring into the space in front of them as Seamus Tully filled their tankards from a jug of ale.

"Everything all right, gents?" he asked. "Only you look like a pair of buggered heifers."

Justy looked at the tankard. His mouth tasted sour, but he knew the ale wouldn't flush it clean. "It's Kerry. She's gone and put herself in a hole."

"What kind of a hole might that be?"

"One full of Mussulmen, with a bloody great wall built around it."

"Ah, shite." Tully reached for Justy's glass and drank a slug out of it. "I had a feeling."

"And you didn't stop her?"

"Easy now. It's not like she told me what she was up to. She just had that look about her. You know, the one where her jaw goes square and her eyes go narrow and she'd as soon drive a coach and four right over you, rather than ask you nicely to step out of the way."

Justy smiled despite himself. "Aye, well, it sounds like that bloody cousin of hers convinced her to dress up like a doxy and sneak inside, to find out the lay of the land for him."

"Owens? The shag. What's he planning, to blow down the wall of Jericho, then steam in and gut every man, mott, and kinchin inside?"

"I wouldn't be surprised. The thing is, she was supposed to leave him a sign that she was safe inside, and there's been nothing. I'm worried for her, and I want to get her out."

"Only there's no way in." Tully took another drink. His eyes appraised Justy over the rim of the tankard. "Or is there?"

"I think there might be. Do you know a candle-maker up by the compound there? Hard by the wall?"

Tully thought for a moment. "There's a few taper-fencers in Canvas Town. But I don't know of one up by the wall. What's the play?"

Justy sat back. "Umar took me and one of my men into Jericho a few days back, through a secret entrance, not through the front. Five gets you ten that's not the only secret entrance to the place. I need to find a way in. Will you ask about for me?"

"If you think it'll help Kerry, I will, of course." Tully emptied the glass and wiped the counter. "We might have more luck up that way if it's someone with a darker skin doing the asking. Why don't you lend me your man Hardluck for the job?"

Justy winced. "I like your thinking, Seamus, but I don't think we'll ever see Hardluck again."

"Certainly not if I see the black joke first," Lars said.

Tully looked back and forth between the two of them. "Have yiz fallen out, then?"

"You might say," Lars said. "He's only been working for his old master the whole time, spying on Justy, no doubt."

"Hardluck?" Tully frowned. "Are you sure?"

"Sure as you're standing in front of me," Justy said. "I saw him driving out of that bloody compound this morning."

"That can't be."

"He went right past me, Seamus."

"Well, he must be a bloody magician, then, for he's been back in the galley the whole day."

Justy flushed. "Impossible. I saw him with my own eyes."

"And I saw him with mine, *a mhac*. Go in the back and see for yourself. Ask Kathleen, she'll tell you. He's been in there peeling tatties all morning, waiting on you to send for him."

Justy strode into the back of the tavern, ignoring the twinge in his knee, and pushed open the kitchen door. Hardluck was sitting on a barrel, his coat off, his sleeves rolled up, a potato in one hand, and a knife in the other. There were peelings on the floor and a bowl full of yellow potatoes on the table beside him. He had the dull-eyed look of a man who'd been doing scut work for hours at a time.

"How long have you been here?" Justy snapped.

Hardluck's mouth dropped open. He swallowed. "Sorry, sir. I didn't mean no harm by it. Kath just said she needed some help."

His eyes flicked across the room. Justy followed the look to see a girl in her midtwenties with her hands plunged elbow-deep in a sink full of linens. "You're Kathleen?"

The girl stood up straight and tucked a loose hank of red hair under her white cap. "Yes, sir."

"When did he come back here?"

"Come back, sir?" She glanced at Hardluck, a puzzled look on her face.

"How long ago? An hour?"

The girl's face reddened. "I'll thank you not to speak so sharp to me, sir. I'm not your maid."

Hardluck stood up slowly. "Forgive me, sir. I thought I was meant to wait for word from you. Was I supposed to meet you back at the Hall?"

The driver's eyes were on the floor. His arms were loose by his sides and his head was down. He looked like a dog about to receive a beating, the kind that was doled out so regularly and frequently that it was just a matter of course.

Justy felt his anger evaporate. He saw how unjust it was for him to be enraged at Hardluck. The man was a slave. He felt a strange sense of relief. There was a chair beside the door. He lowered himself carefully into it, nursing his knee. "Go back to your master, Hardluck."

The driver looked startled. "Sir?"

"Let's not pretend anymore. I saw you today. Up at the compound. But before you leave, I would like to know what Piers Riker was doing up there. Perhaps you would tell me that?"

Hardluck's forehead was as furrowed as a plowed field. "But I've been here all day, sir."

Justy felt irritation pluck at him. "I saw you, Hardluck. Perched on top of your carriage. Riker's carriage, I should say. You drove right past me. I called out to you, actually, but you didn't hear. Or perhaps you merely ignored me. Not that it matters."

"Not me, sir, I swear."

"I know that rig, Hardluck!" The heat was back in his voice. "That paintwork, those ridiculous pennants. There aren't two cabs like it in the city of New York."

Hardluck's eyes were wide. "But there are, sir."

"What?"

"Two cabs, sir, the same. Yours is one of a pair."

"A pair?" Part of Justy knew he sounded like a parrot, but his mind was having trouble grasping what Hardluck was saying.

"One made for Mister Piers, sir, the other for Mister Tobias. Mister Tobias usually keeps his on the estate, as it's too small to carry much more than himself and his papers, but Meriday—that's the driver, sir—he drove the big carriage into a slough a few weeks back, near New Hope, and he twisted the axle, so Mister Tobias had to switch to the smaller rig."

"Two cabs. A pair."

"Yes, sir."

"And you've been here all day?" He looked at Kathleen, who nodded emphatically.

He thought back, remembering the coach driving out of the gates. The same coach, identical in every way, but the driver? He thought about the figure on the top of the cab, hunched over, lashing out with his whip, wrapped in a coachman's robe, with a hood that hid his face.

Not Hardluck at all.

A wave of emotion broke over him. Relief at the fact that he hadn't been duped by Riker, or betrayed by Hardluck. Shame that he had thought the worst of the driver. Anger at himself for lashing out at Kathleen and Hardluck both. And then, a surge of excitement.

"What would Tobias Riker be doing up at a Mohammedan compound in Canvas Town?"

"I couldn't say, sir. But it might not have been Mister Tobias at all. He often has Meriday running up to Jericho for one thing or another."

"Wait a moment. You know about Jericho?"

Hardluck nodded. "Never been there, sir, but I know of it, certainly."

"And Tobias Riker does business there?"

The puzzled look was back on Hardluck's face. "Of some kind, sir, but I don't know what."

"Well, god damn it, Hardluck! Why the good holy hell didn't you tell me?"

"Tell you what, sir?"

"That you know about this goddamned compound! That your old master has been doing business up there! For Christ's sake, I have been racking my brains to find a way into that place, to find out what this man Umar is up to, and to dig the only woman I've ever loved out of the pit that she has fallen into, and you might have had the answers the whole goddamned time!"

The kitchen was silent, except for the drips of water that fell from Kathleen's hands. Hardluck was staring at the floor. "I didn't know any of that, sir. You didn't tell me any of that."

The door creaked open. Lars looked in. "Everything square in here?"

Justy gestured. "Turns out Hardluck here knows all about Jericho. Riker does business up there, he says. His driver . . . what's his name?"

"Meriday," Hardluck said.

"Meriday is up and down from there all the time. All the time!" Justy sat down slowly. He felt as though his head was about to split. Everything he'd said and not seen, known and assumed, spinning in his mind.

Lars patted him on the shoulder. "Well, let's start from the beginning. Who does your man Meriday take up to Jericho, Hardluck?"

The coachman made a hopeless gesture. "I don't really know, sir. Mister Tobias goes up there, and sometimes has friends with him. And then there's the lawyer Meriday brings back and forth. Several times a week, sometimes."

Justy looked up. "Lawyer?"

"A man named Shard."

"Shard?" Lars and Justy spoke at the same time. Hardluck's eyes widened.

"There was a Shard taken to the Almshouse after the fire the other night," Justy said.

Lars nodded. "I know it. I know him."

"You *know* him?" Justly felt the swelling sensation in his skull increase.

"Easy now. I don't *know* him. But I've met him once or twice. At the Bun. And I saw him after he was brought in to the Almshouse the other night. Your lads made a right mess of him. Scrambled his brains, for sure. He was babbling away about the Devil tempting him and the fires of hell. All the usual stuff the plain folk come out with."

Justy held up his hand. "Hold on. He's a Puritan?"

"Ties his hair with a yellow ribbon like a lot of them do."

"What in God's name is one of the plain folk doing in a place like the Buttered Bun?"

Lars shrugged. "He's a human being, ain't he? We all lapse from time to time. Except you, maybe." He winked at Kathleen, who hid a smile behind her hand.

Justy leaned back in the chair, his mind racing. What was Riker doing up at Jericho? What business did he have with Umar? And the lawyer: Why did Riker need to send a lawyer up to Jericho several times a week? And who was the lawyer? Shard was an unusual name. Was it the same Shard who was in the Almshouse? Again, he felt as though he was looking at a puzzle, except that now he was beginning to see the edges and patches of color that made up the image. The skin pricked on his arms and the back of his neck. It was the feeling that something in the sequence of events was beginning to run in his favor, like a tide turning.

He sat up. "Hardluck, I apologize for my outburst. Will you forgive me?"

The driver's smile lit up his face. "Nothing to it, sir."

"Thank you. Now, can you find this man Meriday for me? Ask him about this lawyer?"

The jarvie nodded. "I'll go to Mister Tobias' house directly, sir. I'll say I'm come to pick up some trifles I've left behind."

"Lars, I need you at the Almshouse. Can you persuade them to keep you another night?"

The big sailor lifted his arm. "I won't be lying if I say I need the dressing changed. Then maybe I can keel over or something."

"I'm sure you'll be very convincing."

He pushed himself to his feet. He bowed to Kathleen. "You'll forgive me too, mistress, for speaking to you so."

She colored, and bobbed a curtsey.

Lars squinted at him. "Well, we've got our marching orders. What are you going to do?"

Justy grinned. "Something I usually hate doing."

"What's that, then?"

"Paperwork."

THIRTY

"Long day, Marshal?"

Justy jumped. The nib of his pen jammed and a large blot of ink spread slowly over the paper. "Damn it, Gorton!"

"Sorry." The watchman leaned on the door of Justy's office.

"You look pleased with yourself. Did you get some sleep?"

"I did."

"I don't suppose you had any luck getting Umar to take you on as a spy as well."

"I put the hook in the water, but nothing nibbled."

The Trinity bell began to sound five. One more day before the girl's body was taken out of the Almshouse and dumped in a common grave.

"I need you to make some inquiries for me."

"I'm at your service, Marshal. But you only paid me for two days, and you're already a day in arrears."

Justy grimaced. He tugged his purse out of his pocket and counted out five dollars. Gorton's hand whipped out, and the coins disappeared.

"You and Playfair picked up a man after that fracas last night," Justy said. "Name of Shard."

"Did we?"

"He got rapped over the head. Ended up in the sick bay. I need you to find out who he is."

"Why not just ask him?"

"Because he's still unconscious. Playfair's report doesn't list a profession." Justy shuffled through the files on his desk, then shifted the light so he could read the paper. "Robert Shard."

There was the sound of footsteps in the hallway, and Vanderool's face appeared over Gorton's shoulder. "Evening, Marshal."

"Sergeant. What can I do for you?"

"I need Mister Gorton," Vanderool said. "We're briefing the patrol."

"Take him, then."

Gorton slipped away down the hall. Vanderool lingered.

"What is it, Sergeant?"

Vanderool sucked his teeth. His eyes were like a pig's, sunk deep into his flesh. "You're paying Gorton for extra time."

"That's right. Nothing that will interfere with his Watch duties. I've seen to that."

"I'll bet he hasn't earned his pay."

"And what makes you say that?"

Vanderool smirked. "You want eyes about this city, Marshal, you'd do better to hire a man that's from here and knows the place."

"Like yourself, I suppose."

"At least I can tell you who Robert Shard is." Vanderool showed a row of grubby teeth. "I heard you as I came up the hall."

Justy hid his distaste. "So who is he?"

More of the sergeant's teeth appeared. "What's it worth?"

Justy sighed. "Not much. Gorton will find out eventually, and I've already paid him. But if you tell me now, Sergeant, I'll count it as a personal favor."

Vanderool thought about that for a moment. "He's a lawyer."

"That much I know. Where does he work?"

"Well, that's an easy one. He works here."

"Here?"

"Aye, Marshal." Vanderool smirked. "He's Albany's agent for the southern counties. His office is up on the fifth floor."

Shard's clerk had left for the day, leaving his office secured with a cheap lock that was easily turned. The room was whitewashed and unadorned, as austere as a Puritan lawyer's office might be expected to be. Two identical, uncluttered desks, two hard chairs, and two large cabinets filled with boxes of papers, all neatly labeled and stacked.

Five boxes were marked with the letter *R*. Tobias Riker's name was on a single, thin file that contained just four sheets of paper. There was a statement of ownership of a house on Rector Street, a certificate of purchase for a warehouse on Albany Basin in 1802, a certificate of sale of a few acres of farmland on Wallabout Bay to a Peter Sturtevant in 1801, and a statement of ownership of a 400-acre island in the Helgate of the East River. These were his New York properties. The bulk of his holdings were New Jersey and Pennsylvania estates.

Justy slumped in the lawyer's chair, and looked around the empty room. The desks had no drawers, nowhere to hide any notes or papers. It seemed all Robert Shard did was copy and sign documents brought in by landowners. So why was he riding in Tobias Riker's carriage? And what business did he have in Jericho?

Something snagged in his mind. He thought about the tour of Jericho that Umar had given him. What had he called the place? Mimo. He said it meant several things. Sanctuary. And property. Would Umar have come and filed paperwork like the rest of the landowners in New York? But there was no file marked either Umar or Salam.

There was a tap at the door behind him. A stout, red-faced man in a sturdy brown suit stood in the doorway, a sheaf of papers under his arm. "Mister Shard?"

"No," Justy said.

The man brandished his papers. "I have bills of purchase for lands in Harlem." A strong German accent. "My lawyer says they must be signed. Where is Shard?"

"Mister Shard is very ill, sir. And it is after hours."

"*Verdammt!*" The man slammed the papers on the lawyer's table. "The roads are terrible today. Two carts shed their loads, and a carriage turned over. It is why I am late."

The topmost of the man's papers was a sketch map of the north of Manhattan Island.

"Your map?" Justy asked.

"*Nein.* Mister Shard's map."

The German's purchases were marked in red. It looked as though Shard— or his clerk—had hatched them in red ink when they were prospects, and then colored them solid with a wax pencil when the purchases were complete. The German had bought several parcels, not in the fashionable part of Harlem, where Alexander Hamilton had built a large residence, but further east, on the sloping land that abutted the Horn Hook and the East River. The map showed Randall's and Ward islands, and the New Town promontory by the Helgate, where the German had bought a small plot of land by the upriver shore. Further to the right, on the margin of the map, was a rough circle hatched in red.

Justy pointed. "Is this an island?"

"*Ja*. Riker's place."

"I see you looked at it. Why didn't you buy?"

The German sniffed. "The low ground floods in the spring. The rest is scrub. The *schwarzes* can have it."

"Schwarzes?"

"Blacks. They are living there. Escaped slaves, my neighbor thinks. They hide when I come to inspect the place." He hauled on one of his watch chains. "*Ach!* I am always forgetting which one is the dummy."

Justy failed to hide his smile as the man shoved the dummy back into its fob and yanked on the other chain.

"It confuses the thief," the man said.

"If you say so."

"And it is the fashion, of course." The man's small, piggy eyes glared at the working watch and then at Justy. "Who are you, anyway?"

"I am here to see Mister Shard's clerk. The door was open, but I fear he has already left and simply failed to lock the door." He gestured to the lawyer's chair. "We can wait together."

"*Nein*." The German thrust his watch into its pocket and swept his papers off the lawyer's desk. "I am already late for dinner. I will come back another day."

Justy watched him go, mulling what he had said. Tobias Riker didn't strike him as the type to permit runaway slaves on his land.

Runaway slaves. What had Lew Owens called Umar?

He jumped to his feet, opened the cabinet, and took out the first of the boxes marked *A*. He flicked quickly through the folders.

A file labeled ABSALOM, JOHN was a half-inch thick. The top sheet was a sketch map, like the German's. It showed the area north of the Broad Way, from St. Paul's Church to Greenwich Village. There were several patches of red, concentrated around the area where a line ran inland from the Hudson River, extending Hudson's Kill across the Broad Way and down to the Collect Pond. The Kill was a tidal stream that flooded in the spring. The land all around it was sunken meadow, or marsh, depending on your point of view.

Useless land for building. Good only for fishing eels or growing reeds. And yet it seemed that John Absalom, or Umar Salam, had bought all of it. Justy scanned the papers, looking for the amounts paid, and saw that Umar had borrowed heavily, paying just ten percent of the price of each plot in cash.

The balance came from the Millennium Bank.

Which was owned by Tobias Riker.

THIRTY-ONE

Hays was in the lobby of the Hall, talking with a tall man in a long overcoat, buttoned to the neck. The man's right eye was gone, closed by a thick, pale mass of scar tissue. His good eye glanced at Justy as he approached, then the man nodded to Hays and walked away, the heels of his boots loud on the stone floor.

"Who was that?" Justy asked.

Hays gave Justy a cold look. "I have been looking for you."

"Good. Because I have to tell you something."

"I hope it has nothing to do with either the Riker or the Beaulieu families."

"Then you will be disappointed. Because it has to do with both."

Hays drew himself up. "I told you to stay away from them. My orders were quite specific."

"They were. But as you once told me yourself, High Constable, evidence is evidence, and wherever it leads us, it is our duty to follow."

Hays said nothing for a moment. He stared at Justy, his jaw tight. "Very well," he said. "Come with me."

Rather than turning to go up the stairs to his office, Hays walked out into the street. The sky above them was a like a sheet of pounded metal. Hays went quickly down the steps, turning right up the hill and then right again on Nassau Street. Justy had to press himself against a wall to avoid being spattered by mud as a cart rattled by. He saw Hays duck under the lintel of a small tavern a few yards down.

It was dark inside the drinking hole, and he had to blink several times before his eyes grew accustomed to the gloom. The High Constable was sitting on a low bench wedged into the near corner, under a dusty window set high in the wall. He folded his arms. "Very well. Out with it."

Justy decided not to ask why they were in a Nassau Street boozing ken, and not in Hays' office. He sat down on the bench. "I think Tobias Riker is buying land."

"What of it?"

"The land is here. On Manhattan Island."

Hays shook his head. "Not possible. Tobias Riker is on the Planning Commission. And all Commission members are banned from property purchases in New York County until five years after the plan is made public."

I know. Which is why he's using a third party to buy the land for him."

"Who?"

"Umar."

Hays leaned back on the banquette and peered down his nose. "Explain."

Justy shifted, so that he could look the High Constable full in the face. "Look, Jake, you only have to glance at a newspaper to know the whole city's trying to guess what the Planning Commission's survey will say, and where the main roads will go. And no one wants to know more than your speculator friends in the Tontine."

"They're not my friends. And I have no knowledge of what the commission has or has not discussed, as well you know."

"I do. But don't tell me that every time you go in there some cove doesn't sidle up and ask you to whid the scrap. What do they promise you?"

"The world, usually." Hays looked as though he had tasted something sour. "That bumptious prig Joseph Langham offered me forty percent yesterday, if I could tell him whether it was worth buying the Stuyvesant place. Which is precisely why the Mayor selected men of considerable means to serve on the Commission. They're all wealthy enough that they won't be tempted to indulge in that kind of speculation."

"And what if it turned out that one of them wasn't quite as wealthy as he made out? What if he was close to bankrupt, and therefore highly susceptible to temptation?"

Hays flicked the idea away. "These are public men. It would be impossible for someone to keep up such a pretense for long. And even if he did, how could he get around the five-year moratorium? No. There's no way he could get away with it."

"He could if he were clever. And if he were patient. And if he worked with a buyer with whom he had no connection. Someone invisible."

Hays said nothing. And then he nodded towards the counter at the far end of the tavern. "A stoup of tickle here, if you will, Sam. And a brace of glasses."

They waited until the landlord had set a dusty bottle on the table beside them. Hays poured a viscous amber slug into a glass, and pushed it at Justy. "Someone invisible?"

The liquor smelled like overripe fruit. "When the Mohammedans arrived here, however many years ago, they were led by a man named Absalom. We know him as Umar Salam now, but he's been buying land under a version of his original name."

"I doubt it." Hays' Adam's apple bobbed as he swallowed half his drink. "Legal it may be, but we both know that it'll be a chilly afternoon in Hades before any New Yorker dares sell property to a black man. Or any judge dredges up the sand to sign the papers."

"Which is why Umar does what all wealthy property owners do. He uses an attorney."

Hays was silent. He turned his glass in his hands. "What land has he bought?"

"Parts of the Lispenard estate, up by Canvas Town. The meadows and the marshland that runs up to the Broad Way."

"The compound."

"Not yet."

"Papers?"

"There's a file in the State Comptroller's agent's office. It names a John Absalom as the buyer and Lucius Lispenard as the seller."

Hays sighed. "I'm sure I should ask how you know about the contents of a file that should by all rights be safe under lock and key in the offices of Robert Shard, attorney-at-law."

"Better for both of us if you don't." Justy picked up his glass, and drank it off. Armagnac, thick with sugar and heavy with the taste of Normandy apples. The liquor spread like an oil slick across his tongue and burned a long trail down into the pit of his stomach. He exhaled heavily, tears in his eyes and the afterburn from the liquor scalding the roof of his mouth.

Hays chuckled. "Not bad, eh? Liberated a case of it from a French privateer last year. I pay Sam here rent, and he keeps his mouth shut for me. Another?"

"Why not?"

Hays refilled the glass. "So. Why buy a swathe of marshland that'll take decades to make fit for development?"

"Precisely because of that. The surveyors will tell the Commission that the marshes are practically useless. Which means the city's development plans won't include them. So no one will give a damn who owns them. They'll be worth next to nothing. But what would happen if, in just five years' time, those lands turned out to be suitable for development after all?"

"In five years? They'd be worth a fortune. But how, exactly, would that come to pass?"

Justy leaned forward. "I was up on the Broad Way the other day. There's a great view down over Canvas Town, if you ever care to look. It's hard to pick out the boundaries of the compound, but I noticed a few things. The first is that our friend Umar has extended his walls quite a way north. Much further than you'd think possible, given the marsh. The second is that there are people working the marshlands and the meadow inland."

"Fishing for eels?"

"Perhaps. But they didn't look like eelers to me. It looked like they were digging."

Hays sipped. "Go on."

"Umar told me that he escaped from a coastal island in the Carolinas. There are rice plantations there, whose owners buy slaves from parts of Africa where they've been growing rice for generations, using some very specific techniques. Like land drainage. And flood control."

A slow smile spread across Hay's face. "The sneaky devil! He's draining the meadowlands, right under our noses."

"And not just the meadows. The papers in Shard's office suggest he has his eye on the Collect Pond, too."

Hays laughed. "He's mad. You remember what people said about poor Jacob Brown when he proposed the same thing last year. They laughed him out of committee!"

Justy shrugged. "We know how to reclaim land along the waterfront well enough. Why not do the same thing with the Collect? Turn Hudson's Kill into a canal to channel water from the pond to the river, and just fill the damned thing in."

Hays snorted. "And where the hell would you get enough sand to fill in the pond? Drag it up from the river? Perhaps you'd level Bayard's Mount?"

"I'm not an engineer. But I'm sure Umar has some idea."

Hays sipped his Armagnac. "Very well, then. Say you have this correct, that Umar has bought the meadowlands and plans to make them developable. Where does Riker come in?"

"His fingers are stuck into several parts of the pie. The Millennium Bank is the guarantor of the sale. It lent Umar ninety percent of the purchase price. Riker got Chase Beaulieu a job as a surveyor, more than likely to keep him apprised of how the chief surveyor would classify the meadows. Perhaps even to have Beaulieu survey them himself, and pronounce them undevelopable. Finally, Riker's carriage has been making regular trips up and down to the compound, several times a week. Quite often with a property lawyer on board."

Hays sniffed. "It's all very circumstantial."

"I agree, it is. Until you consider that the lawyer in question is Robert Shard."

Hays blinked. "You're telling me the very man tasked with ratifying and approving the purchases of land in the State of New York is acting as a land agent to a runaway slave? How in God's name is that happening?"

"Well, Shard's a Puritan, but I'm told he has a yen for the seamier attractions of the city. I think Riker found out, and blackmailed him into helping Umar buy the land."

"So that Riker can then buy the land from Umar at a later date?"

"He might do that, although I'm willing to bet that if the plan is to buy from Umar, the deal has already been done, and Riker will just need to back-date the papers, once the moratorium on land purchases has expired. Or, Umar could simply default on his loan, making the Millennium Bank the owner. Then Riker could buy the land from the bank in five years' time."

"At a nice discount."

"No doubt."

Hays nodded. "I see the sense of it. But it's damned risky. What if he gets caught?"

"By whom? You said yourself, no one's going to investigate Riker. He's too powerful."

Hays nodded again, slower this time, as though he was tasting the theory. "This is all very well. But what does Umar get?"

"I don't know. It's the one part of this I can't work out."

"Money?"

"I'm sure, but there has to be more. Perhaps Umar really does have an eye on draining the Collect and building a new compound there."

"It would hardly increase the value of the land if a fort full of Negroes were camped on the edge of it."

Justy shrugged. "I can't think of anything else."

Hays sat in the silence, thinking. "So what can you prove?"

"It depends on Shard. A man like that might prefer to die than stand up in court and confess the kinds of sins he's being blackmailed for. But we can squeeze him a little, to see if he'll talk."

Hays held his glass up to the wan light coming though the grubby window and examined the liquid. "You have built quite a case, Justice. Despite my instructions."

"The evidence—"

"Hang the evidence. You had it out for young Riker over the girl. You just happen to have scraped this up instead."

"I think the two might still be connected."

Hays drained his glass.

"I look forward to seeing what contortions you perform to prove it."

THIRTY-TWO

Thursday

Justy breakfasted on a sweet roll bought from a pannam-fencer on the Broad Way. He ate on the hoof, walking up to the Almshouse, drawing up a list of questions in his head for Robert Shard, attorney-at-law. But when he arrived, the lawyer was still unconscious.

"He wakes up occasionally," Sister Marie-Therese said. Shard had kicked his blankets loose, and the vestal gestured at a novice to pull them back over his feet.

"Does he say anything?" Justy asked.

"Oh, terrible things." Lars stood behind them, orange stubble on his face and scalp, and black bags under his eyes. He grinned. "The temptations of the flesh, the fires of hell. The Devil himself."

Sister Marie-Therese's face was bright red. "And where have you been, Captain Hokkanssen? You've had us tearing this place apart looking for you."

"Did I not say I'd be going out last night, Sister?"

"You did not. And if you had, we would not have permitted it. This is not a hostel for you to come and go as you please." She sniffed. "And where did you go?"

"Just out for a bit of snap."

"For a drink, more like."

He shrugged. "Well, I feel fit enough."

"Consider yourself discharged, then. And whatever befalls you, it's on your own head."

They watched her walk away, her bonnet like a sail in a full wind.

"God save me from landlords and sisters of mercy," Lars muttered. "Now let's get out of it."

They went down into the street, Justy limping slightly, and Lars with his jaw clenched as the stitches in his side pulled with every step.

"Look at the hack of the two of us," the sailor said, when they reached the bottom of the staircase. "Soft as curds."

"Tell me about Shard. Did he make any kind of sense?"

"In the end. Once I'd given him a nip."

"You're joking."

"I am not, indeed. I've seen enough men with the fever of drink to recognize a fellow that's suffering from the lack of it. He woke up at midnight, so I sat him up and handed him the flask and encouraged him to unburden himself. And I'm a good listener, as you know."

"So what did he tell you?"

"A whole mess of things. The plain religion, his marriage, the temptation, the girls. All of that he said was well enough disposed to deal with on his conscience, he said, until the Devil came. It got a bit dark after that."

"Oh yes?"

"He said the Devil made him do terrible things to one girl. Unspeakable things. And then he held those acts over him and made him break the law, over and over, until he was so deep in the pit there was no getting out." He paused. "That grim look on your face tells me you know what he's talking about."

"I think so. Did the Devil have a name?"

"No."

Hardluck pulled the carriage up to the curb. Lars opened the door. "Come on. We need to go see your uncle."

"Why's that?"

"Well, after I said good night to Shard, I took a wander down to the Buttered Bun. Lizzie Toms told me your uncle's looking to settle things over that ruck the other night. Sharpening the knives, she said."

Justy groaned. "Jesus, that's all we need. A pitched battle between Owens and the Bull. We may as well just set fire to the city ourselves."

"Well, that's the interesting part. Owens isn't the one your uncle's after. In fact, Lizzie told me the two of them are teaming up. To go after your man Umar."

"Of course." Justy felt a queasy sensation. "Any idea when?"

"No." Lars hauled himself aboard. He held out his hand to Justy. "But if the working girls know about it, I'd say that means sooner rather than later."

There was no barrier laid across the top of Dover Street, but the moment Hardluck began to make the turn, a man stepped out and grabbed one of the horses by the bridle.

"Get on away out of it, Snowdrop." The man waved a thick length of wood. "There's no one comes down here today."

Justy climbed out of the cab. The man was young and tough, and puffed up by his position. But he was not used to dealing with the quality, and while he would have sent an ordinary citizen packing with a clip around the head, Justy's sleek carriage and tailored clothes made him pause.

"So what is it? A pothole being fixed? Or did a cart shed its load?" Justy asked.

The man looked confused. "Wha'?"

Lars leaned out the cab window. "He wants to know why you've closed the road, son."

"You don't need to know the reason why. You just need to get on out of it."

Justy said, "Do you know the penalty for blocking one of the city's thoroughfares without cause?"

"I know I'll give you a thick ear if you don't fuck off and quickly."

Justy smiled. "I'm a city Marshal, lad, and the beaks don't take well to having officers of the law insulted and assaulted. But if you step back now, I'll let you away with that flagrant display of disrespect. Take a swing at me, though, and you'll end up in Newgate."

Lars grinned. "I'd listen to him, if I was you, son."

But the young man was committed. He hefted the length of wood in his hand, expecting Justy to take one look at it and run. Instead Justy drove himself forward, crouching slightly, fists up.

The man's eyes widened, and he swung. Justy leaned backwards to let the stave hiss past his nose. He grabbed the man's forearm and shoved hard, driving him into a pirouette that twisted the man's left ankle and sent him sprawling on the hard-packed stone.

Lars clapped. "Looks like Owney Clearey taught you a thing or two after all."

"Don't get up," Justy warned the man. But he sprang to his feet, red in the face and breathing hard. He raised the stave, but Justy was already nose-to-nose with him, grabbing his wrist and holding it in the air while he rammed his knee up hard into the man's groin.

The man folded into the gutter. Justy stepped back to see a small crowd of men in waistcoats and farmer's caps crowding the entrance to the street.

"Move out of it."

A man pushed his way to the front. He was tall and broad-shouldered, with a long-skirted black riding coat that flapped around him. His graying hair curled over a forehead bumped with pustules, and a nose that looked as though an oxcart had driven over it.

The young man pulled himself to his feet. "I'm sorry, Mister O'Toole, I—"

O'Toole hammered the side of his bunched fist into the man's temple. The man's eyes rolled up in his head and he went down again, like a fresh-cut tree.

"Justice," O'Toole said, as though they were just passing on the street.

"O'Toole."

"What do you want?"

"I'm here to see my uncle."

"No one passes. Not today. Not even you."

"You can't just block roads in this city when you feel like it."

O'Toole sneered. "I'll remind you, son, this here's the waterfront, which means it belongs to the Bull, not those noddies you work with up by Federal Hall. The Bull put up these buildings and he paved these roads. If we'd have waited for your lot to lift a finger, we'd still be sloshing about in our own filth. So if the Bull wants to close a street for a day, in his part of the town, he'll damned well do it."

He had a point. Since the war, the city fathers had deliberately ignored the poorer parts of the city, and lavished all their attention on the new developments north and east of the city, out to Corlears Hook and along the Bowery. Canvas Town and the East River waterfront, where the immigrants lived, got nothing. But the Bull realized that by diverting some of the river of dirty money that flowed along the waterfront into some improvements bought him goodwill and protection. So he paved the roads with stolen stone, and repaired the warehouses with pilfered timber. And the people loved him for it.

"Fair enough. But I still want to see my uncle."

"Well, he doesn't want to see you. So you'd best fuck off. And don't try going around the back, for my lads have orders to break the arms of any man trying to pass."

O'Toole's face was like a wall, but the men behind him were smirking.

"I know what you're planning," Justy said. "You and the Bull and Owens."

"We're planning to get my daughter back safe, Justice. Your uncle's god-daughter. That black bastard Owens' cousin. Family."

Justy shook his head. "This isn't about Kerry. You and I both know she's just an excuse."

"If you've come to lend a hand, Justice, you're welcome." O'Toole's eyes were as flat and hard as the ice on a Mayo marsh in winter. "But if not, you'd best stand aside while we deal with those filthy heathens."

Justy laughed. "Heathens, is it? And when was the last time you were in church?"

He knew the answer to that one. It was nearly twenty years ago, the day O'Toole's wife had died giving birth to Kerry. O'Toole had taken the squall-ing baby down to St. Peter's church, wrapped her in a piece of green silk, and left her on the altar. And then he went to get drunk.

O'Toole's face shifted in what might have been a smile. "I don't need some cock in a cassock to tell me what's unholy and what's not. These filthy devils are like a gangrened hand. You've to cut it off and burn the stump, if the dis-ease isn't to spread."

"Very poetic." But Justy knew O'Toole didn't speak in riddles. If he talked about cutting and burning, it meant that he fully intended to gut every man, woman, and child in the compound like so many fish, and then reduce the whole thing to ashes.

Justy felt the frustration well up in him. Even if he could put O'Toole down, there were too many others to fight, and he couldn't order Hardluck to try to force the carriage through. The Bull's men would cut the ligaments on the backs of the horses' legs and then slice their bellies open. And then they would pull Hardluck off the cab and do the same to him.

He took a step backwards and his shoe slid on a loose stone. His leg bent awkwardly and O'Toole laughed. "You look crocked, Justice."

Justy felt the blood rush into his face as he remembered his mad dash after Riker's carriage, and then his undignified, painful sprawl in the street. He thought about how the gleaming blue cab had looked as it rounded the corner, its pennants jaunty in the wind. He smiled to himself.

He nodded at the young man lying in the street. "Don't be too hard on the lad, O'Toole. He was just doing his job."

O'Toole sneered. "I don't need to be hard on him. He got dropped by a crocked cossack. He's going to have to live that down every day for the rest of his puff."

Justy turned his back on the crowd. Lars was still leaning out of the carriage. He gave Justy a sympathetic look. "I suppose we'll have to do this ourselves then, *a chara*."

"Aye," Justy said. "I suppose we will."

THIRTY-THREE

"This is a bad idea," Lars said.

They were driving as fast as they could up the Broad Way. The sky was swollen and a light rain was making the driving conditions as bad as they could be. The water on the cobbles mixed with dirt and dung and formed an ooze. A heavy rain would wash it away, but soft weather like this just turned the streets into a treacherous slick of lumpy stone, on which a horse might turn a hoof, or a wheel might slip.

Justy pulled on the sash that opened the window, letting the cool, moist air into the cab. He felt rain on his face.

"It'll work," he said. Although he had no idea whether it would.

It was his memory of the switches bobbing on the back of Riker's coach like an insult that had given him the idea. They had hurried back to Hughson's and he had written two notes, one for Gorton, and the other for Hays that one of Tully's serving boys went to carry to the Federal Hall. Hardluck went hunting, first rummaging in the tavern's rubbish tip, and then out into Canvas Town. It was a half hour before he returned, a huge smile on his face and the two switches clutched in his hand, their long, jaunty pennants still attached.

The pennants bounced at the back of the carriage as it bumped up the Broad Way. Hardluck was hunched on the top of the cab, his cloak on, and his hood up.

"I don't see how," Lars said. "We're just going to drive in there and set to? Me with a fin that I can barely flap and you with a dodgy stump?"

"I'm not aiming to get into a tilt. And if we do, it won't just be the two of us. I've told Gorton to get a crew together. And we'll have Hardluck."

"Oh aye, I'm sure he'll be happy to fight and die for his master."

Justy was stung. "He's not a slave, god damn it!"

"Oh, he's not?" Lars feigned surprise. "I must have been at rug when you paid a visit to the beak, then."

"I promised to free him. But I've been a little pressed for time, in case you hadn't noticed."

"I've noticed you enjoying bouncing about in this fancy rattler."

Justy hammered on the roof of the cab. They stopped. Justy reached over Lars and opened the door. "Get out."

Lars looked startled. "What?"

"Get out." Justy's voice was hard. "If you're not happy with the way I'm going about things, then I'd rather you weren't with me at all."

"I'm only saying—"

"I don't give a damn what you're saying, Lars. I'm trying to help Kerry, and you've not come up with any bright ideas, so I'm going ahead with the best plan I can think of. Unless you've got something else to say, you can get the hell on out of it."

Lars' jaw tightened. "I'll tell you what I have to say. And you'll damned well listen, if you know what's good for you."

"Go on, then."

"You may be right about getting us into that place. They might be fooled into thinking this is Riker's rig. No doubt the weather will help with that. And no doubt your man Gorton will show up with some handy lads who'll help us when the time is right."

"Well, then?"

Lars leaned forward. "Well, what I'm not prepared to watch is you grabbing up some dumb cull and using that chive of yours to persuade them to tell us where Kerry is."

Justy felt himself redden. "You've a better idea? Because I've not heard it, if you do."

"Listen to me, Justy," Lars' voice was soft. "You know this is a bad thing you're thinking of. No good will come of it."

"I don't plan to cut the cully open, Lars." The image of the girl in the alley flashed in his mind. He imagined the boy holding his knife, the razor-sharp end of the blade making a smooth, even cut, the tears flowing down the boy's face. He shivered.

Lars was looking at him, his eyes soft. "Let me do it, *a chara*. Will you promise me?"

The rain was loud on the cobbles. People were hurrying past, clamping their hats to their heads. A gust of wind slapped rainwater off the back of the cab. He felt the mist on his face.

He reached over his friend, and hauled on the leather pull on the door. He knocked on the roof of the cab again, Hardluck flicked the reins, and they moved on up the hill towards Jericho.

By the time they reached Jericho, the rain was pounding the city and turning the unpaved roads to mud. The sentry was huddled in the entryway, swathed in a sodden cape. He squinted up at the black carriage, at the driver hunched on top, and he waved them in.

Justy assumed the compound would have the kind of layout that most houses have to handle traffic inside their walls: a route to a stabling area for the homeowner's own carriages, and a turning circle and waiting area for vehicles staying only a short time.

It had neither. Once they had made the hard turn through the chicane, the carriage halted. Justy pulled the curtain aside an inch and peered out. They were in a kind of large box, perhaps three times the width of the carriage, and less than twice as long. There was no way out.

The cab jolted as Hardluck jumped down. He tapped at the door. His cloak was drenched, but he seemed not to notice the rain as it hammered on his head and poured in a stream through one of the folds in his hat. Justy pulled the sash of the window downwards an inch.

"You have to unharness the horses and spin the rig, sir." Hardluck had to speak loudly because of the roar of the rain on the roof of the carriage. "Then harness them again after."

"A two-man job?"

"Yes, sir. There's a passage at the front of us, wide enough for a horse to pass, but no way to get this thing down it."

It made sense. Umar and his people likely didn't use anything larger than a handcart, so they had built an entrance to their fortress that denied access to anything larger. The turning box gave the most basic accommodation to any visitor that might own a carriage, but as Justy thought about it, he realized it might not even have been built for that purpose. It was similar to the atrium-like entrances to the medieval castles that he had visited in England and Ireland, designed to draw the enemy in and concentrate them in a place where they could be assaulted from above.

Lars peered up through the opposite window. "I'm bracing myself for the boulders and boiling oil." He grinned. "But I don't see anyone out there. You?"

Justy shook his head. He had gambled that they would drive into the center of the compound, or at least to a place where there would be some foot traffic. He had planned to snatch someone up and question them about where Kerry was. But no one would be out in this rain.

Unless they had to be.

"The sentry," he said.

Lars stared at him. "You're cracked. You can't just snag the man in broad daylight."

"Well, it may as well be the middle of the night. Everyone's indoors, trying to keep warm and dry, and they'll stay that way until this stops. Which doesn't give us long."

He stepped out of the carriage. The four walls of the box were about ten feet high, with the wide entrance behind them, and the narrow exit in front. A neat trap.

"Which hand did he wave you in with, Hardluck?"

The jarvie thought for a moment. "His right."

"So we go at him together. Hard and fast. You'll be slightly ahead of me, and slightly to the right, so you'll be a bigger target, and the first in line. He'll go for you, and I'll come at him from the flank with this."

He had taken the knife out of his pocket, and he snapped it open. Hardluck's eyes opened wide at the sight of the sprung steel appearing like magic in the air.

Justy grinned at the expression on the driver's face. The blood was powering through him now, thumping in his temples and his chest, making his legs tremble. "Take your whip. Make it look like a staff. He'll come at you hard, but don't worry. I'll stop him."

They moved off, Hardluck in the lead, his cloak billowing slightly. As they rounded the back of the carriage and moved down the narrow passage of the entrance chicane, the rain slackened. Justy was about to urge Hardluck on, but the driver was already running, the cloak on his back like the wings of a huge raven taking off into the rain, obscuring Justy's view.

And then he stopped.

Justy thrust past him, but there was nothing to do. The sentry was already on his knees in the mud, his hands clawing at his face, blood running down his cheeks.

Hardluck coiled his whip and tucked it back into his belt. He and Justy picked the man up and hurried him back along the passageway. They tumbled him inside the cab. Lars stared.

"Not me," Justy said. He jerked his head at Hardluck. "This one. With his switch."

The man was whimpering. Justy held his wrists and pulled them away from his face. For a moment, he thought the man might have lost an eye, perhaps even both of them. But then he saw how truly skilled Hardluck was. The end of the whip had slashed across the man's forehead, so that the blood had come down in a sheet into the man's eyes, blinding him.

Lars grunted his appreciation. "Makes you wonder what he'd be like with a blade."

Justy sat beside him, facing the man, the three of them in a tight triangle, the sound of breathing loud in the cab, rainwater dripping onto the floor and soaking into the upholstery.

Lars pulled a grubby strip of linen out of his coat pocket and used it to wipe away the blood.

"See now?" His voice was a low rumble. "You're not blinded. Just a wee bit cut, is all. Nothing a soft bandage and a good rest won't see to."

The man's shoulders slumped with relief. And then he tensed up again, as Justy produced his knife and pressed the catch in the handle, and the blade snapped up, like a long, pale flame in the gloom of the carriage. He pressed a finger to his lips. "Not a word, cully. Not a sound, unless you want me to take your eyes for sure."

The sentry was a big man, about six feet tall, swarthy, with a shaved head and face that had about a week's growth of stubble all over it. He swallowed, his eyes on the dancing blade, and Lars leaned forward. "He's not playing with you, pal. I've seen him do things with yon chive. Terrible things. Don't make me leave him alone with you."

The man swallowed again, and then his face hardened, and he spat on the floor of the cab. He stared at Lars, his chin tilted upwards. Defiant eyes.

Lars sighed. "Oh, for heaven's sake, man. You don't even know what I want yet."

"It does not matter what you want." The man's voice was hoarse, sharp with an accent that Justy did not recognize. "You will know nothing from me."

"All right, then." Lars leaned back in his seat. "Cut him."

Justy gritted his teeth. He had hoped that he would sit, silently intimidating their captive, while Lars persuaded him to talk. But he could see that Lars understood that they had no time for finesse. The sentry's absence would be noticed soon enough, and someone would surely spot the carriage before long. They had minutes, at most.

Justy flicked the blade. The man shuddered and closed his eyes, but the tip of the blade dropped and sliced through the string that held his cape in place. The sodden material fell away, revealing a kind of long, loose smock worn over a pair of loose trousers. The man exhaled heavily, and the carriage was filled with the stench of garlic and onions.

"In the storehouse, behind the workroom," he said.

Justy was repelled by the vague sense of disappointment he felt. "What's there?"

"The woman. The prisoner."

Silence in the cab. The rain had all but stopped. The sentry stared. Lars raised his eyebrows.

Justy watched the man, his thumb stroking the blade of his knife. He knew how persuasive the promise of pain could be, but the sentry had given up the goods too fast. Which meant he had been primed. Which meant that Umar had expected some kind of attack, and anticipated the man would be snatched up and interrogated.

It was a trap. The fact the man had immediately told them about a woman prisoner suggested that Umar knew who she was. And the fact that he told them she would be in a storeroom behind a workhouse suggested Umar knew who would come to find her. Someone who knew where both workhouse and storeroom were located. As Justy did.

He felt a cold anger spill through him. His eyes focused on the sentry's. He felt his throat close, and it was suddenly hard to breathe. A sharp pain in his hand made him look down. Blood dripped from a wound on his thumb. He stuck his thumb in his mouth. Felt for the cut. Let the coppery taste of his own blood slide over his tongue. He looked the sentry in the eye again.

"Lars?"

"Aye."

"Get out."

A pause. "I will not."

"You will, Lars. And you'll do it now. This fellow has a good deal more to tell us. And we've no time to waste. So you'll step out, like a good man. And let me go to work."

He was cool now, the sweat like a band of ice on his forehead. He could feel the grain in the handle of the knife.

"Don't, Justy."

"Get out. Now."

The sentry's Adam's apple bobbed like a fishing float. His eyes flickered back and forth between Justy and Lars.

Lars shrugged and turned to reach for the door handle.

"No!" The man's voice was hoarse. "Don't leave me with him."

Lars waited. "Give me a good reason."

The man's eyes were oscillating between the tip of the knife and Justy's eyes. "Abu Umar is waiting. He knows you have been planning an attack."

"How does he know?" Lars' voice was sharp.

"He has spies."

"And where is the woman?"

"Where I said. In the storehouse. With the others."

"Which others?"

The man looked confused. "The other women."

Justy forced himself not to look at Lars, to keep his eyes on the sentry.

Lars said, "How many men? What weapons?"

The man said nothing.

"Very well, then." Lars opened the door, and a rush of cool air swept into the cab. Justy took a deep breath, and readied himself.

"Fifty men." The man's eyes were shut tight. "Knives, swords, and firearms." His eyes snapped open. He stared at Lars. "Please!"

"Fifty firearms?" Lars sounded skeptical.

"I am not lying, I swear!"

"What's the plan?"

"To wait out of sight until all your men are in the square. And then to attack from above, and from the sides."

"Nothing between here and there?"

The man shook his head, his eyes pleading. "Some lookouts. Children. But that is all."

Lars twisted hard in his seat. His elbow cracked the sentry on the temple, and the man slumped like a sack of rice.

He glanced at Justy, a somber look. "Well?"

Justy avoided his eye. His face burned. "They're expecting a bigger force."

"Aye." Lars chewed over what the sentry had told them. "You think he's telling the truth about where Kerry is?"

"Why keep her anywhere else? It would only take more men to guard her. She's a lure."

"We're stroked, then. The three of us against fifty armed hackums? We've no chance."

"Maybe." Justy folded his knife away carefully. "But Umar's braced for a company attack. He won't attack one man."

Lars laughed, drily. "You're willing to take that risk? To just stroll out of here and into the killing ground?"

"I'd say I'd be safe enough. He won't want to show his hand."

"And what then?"

"And then we ask him to hand Kerry over. Convince him it's in his interests to avoid a tilt with Owens and the Bull."

"Convince him."

"I don't see why not. A firefight's in no one's best interest."

Lars acknowledged the point with a grunt. "Right then. But you're not going alone. Hardluck and me'll be behind you."

Justy shook his head. "I can't ask Hardluck to risk his neck more than he has already. And you can't come either. Not with that wound of yours."

Lars reached forward and took the knife from Justy's hand. "I can't see Hardluck staying put back here," he said. The blade flicked up, and he used it to cut the bandage that bound his right arm right against his chest. The arm came free and he flexed his fingers. He handed the knife back to Justy, hilt first.

"As for me, I suppose I'll just have to bleed."

THIRTY-FOUR

The rain had stopped. Justy led the way out of the turning box and into the alley. Lars and Hardluck walked a yard behind him, one on each shoulder. The high walls hemmed them in, and it was an effort to resist cringing over, bracing for an assault from above. Justy could feel the eyes on him. Men watching from high on the walls, doubtless armed and equipped with stones and brickbats, ready to hurl them down on an invader.

Except that a disciplined defender would not attack the vanguard of an invading force. And Justy had no doubt that Umar was a disciplined man. He would have instructed his people to wait until as many invaders as possible were concentrated in a killing ground, to inflict maximum damage. The men on the walls above the turning box were there not to stop men coming in, but to prevent them from getting out again.

The passage opened out onto the wide-open area that Justy had walked around with Umar. He noted the small accommodation building, the kitchen, and the building where he had seen the silent women in their colored shawls.

His hands were shaking. Lars was right. What he was doing was insane. But sometimes it was the madmen that seemed to have it right. He had seen men, crazed with drink and fear, run alone at a line of redcoats. They had disappeared into the cloud of gun smoke and somehow emerged unscathed.

But then what?

He stopped. "This is as far as you go, boys. Stay here and keep your glimms wide for me. Squeak beef if you see anything peery."

Lars shifted in the shadows behind him. "There's nothing I can say to stop this windmill in your head, I suppose."

"I'll be all right, so long as I'm on my sneak. A man on his own is no threat to anyone. But two or three of us in a clutch might draw fire from some nervous cully."

Lars grunted. "And what if you go in and don't come out?"

"Wait until the five o'clock bell. Then you know what to do." He squared his shoulders and stepped into the empty space. His shoes were loud on the loose, gravelly surface of the yard. He could feel the stones through the thin soles. He wondered if his boots had been mended yet. Then he wondered if he would ever get to wear them again.

It was only a few yards to the door of the workhouse, but it felt like a quarter mile. He imagined thumbs pushing down on hammers up on the ramparts of the walls around him. Fifty men. Fifty muskets. He wondered how well Umar's men could shoot.

The Bull and Owens might field a hundred men. Fifty musket balls fired into a crowd that large, crammed into a space this small, would create havoc. Many would miss. Some of the muskets might not even fire, thanks to the wet weather. But the shock would be enough to create panic in the invader's ranks. Some would hold, but the rest would be fighting with each other to get out. Then Umar's men could close in with edged weapons, and cut them to pieces.

The door to the workhouse was made of two wide planks of heavy, dark wood that had been sanded and oiled, then caulked together and painted with resin. The glossy surface was beaded with rainwater. He could see his face in the varnish, and, behind him, the late afternoon sun struggling to break through the clouds.

For a moment, he considered knocking. But then he grasped the handle of the door, the iron cold and wet on his palm. He pressed down on the smooth surface of the latch and felt the bolt snap out of its housing. He pulled the door open.

———◆———

The room looked smaller in the dim light. It was empty, filled with bolts of colored cloth that lined the walls and were stacked to the ceiling. Justy walked across the room to the storeroom door and pulled it open. The room inside was small and square.

Umar sat at a small table, dressed in his white robe. The bodyguard with the scarred face stood behind him. A weapon dangled from a strap around his wrist, a long, straight piece of sharpened metal, crude and brutal, like a cross between a large knife and a short sword. There was a single candle on the table, and a strong smell of incense in the room.

Umar was eating an apple, cutting slices with a sharp, narrow table knife, and spearing them with an old-fashioned, long-tined fork. The skin around his eyes crinkled as he chewed. "You are a brave man, Marshal."

"I was counting on your ability to control your people."

Umar acknowledged the compliment with a nod. "They will do nothing until they are told."

"Until you have all of Owens' and the Bull's men in your trap."

"If they are unwise enough to fall into it. But your uncle is a cautious man. And Owens is no fool."

Justy stepped into the room and let the door swing closed behind him. "You can stop this."

"I can? How?" Umar sounded amused.

"Let me take Kerry out of here. When I show them I have her, that she's safe, they'll have no excuse to attack you."

Umar chuckled. "They don't need an excuse. The O'Toole girl is a convenience for them both. A rallying cry. But she is beside the point."

"And the point is?"

Umar spread his arms. "This. Us. Our land. Our people. Our religion." His eyes glittered. "It is remarkable, is it not, that Negroes and Irishmen, two peoples that have themselves been so brutally oppressed, can behave the same way to a third people."

"You think they want to kill you just because you're Mohammedan? That's madness."

"Is it?" Umar shrugged. "Perhaps you're right. Perhaps it's merely because they want this land. Or perhaps because they fear that I might lead their people astray, as they see it. Or perhaps they just fear what they do not understand."

"In that case, why provoke them? Why take Kerry O'Toole?"

Umar sat silently for a moment. "Would you like to see her?"

"She's alive, then?"

"Of course. She's no use to me dead."

"I don't see what use to you she is at all."

Umar smiled. He turned and opened the door behind him. Justy followed him into a short passageway with a hard-packed earth floor. The only light came from the storeroom behind them. Umar turned left, and the light all but disappeared. It was like walking into a dark tunnel. The smell of incense was much stronger, mixed with the heavy stench of damp. Justy was vaguely aware of a line of doors on his right, but they were an impression, and nothing more. Umar's bulk was a vague shape in the blackness in front of him. He could feel the bodyguard somewhere behind him. His eyes and ears strained. The roof of the passage pressed down on him. The fear he had felt in the yard returned, scrabbling at his guts.

The shuffling of Umar's slippers on the dirt floor ceased. Justy stopped dead. He realized he was crouching slightly, braced for some kind of attack.

Umar pulled a door open, and a triangle of soft light fell into the passageway. Kerry sat on a low cot inside a cell, straight-backed, her legs crossed. Light came from a pair of thick candles, set in sconces on the low walls either side of the tiny room. A man sat on a small bench, close to the door. The candlelight shone on the tattoos on his face. He carried the same weapon as Umar's guard, a brutal, ugly strip of hammered, sharpened steel.

"Inside, Marshal," Umar said.

Justy weighed his options. Umar and the man behind him in the tunnel had trapped him. He could stab Umar and run, but he had no idea where the tunnel led, and the two hackums would be on him faster than rats on a dying dog. Three against one in a dark, unfamiliar place were no odds at all, really.

He stepped into the room. The bodyguard stood up quickly and patted down his pockets. He took out the knife and handed it wordlessly to Umar. Umar weighed it for a moment, and tucked it into the folds of his robe.

"What now?" Justy asked.

"Now we wait." And Umar let the door swing closed in his face.

THIRTY-FIVE

The bodyguard stared. Justy stared back. It was like trying to look through a wall, or a cliff face. The man stood, loose-limbed and easy, holding the long, brutal blade across his body, blade upwards, the handle in his right hand, and the back of the blade cradled in his left.

Justy turned to Kerry. "Are you all right?"

She rolled her eyes. "Come to save me again, have you?"

The anger flared in him. "Jesus, Kerry! Do you not know what's happening here?"

Her eyes burned with contempt. "I ken a sight more than you do, ye clunch. You haven't the first bloody clue."

The look she gave him, fear and anger mixed, was like a bucket of cold water. The low cot squeaked as he sat down.

The guard stepped backwards, pushed open the door with his shoulder and stepped into the dark passage outside. The latch clicked into place, and the door creaked as the man leaned his weight against the wood.

"Does he speak?" Justy asked.

"He has no tongue."

"Well, at least we don't have to worry about him prattling on at us."

Her mouth twitched slightly, and he saw her relax a little. She was wearing the same dress he had seen her in at the gathering. It was a little more crumpled, and a little grubbier, but she still looked good. "So are you all right?"

She shrugged. "No harm done. Except to my pride."

He watched her, until he was sure she was telling him the truth. "I'm glad to see you."

She smiled a little. "Aye, well. Me too."

He glanced at the door. "So how long is it since you practiced your Irish?"

"*Is fearr Gaeilge briste, na Bearla cliste.*" An old phrase: Broken Irish is better than clever English.

"You're right about that," he said, in the same language. "So did you find anything out?"

"You mean, did I do your bloody job for you?"

It was his turn to shrug.

"Well, I did, as it happens," she murmured. "The girl is from here. Her mother spoke to me."

"What did she say? Why didn't she come to claim the girl?"

Kerry snorted. "She's a woman, is why. And women aren't allowed to do anything in this place except sew shawls, cook food, and launch kinchin. They sure as mutton can't go strolling about the streets, visiting with nuns and Marshals and the like."

"And the father?"

Kerry raised her eyebrows. "Her father is the man himself."

"Umar? But why would he not want to claim her?"

"Because he doesn't want people sniffing around this place. And certainly not the law."

"But his own daughter?"

Kerry scowled. "She stopped being kin the moment she filled her pannier. She was worthless to him. And a traitor to his religion. Or his way of practicing it, at least."

Justy sat and thought for a while. "Does the mother know who killed her?"

"No."

"Might it have been Umar?"

"I'd not put it past him, what with all the other things he does in here. But she says not."

"And what does he do in here?"

"It's a baby mill." Her voice was flat. "He has a crew of women go out and recruit young doxies who want to get away from their pimps. White girls. He gives them a load of patter about the true religion, and says they'll have more money than they could dream about. Then he makes them cut with charas, and shuts them up in here."

"Charas?"

"Some kind of drug. You put a ball of it in a silver dish, and heat it with a candle. The smoke makes you feel candy, like you've drunk a whole bottle of geneva at once. And when you wake up the next day, it's like your napper's been cracked wide open. The only thing that makes you feel better is more charas."

"They're drunk on it."

"As David's sow. So Umar can do what he wants with them. And what he wants is little white kinchin."

"What does he want white babies for?"

"Because white ones fetch a higher price, you fool."

"Jesus." His head was reeling. He sat for a while, staring at the door.

She put her hand on his. He was surprised by how cool it felt. How smooth her fingers were.

"We have to get out of here," he said.

"You don't think I've been thinking about that since I got shut up?"

"You don't understand. Your cousin's coming for you. And my uncle. They'll have a hundred men or more. But Umar has set a trap, he's got men with muskets. It'll be a bloodbath."

"We'll be safer in here, then."

"You think? If things go his way out there, there's no reason to keep us quick. And the way the Bull is fixed, I don't think he'll be in the mood to accept a ransom. I can't speak for Owens."

"Depends on how many men he loses."

"Aye. And Umar has fifty barkers. Maybe more."

She was quiet.

"What?" he said.

"I can't go. Not without Tanny. The girl I came in with. Umar has her locked up somewhere. If I pike, he'll hurt her. Badly."

"Where is she?"

Kerry shook her head. "I don't know."

Justy went to the door and put his ear against it. He could hear the sentry breathing on the other side.

"We can't sit here, Kerry. It'll be dark in an about an hour, and that's most likely when Lew and the Bull will attack. We can't be here when that happens."

"But Tanny . . ."

"Tanny is going to be the last thing on Umar's mind when it starts. You'll be the first. He's going to come down here and get you, and you don't want to be here when he does. I'm not saying we forget her. We'll try and find her, but we have to leave here now."

Her face seemed to ripple in the weak light, softening and then hardening. She nodded. "Right, well. How do we get past your man?"

"Is there anything we can use as a weapon?"

"Not unless you fancy breaking up the bed and using the boards."

"I may do just that." Justy smoothed his hand over the wall of the cell. It was the same color as the floor, and appeared to be made of the same hard-packed earth, but as he pushed on it, he felt it give slightly under his palm, and the surface flaked away.

"Roll up the mattress," he whispered. "Double it over, and lay it in front of the door. Then stand to the side."

"What are you going to do?"

"I'm going to use a plank to make a hole in the wall."

"Just like that?"

"I saw some wattle frames outside. They use them instead of bricks, I think. They're pretty flimsy. It shouldn't be too hard."

She made a face. "You don't think he'll hear you?"

"I'm counting on it. He'll be expecting me to try and get a weapon. And he knows the only weapon available to me is the timber in this kip. So he won't come in if he hears me breaking it up. But I'd say me breaking through the wall will be a surprise. He'll try to put a stop to that. And then we'll have him. Is there anything in that bucket?"

She looked at the covered pail in the corner. "Two days' worth."

"Well, let him get halfway in. The mattress will slow him a bit. Make him turn towards you. Scream or something, and then throw that lot in his face. Then I'll crack him one on the napper."

She shuddered. "But that degen of his."

"It's only a knife. Don't look at it. Right now we're worth more to Umar alive than dead, so he won't want to use it. Are you set?"

He stared at her. Her eyes tightened as she gripped herself. Her chin tilted up. "Just make sure you put him down."

"I will."

They tilted the bed over gently. She folded the thin mattress, and heaped it up beside the door. Justy nodded. The guard might trip on it or he might not, but it would definitely slow him.

The cot was a frame made of pieces of old salvage wood, nailed hastily together, with loose planks nailed on top. The wood was oak, but it was thin and weathered, with smears of old pitch on the edges.

Justy wanted one of the sides of the frame of the cot. They were the sturdiest, hardest parts, and therefore the best for use, both as a bludgeon to punch a hole in the wall of the cell, and as a weapon. He gripped one of the stubby legs of the cot and wiggled at it. It squeaked and groaned as the nails worked their way out. Kerry was standing beside the doorway, the pail in her hand.

The leg came free. Sweat poured down Justy's face. He pulled off his damp coat and went to work on another leg. The squeaking seemed impossibly loud in the small space. The second leg came free, and now he had a five-foot length of oak in his hand. He kicked away the flimsy nailed planks and thrust the end of the spar at the wall. There was a loud thump, and the mud cladding splintered around the end of the spar. He hammered again, and the spar punched into the wall, through the frame and the mud and the wattle behind it and into the space beyond.

A woman cried out. Justy pulled hard, but the spar was stuck fast. The remnants of one of the loose planks had snagged in the hole. He wiggled the spar up and down, and a long crack appeared in the wall, but the spar would not move.

The door to the cell slammed open. The guard rushed inside, and tripped on the mattress. He went sprawling on the remains of the cot, but rolled quickly to one side and was on his feet in an instant. Kerry flung the bucket at him, but he barely blinked. He stood, Kerry's waste running down his face, his cutlass in his right hand. He had fallen on his right shoulder, and the nails from one of the loose planks had gone deep into the muscle. The plank hung loose along his arm. He reached up with his left hand and pulled the plank free. Blood soaked his shirt. His eyes never left Kerry's face.

Justy reversed his grip on the spar that was stuck in the wall. He tilted the spar up and leaned on it as hard as he could. There was a cracking, tearing sound, and the whole wall seemed to fall in. Dust filled the room, snuffing out the candles. It was suddenly pitch black. Justy threw himself across the cell. His left shoulder hit the far wall, and he quarter-turned to where he thought the door might be and hurled himself forward again.

He was gambling that the guard would go for him first, to get rid of the threat and subdue Kerry after. But now he was no longer where the guard thought he would be. Instead, he was behind the guard, bearing down on his back. Hopefully.

He launched himself into the air, his hands in front of him like claws, blindly raking the darkness. His left hand glanced off the guard's back. His right hand missed. His head did not.

It had Justy's entire weight behind it. The solid plate of Justy's brow, backed by one and a half hundredweight of bone and blood and muscle, slammed into the side of the guard's head. The man's ear cushioned the blow a little, the skin splitting like a soft fruit, but the sheer force of the assault threw him onto the ground.

Justy fell with him. Something struck him hard on the back. Someone was screaming. His hands were scrabbling at where he thought the man's head should be. His nails splintered and broke. He felt soft tissue under the index finger of his right hand. An eye. He jammed his finger into the socket and pulled hard. The man reared backwards, making a clotted, guttural sound, and Justy's knees thumped into his side as he scrambled to trap his right arm and the cutlass. He wrenched backwards again, and the eyeball burst under his finger. The man bucked again and screeched and flailed backwards with the cutlass, but Justy was on his back now, and hard to hit, and the blade clattered against the floor and the walls.

It was pitch dark, but Justy squeezed his eyes shut, concentrating on what he was doing. He could picture himself behind the guard, his legs wrapped around him, clinging on like a child playing pick-a-back. He changed his grip, hooking the first and second fingers of his left hand into the man's eye sockets and hauling backwards. He felt the mess of one destroyed eye under one finger, and empty space under the other.

The guard was weakening. He was moaning, but there was still fight in him, as he tried to buck Justy off, and hack at him with the blade. Justy's right hand was free now, and he waited until the guard chopped back, and then caught the man's wrist. He pulled it back until he could feel the man's elbow against his knee and leaned hard until, with a crunch, the joint gave way.

The man made a choking sound, and his arm flopped loose. Justy grabbed the cutlass, tore it loose and hacked it across the man's chest, over and over, until he could feel the blood gushing warm over his hand and the man lay still.

He rolled off, gasping. He was bathed in sweat. He could feel the slime of the man's ruined eye on one hand, his blood on the other. He smelled the iron stink of fresh blood, the stench of shit. He dropped the blade and crawled backwards, away from the body. He rolled over and vomited until his stomach was empty.

"Get up!" Kerry was pulling at his shoulder. She held one of the thick candles in one hand. She looked like a nightmare, her hair in rats' tails, her face and clothes covered in dust.

Justy got to his feet. The guard's body was sprawled in the passage. His chest was a black hole. His eyelids, mercifully, were closed. Kerry pushed her face close. "Are you hurt?"

He shook his head. The light from the candle glinted on the dull blade. He bent to pick it up.

There was a muffled cough. Kerry held up the candle. The light reflected on the eyes of someone in the adjoining cell. She stepped forward, and Justy saw a young girl, dressed in a thin shift, hugging her knees to her chest. Her pale face looked jaundiced in the wan light. Her hair was copper. She looked dully up at them.

"You're all right," Kerry said, softly. "What's your name?"

"Martha."

"Come on, then, Martha. Up you get."

The girl stared, blank-eyed. "Do you have my baby?"

Justy and Kerry looked at each other.

"We can't take her," Justy said.

"We can't very well leave her here. In the dark. With a bloody corpse. She'll go spare."

"What about the other cells? Can we put her in one of them?"

Kerry shrugged. She put her arm around the red-headed girl, and led her carefully out of the ruined room, down the passageway. The girl's legs looked like they were made of matchsticks. Kerry opened the door to the next cell. A dark-haired girl was lying on the bed, the blanket pushed back, her hands folded over her distended belly. Sweat stained the armpits of her shift. She had a cloth laid over her forehead.

"What's all the noise?" Her voice was thick, as though her tongue was swollen.

"Nothing." Kerry pushed the red-headed girl into the room. "This is Martha. She'll be staying with you for a spell."

She closed the door before the girl could speak, and led the way down the passage, away from the storeroom. Justy limped after her. The blade was heavy in his hand. His entire body ached. His eye was swollen where the guard had caught him with the back of his head. And his knee felt as though it had been pulled apart and roughly reassembled by a drunken plumber.

He began counting doors. The passage seemed impossibly long.

"How big is this place?"

"A lot bigger than you think," Kerry said. "They've been building for years, draining the marshland yard by yard."

"How many of them are there?"

"I don't know. I've not seen the whole place. Just the outbuildings. And this hellhole."

They had come to the end of the passageway. Her candle reflected on another resin-varnished door. She waited until he had caught his breath. "Ready?"

THIRTY-SIX

The rainclouds had cleared, and the evening sun had almost slipped below the horizon. It was dusk, but after the pitch black of the cell block, it still took a moment for Justy's eyes to adjust to the light. The door opened onto a small courtyard. Four high walls, with a wooden platform that ran the whole way around the yard, four feet below the top. The platform overhung a number of benches arranged against the walls of the yard, and on the benches sat a group of women, perhaps twenty of them, in robes of every shade of red and blue and brown and green. The women sat silent, their faces covered.

"Umar's womenfolk," Kerry whispered. She was covered from head to foot in dried mud. She looked like one of the witches the old Irish folk told about in their fairy tales. Justy looked down at his own clothes. The entire right side of his body was soaked in blood. The blade was streaked with it. His hand had what looked like raw egg smeared over the back of it.

He followed Kerry, limping on his damaged knee, feeling the eyes of the women on him. This was a second compound. He could see it now. The high walls of the space Umar had shown him screened this second area from view, both from the Broad Way and from the stream north of the marshes. It meant Jericho was twice the size he thought it was. Perhaps even bigger.

They were halfway across the courtyard, and still not one of the women had made a sound.

"Why don't they speak?" he whispered.

Kerry shook her head. "Just keep moving."

He limped on towards the door in the far wall.

It opened, and Gorton stepped through into the yard. He had his coat off, and his sleeves rolled up, and his shirt open at the neck. He had untied his hair, and it tumbled in a gray wave over his shoulders. There was a half smile on his face, a pistol in his belt, and one of the long, crude blades in his hand.

"Evening, Marshal," he said.

Kerry looked back.

Gorton shook his head. "I wouldn't, if I were you, girl. There's a whole platoon of lads back that way. I can't vouch for your safety if you run into them."

Justy was cold. His head was singing. "You scum. You bastard traitor."

"Traitor to who, Marshal? To you? To the great city of New York?"

Justy used his own blade to point at the door behind him. "Do you have any idea what's going on in there? What he's doing?"

"Course I do, jack. It's one of the perquisites." Gorton grinned. "As your titter will be, once I've made you easy."

He stepped forward, spinning the blade in his hand, catching it, spinning it again. The grin was plastered to his face. It didn't make it to his eyes. Justy stepped to the side, away from Kerry, trying to find a line of attack. The odds were long. He was injured; Gorton was not. They were both armed, but he was no swordsman, and Gorton looked strangely comfortable with the wide, brutal blade.

He glanced around, saw nothing but eyes watching him.

"A rum lot, ain't they?" Gorton said. "They waft about the place like ghosts. Won't say a word to a white man, or let him see their face. Not that I gave a damn. I've spent enough time in coal holes to know dark meat ain't to my taste."

He winked at Kerry. "Although I'll make an exception in your case, girl."

He spun the blade in his hand, and Justy lunged, a desperate thrust at Gorton's throat. Gorton rocked back, but recovered fast, his blade swinging up to hit Justy's cutlass a glancing blow that sent it sliding over his shoulder.

Justy stepped back quickly, then right and right again, keeping an eye on Kerry. And then he attacked, driving off his left foot. The two cutlasses crashed together, and Justy was thrown back, his hand numbed by the violence of Gorton's strike. His leg crumpled under him, and Gorton came on with a fast backhand. Justy scrambled back further, into the center of the courtyard, avoiding the blow. He jabbed again, but Gorton twisted sideways and hacked upwards. Justy felt the tip of the blade brush his shirt, just under his chin. He flailed with the cutlass, but his arm was weak and there was no force behind the swing. Gorton caught the back of the blade with his left hand, and used his own cutlass to cut the strap around Justy's wrist. And then he shoved Justy hard, and sent him sprawling.

Gorton's face was bone white. He had switched his cutlass to his left hand, and was holding the pistol in his right. He jammed the muzzle into Justy's temple, forcing his head over. "Scum, am I? You madge. Get up."

Justy got slowly to his feet. Kerry's face was a mask. The women watched, dark-eyed and soundless.

Gorton picked up Justy's cutlass. He smiled his half smile. "You're lucky the chief cock wants the both of you alive."

He motioned with the pistol towards the door he had come through. "You first, missy," he said to Kerry. "And don't try to chouse me, or I'll blow a hole in his backbone."

Kerry pulled the door open. She recognized the comfortable chairs and the dining table with the big pewter box and the five-taper candelabra, fitted with fresh candles, their wicks pointing upright, as straight as soldiers. It was the room where Umar had served her the drugged mint tea.

"Nice, innit? This is where he entertains the nobs. Before they entertain their knobs." Gorton laughed. He dropped the cutlasses by the door. "A nice little side business it could be, if he charged them. Now sit." He nodded towards a chaise placed against one wall. "Side by side."

He sat opposite. His pistol looked oiled and cleaned and well cared for. It was fully cocked, and as steady as a rock in his hand. Justy tried not to look at the black hole of the muzzle. "He doesn't charge them?" he asked.

Gorton shrugged. "Cakey, innit? But I suppose he knows what he's doing."

"Making white babies for sale."

"That's right. And worth their weight in gold they are, too. What's a slave cost these days? Four hundred ducats? Umar's got coves'll pay ten times that for a pale-skinned kinchin-mort. More if they're paying in kind."

"In kind?"

"Aye. Slave captains in Africa will trade twenty grown bucks for one. And we've got twenty girls back there, each turning out a little white chit every twelvemonth. Quite a hallow thing."

Justy thought about the girl he had seen in the cell. The tiny smoke-filled room, her distended belly, the thick sound of her voice.

"How much did it take to buy you?" He let the contempt curdle in his voice.

Gorton smirked. "Well, I didn't come cheap, matey. I've got a neat little share of the business, and a nice fat stipend. Plus use of the facilities when I choose, if you get my meaning."

"And what does Umar get in return?"

"Information. A man on the inside. Someone to take care of any scrapes that might arise."

"Like a girl getting loose from this place."

Gorton smiled faintly. "Aye. Like that."

"Did you kill her?"

The smile disappeared. "I don't kill kinchen."

"But you're happy enough to sell them."

"They do all right. Better than I did when I was a chip."

"And how do you know that?"

"Stands to reason, don't it? The ones he trades with the Africans are like trophies. They won't have to work in the fields or the mines or stand in the ranks with the other cannon fodder. It'll be the best food and a soft bed for them, for the rest of their lives. The color of their skin will see to that. And the ones he sells here? They're made."

Kerry started. "He sells children here? In New York?"

Gorton grinned. "Yes he does, darlin'. Not many, for it's risky and he doesn't want to be caught, but you'd be surprised how many fat culls can't have kinchen of their own. And how much they're willing to cough up for the privilege."

Justy could feel Kerry vibrating beside him, like a mill engine building a head of steam. His own anger seemed to have gone. He smelled his own sweat drying, the blood on his sleeve. He felt the rough silk of the chaise upholstery under his hands. He heard footsteps.

The door opened. Umar stepped inside. The scarred man was behind him. Umar picked up the cutlass Justy had used on the guard in the cell. He stared. "You killed Carthy."

Justy said nothing.

"He was with me from the beginning," Umar said. "We took the boat into the eye of the storm, the three of us. Me, Carthy, and Jason here. The women holding on to each other in the bows, screaming and praying. The lightning cracking around us. The boat filling with water. We rowed until our hands split and our arms tore, and we thought we were in hell. But we lived. We were brothers. And you killed him."

"It was my pleasure." Justy leaned back on the chaise. "Absalom."

Umar made a growling sound, deep in his throat. His eyes darkened, as though he had pulled a blind behind them, and snuffed out the light.

"Kill him." He thrust the cutlass at Gorton. "Use this."

Gorton shoved his pistol into his belt and took the blade. "You want me to cut him up a bit first, then? See if he's got anything else to tell us?"

"He knows nothing of use. He did not speak to his uncle. Kill him, and burn the body. Make sure there is no trace. We must leave no one any reason to come after us."

"What about Old Hays? He'll suspect."

"But he will not know. You said yourself he is a stickler for correctness. He will do nothing without evidence."

Gorton glanced at Kerry. "And her?"

"She stays with me."

Gorton spun the cutlass in his hand. He took a step towards Justy. "You heard the man, Flanagan. Up you get. Time for you to walk the plank."

———————

Justy did not get up. He got on his knees, sliding slowly off the chaise onto the rug. It was thick and tufted, a series of geometric shapes woven, over and over, in red and gold on a pale blue background. His eyes darted from the cutlass to Gorton's face and back again.

"Please," he said. "Don't."

Gorton sneered. "I didn't think you'd want to go out on your knees like a Smithfield bunter, Marshal, but so be it."

He raised the cutlass. Justy threw himself flat. "Please, Jeremiah," he wailed, reaching for Gorton's boots, scrabbling forward like a man begging for his life.

"Ah, for Christ!" Gorton stepped back sharply. "Be a man."

"Please!" Justy clawed at his breeches. Gorton struck out with his boot, shoving Justy back against the table and sending the candelabra and its tapers spilling in all directions.

"Kill him!" Umar roared.

Gorton growled in frustration. He hacked down hard with the cutlass, but the table was in the way now, impeding his swing, and Justy rolled to the side, avoiding the blow.

He rolled into a ball, on his knees, hunched over, head down. He moaned. He begged.

"Please, Jeremiah! Please!"

"Gutless cunt," Gorton muttered. "You're a goddamned embarrassment. A white man, groveling so in front of these darkies." He squared off, one foot either side of Justy's head. He raised the blade in both hands, poised for the strike that would cleave Justy's head in two.

Below him, curled up on the ground, Justy was waiting.

But not to die. He had closed his eyes. He was counting. One for Gorton to position himself. Two for him to raise the blade.

Three.

He launched himself upwards, jackknifing off his knees, driving the toes of his shoes into the pile of the rug. Aiming for Gorton's throat.

From the moment he had stepped into the room, he had been looking for any kind of weapon. The cutlasses were too far away; he had no idea whether there was any cutlery in the pewter box on the table, and the furniture was too sturdy to break apart easily. Which left the candelabra on the table, and, more importantly, the candlesticks themselves. Six-inch cylinders of hardened wax, a half inch wide at the base, tapering to a rounded point. No one's idea of a weapon. But as Owney Clearey had taught him that last day in his basement gymnasium, anything could be a lethal instrument, properly aimed, properly applied, with maximum force, speed, and aggression.

He had groveled about on the floor, trying to upset the table and grab a taper, and Gorton had helped. The candleholder had toppled and the tapers had spilled onto the floor. Justy had rolled to grab one, then rolled back as Gorton hacked down. Now the taper was cupped in the heel of his right hand and held in place with his left. The moment Gorton struck, Justy was off his knees, thrusting out his arm, making a straight line through his shoulder and his elbow and his wrist to the point of the candle, aimed at the soft hollow at the base of Gorton's jaw.

One chance. To drive the taper up, through the thin layer of skin and muscle under Gorton's tongue, through his mouth and his palate, and up into his brain.

One chance.

And he missed.

When Gorton swung the cutlass, the movement tilted him forward, not much, but enough that the point of the candle was intercepted by the hard plateau of his sternum, where his shirt gaped open. A miss. But not a catastrophic one. If it had been a knife in Justy's hand, that would likely have been the end of it. A knife might have cut the skin, even penetrated a short way into the bone. But then it would have stuck there, or broken or glanced off.

But the unlit candle was rounded at its end, not sharp. Driven by the tremendous force of Justy's strike, with his full weight behind it, the candle slid smoothly up Gorton's sternum without breaking. It followed the line of Gorton's neck, and slipped easily into the jugular notch above his clavicle. Justy felt the resistance on the heel of his hand, a fraction of a second, and then it was gone, and he rammed the candle home into Gorton's windpipe.

Gorton dropped the cutlass. He swayed backwards, choking, clutching at his throat. A half-inch stub of candle protruded above his collarbone. He clawed at it, his face turning purple.

Justy pulled the pistol out of Gorton's belt, cocked it, and stepped back.

Umar was backing towards the door, dragging Kerry in front of him, a knife at her throat. The scarred bodyguard pushed past him and bore down on Justy, his cutlass swinging, howling a hoarse, wordless scream. The scars around his mouth were white. His eyes were bloodshot. His mouth was like a monstrous cave, fringed with the ragged stumps of his teeth. There was nothing inside it. His tongue had been cut out.

Justy swung the pistol up and shot the scarred man in the face. The man dropped, his shoulder catching the edge of the table and upending it. There was a great crash as the cutlery box spilled open, and dozens of knives, forks, and spoons went skittering across the floor.

Gorton was on his knees, making a strangled sound. His face was the color of a bruised plum. His fingers were plucking at the stub of candle, his ragged nails too short to dig into the wax. Justy watched him for a moment. He picked up the cutlass and spun it in his hand. He smiled. "I told you biting your nails was a bad habit."

THIRTY-SEVEN

Justy limped into the yard. There was only a trace of light left in the sky. The women had clustered at the far end of the space, like a flock of multicolored birds, staring and squawking. Umar had forced Kerry up a shallow set of steps built into the wall, and was herding her along the wooden parapet. Justy staggered up the steps, his knee shrieking.

Kerry was slowing Umar down. The wall of the cell block was in front of them. It was double the height of the parapet, and for a moment it looked as though there was nowhere for Umar to go, but then Justy saw the gaps on either side of the wall, just wide enough for a person to pass. Umar shoved Kerry through.

Justy lurched after them, and found himself in a wide, open space, the roof of the cell block. It was thirty feet wide, and perhaps a hundred feet long. The walls that bordered it were four feet high, level with the parapet, except for the high back wall that he had passed through. There were fifty or sixty men in the space, hurrying to positions on the parapet. Some wore robes like Umar, others were dressed like field workers, others looked like merchants. Some were white and some were black. Some were bearded and some were clean-shaven. All were armed with Brown Bess muskets, which they propped against the wall, ready to deploy. They knelt down beside them, peering over the wall that flanked the inner courtyard of the compound on two sides. They had oversight of the kitchen area, the side of the living quarters, and the entrance to the storeroom. But the parapet hid them from view by anyone in the courtyard below.

Four men blocked Justy's way. They all carried cutlasses, and all had the same strange tattoos on their faces as the man Justy had killed in the cells below them. Umar stood behind them, holding Kerry by the arm. "Your friends have set a fire at the gate," he said.

There was a glow in the darkness behind the far wall, then a fountain of sparks and a column of smoke.

"Your carriage?" Umar asked.

Justy nodded. The plan had been to somehow find Kerry and bring her out and stop Owens and the Bull from assaulting the compound. The backup was for Lars and Hardluck to block the entrance to Jericho with the carriage, to rip the stuffing out of its seats and set fire to it.

"You think this will stop anything?" Umar asked. He seemed genuinely curious.

"I think half the citizens of New York are converging on this place right now. And that will scupper whatever it is you had planned."

Umar laughed. Kerry took the opportunity to try to twist away, but Umar held her tight. She grimaced as he squeezed her arm.

"You are slippery," Umar said. "Like your cousin. A small fire will not stop him. And that will not stop me."

"From doing what?" Justy asked.

"From creating a paradise for my people."

"And how does this help you do that? No matter how many men you kill today, you won't be left in peace. The natives who run this city hate anyone who's not white and Protestant, so you can bet there'll be a pack of them up here before long, and these wall of yours won't hold them."

"I am not a fool, Marshal," Umar said. "I have no intention of staying behind these walls."

It came to Justy slowly, like smoke filtering under a door. He saw the map in Shard's office, the red hatches around the land prospects: the Collect Pond; the island by the Helgate. He heard the fat farmer's voice, "The schwarzes can have it."

"The island. That's the deal. You give Riker the meadows: he gives you his island."

"Very good, Marshal. I shall build walls ten feet high around it, and my people will live in peace. The natives will be content to have us off their island and on our own."

"The gangs will come after you."

"The gangs will die tonight." Umar pointed into the compound. "Down there."

"You can't hope to do that with just fifty muskets, even if they do fall into your trap. There are hundreds of them."

"Indeed there are. But my men are just the powder in the touchhole. The real explosion will follow. As you are about to see."

A roaring noise came from below them, what sounded like a hundred men cheering a winning horse. The wall on the far side of the courtyard seemed to bulge outward. And then it disappeared completely, in a cloud of dust. Owens' people had been taking the wall apart from the outside, under cover of the shanties. They had scraped away the exterior stucco, and removed the wall, brick by brick, until there was nothing left but a thin skin of brick and mud, that a man need only lean on to knock over.

"Ready!" Umar roared, and every second man poked his musket over the parapet. They were perfectly arranged, lined up along the tops of the walls opposite, aiming directly at the gaping tear in the wall. Umar smirked at Justy. "I told you I had eyes all over this city."

Justy held his breath. He could feel the tension coming off the men on the parapet. He knew what they were feeling, the tightness in their necks and chests as they strained to see through the darkness and the dust. The cramp in their fingers as they took up the pressure on the triggers of their muskets. The loose feeling in their guts at the prospect of combat. He had felt all these things himself, many times.

Everyone was staring, even Kerry and Umar. They waited, bracing for the charge, for the sight of dozens of men forcing themselves through the gap, screaming as they ran into the killing ground.

But no one came. There was just the dust and the darkness.

And then something moved.

There was a ripple along the ranks of men, as they braced their weapons again. Held their breath. Fingered their triggers.

The dust thinned, and the movement came again. Not a rank of charging men. A flicker of activity, small and close to the ground. They strained their eyes.

A chicken appeared on the rubble. It peered around, head jerking as it took in its surroundings. It took a single uncertain step, slipped, and flopped into the compound in a flurry of wings.

There was a loud bang, then two more, and then Justy heard a volley of curses come from the far parapet. He glanced into the compound. The chicken was still alive, making its way uncertainly across the space.

Justy grinned at Umar. "It looks as though Owens may have had eyes of his own in here."

Umar took a step backwards, pulling Kerry. The moon was rising now, and his eyes were hooded by the shadow, but they flickered as a muffled drumming sound filled the air.

Justy knew what it was. It was the sound of men running along a wooden platform, preparing to hurl themselves through the gap in the wall behind him. A breach, but not where Umar had expected. Riskier, because the gap that led from the parapet to the rooftop was tiny compared to the hole in the outer wall below. But it had the element of surprise.

It all depended on who came through the gap first, and how Umar would react. Line his muskets up in ranks, use disciplined volley fire, and the invaders would have no chance.

But Umar was not a soldier.

A wild howling came from the darkness behind Justy. O'Toole burst through the gap, an ax in one hand and a club in the other. He looked huge, lit by the moon, his face streaked with what looked like blood, his coat unfurled behind him like the wings of some nightmarish bird of prey. The nearest man on the parapet fired his musket, and O'Toole was engulfed in smoke. For a moment Justy thought he might be hit, but then he roared out of the smoke and felled the man.

Men poured through the gap after him, all screaming and cursing, open mouths and wild eyes. They spread out around O'Toole and began hacking and bludgeoning their way along the parapet. Umar's men were still frozen in place, as though they could not believe that the enemy had not done what they expected them to do. They were easy prey. A few muskets barked, but not one of O'Toole's men fell back.

Umar ran. He dropped his cutlass, let go of Kerry, and made for the gap in the other side of the wall. His men followed.

Justy caught Kerry's arm. "Are you all right?"

She threw him off. "I wish men would get over grabbing me. I'm fine."

She looked at her father. O'Toole was standing in the middle of the rooftop, directing his men. He saw her and nodded. She turned away, picked up the discarded cutlass, and walked through the gap in the wall that Umar had taken.

"Kerry!" Justy called out.

She ignored him, and he limped after her. Umar and his men were running along the platform to the steps. O'Toole had left a handful of men behind him in the courtyard to cover his rear. One man was climbing the top of the steps when Umar's group reached the end of the platform. A blade swung, and the man fell backwards, his head lolling. The four scarred bodyguards hurried Umar down the steps, and formed a wedge around him at the bottom. O'Toole's men circled them. Two were Irish boys, wearing flat caps and carrying staves. The other three were Owens' men, all big lads with long knives.

Umar's bodyguards swung their cutlasses, fending the men off as they inched across the courtyard. One of them lunged forward, hacking at the face of one of Owens' trusties, hoping to cut him down and carve a way out. But the man stepped aside, dragged him off balance, and slid his knife deep into the man's chest. The two Irishmen stepped into the gap, attacking together, one swinging at the head of the scarred man on Umar's right, the other hammering his stave into the man's spine. There was a sharp crack, and the man crumpled. Then it was an Irishman with a club and a black man with a knife to each bodyguard, and a few seconds later Umar stood alone.

He stared at Justy. And then he clapped his hands. "Well done, Marshal. You have helped rid the city of a pestilent religion, and consolidated the power of the gangs. Not quite what the city fathers would imagine your role to be. But I'm sure your uncle will be pleased."

Justy looked up at the roof, wondering what kind of havoc O'Toole was wreaking. "This is your doing, Umar. Not mine. You're the one who provoked the gangs. You set the trap. You baited it. You made a shambles of it. All that blood being spilled up there? That's on your hands. As for my role, part of it is to stop bastards like you from trafficking in human beings, and making money out of their misery."

Umar laughed. "Your uncle is no different. Nor is Owens."

"They're not slavers. They don't breed children for sale."

"Do they not? They have their stables of whores. Some of whom are little more than children. Would you call them free?"

"It's not the same thing."

Umar shrugged. "You will tell yourself what you need, to keep your conscience easy."

Justy felt himself redden. "The fact remains, you are a slaver, and a pimp."

"And a murderer."

A woman stepped into the yard. She wore a bright yellow robe, and a shawl of the same color, draped over her head and wrapped around her face, so that only her eyes showed. They glittered in the moonlight.

She stopped a few paces from Umar. She pulled away her veil. "You killed Rumi."

"I did not, Sahar," Umar said, softly. "I did not kill her."

"You cast her out. Your own daughter. You gave her to that man. You made her a whore."

"She was a whore!" Umar's voice was loud. "She gave herself away. She broke the laws. She defied me. For my honor, she should have been stoned to death, here, where I stand. Her body should have been burned and the ashes thrown into the sea. But I spared her."

"Spared her for what? To be gutted like a pig and left to bleed in a stinking alley, where men and women relieve themselves?" Sahar's face was rigid. "I hope they bury you alive."

Behind her, Owens and the Bull stepped out. Then the huge bulk of Jonty and finally Tanny, dull-eyed, holding fast to Jonty's massive hand.

Owens grinned. "How now, Absalom."

Umar's eyes were dark. "God forgive you, Sahar."

"God?" She laughed. "You claim to be a man of God, and yet you imprison women. Drug them. Prostitute them. And then sell their babies. You, who were a slave, have become what you most despised."

"I carried you out of hell, Sahar."

"And traded me one hell for another. How long before you started fumbling at me, do you remember? I do. It was not even a year. I was seven years old. Seven. When I became a woman, when I began to bleed, I thought perhaps you would stop. Perhaps you would be disgusted by me. But no. You kept on, and you made me hate myself. I dreamed of death, every day, until the miracle happened and my belly began to swell. And then Rumi was born, and everything changed. Nothing mattered then, your blasphemies, your goatishness, even when you brought those women in here and began your filthy business, none of it mattered because I had Rumi. My beautiful child. And you took her from me. You killed her. And for what?" She sneered. "For your honor."

She spat in his face. He let the saliva trickle into his beard. "I should kill you."

Justy had not forgotten about the knife that Umar had taken from him in the storeroom. He was already moving when Umar's right hand flicked out, and the sprung blade snapped open. The steel gleamed like a fish jumping as Umar lunged. He was quicker and closer than Justy, and Sahar yelped as the blade sheared through her robe. She staggered backwards, her arms flailing, and cannoned into Justy. He dropped the cutlass, held her tight, and turned sharply away, gritting his teeth as his knee collapsed under him and he went down, Sahar under him, his back to Umar, braced for the knife.

Umar's scream was high-pitched, like an animal with a broken limb. Justy dragged himself to his feet. Umar was writhing on the ground, clutching at his back. Kerry stood over him, the cutlass in her hand.

Justy crouched over Sahar. He looked for blood, but there was only a ragged cut in her robe. She shook her head. He helped her to her feet.

She walked over to Umar. He had stopped moving now. He lay on his side, his breath coming in shallow spurts. His robe was soaked with blood.

Sahar turned to Kerry.

"No!" Justy shouted. But the cutlass was already in Sahar's hand. She put it against Umar's throat and thrust down hard. The sharp edge cut smoothly through the skin and muscle and cartilage. He made no noise, not even a sigh, as his blood drained into the dirt.

Sahar dropped the blade on his body.

"For my honor," she said.

THIRTY-EIGHT

The moment he had seen the wall come down, a single question had begun nagging at Justy. He stepped up to Owens. "When did she start spying for you?"

"Why do you care, Marshal? It's all worked out nice, ain't it?"

"Tell me! Was it before or after you came bleating to me in your damned carriage?"

A smirk. "A shade before."

It was like a punch in the stomach. "You lied to me."

"I told you Kerry didn't mark any of the carts, like we agreed she would. And she didn't. But she got Sahar to come out to us. And she told us everything."

Justy turned to speak to Sahar, but she had disappeared, and all the other Mohammedan women with her.

"Umar knew about the wall," he said. "One of your people talked."

Owens jerked his head at the big man looming behind him, like a hole in the darkness. "That was Jonty here. Singing like a bird, on my instruction. He came up a few months back with two escaped slaves from Charleston. I didn't have work for them, so they went with Absalom. He stayed in touch."

Justy's face burned. "Quite a scrap you came up with. Why the hell did you involve me?"

"You involved yourself, bach. I knew Absalom had some kind of land scheme cooking because one of my conks overheard young Mister Lispenard blabbing about it in his cups. I was set to take care of things myself, but then that lass got milled and you and Kerry started poking your trunks in, and that put Absalom on guard. I needed a diversion, something to keep him off balance. I estimated you'd do the trick nicely. And so you did."

Justy shifted his gaze to the Bull. "You knew about this?"

"Not until yesterday."

"And you were content to let it happen."

The Bull grunted. "There's not much can stop you, once you get going, Justice. If we'd given you your head, you'd have whiddled the whole scrap. We thought it better to just divert your attentions a nipperkin, and no harm done."

"No harm?" The anger was like a spike in his chest. "I was nearly killed. Twice."

The Bull's face shifted into what passed as a smile. "You weren't, though, were you? You're a hard man to make easy."

He looked at Kerry. She shrugged and said nothing. His face flared. "God damn, but I should arrest you all. For murder, for conspiracy, and for causing a riot."

Owens smirked. "Self-defense, bach. We were conspiring, certainly, but only to rescue my cousin from a shameful fate." He nodded at the corpses littering the courtyard. "These rogues just got in the way."

There was a creaking, clattering sound above them. O'Toole led his troops along the platform and down the steps into the courtyard. His shirt and breeches were spattered with blood.

"All clear up top," he said to the Bull. "But the cavalry's here."

The Bull nodded. "Right on time. How many dead?"

"Of ours? Two. Patsy Fagin caught a ball in the face. And that's Jem Clancy lying there with his swede half off."

The Bull glanced at the body crumpled at the bottom of the steps. "What about their lot?"

"We put down a handful or so. Plenty more with cracked costards and broken rammers. The rest put their hands up quick enough. Quiet as lambs now."

"The muskets?"

"The lads have them."

"Let's pike then, before the swoddies get past the gate." The Bull nodded at Justy. "That was fast thinking, blocking the gate like that. You did us a favor there."

Justy said nothing. He watched, helplessness and uselessness and anger all curdling inside him like a bad dinner, as his uncle and Lew Owens led the troop of men through the withdrawing room door, most of them now armed with brand-new Brown Bess muskets.

Tanny was leaning against the giant, Jonty, still holding his hand. Her eyes were glazed, and her skin was gray. Kerry embraced her, but her arms were limp. It was like hugging a doll.

"She was in the room beside where we made the breach," Jonty said. "She was tied up there."

"Was she hurt?"

He shrugged, and followed the last of Owens' men out of the yard.

Umar's white robe was now black with blood. Justy dropped his cutlass and squatted beside the corpse, wincing at the grating sensation in his knee. He pried Umar's fingers off his knife. He wiped the dirt off it, folded it carefully and slipped it into the pocket of his breeches.

He looked around at the litter of dead bodies. "Well, at least I know who did it this time."

"You won't go after her," Kerry said.

"I won't? And why not? She murdered a man. In cold blood. Right here in front of me."

"You heard what he did to the girl."

The girl. Justy thought back to what Sahar had said. That Umar had cast his daughter out. That he had prostituted her. That he had given her to a man. The man that had seen her last. That man that had probably killed her. But who was he? Umar couldn't tell him. And Sahar was gone.

There was a grating sound as the door to the cell block opened.

"So there you are!" Lars grinned at him, relief behind his smile. Hardluck stood behind him, looking around the courtyard, his eyes bulging.

"Quite a mess you've made in here," Lars said. He walked across and prodded Umar's body with his toe. "Was this the big man, then?"

"It was."

Lars grunted. "Good riddance, I'd say. Now, we've to be out of here, if we're not to get snatched up by the soldiery. They're right behind us. Is there another way out?"

"This way."

Justy dropped his cutlass. He led the way into the withdrawing room. The scarred bodyguard's corpse had been shoved into a corner of the room. There was no sign of Gorton.

"What?" Lars asked.

"Nothing." Justy led them on, through the room, and into a short passage-way that led to a small atrium. There was a huge hole in the far wall, screened by what looked like a large black sail. Justy walked gingerly over the rubble and pulled the sail to one side. He saw a small shack with a dirt floor and hundreds of bricks, piled neatly to the ceiling, with a pathway to the street.

They walked as quickly as they could through the lanes, Justy leaning on Hardluck, Kerry leading the way. Once she had her bearings, she took them along the side of Jericho's walls towards the front gate. A crowd had gathered and they stood in the shadows, watching a group of cavalrymen dragging the smoldering remains of the carriage beyond the gate.

"Sorry, Hardluck," Justy murmured. The driver smiled sadly and said nothing.

The soldiers looked nervous, and stood with their swords ready, as more people gathered to see what was going on.

"Where are this lot usually garrisoned?" Lars asked.

"Fort Washington."

"They got here quare fast then, didn't they?"

An officer strode out, snapping orders at the soldiers. He pulled himself up onto a white mare. The moonlight caught his face, showing one good eye and a white hollow with a mass of scar tissue where the other eye had been. And Justy felt another piece of the picture swim into focus, as clear as printed words under a magnifying glass.

THIRTY-NINE

He had the sneaking suspicion that going to the Almshouse was a waste of time. There was always the chance that now Umar was dead, and Sahar was free, she might go to claim her daughter's body. But he wasn't surprised when the young novice on the door told him the corpse had been taken by a man claiming to be her brother.

"One of Owens' men, no doubt." Justy looked at Kerry. "But you knew that already, didn't you? That would have been part of her deal."

Kerry shrugged and said nothing. They sat on the steps of the Almshouse with Lars and Hardluck, an awkward quartet, ragged and filthy.

"A pity we'll never find out who killed the girl," Justy said.

Kerry frowned. "And why would you say that?"

"Because if there's no body, there's no crime. And where there's no crime, there's no investigation."

"What do you mean, no crime?" Kerry snapped. "She was stabbed and left to bleed to death. You saw her. I saw her."

"It doesn't matter. Even if we knew who killed her, a judge would demand that we produce the evidence. That means a body. Or a grave, if we'd buried her. And I can't produce either."

Kerry ground her teeth. Her face was white.

Justy stood up, wincing as the bones grated in his knee. "You did what you set out to do, Kerry. You found out who she was. She was claimed, and no doubt her mother will tuck her up properly, in her way."

"But the bastard who killed her is still out there."

He spread his arms. "I don't like it any more than you do, Kerry. But what can I do?"

"You can find him."

"I don't see how. I probably won't be a Marshal much longer, after today. And even if I was, and I did find him, he wouldn't get justice."

"There are other kinds of justice."

"Marshal or not, I'm not about to go after a man on the cross, Kerry," Justy said, quietly.

Her eyes blazed. "Well, you're no use to me, then. You're full of fine words about making this city a better place, and for everyone who lives in it, but when it comes to doing right by a Negro titter, you're as careless as the rest of them."

"That's not fair."

"Is it not? Well then, I'll bid you good night, Justice Flanagan, and pleasant dreams. If you can sleep."

She stormed away down the steps, the blue dress billowing behind her like a dirty cloud.

"Should I see her home?" Lars asked.

Justy shook his head. "She wouldn't thank you if you asked."

They walked down to Justy's boarding house.

"So what now?" Lars asked.

"Did you not hear what I said to Kerry?"

Lars grinned. "I heard. But I know you well enough to ken you'll not let this lie."

Justy shrugged. "Right now all I know is that I need a bath and a bed, and a surgeon to look at this goddamned knee."

"The fella who fixed me up isn't too bad. I'll take you to see him in the morning." Lars glanced sympathetically at Hardluck. "It's a pity we'll not be able to go in that rig of yours."

The coachman shrugged. "It was never mine, sir."

"No, but I meant it to be," Justy said. "Come with us tomorrow, and I'll remedy your situation for once and done."

Hardluck said nothing. He looked lost.

"I can't have a slave, Hardluck," Justy said, softly.

The driver nodded. Lars slapped him on the back. "Come on, matey. Let me buy you a drink at Hughson's. Happen we could find a place for you on board the *Netherleigh*, a strong fella like yourself. Have you ever thought about going to sea?"

He winked at Justy, and led Hardluck away down the street.

It was dark in the hallway of Mrs. Chow's house, and Justy had to fumble to find a match to light the candle in the sconce beside the door. He wiggled the taper free, and walked slowly past the parlor and along the hall.

And then he stopped. The hairs rose on his forearms and the back of his neck. It was a moment before his brain registered what was out of place. A smell. Not the jasmine that Mrs. Chow favored, and not the lingering smells of spice from the kitchen. Something darker.

And then a sensation, the faintest vacuum in the air as the door to the parlor swung back, making the candle flicker.

He did not hesitate. If his knee had not been a wreck, he could have run for it, through the kitchen and out into the back yard. But he knew he could not run five paces without collapsing. So there could be no retreat, only attack.

He turned quickly, threw the candle down the hallway towards the front door, and took two quick steps backwards at the same time. The candle went out, but not before he had seen the dark shape of someone standing just inside the door to the parlor, and the light reflecting on something long and narrow. A sword against his knife. Not bad odds, because they were indoors, which meant close quarters. And the tighter the clutch, the shorter the blade.

He slipped the knife out of his pocket, pressed the metal catch and used his other thumb to ease the blade open under control. It snicked quietly into its housing. He held the blade outwards, level with his waist, and leaned forward, straining his ears. He stared at the doorway to the parlor. The hallway was as dark as a cellar, but he was sure he could see the corners of the door in the blackness. And the shape of a man moving there.

He was coming out. The earthy smell was suddenly much stronger, and Justy realized it was blood he had smelled, mixed with sweat. The darkness seemed to shift again, and then Justy heard the sound of breathing, hoarse and labored.

Gorton.

And then everything changed, because Justy heard the telltale double click of a hammer being cocked, and he realized that Gorton had brought both a sword and a pistol, and that when a man thought to bring one pistol, he often decided to bring two.

Everything happened very slowly. He wasn't even aware of making a choice, and it was almost as though his body had made the choice for him, his hand flicking the blade underarm, forward into the blackness. He was not conscious of where he threw the knife, only that it seemed to be the right place to aim it.

The pistol fired. Justy was already falling, using the momentum of his throw to carry him out of Gorton's aim. A long tongue of flame licked at him, scorching his left shoulder as he went down. He rolled to his right, and then sprang to his feet.

Or he would have, had his knee not given way under him. It seemed to take forever to stand, and when he was finally upright, Gorton was on him, wheezing and choking, his fist and the butt of the pistol like an iron flail on Justy's head and shoulders. Justy shoved hard, driving Gorton back into the darkness of the parlor.

There was the sound of a chair turning over, and then Gorton getting to his feet in the dark. This was Justy's home, and he knew the layout of the parlor well. Much better than Gorton, who had perhaps taken a single glance around it before putting out his light and waiting in the dark. He thought about how Gorton had fallen through the door and which chair he would have upset. Where he would be standing now. Blind in the darkness, listening.

Justy took a single step forward, until he felt the edge of a rug under his feet. He took a long step right, and then forward again, guided by the back of a chair under his left hand. Gorton was moving too, far to his left, close to the window. He wondered how much damage the candle had done when he had shoved it into Gorton's throat. And how the hell he had managed to get it out.

Justy took another step forward. He could smell the cold ash in the fireplace. He reached down slowly, his fingers feeling for the poker that was usually left resting against the wall.

The brass felt cool in his hand. He smiled to himself, because he knew now that he had won. He could hear Gorton stepping backwards, uncertain, his boots scraping on the floor where the rug ended. Justy knew exactly where he was. In his mind's eye, he imagined the parlor, the chairs facing each other, grouped around the low square table in the center of the room. Justy had to take two steps forward and a quarter turn to the left, and he would have an open line of approach. Five fast, hard steps. Maximum aggression. Never mind his damaged knee. Gorton would never know what hit him.

He took the two steps forward. He made the quarter turn. He readied the poker.

For a moment, Justy thought Gorton had fired blind, and the powder in his pistol had somehow lit the room. But the bang was the sound of the front door slamming open. And the illumination was moonlight, streaming in from the hallway. There was Gorton, frozen, his sword in one hand, his pistol in the other. And there was Hardluck, picking himself off the floor of the hall.

Gorton spun around, his pistol swinging up. Justy threw the poker. There was another loud bang, and the room was instantly full of reeking smoke. Justy ran at Gorton, grabbing the candelabra off the table. Gorton spun towards him, swinging hard with his sword. There was an immense clang as Justy caught the blade on the pewter candlestick. Justy went down on his injured knee, his arm numb as far as his elbow. One of the arms had sheared off the candlestick. Gorton raised his sword again. He made a muffled sound. He was laughing. He had dragged the wax taper out of his throat and bandaged the hole. The blood was a black blot on the white cloth.

And then Gorton stopped laughing. His head tilted slightly, as though he was listening for something, and his sword slipped out of his hand, and his knees gave way, and he fell onto one of Mrs. Chow's uncomfortable chairs.

Hardluck stood behind him, the poker in his hand.

Justy knelt on the floor, his lungs heaving. It was a few moments before he was able to drag himself to his feet, for what seemed like the fiftieth time that day. He staggered to the window and pulled back the heavy drapes, so that the parlor was flooded with moonlight.

Hardluck stood by Gorton's body, staring at the poker in his hand, and the clotted mess of blood and matter on the handle.

Justy put his hand on the jarvie's shoulder. "Thank you."

Hardluck nodded, numbly.

Justy took the poker from him. "What brought you back?"

"I wanted to talk to you, about going to the beak. I heard the shot, so I charged the door."

He looked at the body, slumped on the seat of the chair. Gorton had wrapped a rag around the hole in his throat, and stuffed another into his mouth, to staunch the blood from the wound the end of the candle had made when it speared the soft tissue around his nose and his gullet. Justy shivered, imagining the excruciating pain. He opened Gorton's waistcoat, looking to see if his knife had hit its target. He had missed by a mile. He looked around, and saw it, embedded at head height in the parlor door.

Hardluck groaned, and put his face in his hands.

"Why so maudlin?" Justy asked. "You did a good thing today. Saving my life is only the half of it. That man was the worst kind of criminal, and you stopped him. There will be a reward from the city for that."

"A reward is no use to a dead man," Hardluck said, though his fingers.

"A dead man? What are you talking about?"

"I killed a white man, sir. That means mortal trouble for me."

He was right. A judge would have little sympathy for the argument that Gorton was part of a criminal conspiracy, and had protected a pimp, a slaver, and a swindler, all while pretending to serve the city. He was also a white man, and even following the gradual ban on slavery in New York, the men who ran the city were loath to encourage the idea that a black man could get away with killing a white man, for whatever reason.

And then he smiled.

"Don't worry." Justy went to the parlor door and pulled the knife out. He tested the point and folded it away. He patted the big man on the shoulder. "You'll be fine. Trust me."

FORTY

Friday

The judge studied the papers on the desk in front of him. Roderick Thorne was a dried-up husk of a man, with pale skin speckled with light brown splotches that made it look as though someone had thrown a spoonful of thin beef gruel at him. His eyes were a watery blue, his nose long and hooked. He wore a wig that was at least a size too large, and a coat that was shiny with grease on the lapels and use on the elbows. He smelled of mothballs and dried sweat.

He snorted and picked his nose. "Hardluck. What manner of a name is that?"

Justy said nothing. He knew the judge didn't expect an answer.

Thorne shifted his ill-fitting wig and glared at Justy. "This seems perfectly clear. The Negro Hardluck killed a man in cold blood. Clearly not a case of self-defense, because his life was not being threatened. Yours was, by your own account. Had you killed the man, self-defense it would have been. But no. This is manslaughter."

Justy had spent most of the night dealing with the situation at his boarding house. He had first hunted for Mrs. Chow, and found her in her bedroom, gagged and bound, but otherwise unscathed. She had calmly gone to the kitchen to make tea. Hays had appeared, but said nothing to Justy, other than to instruct him to appear before the duty judge in the morning.

Justy was not under suspicion. Hays had provided a written statement testifying that Gorton had been a turncoat, that he had clearly threatened Justy's life, and that Justy could produce witnesses if required. The problem was Hardluck. But Justy knew the law, and the law was on Hardluck's side.

"New York versus Cullen, Your Honor," he said.

The old man's head snapped up, so fast that his wig slid down his brow. He pushed it back up. "What the devil are you talking about?"

"Cullen was a slave, owned by a Johan de Vries, of Orange. He shot a man named Thomas Stark—"

"I know the damned decision, man! What of it?"

"Then you'll know that de Vries believed Stark was going to kill him. Just as I believed Gorton was going to kill me."

"And?"

"Well, Your Honor, as you'll recall, the court ruled that a slave is the extension of the hand of his master. Therefore, when Cullen killed Stark, he was acting as de Vries' own hand. And because de Vries was in fear for his life, the killing was therefore self-defense."

The splotches on the judge's face had darkened. "I fail to see what this has to do with the case at hand, Mister Flanagan."

Justy smiled. "Hardluck is my slave."

Thorne's face sagged. "What?"

"My slave, Your Honor. And as you noted, I was in fear for my life. Which means when he killed Gorton, he was acting in self-defense."

"This is preposterous!"

"Not at all. I am his legal owner. The papers . . ." He pulled two envelopes from the inside of his coat, opened one and laid a document on the table.

Thorne read it, grunting and mumbling to himself. "Piers Riker? This very week?"

"Yes."

The judge looked up, a mean look creasing his face. "In which case, the offense is doubled. The purchase or sale of slaves is illegal in New York, so if this document is true, it means you have broken the law. Moreover, because the traffic in slaves is illegal in this state, the transaction is legally void, which means the Negro named Hardluck is not your property. Making him guilty. As are you, Mister Flanagan. Guilty of buying a slave. A trifling offense, in comparison, but one which carries with it a significant fine." He pushed the document across the table.

Justy pushed it back. "Except that Hardluck was not sold. He was a gift."

"A gift?"

"Indeed, Your Honor. No money changed hands." Which wasn't quite true, but if it came to it, he could argue the technicality. That he had wagered for the carriage, and Hardluck had been added to the prize without his knowledge.

The judge's face was pinched, his eyes and mouth drawn tight around his nose. "And Mister Riker will testify accordingly?"

"He will."

A long pause. "Well, in that case, I suppose . . ."

"May I order him released?"

Thorne cleared his throat. He rubbed his hands dry on his lapels. "Yes. Yes, you may."

Justy turned to the guard standing behind him at the door. "Bring up the prisoner that goes by the name Hardluck."

The man nodded and disappeared.

Justy waited.

"Why the devil are you loitering?" the judge snapped.

"Just one more piece of business, Your Honor."

"Well, then, out with it. There is still a great deal of the city's business to do."

"Of course." He opened the second envelope. He made a show of reading the papers. The judge held out his hand. "Come on!"

"Just a moment." Justy leafed through the pages until he heard the sound of boots on the floors of the hallway behind him. Then he handed over four sheets of paper to the judge. "Certificates of emancipation, Your Honor." He smiled. "For the Negro, Hardluck."

The judge snatched the papers up. The blotches on his face seemed to swell as he read the documents, and then read them again. But Justy had been careful. He had come in at dawn and got to work ensuring the papers were correct in every detail.

The footsteps stopped behind him. The guard held Hardluck tight by the arm. The jarvie looked disheveled. His face was grizzled with stubble, his eyes were red. He wore a loose shift and his shoes, and nothing more, which told Justy the Watch had come for him in the night, and not done him the courtesy of letting him dress. But then, he was a slave, and a Negro and a presumed murderer, so that was not surprising.

"You may let him go," Justy said, and the guard reluctantly loosed his grip. Hardluck stared into the room. Justy nodded and turned back to the judge.

"You wish to give up all legal rights to this man and set him free?" Thorne asked the formal question. His tone was grudging.

"Yes," Justy replied.

Ink splashed as Thorne jabbed his pen into its well. He scribbled at the bottom of the first document, and then the second. He paused at the third, and gave Justy a baleful look.

"Just in case, My Lord," Justy said.

The judge signed the remaining two certificates and pushed the papers away. Justy examined them. Date, name, title, signature. He could feel Thorne twitching and boiling a few feet away. He ignored him. He wanted to make sure there were no errors. He handed one of the documents to Hardluck. The second and third he folded and put in his pocket. The last he placed back on the judge's table.

"This one's for you. For your records." He smiled. "Your Honor."

FORTY-ONE

Justy and Hardluck walked slowly down the stairs to the mezzanine above the lobby. It was crammed with petitioners hoping to see the Mayor, who once a month held a special session to hear appeals against City rulings. A long line snaked around the ornate stone floor, men and women of all sorts, from wealthy merchants in fur-lined coats to servants dressed in their black-and-whites. Everyone was chattering, complaining, hurling insults, laughing. The noise was deafening, like a huge waterfall, amplified by the acoustics in the high-ceilinged lobby. Justy had the impression of a hundred birds in a nest, all with their beaks wide open.

Hardluck was staring at the paper in his hand.

"Can you read?" Justy asked.

"A little, sir. The Rikers like their people to have their letters."

"So you know what it says. You're free. You don't have to answer to anyone, anymore."

The big driver had tears in his eyes. "I'm grateful, sir. But—"

"I know, you said before, you're frightened about making your way. But I believe you will, carriage or no. So until you get your feet under you, you'll stay at Hughson's, on my account."

"I can't let you do that, sir!"

"It's the least I can do. I burned that carriage, after all, and my intent was to give it to you."

"I'll pay you back, sir. I promise you."

Justy grinned. "I believe you would, but there's no call. Now, there is one more thing for you to do here. It might be better if you were dressed, but this can't wait." He was still holding the second envelope. He took three sheets of paper from it. "You need a new name."

"Sir?"

Justy held up his hands. "I'm not saying Hardluck isn't a perfectly good name. It's your name. But you need a surname to go along with it. For legal purposes."

"What name should I use?"

"Many freedmen use the name of their former master. But I'm not sure how you'd feel about being called Riker."

"Flanagan, then?" Hardluck looked doubtful.

"I'd be honored, Hardluck, but I think it should be a name of your choosing."

"And it can be anything I wish?"

"So long as it's signed by the registrar and a witness in good standing."

Hardluck thought for a moment. "Cross," he said. And suddenly there were tears in his eyes. "Because the Lord Jesus has delivered me out of bondage."

The registrar's office was on the mezzanine level. He was not busy, so they had the papers signed immediately. Justy left copies of the name change and the certificate of emancipation with the registrar and took copies for himself. As they walked down the stairs to the lobby, he folded Hardluck's documents into an envelope. "Keep them with you always. There are slave-catchers here, men who will try to snatch you off the street and sell you back into bondage if they can. These freedom papers are your surety. If you lose them, or anyone takes them, you can appeal to the Hall. They have records here, as you see, and you can have a copy made by the scrivener. Or come to me. I will keep a copy, and I can vouch for you." He smiled, and put out his hand. "Mister Cross."

Hardluck's hand was rough and strong, ridged with calluses from handling ropes and reins. It was like grasping the branch of a sun-warmed tree. His smile was so wide, it looked as though it might split his face. "Hardluck Cross." He rolled his name around his mouth. "It sounds well?"

"It'll be a hit with the ladies at chapel, I'd say."

Hardluck's eyes opened wide as the world opened up before him. And then he laughed, a deep, booming sound, like a bass drum pounding, and the crowd in the lobby of the Hall went quiet and stared at the man on the stairs, in his grubby gray shift and scuffed white shoes, whose life had just begun.

All trace of the previous day's storm had been swept away. The sun glittered in a brittle blue sky, and the wind was a knife, slicing up Broad Street from the docks. New Yorkers hurried up and down Wall Street, some swathed in scarves and hats and heavy coats, others hugging themselves in their summer rig, taken by surprise by the sudden onset of autumn.

Justy had no overcoat, but he didn't have far to go. He let gravity pull him down the hill to the Tontine Coffee House, and then up the flight of teak steps to its front door.

There were no limits to when traders could do business in New York, but many of the city's money men liked to decamp to their country homes on a Friday afternoon, and return late on Monday morning. So the Tontine was quiet, but Justy was gambling that Tobias Riker would be there, taking stock of the news that Umar was dead, and doing the necessary business as quickly as possible.

The grand foyer was empty, and as Justy passed the dining room, he saw just two members seated at the table, reading newspapers and sipping coffee. Riker was in the Club Room with two others, their chairs drawn up tight around a small table cluttered with empty cups. Justy stopped just inside the doorway and looked around. The room hadn't changed at all since he had last stepped inside it. The royal-blue rug was like a cloud under his feet. The air smelled of polished leather, from the armchairs, and cedar, from the precisely cut wood piled up beside the fireplace.

He waited until Riker raised his head and looked at him. The man was the image of his son, with the same sharp face and widow's peak. But the hair was grayer, and the eyes were harder. He barked at Justy, "You are?"

"Flanagan. Mayor's Marshal."

The eyes watched him for a moment. "City business?"

Justy thought about that. "Yes."

"Then it can wait until Monday."

"No. It cannot."

The two other heads turned. Riker stood up. He was immaculately dressed in a subtle navy-blue suit of fine worsted wool, coat, breeches, and vest. His shirt and cravat were made of white silk, and there was a gold pin with an onyx stud thrust through the knot of his tie. It was his only concession to fashion. Everything else about him was sobriety personified: the buttons on his coat were black, and he didn't even wear one watch chain, let alone two.

"Flanagan. Yes. Of course."

Justy watched him approach, his shoes silent on the soft carpet. He was thin and narrow-shouldered and a few inches shorter than Justy, but he carried himself like a much taller man. Close up, he looked like someone who enjoyed all the pleasures of life. His cheeks and nose were veined and even his immaculate tailoring couldn't hide the hard ball of his potbelly. His eyes were pale blue and his face was narrow and pointed, like a fox.

"And what can I do for you, Marshal Flanagan?" The bark was gone. The voice was smooth.

"Your scrap is come untwisted, Mister Riker."

"My scrap?"

"This scheme of yours, to secure land before the commission gives its report."

Riker raised a thin eyebrow. "That's quite a charge, Marshal. Have you any evidence?"

"Plenty. Your extortion of Mister Shard. His frequent trips up to the Mohammedan compound in your carriage. The sales contract documents in the recorder's office signed by John Absalom. Also known as Umar Salam. Sales that include loans from your bank. I wonder if we issued a writ of subpoena to your executives what we might find."

Riker shrugged. "I am not familiar with a Mister Shard. He sounds like a most unfortunate creature, to be preyed upon so. But I can assure it was not by me. And this talk of my carriage? Carriages are easily confused. Doubtless he has, or has been using, a carriage similar to mine. As for the Millennium Bank being involved in transactions that you claim are dubious, again, that has nothing to do with me. I am the majority shareholder in the bank. I am not privy to its doings, nor am I familiar with its clients. But by all means, do question the executives. And do it now, if you wish."

He stood to one side. The men who had been sitting with him were now standing. One was the picture of a Wall Street man, tall and lean, with a long face like a bloodhound. He wore a sharply cut black coat, and small powdered wig. The other was Charles Shotwell, looking fleshy and ruddy, as though he had just come in from the cold. The razor cut still showed, thinner now, but still livid across his cheek. He was dressed in a lovat coat and tan breeches. The single watch chain running from his middle waistcoat button to his right fob pocket looked even tighter than the last time Justy had seen it. The banker thrust his thumb into the vacant fob and flashed Justy a nervous smile.

Riker's smirk was the image of his son's. "It doesn't look as though you have much evidence after all, Marshal. In fact, it seems as though you have been wasting your time. New York's time. I shall have words to say to the High Constable at the next budget meeting. He is a strong proponent of a policing force for the city, but if your efforts are any example, it strikes me that would be a monumental waste of money."

"You will not be attending the next budget meeting, Mister Riker."

"I shall not? Why not?"

"Because while I may not have evidence enough to convict you in a court of law, I have more than enough to destroy your reputation. I have friends among the newslettermen. And you have left a juicy trail for them to start sniffing after. I shall point them in the right direction, and they will piece it all together. Some will dismiss the reports, but there will be an inquiry. And when Jake Hays starts uncovering evidence, you'll be cooked. I'm sure you can call in enough favors to keep yourself out of court. But you won't be able to erase the stink of corruption. That'll be too much for most of your peers in the city. They'll vote to have you removed from the Council and all other roles of influence. People will stop doing business with you. You'll be a pariah. You'll be banished to your bankrupt estate. Or perhaps to your wee island."

Riker stared. His eyes were glassy and hard, like a snake's. Justy expected to see a forked tongue appear between his lips at any moment. "What do you want?"

"I want you out of New York, but I'll settle for having you out of New York's business. I want you to retire from public life. From the City Council. And the Planning Commission. And any other public offices that you hold. If you resign all of your duties on Monday morning, I'll forget everything I know, and you'll never hear about any of this from me again."

Riker didn't blink. Justy could almost see the mind racing behind the marble eyes.

"And my contracts with Mister Absalom?"

"So you don't deny them?"

"Would it make a difference if I did?"

Justy shrugged. "Keep them. Deal with his heirs. If you can find them. I don't give a damn how much money you make, I just don't want you befouling my city."

Riker nodded, as unruffled as though he was discussing a point of order in the Council. "A moment, if you please."

He went back to the cluster of chairs and huddled with Shotwell and the long-faced man. He spoke for a long time. The long-faced man shook his head, vehemently. Shotwell looked stunned. He pulled his watch out of its pocket, glanced at it, then tucked it away again. He said something, and then the tall banker pulled out his own watch. They all nodded.

Riker walked back slowly towards Justy. He stopped a few feet away. "Very well, Mister Flanagan. I shall resign all my commissions on Monday morning. In return, we shall consider this case closed. Agreed?"

"Agreed."

"In that case, our business is concluded."

"Not quite."

"What?" Riker's jaw was tight.

"Your carriage."

"What about it?"

"I want it. The cab, and the horses with it."

For the first time, Riker looked surprised. "I'm not giving you my carriage."

"In that case we do not have a deal."

He shook his head. "I don't understand."

"It's quite simple, Mister Riker. I want your carriage. Today. Consider it a commission, if it makes it easier for you."

"The carriage." Riker stared. "And then we are complete?"

"Yes."

"Very well. I will inform my driver. You may collect it from here this afternoon."

He was on the point of turning away, when something stopped him, as though another part of him had taken hold. He leaned close, baring his teeth. "You will regret this."

"Just as Chase Beaulieu did?" Justy leaned in, so that their noses were almost touching, and he could see a yellow tint in the bloodshot whites of Riker's eyes. "You got him the job so you would know what the surveyor's recommendations would be. You thought he was a dolt, but he was cleverer than you expected. He pieced it together. And you killed him for it."

"Chase Beaulieu was a drunk. He fell in the river and drowned."

"So everyone says. Even his father. But you and he and I all know the truth."

The snarl became a sneer. "You claim to know a truth, yet you have no evidence."

"No. But that might change, if a story came out. The family might decide a postmortem is appropriate after all. And who knows what truths we might uncover then."

Riker blinked, and his eyes seemed to clear. He swayed backwards, the emollient, persuasive part of him now back in control. He gave a bland smile. "Good day, Mister Flanagan. I hope never to see you again."

Justy nodded. "The feeling, Mister Riker, is mutual."

FORTY-TWO

He sat at the counter in Hughson's Tavern, drawing circles on the polished wood with the spillage from his glass. He had taken the long way around from the Tontine, not wanting to bump into Jake Hays. He had written a brief report and left it on the High Constable's desk, but he knew Hays would have a great many more questions. About Gorton, about Umar, and about Jericho. He had questions for Hays, too, but they would have to wait.

Because he still had to find out who killed the girl. Lars was right, he could not let it go. It would nag at him, every day, until he was able to put together all the pieces of the puzzle in his head. Rumi had rebelled. She had slept with an Irish boy, become pregnant, and been discovered by her father. His religion required that she be killed by stoning, but he had whored her instead.

Was that all he knew?

He had the sick feeling that he was as far from the truth as when he had started. The biggest pieces of the puzzle were held by Umar, but he was dead. Sahar might be able to offer more that she knew, but she was gone. And yet he was sure he knew more himself, just that he hadn't seen it yet.

He felt a familiar weight on his shoulders. Lars squeezed his neck and eased onto the chair beside him. He mimed to the barman to bring him a tankard. "I heard what happened with your man Gorton."

"News travels fast," Justy said.

"Not really. I was sat right here when they came and hauled poor Hard-luck away in his nightshirt."

"So you were up all night drinking?"

"Well, not just drinking." Lars winked. "How did your account of things play down at the Hall?"

"I've no idea. I wrote a report and got out of it before Hays came in. I did go to see Riker, though."

The barman arrived with a tankard. Lars sucked the froth noisily off the top of the beer. "And how was that?"

Justy told him. Lars chuckled. "You've made an enemy there, lad."

"I'll just add him to the list."

"Do you think he killed this fella Beaulieu?"

"It was a bit convenient, wasn't it? The inside man in this scrap of Riker's suddenly going facedown in the river? And only hours after he whispers to me that he wants to meet."

Lars grunted. "Convenient's one word for it." He swallowed a mouthful of ale.

"Exactly. But I've no proof. So I have to let it go."

Lars looked sympathetically at him. "Leaves a bad taste, I suppose."

"The kind all the ale in the world can't wash away."

They sat for a while, looking at the shelves of cups and crockery on the wall opposite.

"What about the other thing?" Lars asked, eventually.

"The girl?" Justy shrugged. "I'm stuck on speaking to the mother. She's the key to the whole affair, I'd say. But I don't expect I'll ever see her again."

"And why not? She's sure to be in the city still. It's just a question of finding her."

"Why would she still be here?"

Lars scoffed. "Because she's a Negro and a woman and a Mohammedan, of course. It's not easy to get about this glorious country of ours with just one of those handicaps. No. She'll be here, somewhere, hiding out."

"You think Owens knows where she is?"

"Not if she has any sense at all. She'll steer clear, now that she's no use to him. And that means staying clear of her people, too. If he wanted to quiet her, that's the first place he'd look."

"So where, then?"

Lars looked sidelong at Justy. "Your noggin really is baked today, isn't it?"

"I didn't get much sleep last night either, remember."

Lars grunted. "Well, I'd say she's with a friend. Someone who's not of the religion, if you're with me."

"But Umar kept his women locked up like caged birds. Sahar doesn't know anyone outside of the religion."

Lars picked up his tankard. His Adam's apple bobbed as he swallowed half the pint. He belched softly. "Except that she does now, doesn't she?"

———————

Kerry opened her door at the second knock. She was wearing a man's breeches, hose, and shirt, but her hair was loose, hanging coiled over her right shoulder like a chestnut rope.

For a moment, Justy felt lost. Kerry leaned on the jamb of the doorway and folded her arms. Her green eyes looked somewhere between wary and amused.

"Been reading?" Justy asked.

"Not much else to do now," she replied.

"Can we come in?"

She stood aside and they walked into the tiny front room. Her bedroom door was closed. Justy and Lars sat down, and Kerry poured water out of an urn into three cups. She put them on the table in the center of the room and sat down, her back straight as a rod. "So."

Justy nodded to the closed door. "Do you have a guest staying?"

An eyebrow ticked up. "And if I did?"

"I'm only asking."

She flicked dust off the knee of her breeches. "Well, it's none of your business either way."

He sighed. "Is it Sahar?"

She burst out laughing. "In this house? With Lew Owens a step away? Are you spooney?"

"I thought they were friends. Allies, at least."

"They were until he was done with her. But if you lot up at Federal Hall make any kind of a rumpus about last night, she'll be a problem for him, won't she? Better to hush her now and be done with it, so she can't tell any tales. That's how Lew sees things."

"You warned her?"

"Of course I did. The poor judy's been tasked her whole life. It was about time someone looked out for her."

"So who is in there?"

She folded her arms. "Who do you think?"

Justy remembered the glazed look on the young woman's face the night before. The way Kerry had held her hand. "Your friend Tanny?"

"You'll make a detective yet."

Justy leaned forward in his chair. The horsehair made a creaking sound under him. "Where's Sahar, Kerry?"

"Why do you want to know?"

"You know why. She's the only one who can tell me what happened with her daughter."

Kerry stood up and went to her window. The glass was screened with a muslin curtain, and she twitched it aside to look into the street. Then she turned to look at Justy. The light was behind her, silhouetting her and throwing her face into shadow.

"I've hidden her away. Somewhere you can't get to her."

"And what does that mean?"

"It means she's in as much danger from you as she is from Owens. I know you, Justy. You're a law man, and the way you see it, Sahar broke the law when she killed that bastard."

"And how do you see it?"

"That he got what was coming to him. He was a rapist and a pimp and a murderer. Sahar told me he killed the girls who couldn't produce kinchen for him, or who tried to run away. He gave them to his men first, then he had them killed and buried up the island somewhere. God alone knows how many. He would have killed Sahar, after what she'd done, so as far as I'm concerned, it was self-defense."

Justy looked at his hands. "I wasn't going to arrest her."

"Oh, you weren't?" Kerry's voice was heavy with sarcasm. "You were just going to let her walk away, after she topped a man, right in front of you?"

"I wasn't sure what I was going to do. Because if I was going to arrest her, I'd have to arrest you, too. It was you put him on the ground, remember?"

She said nothing. Her eyes were hooded, but he could feel the anger radiating from them.

He sighed. "I swear, I don't know what I was going to do. The report I wrote for Jake Hays last night? I left that part out. And you know what that makes me? An accessory."

"You could write another report."

"I could. And I should. Because what she did was murder, plain and simple. But right now I'm more concerned about another murder. Which is why I want to talk to her now."

"You won't arrest her."

"Not today."

She stepped towards him. "Not ever, Justy. You let her go free. Or she's gone for good."

Behind her, in the street, the sun came out from behind a cloud, and the light turned her hair into a dark halo. He felt as though someone had grabbed him by the throat. "You'd let Rumi's killer go?"

"If it saved Sahar's life, yes."

"Jesus, Kerry!"

It was hot in the small room, stifling. He could feel the sweat soaking his shirt under his arms. He wanted to wrench the scarf from around his neck so that he could breathe. Kerry was like a statue, dark and cool as marble. He felt the mad urge to tear off his coat and press himself against her, to rest his burning cheek on hers.

He pulled a handkerchief out of his pocket. He twisted it in his hands, resisting the temptation to mop his face. "I won't arrest her."

"You swear it?"

"I swear."

She waited for a moment, very still. And then she made up her mind. "I'll take you."

They waited in the street while she changed. Justy leaned on the wall of the warehouse building opposite and let the sweat dry on his forehead.

"Is it always like that with you two now?" Lars asked.

"Like what?"

"Like you looking like a wee puppy and her deciding or not whether to jump you?"

"What?"

Lars snorted. "I wish the two of yez would just get it over with and dab it up already. There'd be a good deal less tension."

Kerry's front door rattled and she stepped out. She had pulled her hair up and pinned it, so that it showed off her long neck above the ruff of the high collar of her black dress. She looked at them, sharp green eyes. "What are you two scheming?"

"Nothing." Justy could feel the flush creeping over the top of his head.

She looked him up and down. "This way, then."

They followed her down towards Chapel Street, and then into the lanes of Canvas Town. For a long time they walked through the busy markets, dodging shoppers carrying bags and messengers carrying loads as the lanes twisted left and right under the colored awnings.

And then they burst out of the shade and into the sunlight and Justy blinked. "Here?"

They were standing outside the waterfront entrance to Hughson's Tavern. Kerry led them up the exterior staircase and through a first-floor doorway. A maid bobbed a curtsey as they passed her on the landing. Kerry tapped on a door.

There was a single bed, a small table with a three-spike candleholder, a threadbare wooden chair with spindly legs, and a wardrobe. And nothing else.

Justy felt his face redden. He spun around. "Where is she?"

Kerry leaned on the door. "No arrest. You swore it."

"Yes. I swore. Now produce her, Kerry."

She smirked at him, and opened the door.

It was a moment before Justy recognized Sahar. She seemed smaller than the night before, without her bright robes. She was dressed in a maid's uniform, and the white of her mob cap made her skin look darker. She looked just like a hundred other black servants in the city. Justy might walk right past her in the street and never notice. He smiled, despite himself.

"She was on the landing, when we came in, wasn't she?"

Kerry nodded. "Did you twig her then?"

"No. I never would have. It's a good disguise."

Sahar sat on the bed, Kerry beside her. Lars leaned his bulk against the door.

Justy sat carefully on the spindle-legged chair and faced Sahar. "You're in no danger from me. I'm not here to arrest you. Has Kerry told you that?"

Sahar nodded. She had a small, heart-shaped face, with large, oval eyes and dramatically arched brows, a long, thin nose, and a tiny purse of a mouth. Justy had calculated she must be nearly thirty years old, but she looked at least ten years younger. She was looking at her hands, folded in her lap, narrow palms and long fingers, lighter close to the knuckles where she had taken off her rings. That gave Justy an idea.

"Sahar, I need you to tell me everything you can about the night Rumi was killed. Can you do that?"

"Yes. But I know very little. I was locked in a room."

"Why?"

"Because Absalom wanted to be sure I would not try to stop him whoring my daughter."

He saw the fire in her eyes then, the strength she had used to cut Umar's throat. "Last night, he said he saved her from being stoned to death. Did that happen often?"

"Only once. A few years ago. A man was stoned for raping a boy."

"I see. And Rumi's crime was bad enough for her to be stoned?"

"So he said."

"So why wasn't she?"

"Because he wanted the child."

Justy nodded. "He had to punish her, though. To keep everyone else in line."

"He disowned her," she spat. "He wanted to put her in her place. He told her he would whore her, then take her child and make her a serf, cleaning the bog houses."

Kerry took one of her hands.

"So what happened?" Justy asked.

"I don't know. I was locked in. But I heard the noise. A crashing sound, like glass breaking. People shouting. I was told Rumi had stabbed the man and run away." She looked down. "It was only later I heard it was not she who had stabbed him, but the other way around."

She gripped Kerry's hand, skin on her knuckles turning pale. Justy waited for a moment.

"Do you know who the man was?"

She shook her head. "One of the wealthy men that came up every few weeks, to drink and smoke and plough the white women. I never saw their faces. I don't know their names. The angels served them."

"But Rumi wasn't white."

Sahar's eyes filled with tears again, so that her pupils looked magnified. "When Absalom locked me up, he said one of his visitors wanted a dark-skinned woman for a change. But he feared getting the pox from a Canvas Town whore. Rumi was perfect because she was clean." Her voice wobbled.

"Thank you, Sahar." He sat back, gingerly. He had the feeling the chair was going to collapse under him, but it was surprisingly sturdy. "Now it's my turn to try and help you."

A faint smile. "How can you help me?"

"Umar . . . Absalom . . . was Rumi's father. But was he your husband also? Were you pledged to each other?"

She looked up. The whites of her eyes were brilliant, as though her tears had washed them clean. "Why do you want to know this?"

"It may help you."

She shrugged. "He took my innocence when I was young. We had a child together later."

"Was there a formal marriage? Some kind of ceremony?"

"When Rumi was born, there was a ceremony. We were pledged to each other then."

"Who witnessed it?"

"Everyone."

"And did Umar have any other children? Or was Rumi the only one?"

"She was the only one."

Justy nodded. "That's very good, Sahar. Now we need to find some of the other people who were at the ceremony. They can testify that you and Umar were husband and wife."

"And why would I want this?"

"Because if you are his wife, in the eyes of the law, you will inherit an estate that could be worth a great deal of money. Enough to get to a safe place and build a new life. For you, and anyone else you wanted to bring with you."

She looked at Kerry. Kerry nodded, and squeezed her hand.

Sahar's face darkened. "But what about Owens?"

"You will have to be careful. Stay hidden. Have Kerry look for your witnesses. You and they have to see a lawyer and sign some papers."

He made to leave.

"One thing." Sahar was standing by the bed, holding her head up. "When my friend came to tell me Rumi had stabbed the man, she said the angels, the white women, gave him a nickname."

"What was it?" Justy asked.

"Firkin."

FORTY-THREE

"Could be anyone." Lars was wedged into the backward-facing seat of a public hansom, shoulder to shoulder with Hardluck and facing Justy, who had the uncomfortable sensation that the cab might come apart at any moment. The wind whistled in around the sides of the doors and through a hole in the flimsy leather roof, and there were gaps in the floorboards, so wide that he could see the cobbles on the road.

A firkin was a barrel. So the man might be barrel-chested, or barrel-bellied. That could describe half the men in the city. Or perhaps it was a reference to the man's appetite for food. Or drink. It was a neat description for Jake Hays, now that he thought about it.

He felt a chill. Hays had warned him away from Jericho. He had forbidden him to talk to Umar. And Riker. And Beaulieu. Could Hays have killed the girl? It seemed impossible. The High Constable was a happily married man, with two daughters of his own. But Justy knew from experience that apparently happily married men were capable of all kinds of depravity.

"It could be anyone," he said to himself. Except that it could not be anyone. Umar had managed to keep his brothel-cum-infant farm a secret. So secret that even Seamus Tully, a man who knew almost everything that went on in the city, had never caught a whiff of it. Which suggested a small, exclusive group. And Rumi's killer had been a frequent visitor, which suggested he was wealthy or influential enough to be worth cultivating. A man of a certain class. And not of the class of men that took their pleasure in Canvas Town. So not just anyone at all.

And how did he get to Jericho? Not in a hackney: such a man would not want to risk being seen in public. And not in his own carriage either, because servants talk, and a driver might tell a housemaid, who might let it slip to her mistress. Another man's carriage, then.

And that thought made Justy smile, because they were drawing up to the Tontine, the horses sweating and farting as the hack lurched to a halt. He climbed out and flicked a coin to the driver, who rubbed it tenderly with his thumb and tipped his beaver hat in thanks. Then Justy led Lars and Hardluck around the corner of the Tontine to the stables.

Tobias Riker's carriage was drawn up to the side. It was identical to the one Justy had won from Piers Riker, except that it was, if possible, in even better condition. The paintwork gleamed in the afternoon sunlight, and the pennants flickered like snakes' tongues in the breeze.

The driver, dressed head to toe in white, had his back to them, and was leaning into the cab. Justy quickened his pace.

"The jarvie there, what's his name again?"

"Meriday," Hardluck said.

"Meriday is going to tell us everything we need to know. Who went where, and when."

The driver was almost flat on his stomach now, reaching for something deep inside the cab. There was a grunt of satisfaction, and he pulled himself upright. He was a big man, about fifty years of age, with a crown of white hair. He sweated freely, the beads of perspiration standing out on the dark skin of his brow. He grinned, a wide, white smile, and showed Justy what he had found. It was a small gold watch. He wound it up as he spoke.

"All the way down the side, it was," he said, in a deep voice. "It winked at me as I was wiping down the seats. Mister Riker will be pleased I found that." He lifted the watch to his ear, laughed, and slipped it into his pocket.

"I want to ask you about the people who have been using this carriage," Justy said.

Hardluck stepped up behind him. "Sir, I—"

Justy waved him back. "A moment, please, Hardluck."

"But this isn't Meriday."

Justy felt as though all the air had been sucked out of his lungs. The driver flashed his wide smile again. "I'm William, sir."

"Where's Meriday?"

"I don't know, sir. Taken ill, perhaps. I ain't seen him since yesterday. Mister Riker told me to take on his duties this morning. He didn't say why."

Justy wanted to curse and swear and stamp about the stables, but he contented himself with groaning inside. Riker might have no idea who knew what about his relationship to Umar, but he was clever enough to realize that it was better for everyone if he erased all trace of it. And that included squirreling away his driver, who must have seen every face, and knew every address. And where was Meriday now? Shipped back to the farm was one possibility. Facedown in the Helgate was another.

"I'm Justice Flanagan. Did Mister Riker tell you of our arrangement?"

The driver nodded. "She's all washed and swept and ready to go, Marshal. I expect young Hardluck here will be driving her for you."

"He will be driving, yes. Although not for me. This is now Mister Cross's carriage."

"Mister Cross, sir? Is that this gentleman?" William turned his wide smile on Lars.

"No. That is this gentleman." Justy slapped Hardluck on the shoulder. "Allow me to present Hardluck Cross, a free citizen of the city of New York."

William's mouth fell open, into a huge O, and his eyes opened wide. Hardluck was grinning, his eyes shining, and it was a moment before William had gathered himself. "It's true, then?"

"True as the nose on your face, Willum."

The older man's face seemed to melt slightly, and his eyes were suddenly wet. He cleared his throat. "That's wonderful news, Hardluck. Best news I've heard in I don't know when. Carly will be fair betwattled when I tell her. And Tilly, too."

"You give them my love, now."

The driver smiled his wide smile. "I'll do that. I certainly will."

He shook Hardluck firmly by the hand, then turned away.

Hardluck watched him go. "Willum's normally a footman. Can't drive worth a damn." His voice was tight.

"You're good friends?"

Hardluck nodded. "I've known him since I was a chit. He's like an uncle, more or less."

"He seemed pleased to have found Mister Riker's watch."

Hardluck shook his head. "Not Mister Riker's. He doesn't stand for jewelry. Him and Master Piers had a terrible fight about it once. He says it draws attention."

Justy watched William climb the steps to the servant's entrance at the back of the Tontine.

Hardluck was staring at the carriage, and the two chestnut mares, standing quietly in their traces. "Are you sure about this, sir?"

"I am, Hardluck. I felt awful about asking you to torch the other one. And it's the least I can do in return for your help last night. You'll do me the honor of taking it and saying no more."

"I will, sir."

"And you'll stop calling me sir, please. I'm Justy, to my friends." He held out his hand.

Hardluck shook. "Thank you, Justy."

Now Justy had to clear his throat. "Right then. Let's get on out of here, before Riker changes his mind."

"Where can I take you?" Hardluck asked.

Justy shook his head. "Lars and I are taking Shanks' pony from here, but there is one thing you can do for me, if you don't mind."

"Name it."

"I need you to take a message to Kerry O'Toole."

FORTY-FOUR

The working week was now over, and Wall Street was a shadow of its normal self. There were plenty of people in the dress shops and fancy goods stores up and down the hill, but the usual crush of traffic was a memory, and it was an easy task to cross the freshly swept street.

Justy walked alone down William Street. The whole way down the hill he felt his insides drawing tighter, until he made the right turn and arrived at the High Constable's house. There was neither a door knock, nor a bell pull, so he rapped on the dark green paint with his knuckles. A moment later the door was hauled open and Hays was glaring at him.

"And where the rotting cod have you been?" he demanded.

"I'm sorry, Jake, I—"

"It's 'sir' to you, until you've explained yourself, young man."

Justy flushed. "And should I do so on your front step with all the glimms in the street a-peeping?"

Hays scowled. He led Justy down to his study. It was a small, brown, airless room, crammed with books, with barely enough room for a desk and chair. It was lit by a single window, set high in the wall.

Hays closed the door. "Well?"

"I'm sorry I didn't come to see you this morning."

"You'd damned well better be sorry. You're making it increasingly difficult for me to make the case that you should remain in the city's service. What am I to make of the report you left me? You admit to taking part in a riot that left nearly ten men dead. You admit to setting a fire inside the city bounds. You tell some wild story about your own protégé trying to attack you, ending in a fight that leads to his death at the hand of your own goddamned slave."

"May I explain?"

"You may try."

Justy looked up at the window. A fly was buzzing against the glass. "I didn't come to see you because I knew you would stop me from doing what I had to do."

"Which was?"

"Talk to Tobias Riker."

"Riker!" Hays face turned a shade closer to purple. "God damn it, Flanagan, I—"

"Riker is at the heart of this thing. I told you I would connect his scheme with Umar to the girl's death, and now I believe I have. Umar was running a unique kind of brothel in Jericho, prostituting young white girls to wealthy men, getting them pregnant, and then selling their babies. And Riker knew all about it."

"What?" The color had drained from Hays' face.

"Umar was selling children. Infants. To slave takers and tribal chiefs in Africa. He traded them for money or other slaves, which he then sold himself on the markets, probably in New Jersey or down south. He also sold some children here, in New York, to wealthy families who couldn't have children of their own. Riker knew about the whole scheme, because it was the source of income Umar used to make his primary payment for the land purchases from Lispenard. Riker's bank paid the rest."

Hays leaned on his desk, clutching the edge. He looked as though he had been punched. Above him, the fly began to hurl itself at the glass, over and over. "How do you know this?"

"Kerry O'Toole found out. She disguised herself and went in there a few days ago. She met the dead girl's mother, who told her the whole thing. The girl's name was Rumi, by the way. Umar was her father."

Hays sat and thought it through. Justy could almost see him slotting all the pieces of information into place in his head. Slowly, the color came back into his cheeks. "Very well," he murmured. "Very well. But even suppose Riker knew about this noxious business, what does he have to do with the girl's death?"

"Umar was playing a very long game. He wasn't interested in money from prostitution, which wouldn't amount to so much. It was the children and the associated trade that brought in the real chink. The mothers were easy to find. There are so many desperate young women arriving every day in this city that no one notices when a few disappear. But to make white babies, he needed white men as well. He couldn't very well hang out a shingle and let in every jack tar and swoddie in the city. Word would get out immediately, and what would New Yorkers think of a black Mohammedan keeping two dozen white girls foxed and locked up in a fortress?"

"Not much."

"No indeed. So he needed a small group of men, the kind that are used to keeping secrets. Wealthy men, with a lot to lose, so if they were tempted to turn conk, Umar had plenty to threaten them with. And he needed someone to find these men for him."

"And you think that man is Riker."

"I'm sure of it. I saw his carriage going up there, remember."

"But you said that was the lawyer."

"Yes. But Riker's driver told my man he was ferrying folk up and down from there all the time. And how else would these men get to Jericho? Not on their own."

"No." Hays was rubbing his chin now, his mind racing. "Go on."

"The girl's mother told Kerry that Umar was furious when he heard she was pregnant. He excommunicated her from his church, or whatever he called it, and disowned her. Then he prostituted her. To one of his visitors. Some cove who fancied a roll with a cherry-colored cat for a change. He was skittish about being tipped a token if he went down Canvas Town, so he wanted a girl who was guaranteed to be clean. Umar gave him his daughter."

Hays was very quiet.

Justy went on. "The Corrigan lad said she was a spirited girl. She must have fought back. There was a kickup, and someone said she stabbed the man, but they got it confused. He stabbed her, as we know, but not badly enough to kill her there and then. Somehow she was able to get clear of the place, and make it to the alley."

"So the killer is an associate of Riker's."

"Yes."

"And Riker's protecting him?"

"I think so. He has to, because if we catch him, the whole scheme is blown. Riker will be disgraced, not just because of the fraud with Umar, or even the murder, but association with a baby-trading scrap? White slavery would be a shade too dark, even for his Wall Street messmates."

"Yes. Yes, I see." Hays pushed himself off the desk. "So how do we get to Riker?"

"We don't. At least not in any way I can see. He's covered his tracks too well."

"But he guaranteed Umar's loans, didn't he?"

"His bank did. But there's nothing to say he knew anything of it. Riker's sharp. He'll have used someone else to grease the lawyer, Shard. He won't want any kind of connection there. He made a mistake getting Chase Beaulieu a job with the surveyors. He underestimated him, and I think Chase twigged what was going on. And that got him killed. Riker's driver knows who the men are—he would have picked them up and dropped them off. But Riker has paumed him. Hidden him, or hushed him. Either way, he's not to be found."

"What, then?"

"We have to go about this the other way. There can't be that many men who Riker trusts enough to let into a scheme like this. Rumi's mother said they nicknamed him: the firkin."

Hays slid his fingers into his waistcoat. "Well, that could mean anything."

"Yes. And there are plenty of barrel-shaped coves that frequent the Tontine. But how many are that close to Riker? That's where we have to start."

Hays sighed. "And Riker? He just gets away with all of this?"

"For now, yes. But there is a silver lining."

Justy told him about the deal he had struck. Hays' face was a picture of indecision, his forehead furrowed and his lips pursed tight as he suppressed a smile.

"That's highly irregular, Justice. You had no authority to make such a bargain."

"No indeed. And nor would you have given it me. But this way Riker is out of your hair, and the city's business."

"The bloody rogue still stands to make a great deal of money."

"Perhaps. That's up to Umar's heir." And he told Hays about his plans for Sahar.

Hays' eyebrows flew skyward. "My God! That won't go down well."

"No. But by that time it won't make much difference either way. We'll either have caught our man and he'll implicate Riker and they'll both be in clink, or we won't, and the bastards will all be scot-free."

"Which present us with a situation of extreme urgency, wouldn't you say?" Hays' eyes were sharp and clear, and burning with energy. "Riker's a careful man. He won't want to sit to see if we can catch this fellow. Quite the contrary. He'll want to sew things up as quickly as possible. He's going to kill him."

He disappeared for a few moments, and returned wearing a long leather coat and pushing a hat onto his head. They walked quickly up the hill towards the Federal Hall, the breeze from the docks at their backs.

"We must secure all of Mister Shard's papers, immediately. And Shard along with them. If, as you say, he hasn't had any contact with Riker, he's probably not in imminent danger, but still." He ran up the steps of the Hall, calling for the Watch commander.

Playfair presented himself, his chest puffed out, his chin jutting like a rail spike. He slammed to attention in the doorway of Hays' office.

"Excellent!" Hays' eyes sparkled. He squinted at the watchman, whose eyes were rimmed with red, and whose cheeks were heavy with stubble. "A long night, was it, Mister Playfair? Were you out rousting rogues or drinking with them?"

"A little bit of both, if I'm honest, sir." Playfair's voice was gravelly.

Hays laughed. "Well, listen carefully, now. I have a task for you and your men."

A moment later, Playfair was hurrying back down the stairs with his orders. Hays slumped into his chair.

"Is there anything I have forgotten?"

"Almost certainly."

The High Constable acknowledged the point with a smile.

Justy went to the window. Below him, a carter was heaving on the arms of a wagonload of split firewood as he tried to get it around a corner to the back of the Hall. "Why did you want to keep me away from Jericho, Jake?"

Hays was quiet.

"I've spent days trying to piece it together, and I still can't. So tell me why. Why warn me away from Umar and his compound? And while you're at it, you can tell me why you've been huddling with cavalry officers the past week, and how it is that they managed to get to Jericho so damned quickly, given their quarters are more than an hour's ride away in Fort Washington."

The High Constable sighed. "I was under orders."

"From whom?"

"The Mayor." He fiddled with his fingers. "He knew Umar was buying land."

"What?" It took a second for the implications to sink home. "So yesterday, when you were filling me with Frog stingo, and I was telling you about the scrap, you already knew all about it?"

"Not all. Nothing to do with Riker or any of that. Just that Umar was buying up the meadowlands."

"How did the Mayor twig it?"

"Someone up at Albany audited Mister Shard's papers and noted those sales. I think the name Absalom struck them as unusual, and they asked the Mayor's office to look into it. He found out who Absalom was, but rather than expose the thing, he decided to use it as leverage."

Justy was cold. "Against who?"

"Against Umar. He came up with a plan. A mad, windmill-headed scheme. I was against it, of course, but he was adamant. And I was sworn to secrecy. No one knew, apart from me, the Mayor, and Major Swift. And Umar, of course."

"What was the plan?"

Hays shook his head. "As you know, the Mayor is under a great deal of pressure from the owners of the land that Canvas Town stands on. They want the squatters gone, but Lew Owens is making it impossible. He will not be bought off, and the bailiffs charged with moving the squatters are afraid to do their work, lest Owens' men beat them within an inch of their lives, or worse. So the Mayor has been seeking a solution, and, in his eyes, Umar provided one. He told Umar that he would not inhibit his purchase of land, on two conditions. That Umar agree to vacate his compound, and that he come up with a way to lure Owens and your uncle into a trap."

"Jericho."

"Precisely. His plan, clearly flawed as it was, was to get as many men as possible into the place, pour a volley into them, and allow panic to ensue. Then Major Swift's men would move in and put as many of the invaders to the sword as they could. A *coup de main*, he called it."

"I saw Brown Bess muskets there. Did the cavalry provide them?"

"Yes. The idea was for them to recover the weapons after the attack."

"A bloody stupid idea. Owens and the Bull have them now."

Hays sighed, and slumped in his chair. Justy leaned back against the window. The sun was setting, and the white walls of Hays' office were now a pale pink. "The riot on George Street. Did you know that was Umar?"

Hays looked away. "I wasn't certain, no."

"Damn you, Jake! I was nearly killed!"

Hays flapped his arms. "Umar overreached. I'm sorry. I told the Mayor, over and over, that this plan of his was madness. He wouldn't listen."

"You could have told me. I'm supposed to be your right hand." Justy's voice was cold. "Or are you of the opinion that blood is thicker than water?"

Hays looked at the papers on his desk.

"I see." Justy felt a churning, deep in his chest. "I think perhaps Tobias Riker won't be the only one resigning his commission on Monday."

FORTY-FIVE

Lars was waiting for him in the alley opposite the Millennium Bank. It was a new building, three stories high, made of brick, with a bright yellow door.

"Anything?" Justy asked.

Lars rubbed his hand over the stubble on his head. It made a sound like a ship's hull being sanded. "No one's come or gone. Through the front, at least. But there's someone inside. I've seen him moving about in there. How did it go with Hays?"

"About as expected. He as good as admitted that he suspects the Bull and I are confederates."

Lars nodded at the yellow door. "And this?"

"Let's see."

They walked across the street to the bank. The yellow door had a large black knocker at chest height. Justy was about to use it when Lars tried the handle. It turned easily.

The entire ground floor of the bank was a single, large room, dotted with islands of chairs and tables. The walls were painted a pale yellow, and the wainscoting and trim was all brilliant white. The effect was bright and airy. A creaking sound came from above them. A set of stairs in the corner of the large room led up to the first floor. They went up carefully, but there was no hiding the sound of their tread on the landing, and by the time they had opened the door to his office, Charles Shotwell had composed himself.

He sat behind his desk, his hands folded over his stomach, and flashed a weak grin. "Marshal Flanagan. What a surprise."

Justy nodded to Lars. "Wait downstairs." He stood in the doorway, his eyes on Shotwell, waiting until Lars reached the bank's ground floor. The room was as light and airy as the lobby, with the same bright yellow walls and white trim. Shotwell's heavy mahogany desk and overstuffed chair looked out of place.

"I would have thought you'd have gone down to the country by now, Mister Shotwell."

The grin flashed again. "Well, I was about to go. I was indeed. But duty calls, eh?"

"Tobias Riker called, you mean."

"Yes. Well. He is the owner of the bank. So it rather amounts to the same thing."

"Of course. And after I left him earlier, he asked you to cover your tracks, didn't he? Just in case."

Shotwell tutted a laugh. He swallowed. "Not sure what you mean, old stick."

"I mean in case there are any issues with Umar's estate. If he has heirs, they will inherit the land he bought from Lispenard. If not, the land will revert to the city. Either way, you'll have a plague of lawyers looking for the documents detailing the sales. Documents with your bank's name all over them. Awkward for Riker. And better for him if those documents ceased to exist. At least until after the moratorium. No doubt he is talking with Mister Shard right now about setting his copies of the papers aside. And you're here today doing the same. Just in case some nosy city official like me decides to do an audit."

"Preposterous." Shotwell's face had grown crimson. "That would be illegal."

"Indeed it would."

He let the silence fill the room. The color seeped slowly out of Shotwell's cheeks. A pigeon settled on the sill of the window.

Shotwell opened his mouth, then closed it again as Justy held a finger to his lips.

Below them a door opened. There was the sound of murmured conversation, and then of two sets of boots on the stairs and along the landing.

Lars stepped into the room, followed by Kerry in her apprentice's clothes and green caubeen hat. She leaned on the doorway, her hands in her pockets.

Shotwell was now as pale as the trim running around the ceiling of his office. He shrank into his chair.

Lars grinned. "He thinks we're going to kimbaw him."

"Don't worry, Mister Shotwell," Justy said. "We're not going to hurt you."

He turned to Kerry. "How's your skills?"

"Sweet as a nut." She held out her hand. Nestled in her palm was the gold watch William had found in the carriage. "Bumped him in the stairwell at the Tontine. He didn't feel a thing."

It was an expensive piece, two inches across, but less than a half-inch thick, with a push clasp that held the two sides of the gold clamshell together. Justy flipped it open, to reveal a white-faced dial with delicate black numbering, and minute and hour hands made of gold. Engraved on the inside of the clamshell were the letters CRS.

He held up the open watch for Shotwell to see. The banker's eyes bulged.

"What does the R stand for, Charles? Robert? Richard?"

"Reginald." Shotwell's voice sounded strangled.

Justy sat on the edge of the desk. He grabbed Shotwell by the chin. He turned the banker's face to the side, and examined the cut on his cheek. "It's almost gone now, that little slice of yours. Tell me again how you got it."

"Shaving." It was hard for Shotwell to speak. His eyes flickered.

"Shaving." Justy let him go. "Why was your watch in Riker's cab, Shotwell?"

The banker wiped his hands on his waistcoat. "Why shouldn't it be? He's the president of this bank."

"And does he often ferry you about the city?"

"No. But occasionally he will send the carriage for me, if he wants me to meet him."

"Where? The Tontine is across the street. His house is a stroll away. As is yours, I imagine."

He had no idea where Shotwell lived, but he guessed it was in the better part of the city, close to Wall Street. The twitch on the banker's face told him he was right.

"Hughson's?" Shotwell's voice rose, as though asking for approval.

Justy smiled. "So Mister Riker is a frequenter of taverns, is he? And when did you lose this pretty montra of yours?"

Shotwell glanced down at the papers on his desk. "Two weeks ago."

"Two weeks? And was that on a trip to Hughson's?"

"It was."

He gave Shotwell a long look, and let the silence in the room do its work. The banker's eyes flicked between him, Lars, and Kerry, who was still leaning on the door, her arms folded now, her eyes like chips of jade.

"Very well, we'll come back to the watch presently," Justy said. "Tell me about your child."

Shotwell twitched. "My what?"

"Your child. Your baby. What's its name?"

"James."

"How original. Where did you get it?"

Shotwell's mouth fell open. "I don't know what you mean."

"Where did you get it? Not the natural way. You've been trying for too long for that. No doubt you assumed it was because your wife is too old, but I'm willing to wager that you're the problem. But Riker had a solution for you, didn't he? A supply of clean, healthy white babies for you to shop from."

"I . . . ah . . ." Shotwell was perspiring now, beads of sweat leaping out over his forehead.

Justy leaned in. "I met the mother, you greasy scut. She might have been fourteen years old. They kept her drugged and shut up in a cell, about the size of your desk. But you know that, don't you? Because you've been to Jericho, many times. And you were there on Saturday night, were you not?"

"No! I swear."

"Riker knew he could trust you. God knows what manner of frauds the two of you have cooked up using this bank over the years, so you were a natural choice to join his tight little crew of rapists. Did you go through the girls in rotation, Shotwell, or did you have favorites?" He didn't wait for an answer. "But that wasn't enough variety for you, was it? You fancied yourself something a little darker. But there's all sorts of risks that come with laying with a cherry-colored cat. She might turn out to be a fire ship, and a married man like yourself doesn't want to find himself peppered, because how could you explain that? So you asked Umar, and because you've been such a good little rapist, and such a good customer, he promised you a clean Negro wench for your pleasure."

Shotwell's head was hanging now. His eyes were closed.

Justy stood up and leaned over the banker, white knuckles on the desktop. "Only this one wasn't drugged to the eyeballs, was she? This one fought back. You were in Umar's withdrawing room, weren't you? Umar left you there with her, because the poor lass didn't have her own cell. You went to grab her, but there was a ruck. You knocked over the table and upset the cutlery box, and she grabbed a knife and took a swipe at your face, and even though it was a poxy table chive, it had a good enough point on it to gouge you. And that made you see red, didn't it? Goddamned nigger whore going for you with a blade, so you slapped her and snatched the knife, and you pushed her back and you stabbed her. You fucking stabbed her . . ."

Lars pulled him back, dragging him away from Shotwell, off the desk and into the center of the room. Justy shook him off, his chest heaving, stars bursting in front of his eyes.

Shotwell was crying, snot like a carpet under his nose, his cheeks slick with tears. "It was an accident. An accident. I swear it. The girl—"

"Rumi," Kerry snapped. "Her name was Rumi."

Shotwell shook his head. "It was the drug. The charas . . . I would never . . ."

Kerry crossed the room in three quick strides. Justy felt her brush past him, and instinctively reached for his pocket, but she had already slit the bottom with the tiny blade she carried, and caught his knife as it fell. The blade clicked out, and she slid hard across the desk, sending papers flying to the floor as she slammed into the banker and put the knife to his throat.

"Rumi," she hissed. "Say her name."

Shotwell's mouth flapped open, like a fish gasping. "Rumi."

"I should tear your throat out for what you did. But it would be too quick." She slid the point of the knife down over the bulge of his belly, straining against the waistcoat as his breath came hard and fast. "Perhaps I should do to you what you did to her. Make a little hole in your guts and let your life leak out." She sneered. "Or maybe I'll just cut your cock off."

"No!" Shotwell squeaked. "Please! What do you want?"

"I want you to confess, Shotwell," Justy said. "I want you to come with me to the Hall, and I want you to write out a full confession. The girl, the scheme, Riker, everything."

Shotwell was shaking, cringing away from Kerry and the knife in her hand. "I didn't mean to hurt the girl. I swear. It was an accident. The drug. I wanted to scare her. It was a mistake. I'll confess." He swallowed. "But Riker . . . I can't . . . he'll kill me."

Justy shrugged. "As you wish. In that case we'll leave you with her."

Kerry grinned. She slipped the blade under Shotwell's waistcoat and slid it upwards. A button popped off and rattled across the desk. And then another.

"Stop." Shotwell's face was running with sweat. "I'll tell you. I'll tell you everything."

"Now that's a pity."

Justy and Lars spun around. Playfair was standing in the doorway. He had a long knife thrust into his belt and a pistol in each hand. One was pointed at Justy's stomach, the other at Shotwell's chest. He chuckled at the look on Justy's face.

"What?" he said. "You didn't think that soft peg Gorton was the only one on Riker's roll, did you? A man as fly as Mister Tobias don't take chances."

Justy's chest was tight, his legs like water. He couldn't stop staring at the small black hole at the end of the pistol barrel. "But Gorton was Umar's man."

"Mayhap he thought as much, but it was Riker's money, and that made him Riker's man. He'd have twigged in time." The pistol aimed at Shotwell twitched upwards, to point at Kerry. "Drop the chive now, lass. Nice and easy, on the floor."

She swung her right hand out slowly, holding the hilt of the knife between her finger and thumb. She let it fall, point down, so that it stuck in the floorboards.

"You braced Shard," Justy said.

"That I did. Likes a tipple and a wench, does Mister Shard. So I gave him both, and had him tied up, and then we talked. He came around easy enough."

"He called you a devil."

"Did he, now?" Playfair grinned. "I'll take that as a compliment."

"Is he dead?"

"Not as yet. Word from the Almshouse is we might not have to bother with him, as the good Lord looks set to carry him off for us. But either way, he'll be stiff before long."

Justy smiled to himself. The Almshouse was as safe a place as any. A killer would find it hard to get past Sister Marie-Therese. He watched Playfair. The big watchman was trying to come up with a solution to the obvious problem in front of him. He had two pistols, but there were at least three people to kill. Four if he wasn't under orders to save Shotwell for Riker. The obvious solution was to pot Lars and Justy, then take the knife out of his belt and use it on Kerry. After that, dealing with Shotwell would be easy. Except that Kerry might pick up the knife and put up a fight, and that might give the banker time to run for it.

The other option was to shoot Kerry, because she had a weapon to hand, and Justy because he was closest, then go for Lars with the knife in his belt. But Lars was a big man, bigger than Playfair, and a sailor, which meant he likely knew how to handle himself in a clutch. Neither situation was ideal.

He dealt with the Shotwell problem by stepping into the room and kicking the office door closed behind him. Then he leaned on the door. "Behind the desk, jack," he said to Lars, keeping the pistol in his right hand on Justy.

"Nice and easy. Any malarkey and I'll give the Marshal here a plump in the breadbasket."

Lars walked slowly around the table. Playfair was herding them into a single cluster. A good plan, Justy thought, because it made them all easier to watch. And to kill, if it came to that. The desk was a nice touch. If they wanted to attack Playfair, even together, they would all have to navigate the obstacle, and the extra second or two might give him an edge.

The only flaw in the plan was that it would bring Justy closer to his own knife. The big blade was not well balanced for throwing. The handle was too heavy and bulky. But Justy had practiced enough to be lethal over a distance of up to twenty feet.

And Playfair was just ten feet away.

The big watchman grinned. His teeth were ragged and tobacco brown. "You want that chive, don't you, Marshal? Think you can spear me in the tripe, and mayhap you could, if I let you near it. But I didn't come up the East River on a fucking banana boat. So get yourself back there beside the tar."

Justy took a slow step backwards, his eyes on the gun. He had to move slightly left to round the desk, widening the angle between the two points of aim of Playfair's pistols. The watchman was focused entirely on him, and Justy knew that if Lars was going to move, now was the time.

There was the briefest flicker of light in the corner of his right eye, like the sun reflecting on the window of a carriage. There was no time for his mind to work, but his instinct told him that if he was distracted, then so was Playfair, and he hurled himself to the ground.

Playfair fired both pistols together. There was an enormous bang, and Justy felt something snatch at his side. Just his coat, he thought.

The room was full of smoke. He was lying on his back, thinking that he had to get up and close with Playfair, but his arms and legs, even his head, seemed to be fixed to the floor. There was a blur of movement. He could hear a choking, rattling sound, and then Kerry's face was floating above him. Her hand was cool on his cheek. He could feel someone tugging at his clothes. Kerry was talking to him, but he couldn't hear anything over a rushing sound in his ears. Her hat was off, and her hair was hanging over her shoulder. Like a waterfall at night, he thought, with the moonlight reflecting on it. Her eyes were wet and the rushing in his ears became a roar and she seemed to shrink away from him, all the way down to the end of a long tunnel. And then, darkness.

FORTY-SIX

Saturday

He knew he was alive, because he could smell bacon. He had the feeling he had been wrapped in it and was being basted in fat. He couldn't open his eyes. He couldn't even move his face. The flesh felt heavy on his bones, smeared into place. Perhaps someone had put bacon on his face, too. Heavy slabs of ham, laid over his mouth and nose and eyes.

"How much did you give him?"

Lars' voice. His old friend. Lars liked bacon. He had seen him eat an entire piglet once. They had stolen it from a farm near Naas when they were on the run from the redcoats. How many years ago was that? Lars was wounded, so Justy had left him in the woods and hopped into the sty and chased the little bastard around in the mud for ten minutes before getting a grip on it and cutting its throat. The piglet's blood had sprayed into his face, warm and salty. The farmer had come after him, but the sight of Justy, covered in mud and blood and pig shit might have made the farmer think he was a *sluagh*, an evil fairy, and not a human being. So he let him go, and Justy and Lars lit a low fire and cooked the pig, and Lars devoured the whole thing, except the head, which Justy ate.

Maybe he had a pig's face, then. Maybe that was what the bacon smell was all about.

"How much?" Lars asked again.

"It was a mistake," a woman said. "He was given a dose when he came in, but it wasn't recorded, and so he was dosed again. I'm sorry."

"You're sorry? That much opium could kill him!"

Calm down, Lars, he wanted to say. *Calm down, my old friend, and have some bacon.* But his lips wouldn't work, and the words wouldn't come and he felt himself drifting away, like a boat being pulled towards a waterfall. And then he tipped over.

He knew he was alive because he was vomiting, and dead men didn't shoot the cat. Although he might be dead, a small voice inside him noted, if he kept on spewing in the same manner for long. He felt as though the Devil had thrust a gnarly hand down his gullet and was pulling his entrails out.

There was a hand rubbing his back. "Get it all out, now," a soft voice said, and he wanted to scream that there was no more to come out, that he was retching dry, but at that very moment, the Devil gave one final tug, and a stream of black bile spilled out of his mouth, burning his tongue and his gums as it spattered into the wooden bowl that was being held under his face.

He spat, tears in his eyes, and rolled onto his back. He was naked under a sheet and a blanket, with a wide bandage wrapped around his middle. Lars and Kerry were standing over him. Kerry was dressed in her teacher's clothes. Her hair was up and her arms were folded. Her lips were pursed and her eyes were the color of fresh-cut grass. Lars was dressed for the sea, his head freshly shaven, and his tricorn hat under his arm. He grinned. "There he is, the man himself. I knew a wee drop of the poppy wouldn't hurt you."

Justy's mouth tasted like the inside of a rat's nest. "What time is it?"

"Five o'clock of a Saturday evening, or thereabouts. You've been away with the fairies a whole day. How was your trip?"

Justy shook his head. He tried to sit up, but pain shot through his groin. He gasped, and lay back, sweat cooling on his face.

"You caught a ball in the hip," Lars said. "The nimgimmer says you were lucky. It chipped off a chunk of the bone and bounced out. The bone with it. He says you'll mend in a few weeks, if you take it slow."

"It hurts like the Devil's peg." His voice was a rasp. "And what's that bacon smell?"

"Lard." A nun was standing beside him holding the wooden bowl. "We use it in the poultice. It holds the herbs together."

"I thought I was being roasted." He tried to sit up again, and the nun stepped forward to help. She thrust a pillow under his back, and then another, and propped him up. He blinked and looked around. He was in the long ward at the Almshouse, in the same bed Lars had been.

"What happened?"

"You don't remember anything?" Lars asked.

"Not much."

"Kerry here pinked that hackum with her wee chive."

Justy remembered the flash of light that had made him drop to the ground. "You threw it?"

Kerry said nothing.

Lars laughed. "Well, if you won't tell the tale, I shall. She was quick as a snake. Caught him right in the glimm. He fired both his barkers and we went for him at the same time, as soon as we realized we weren't plugged. He was clutching his eye with one paw, but had that toaster of his out with the other." He glanced at Kerry. "So I had to stick him with your knife."

"He's dead?"

"As good Queen Bess."

He took something out of his pocket and tossed it onto the bed. Justy looked down and saw his knife on the sheet, cleaned and oiled, the blade folded away, the brass fittings gleaming.

"And Shotwell?"

Lars shrugged. "He caught the other ball. Plumb in the fizz. Made a right hairy mess of him."

Justy's temples were throbbing, a pulse like a bullet ricocheting inside his skull. He closed his eyes, but it only made it worse. "That's it, then."

"What?"

"Without Shotwell, we can't get Riker. The bastard's going to get away clean."

"I thought you struck a deal."

"We did. But without Shotwell it won't hold. The only evidence against Riker's the paperwork, which can be interpreted any way he likes. Hardly enough to create a scandal."

"What about the lawyer?"

"Jesus!" Justy sat up, ignoring the pain in his side. "I'd forgotten about him. Is he here?"

"He is. They have him upstairs, isn't that right, Sister?"

The nun nodded. "Someone came and paid for him to be placed in a private room."

"Riker." Justy's mind ground into motion, like a rusty gearwheel. "Is there a guard on the door?"

Lars looked at the nun. She shook her head.

"We need to tell Hays," Justy said. "He needs to get a man up here now. Riker wants Shard on his own. He's easier to get to that way. And Riker will want to get to him."

"But you said he's likely never even met the man."

"No, but he has met Playfair. You heard Playfair admit he braced Shard and he worked for Riker. If we can get Shard to identify Playfair, then it puts Riker in the box. And Riker's sharp enough to know it."

"Right you are then," Lars said. "I'll send word down to the Hall. And I'll keep watch myself until a man comes." He strode away.

Kerry was still watching Justy, arms folded, an amused look on her face. She glanced at the bowl of vomit in the young nun's hands. "Shouldn't you empty that?"

The nun opened her mouth to reply, but Kerry's eyes flashed, and the nun hurried off.

"That blade of yours came in useful," Justy said.

"It was a lucky toss. I saw what you were up to, and figured we'd have no better time to rush him. I only wanted to put him off kilter."

"You saved us. He would have put a hole in the two of us and gone to skewer the third. Thanks."

She said nothing, but her eyes gleamed.

"Would you sit down, instead of looming over me like a schoolmarm?" Justy asked.

She gave him a cool look. "I would, but you might think I cared about you."

She sat down. Through the high Almshouse window, a long bank of cloud was turning several shades of orange and red as the sun set.

"We got him, then," she said.

"I'd have preferred to have him in front of a beak, but yes. We got him. Thanks to you buzzing that driver's sack."

She was almost smiling. "How did you know it was Shotwell's montra?"

"I didn't for sure, not until I saw the initials. But both times I met him, I saw him check his watch, then ask someone else for the time. I figured it was just broken, but when I saw the driver fish that onion out of the cab, I got the idea that maybe Shotwell was a twin-chain man, that he'd lost the working watch and the one he kept checking was the dummy. Once I had that in my head, and put him in Riker's carriage, everything else fell into place. His miracle baby, his position at the bank. And then I remembered what Sahar said, that someone told her that Rumi stabbed the man he was with. I thought maybe he wasn't stabbed so much as cut. And I remembered that cut on Shotwell's face was fresh and deep the first time I met him. Nothing that would stand up in court, mind you."

"The filthy murdering bastard didn't deserve a day in court." Kerry's voice was low. The half smile was gone. "He didn't deserve another breath. Not after taking two lives like that. If that hackum hadn't of plugged him, I'd have gut him myself, neck to nuts."

A veil seemed to fall over her eyes. He wanted to reach out and take her hand, but his arms felt as weak as a child's. She seemed to sense it, and she pushed her hands deeper into her lap.

"That's not you, Kerry." The words stuck in his throat like bits of dry bread.

"Is it not? You of all people know full well what I am."

"I know what you tell yourself. But what you might have been forced to do once, doesn't make you who you are now."

She was quiet for a moment.

"I killed Playfair," she said.

Justy felt the sweat start on his scalp. "Lars said—"

"The big clunch was spinning a dit, and you know it. You know where the knife was. There was no way he could have got past Playfair to get it."

"You passed it to him."

"Don't be soft. How would I have had the time to do so? And why would I, when I know rightly how to use a chive? Lars kept Playfair busy for the time I needed to get around on his blind side, and I stabbed that thing up under his arm." She gave a half smile. Distant eyes. "You do keep that yoke sharp. It went in like silk. Near took his feckin' fin off."

He tried to sit up further, gritting his teeth. "Kerry . . ."

She shook her head. "Are we not the sum of our deeds?"

"If you believe that, then look at your own deeds. Look at the work you've done in that school. The difference you made in those children's lives. You've done more of that than you have the other."

"You can use the words. Killing. Whoring."

"You were never a whore, Kerry. You were young, and you were forced. As for any killing you've done, it was in self-defense. And you saved my life by doing so. Both times now."

She turned her face away from him and held up her hand as though pushing him away, even though he could barely lift a finger. He had a memory of her as a child, making the same gesture, closing in on herself, holding him off until she had her emotions in check and her armor on.

"Don't do that, Kerry. Not to me."

She turned back to him. Her eyes were full of tears, magnified and luminous. He had once gone swimming in an old copper mine. He had the same feeling now as he had then, leaping off a high cliff, plunging into the cool, turquoise water.

"Would you prefer this?" She blinked, and the tears plunged down her face, and she trembled, still holding herself, her knuckles white in her lap, her eyes like two great lakes of pain.

"I love you," he said, the words tumbling out before he could stop them. And he lay there, aghast, his heart hammering in his throat.

Her fingers were cool on his cheek. She leaned close and kissed him, gently, and then pressed her cheek to his.

"And I love you," she whispered, and stayed for a moment. And then she was gone.

FORTY-SEVEN

Monday

It was another week before he could walk more than the length of the ward. Lars had gone back to sea. Kerry had gone back to the school. Teasman had been inclined to fire her for skipping out on her duties, but Justy had spoken to Hays, who had spoken to the Mayor, who had told John Teasman that he was looking forward to inspecting the African Free School and had heard great things about his female teaching assistant.

Shard had died. The doctor said the injury he had sustained in the riot on Laycock Lane had caused a brain hemorrhage, small enough to go undetected initially, but serious enough that it continued to bleed, and eventually killed him.

Riker was safe.

Justy walked slowly down the steps of the Almshouse, matching his pace to the slow toll of the nine o'clock bell at Trinity Church. Kerry had brought him his boots, fresh from the cobbler, and they fit like a new pair of kidskin gloves. But they couldn't stop the twin aches in his knee and his side, and he had to lean on an old, twisted blackthorn stick lent him by one of the nuns. Sister Marie-Therese watched from the top step, her hands tucked into the sleeves of her pristine surplice, like a seagull perched on a roof.

Hardluck met him at the bottom, and opened the door of the cab. The brass and the paintwork glowed, the leather was supple and smooth. Justy slid carefully onto the seat. He took a deep, grateful breath. "How much is a ride in this brothel chariot going to cost me?"

Hardluck grinned. He was wearing new whipcord breeches and a long leather driver's coat, with a waistcoat underneath, as red as a robin's breast. He was growing out his hair, and the beginnings of a small, neat beard.

"Your money's no good here, Marshal," he said, and before Justy could respond, he was on top of the cab, and clicking his tongue at the twin mares in the traps.

It was slow going. An oxcart had shed a load of apples on the Broad Way, and the carter was desperately trying to control the frightened animal as it lumbered back and forth, roaring and trampling the bright green fruit under its hooves. Both pigs and people fought over the loose apples as they rolled into the gutters and down the hill, and it was a few minutes before Hardluck was able to open a gap in the traffic and make a hard turn west.

Beekman Street was a quiet road, well kept by the residents, with none of the dead dogs and other rubbish that cluttered so many of the side streets in the quarter. At the bottom of the shallow hill, at the junction with Cliff Street, there was a small chapel, and Hardluck had to slow as a black trolley pulled by an enormous Shire horse swung up to the chapel gate.

A small procession had walked up behind the hearse. There were three men, one leading and two bringing up the rear. Between them was a group of four women who were holding on to each other, handkerchiefs pressed to their faces. As they waited for the undertakers, they clustered together. The leader was stocky and broad in the shoulders, but he was stooped over, his head bowed, so that his steel-gray hair flopped over his face. As he went to comfort the women, he glanced up, only for a moment, but long enough for Justy to recognize Franklin Beaulieu.

It was a Friday, so the lobby of the Federal Hall was as crowded as a carnival. Justy had to use his gnarled blackthorn more than once to reach the stairs. A tall watchman that he didn't know stopped him, but let him through when he told him he was there to see Jacob Hays.

The High Constable jumped up when he saw Justy, his red coat flying behind him as he hurried around the desk and ushered him to a chair. He poured a glass of something golden from an elaborate decanter and pressed it into Justy's hand.

Justy sipped. He grimaced. "Not your French tipple."

"Sherry. Birthday present from my cousin. It is a bit sweet."

Justy shrugged. "Forgive me for forgetting your birthday."

Hays smiled. He was perched on the edge of his desk. "You had other things to worry about. How are you feeling?"

"Much improved."

"Ready to come back?" Hays gulped his sherry.

"I'm not sure I should, Jake." It was an effort to lean forward far enough to place his glass on the table beside him. "I'm not sure I have your trust."

Hays reddened. He put his glass down and gripped the edge of the table. "Of course you do, Justice. There's no question."

"There did seem to be a question over this Jericho business."

"Yes." Hays dropped his head. "That was my mistake. One that I shall not make again. If you will give me another chance."

The Trinity Church bell began to ring the tenth hour.

Justy said, "I just saw Franklin Beaulieu leading a funeral procession, down at St. George's. Have they really kept his son above ground this long?"

"Good God, no. He was buried two days after they found him. That was the mother's funeral you saw."

"The mother?"

Hays' face was grim. "She killed herself. An overdose of laudanum. She was devoted to the boy, I'm told."

Justy's gut twisted, as he remembered his bizarre opium-induced dream in the Almshouse, and the black bile he had brought up after. "How did you find out?"

"The servants. They found her with the empty laudanum bottle by her bed. Difficult to keep that sort of thing quiet when the help's involved."

"Yes." He thought back to the scene outside the chapel. He had only seen Beaulieu's face for a moment, but he could still see the slack cheeks, the dark circles around the eyes, the way he was stooped over, as though for that moment, he was carrying all the sorrow in the world.

Hays reached for the sherry decanter. "Now, I'll be frank with you, Justice. We're in a hard spot. The Mayor has taken this carry-on with Playfair and Gorton and drawn all of the wrong conclusions. And Tobias Riker has done a fine job of turning things to his advantage. There's nothing to connect him to either man, so now he's been raising a fine hullaballoo about corruption and the recruitment of criminals into the Watch ahead of the Council meeting today. We're on our back foot, and no mistake."

"There's a meeting today? I thought the Council only met monthly."

"Riker has raised a special agenda. Specifically to do with policing and the Watch. We meet after luncheon."

Justy sighed. "I'm sorry. I thought I had Riker trussed up."

Hays smiled. "It was a damned close thing. But the cards all fell his way. Playfair, Shotwell, Shard. If any one of them had lived, he'd be in the bag. He was lucky, that's all."

Justy's knee was aching. He shifted in his chair. "There may be more, you know."

"Like Playfair? Oh, I know." Hays looked stern. "That's why I need you, Justice. You're the only man in this damned hall that I can really trust. This whole entanglement has shown me that, as clear as glass."

He tugged on the lapels of his red coat, as though he was pulling on some kind of armor. "The Mayor doesn't want you, you know. He has it in his head that you're a Fenian spy, or some such rot. But I told him what I believe, that you're the future of this city. That you understand it better that any of the spread-bellied Wall Street men and money-grubbing politicians that circulate between here and the Tontine. New York is going to grow, Justice. I know it and he knows it, and we both know that we don't know a damned thing about the people who are stepping off the ships in their hundreds every day, and will soon be thronging this island, from the Battery to Fort Washington. But you know them, Justice. You understand them. You are one of them, and we need you."

"Because I have a foot in both camps."

"Because you can move easily between them, yes, that's part of it. I won't deny that's useful to me."

"And my allegiances on either side?"

Hays laughed. "The only evidence of allegiance I've seen is to yourself. In another man, that might be dangerous, but in a man of your integrity and character, with your respect for the law, I consider it an asset."

Justy felt awkward. "You give me too much credit. I've done things—"

Hays waved his hand. "We've all done things. The question is why we do them. You do them because you believe they are right. Not for profit, or advancement, but because it is the moral thing. It makes you a bad politician, but if you let me play the politics, then we can do good work together, you and I." He thrust out his hand. "Will you reconsider?"

Justy felt a wave of affection for the stubby, florid-faced man in the red coat. He smiled slightly. "I want more money."

"You shall have it."

"And a dedicated assistant."

"Done."

"And my own carriage . . ."

"Oh for God's sake, man!" Hays roared, and pulled him out of his seat and hugged him.

The floorboards creaked behind them. Hays let Justy go.

"A touching scene."

Tobias Riker stood in the doorway. He was dressed simply, in banker's black, with the onyx pin through his white silk necktie. A thin smile had twisted his lips. "Celebrating something?"

"The renewal of Mister Flanagan's contract with the Marshal's service of the city of New York." Hays smoothed his coat.

Riker smirked. "Much good it will do him. By the time the day is done, there won't be a Marshal's service for him to contract with. And you'll be lucky if you still have a job."

"You overestimate yourself, Mister Riker," Hays said. "Your supporters may be fool enough to think that a city this size can do without some body of law enforcement, but the Mayor does not, and nor do the majority of the Council. Whatever arguments you make will soon be outweighed by the sheer volume of crimes that will inevitably increase as the city grows."

"Crime is a civic issue. It does not justify the creation of the police force that you advocate. A force that will amount to a standing army, with a remit to inhibit the freedoms of the citizenry. There are enough members of this Council who do not wish to see a return to the days when the soldiery patrolled New York's streets."

Riker spoke with an almost weary formality, as though these were well-worn arguments that he was becoming tired of repeating.

"No one is suggesting we create an army," Hays said. "But we need some kind of law enforcement body if we are not to become like London, where entire wards of the city are regarded as too dangerous for a gentleman or his lady to set foot. Or is that what you would prefer, Mister Riker?"

Riker flicked his hand. "I care not if the dregs of this city feed off each other in whatever depraved manner strikes them."

"And what if it's the quality indulging in the depravity?" Justy said. "Who polices them?"

Riker swiveled his gaze to take Justy in. "You've been in the wars, I see."

"You're only getting away with your part in all of this because Shotwell and Shard are dead."

"Inconvenient for you." The thin smile was gone now, and the eyes were burning.

"Perhaps. But not as inconvenient as having Umar's wife and heir vanish, is it? That property deal of yours has gone up in smoke. All that chink down the drain. And you on the verge of becoming a public man."

Riker said nothing.

"Oh yes," Justy went on. "I know all about your estate in New Jersey. I expect the bank is providing you with a long line of credit to keep it from going bankrupt. But you can't keep that going forever. You'll be looking for a new lock to fight. And, Marshal or not, I'll be watching and waiting for when you put a foot wrong."

"I'll finish you, Flanagan!" Riker was already halfway across the room, his face as white as paper. Justy was reaching for his knife, ready to pull it free from his boot, already calculating how to turn Riker so that he could slide the blade up between his ribs and into his heart.

But Riker stopped. Justy stood up, slowly, watching as the man forced his rage down inside and contained himself. It was a remarkable transformation, like watching a snake slide free of its sloughed-off skin. Riker took a single long, slow breath, and then he was himself again, as cool and pale and impenetrable as porcelain.

His eyes flicked away from Justy. He nodded curtly to Hays. "I shall see you at the meeting, High Constable. Until then."

And he turned on his heel and left.

Hays exhaled in a low whistle. "I've never seen that side of the man before. You shook him, Justice. You shook him mightily."

"Not enough to make him do what I wanted."

"And a damned good thing too. I saw you going for that knife of yours. What do you think would happen if I had to report to the Mayor that one of his councilmen was lying dead on my carpet, and one of my own Marshals the doer?"

"I would have thought he'd be relieved."

Hays laughed.

The sound of shouting came from the lobby. Not the loud banter of the petitioners, but something more urgent. Hays strode out of his office, with Justy hobbling behind, and they both leaned over the mezzanine balcony to see what was causing the fuss.

The petitioners had backed out of the center of the lobby of the Hall. Franklin Beaulieu and his manservant, Caraway, stood in the clearing. Beaulieu appeared to have come straight from the chapel, and was still dressed from head to toe in mourning black. Caraway was similarly attired, except that he had two pistols shoved into his belt. He stood like a statue, only his eyes moving as they scanned the crowd around them, while his master raged and screamed at Tobias Riker.

"Murderer! Murderer! First my son! Now my wife! You killed them both." Beaulieu's heavy face was crimson, and his gray hair flopped over his forehead.

Riker stood a few steps up the staircase. "I did no such thing!" His voice echoed around the chamber, and the Hall was silent. "Your son was a drunk who tipped himself into the river, and your wife was a sot who drugged herself to death. If any blame attaches, Beaulieu, it attaches to you."

Beaulieu's breathing was ragged, his body bent. He looked as though he had run the whole way up the hill from the church. "It was your scheme, Riker. You lured my boy in. But he found you out, didn't he? You may not have been the one who broke his head before he went into the water, but it was one of your cronies, sure as day."

"I warn you, Franklin." Riker's face was tight. "You are bringing disgrace on your house by making slanderous accusations in public. Think where this could lead in court. Think of your family."

"Family?" Beaulieu was suddenly upright. His face was drained. "What family? My family is dead."

Riker seemed to realize he had gone too far. He took a step backwards, up the stairs.

Beaulieu held out his hand to his footman.

"No!" Justy shouted.

But it was too late. Caraway pulled one of the pistols out of his belt and laid the grip in his master's hand. In a single, smooth movement, Beaulieu cocked the weapon with his thumb, made a half turn, leveled it with a straight arm, and fired. The crash was enormous, the pistol belched smoke, and Riker was thrown backwards, his head striking the marble staircase with a sharp crack.

The Hall was silent. Beaulieu's face was pale and set. He held the pistol out to the side again, and Caraway took it and thrust it back in his belt.

Hays raced down the steps, his red coat flying behind him. Beaulieu's hand was still outstretched. He clicked his fingers, and Caraway frowned and leaned forward and whispered something.

"Just give it to me, man!" Beaulieu said, and Caraway laid the other pistol in his master's hand.

Beaulieu stood, the pistol down by his side, waiting as Hays examined Riker. A thin stream of blood was trickling down the marble.

"Have I killed him?" Beaulieu called out.

Hays looked up. His face was pale. "You have, sir. You have indeed."

"Good." Beaulieu turned towards Caraway, who was already holding his hand out to take the pistol back. And then he turned back to Hays.

"You must place me under arrest, I presume?"

Hays stood up. There was blood on his hands. He used a finger and thumb to pull a handkerchief from his cuff. "You presume correctly, sir. And directly, if you please."

"That won't be necessary." Beaulieu gave a faint smile. "I have no wish to waste the court's time."

The sharp double-click of the pistol's cocking action was like a whip cracking in the silence of the Hall.

"Look after things, Caraway," Beaulieu said, softly. "My will is in an envelope on my desk."

The big man lunged at him, but too late. Beaulieu had already fitted the end of the long muzzle under his chin. And then he squeezed the trigger.

FORTY-EIGHT

January 1805,
Eighteen Months Later

It had snowed in the night, and the long hole in the ground looked like an open wound in a dead man's belly. Justy stood back from the lip as Sergeant Vanderool climbed up the ladder and out of the pit. The sergeant took a few steps to one side and vomited.

Justy handed him a flask, and Vanderool swilled and spat, then drank again. He nodded his thanks.

"How many now?" Justy said.

"Fifteen."

The builders had begun to dig along the edge of the marshland north of Hudson's Kill in the New Year. They had stopped a week later when they found the first skull. Justy wasn't surprised when he got the word. He remembered what Sahar had said, that Umar had murdered at least a dozen women when they had proved troublesome, or unable to conceive. He knew it was only a matter of time before they were found.

He had not seen Sahar since that day in Hughson's. She had disappeared, and he had not asked Kerry where she had gone. He did not even know whether she had tried to inherit Umar's estate. Better not to ask, he thought. Better to wait for Kerry to tell him, if she ever would.

New York was growing fast. Canvas Town, meanwhile, was shrinking. The developers were becoming more aggressive, and the City Council had granted them the support of the constabulary, so it was harder for the gangs to hold them back. But Owens and the Bull had their eyes on new pastures. The plan for the development of New York still had not been released, but speculators were buying land regardless. The city had already given its blessing to plans to drain Hudson's Kill and the marshes, and fill in the land. The idea to develop the Collect had been raised again, by an engineer who claimed that he could level Bayard's Mount in less than a year, drain the pond with a canal, and use the spoil to fill it in.

Developers were already building, buying farmland and displacing farmers who brought their families and their livestock into the town, so that the streets now teemed with pigs and hens and smelled like a barnyard. Meanwhile, immigrants continued to flood in through the docks, fresh meat for the mills and the breweries, and prey for the gangs.

Hays had been prescient. The city was becoming more violent as more and more people crammed into it every day. New gangs were rising up, in particular nativist groups who were beginning to make a habit of making drunken sallies into the Irish or black areas of the city, to beat and rape and steal. Murder was becoming a fact of life in New York, although nothing on the scale of what was in the pit that Justy peered into.

"At least they'll get a decent burial," he said.

"What kind?" Vanderool said. He rubbed his hands together and blew on them. "We don't know what religion they were."

He was right. They knew nothing about the women. No one had noticed when they disappeared into Jericho, and no one had missed them once they were gone. They had no names. They were unremarked.

"It doesn't matter," Justy said. "Just so long as we remember them."

ACKNOWLEDGMENTS

They say the second book is the hardest, so I suppose I've been lucky. Long before I had finished the first of Justy and Kerry's adventures, the ideas for more came bubbling out of me. It was just a question of catching them, like a man running madly about a meadow with a butterfly net.

And getting them into the jar, if that's what butterfly catchers do. That part wasn't so easy, and I had a lot of help. Eileen gave me love, support, and encouragement, day in and day out, throughout. My agent, Lisa Gallagher, answered every one of my dozy questions, sometimes several times over. Michael and Monica were always there, like pinnacles of rock for the exhausted sailor to tie up to when he needed a well-marbled steak, or a strong gin. They may have been on the other side of the Atlantic, but Esther and Damien, and Michael and Andrea, kept me strong and filled me with faith. And I have so many other supporters to thank, from San Francisco to Singapore, including Kirsten and Richard di Patri; Mark and Rebecca Sorensen; Mary, Kathleen, and Amy Kelly; Rodney and Kalika Yap; David Willis; Dan Drake; Candice Fox; Kim Howe; Barbara Bogaev; Jeremy Hobson; Kazandra Santana; Brian Heller; Mark Laughlin; and, for always reminding me to keep my eyes open, Delilah, Sonia, and Adam.

I wrote this book in coffee shops and libraries. Margaux Ryan and her crew at Starbucks in Los Feliz were most hospitable, as were the staff of the libraries in Glendale, New York, Singapore, West Hollywood, and right across Los Angeles—and in Silver Lake in particular. Thanks for having me!

This book would never have been written if I couldn't earn a crust at the same time, and because I was freelancing, I owe a great number of people a great deal of thanks for keeping me employed: at Gimlet, Alex Blumberg,

Nazanin Rafsanjani, Matt Shilts, Abbie Ruzicka, and Rikki Novetsky; at Panoply, Matt Berger, Whitney Donaldson, Michele Siegel, and Raghu Manuvalan; and at NPR, Sarah Gilbert, David McGuffin, Sarah Robbins, Jacob Conrad, Miranda Kennedy, Stacey Vanek Smith, Cardiff Garcia, Darius Rafieyan, Alex Goldmark, Angie Hamilton-Lowe, Denise Rios, Melissa Kuypers, Danny Hajek, Justin Richmond, Arezou Rezvani, Marcia Caldwell, Leo del Aguila, and Theo Mondele.

As anyone with any experience of publishing knows, the coming up with the story and the getting down of the words is only half the battle, and I'm fortunate to be part of such a great team, both at Tor/Forge in New York and Corvus in London. I owe my editors, Diana Gill and Sara O'Keeffe, particular thanks for chiseling the manuscript into shape, but I also want to thank Alexis Saarela, Lucille Rettino, Linda Quinton, Ken Holland, Kristin Temple, Lili Feinberg, Beth Parker, Clive Kintoff, Karen Duffy, Simon Hess, and Declan Heeney for all the hard work they've done to get this book out of the door and in front of you.

GLOSSARY

The following glossary is compiled from a variety of sources, including *The Memoirs of James Hardy Vaux,* by James Hardy Vaux; the *Modern Flash Dictionary,* by George Kent; the *New Dictionary of All the Cant and Flash Languages,* by Humphry Tristram Potter; the *Classical Dictionary of the Vulgar Tongue,* by Francis Grose; the *Universal Etymological English Dictionary,* by Nathan Bailey; and *A History of Cant and Slang Dictionaries,* by Julie Coleman.

I have given a short interpretation of each term or phrase, and, where the source material provides a more colorful definition, I have added it in italics, for the reader's entertainment.

A
abram—naked. Also, one who feigns madness.
a chara—my friend
a mhac—my brother; my friend
at rug—sleeping. Also, safe. *It is all rug. It is all right and safe, the game is secure. (Grose)*

B
bach—Welsh term of endearment. Literally, "little one."
bairn—child
baked—foolish; mad
Ballum Rancum—orgy. *A hop or dance where the women are all prostitutes. NB The company dance in their birthday suits. (Grose)*
barker—a pistol

bawbels—*trinkets; a man's testicles. (Grose)*

bawdy-house—a brothel

beak—a judge or magistrate

black joke—a woman's privates. *Her black joke and belly so white. Figuratively, the black joke signifies the monosyllable. (Grose)*

bloodnut—redhead

blowen—woman. *A mistress or whore of the gentlemen of the camp. (Grose)*

bob—dollar; unit of currency

boozing ken—an alehouse or tavern

bowsing ken—an alehouse or tavern

brace—a pair

breech—backside

breech'd—flush with money

Bristol milk—sherry

bunter—prostitute. *A low dirty prostitute, half whore and half beggar. (Grose)*

buntlings—petticoats. *Hale up the main buntlings: throw up the woman's petticoats. (Bailey)*

burick—prostitute

buzz—steal. *To buz a person is to pick his pocket. The buz is the game of picking pockets in general. (Vaux)*

C

cakey—good

candle-fencer—a merchant who sells candles

case-vrow—*a prostitute attached to a particular bawdy-house. (Grose)*

cat—a cat o' nine tails or a whip

chatter broth—tea. *Also 'cat lap' and 'scandal broth.' (Grose)*

chink—money

chip—child

chit—child

chive—knife

chonkey—pastry, usually stuffed with meat

chouse—to cheat or trick

clobber—clothing. Also, to strike.

clunch—fool or idiot

clutch—fight

conk—informant. Also, nose.

cooler—woman. Also, prison. Also, the buttocks. *Kiss my cooler. Kiss my a-se. It is principally used to signify a woman's posteriors. (Grose)*

costard—head

costard monger—a dealer in fruit, particularly apples

couch—to sleep

couch a hogshead—to take a nap

coup de main—a swift attack that relies on speed and surprise to accomplish its objectives in a single blow

cove—man

covey—collective for prostitutes. *A covey of whores. What a fine covey here is, if the Devil would but throw his net. (Grose)*

crack—to break open

cracked—mad or foolish

crackers—trousers

crib—to steal. Also, house.

crocked—broken

cross—*illegal or dishonest practices in general are called the cross, in opposition to the square. (Vaux)*

cull, cully—man

curtezan—prostitute

D

dab it up—*To dab it up with a woman, is to agree to cohabit with her. (Vaux)*

dairy—breasts

degen—a sword

dimber—pretty

dit—a story

doxy—prostitute

drab—prostitute

dragoon—heavy cavalry

drumbelo—*a dull, heavy fellow. (Grose)*

ducat—dollar (slang), unit of currency

duds—clothing

dumb glutton—a woman's privates

E

eagle—a five-dollar coin

F

fadge—a farthing. Also, sufficient. *It won't fadge; it won't do. (Grose)*

fin—an arm

flash—*to be flash to any matter or meaning, is to understand or comprehend it, and is synonymous with being fly, down, or awake; to put a person flash to any thing, is to put him on his guard, to explain or inform him of what he was before unacquainted with. (Vaux)* Also, underworld slang

flog—to sell

florence—generic term for a wealthy woman

foxed—intoxicated

G

gaffer—a boss

galleon—a large ship

games—legs

gelt—money

geneth—girl (Welsh)

gentry-mort—a gentlewoman

giggler—a girl. Also, a prostitute.

give the hoof—kick

glimm—an eye. Also, to look.

go snacks—to be partners. *To . . . have a share in the benefit arising from any transaction to which you are privy. (Vaux)*

grot—a dwelling or house

grubshite—a fool, a worthless person

guinea—black

gun—a look

gundiguts—*a fat, pursy fellow (Grose)*

H

hackum—a thug

hatchet-faced—a long, thin face

heavers—breasts

hot—angry

How dost do?—hello; a greeting

hugger-mugger—*by stealth, privately, without making an appearance. (Grose)*

J
jakes—toilet
jarvie—driver, coachman
judy—woman

K
kemesa—shirt
ken—dwelling. Also, to understand. (Scots)
kimbaw—to trick or cheat. Also, to beat. *Let's kimbaw the cull and get his money. (Bailey)*
kinchin; kinchen—a child; children
kip—home. Also, slum.

L
libben—a home or house

M
mab—*a Wench or Harlot (Bailey)*
madge—*the private parts of a woman (Grose)*
make easy—kill
malarkey—foolishness
matelot—sailor
mill—kill
mollisher—woman
mott—woman. Also, a woman's privates.
mutton-monger—*a man addicted to wenching (Grose)*
my buff—my friend

N
nab—cloth
nick—to steal. Also, jail.
nimgimmer—a doctor or surgeon. *Particularly those who cure the venereal disease. (Grose)*
nob—a wealthy gentleman
nose gent—a nun
nug—love, a word of love
nug it up—make love

P
pannam—bread
pannier—a basket. Also, womb. *To fill a woman's pannier: to impregnate a woman. (Green)*
paum—to hide
peep—to spy
peg—penis. Also, leg.
pig, in—be with child
pike—to run away
pike on the bene—*run away as fast as you can. (Bailey)*
pit—a pocket
pizzle—a penis
plate—silver plate. Also, money.
Pompey—Portsmouth, England
prancer—a horse. *A snaffler of prancers, a horse stealer. (Bailey)*
primero—a card game
privateer—a pirate
puff—life
put a hole in the bucket—cheat

R
rag—money
rammer—an arm
rantallions—testicles. Also, a rantallion is *one whose scrotum is so relaxed as to be longer than his penis, i. e. whose shot pouch is longer than the barrel of his piece. (Grose)*
rattler—a carriage
rig—a carriage. Also, clothing.
rook—a cheat, a thief. *To rook: to wipe one of his money. (Bailey)*
rookery—slum
rotan—a carriage
rum—good
rumpus—a disturbance

S
scaly—miserly. Also, sordid.
scowre off—run away

scrap—a plan, a scheme

scratcher—a bed

scut—a woman's privates. Also, slattern.

shab off—*to go away sneakingly (Bailey)*

Shanks' pony—on foot

simkin—a simpleton

smicket—*a woman's inner garment of linnen; the o changed to an i, and the term et the better to fit the mouth of a prude. (Bailey)*

Smithfield—London district, close to the notorious Liberty of St Katherine's-by-the-Tower

sneak—*The sneak is the practice of robbing houses or shops, by slipping in unperceived, and taking whatever may lay most convenient; this is commonly the first branch of thieving, in which young boys are initiated, who, from their size and activity, appear well adapted for it. (Vaux)*

snitch—to spy. Also, a punch on the nose.

soused—drunk

spider-shanked—thin-legged

spin a dit—tell a story

spooney—mad

squeak beef—raise the alarm

squirrel—a prostitute

stingo—strong drink

stoup—a drinking vessel

stoup of tickle—a glass of strong liquor

strap—to masturbate

stroke—to copulate

stump—a leg

swede—a head

T

Taffy—a Welshman

taper-fencer—a merchant who sells candles

tar—a sailor

tib—a girl

tickle—strong drink

tilly-tally—nonsense

tilt—a fight

tod—alone
togs—clothes
tol-lol—well enough
top lights—eyes
topping man—a boss
tumble—to have intercourse
twig—to realize, understand, or discover

V

vaulting school—a brothel
vellum—paper
vestal—a nun

W

ware—beware
ware hawk—*the word to look sharp, a bye-word when a bailiff passes. (Grose)*
wear the bands—*to wear the bands, is to be hungry, or short of food for any length of time; a phrase chiefly used on board the hulks, or in jails. (Vaux)*
well-breeched—wealthy. *The swell is well breeched, let's draw him; the gentleman has plenty of money in his pocket, let us rob him. (Vaux)*
whid—a word
whid the scrap—*he whiddles, he peaches. He widdles the whole scrap: he tells what he knows. (Grose)*
windward passage—the anus

ABOUT THE AUTHOR

PADDY HIRSCH is an award-winning journalist and online video host who produces the NPR podcast *The Indicator* from *Planet Money*. The author of *The Devil's Half Mile* came to journalism after serving for eight years as an officer in the British Royal Marines, and lives in Los Angeles. He is also the author of a nonfiction book explaining economics, *Man vs. Markets*.

www.paddyhirsch.com
twitter.com/paddyhirsch
www.facebook.com/paddyhirsch101
www.instagram.com/paddyhirsch